Peter Tremayne is the fiction pseudonym of Peter Berresford Ellis, a well-known authority on the ancient Celts, who has utilised his knowledge of the Brehon law system and seventh-century Irish society to create a new concept in detective fiction.

The International Sister Fidelma Society regularly produces a journal entitled *The Brehon* that is packed with news and fascinating information about Fidelma's world. Details can be obtained either by writing to the Society at PMB #312, 1818 North Taylor Street, Suite B, Little Rock, AR 72207, USA, or by logging onto the society website at www.sisterfidelma. com.

Praise for the widely acclaimed Sister Fidelma mysteries:

'The Sister Fidelma books give the readers a rattling good yarn. But more than that, they bring vividly and viscerally to life the fascinating lost world of the Celtic Irish. I put down *The Spider's Web* with a sense of satisfaction at a good story well told, but also speculating on what modern life might have been like had that civilisation survived'   Ronan Bennett

'Rich helpings of evil and tension with lively and varied characters'
Historical Novels Review

'The detail of the books is fascinating, giving us a vivid picture of everyday life at this time . . . the most detailed and vivid recreations of ancient Ireland'   *Irish Examiner*

'A brilliant and beguiling heroine. Immensely appealing'
Publishers Weekly

'Tremayne's super-sleuth is a vibrant creation, a woman of wit and courage who would stand out in any era, but bri_____ _____ ___ _____ the wild beauty of med   Llywelyn

PETER TREMAYNE

BLOODMOON

HEADLINE

The right of Peter Tremayne to be identified as the Author of
the Work has been asserted by him in accordance with the
Copyright, Designs and Patents Act 1988.

First published in Great Britain in 2018
by HEADLINE PUBLISHING GROUP

First published in Great Britain in paperback in 2019
by HEADLINE PUBLISHING GROUP

1

Cataloguing in Publication Data is available from the British Library

ISBN 978 1 4722 3872 6

Typeset in Times New Roman PS by Palimpsest Book Production Limited,
Falkirk, Stirlingshire

Printed and bound in Great Britain by Clays Ltd, Elcograf S.p.A.

Headline's policy is to use papers that are natural, renewable and recyclable products
and made from wood grown in sustainable forests. The logging and manufacturing
processes are expected to conform to the environmental regulations of the
country of origin.

HEADLINE PUBLISHING GROUP
An Hachette UK Company
Carmelite House
50 Victoria Embankment
London EC4Y 0DZ

www.headline.co.uk
www.hachette.co.uk

*In memory of the struggle against
the Laestrygonians, Cyclops and
the Wild Poseidon . . .
Temporarily becalmed off shore.
March 2017–January 2018*

Sol vertetur in tenebras et luna in sanguinem antequam veniat dies Domini magnus et horribilis.

The sun will turn into darkness, and the moon into blood, before the great and terrible day of the Lord comes.

Joel 2–31
Vulgate Latin translation of Jerome, 4th century

pRINCIPAL ChARACTERS

Sister Fidelma of Cashel, a *dálaigh* or advocate of the law courts of 7th-century Ireland

Brother Eadulf of Seaxmund's Ham, in the land of the South Folk, her companion

Enda, warrior of the Nasc Niadh or Golden Collar, the King of Cashel's bodyguard

At Cluain, in the territory of the Uí Liatháin
Grella, wife to Cenn Fáelad, High King of the Five Kingdoms
Cairenn, her companion
Loingsech, bodyguard to Grella
Antrí of Cluain

At Finnbarr's Abbey, Corcaigh
Abbot Nessán
Brother Ruissine, the abbey steward
Oengarb of Locha Léin, a lawyer
Brother Lúarán, a physician
Imchad, a ferryman

In Ciarraige Cuirche territory
Tassach, a farmer
Anglas, his wife

Cogadháin, an innkeeper
Cogeráin, his son
Fécho, captain of the *Tonn Cliodhna*, coastal vessel
Iffernán, his chief helmsman

Ard Nemed, the Great Island
Artgal, Prince of the Cenél nÁeda
Corbmac, his *rechtaire* or steward
Murchú, captain of a Cenél nÁeda warship

At Ros Tialláin
Tialláin, the chieftain
Gadra, his second in command
Prince Aescwine, commander of a Gewisse (Saxon) warship
Beorhtric, Aescwine's second in command
Áed Caille, an Uí Liatháin bow-maker and a prisoner
Fínsnechta, son of Dúnchad

At Baile an Stratha
Mother Báine, keeper of a hostel

At the community of Doirín
Éladach, an Gréicis (the Greek), brother to Glaisne, a prince of the southern Uí Liatháin
Pilib, his *rechtaire* or steward
Petrán, a warrior

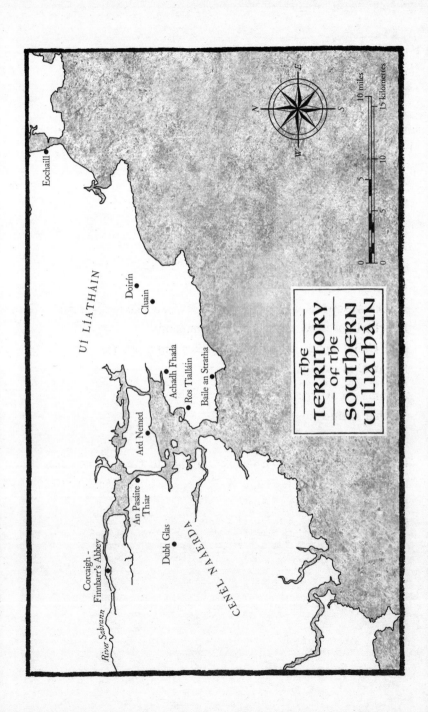

AUThOR'S NOTE

The events in this story follow in chronological sequence from *Night of the Lightbringer*. The year is still AD 671 and the month is known in Old Irish as Meadhónach Gaimrid (sometimes Geamhrad), the 'middle of winter', which equates with the month we now call December, after the Latin 'tenth month' (*decem*) of the Julian calendar.

The setting is mainly in the territory of the Uí Liatháin in what is now east Co. Cork. The chief fortress was in the north of the territory at Caisleán Uí Liatháin (fortress of the Uí Liatháin), Anglicised today as Castlelyons, but most of the action takes place on the southern coast.

The Anglicised form of Cork was derived from 'Corcaigh', the Great Marsh of Munster. The River Dabrona, as recorded by Ptolemy, was later known as the Sabrann but became the Laoi and hence to be Anglicised as the River Lee. Cluain is now Cloyne, 'the meadow', and Eochaill, 'the place of the yew trees', is Youghal. Eochaill stands at the estuary of Abhainn Mór, the Great River, which the English came to call the Blackwater, running 169 kms (105 miles) from its sources in the mountains of Mullach an Radhairc through the province of Munster to empty into the sea.

CHAPTER ONE

'Why have we stopped?'
The imperious tone of the woman leaning out of her ornate carriage made the young warrior, who had signalled the halt, turn his horse and ride the short distance back to the vehicle to answer her.

They had emerged from a thick forest onto a narrow track at the head of a wild and windswept valley. The weather was bleak and cold, a typical midwinter day. The craggy hills on either side of the valley before them were bare of growth, and granite rocks protruded, dominating the landscape. There were only a few trees here and there, and the landscape was brown with dead bracken and patches of thorn bush. There was little of the winter green that one might expect to see in this southern area, as in the forest they had just travelled through.

The warrior, Loingsech, looked tired and cold, in spite of his heavy woollen cloak trimmed with badger fur. But he halted his horse by the carriage and saluted the woman respectfully.

The carriage in which she sat was a four-wheeled one, called a *cethairríad*, drawn by four strong horses. It was clearly no ordinary vehicle, for it was of red yew panelling on a heavy oak frame, carved by expert craftsmen and with gold ornamentation. Moreover, it was an enclosed vehicle, except for the box on which sat the *ara*, or driver, and a *cairpthech*, or chariot-warrior, whose job was to act as guard. The ownership of such a valuable vehicle could be deduced, by those with knowledge, for there was an *aurscarted*, a carving, on the red yew of the door of the carriage. It was an upraised hand, the symbol of the Uí Néill, the High Kings of the Five Kingdoms of Éireann. The single riderless horse tethered at the rear of the carriage was a curiosity.

The woman who leant out of the vehicle was tall, in her late twenties, with hints of fiery red in her otherwise blond hair. She was attractive, but worry lines could be discerned around her eyes and the corners of her mouth. There was an expression of anxiety about her features though her demeanour showed that she was used to giving commands and, moreover, to having them obeyed. She fixed the young warrior with icy blue eyes.

'Loingsech, why have we stopped?' she demanded again.

The young man inclined his head in respect. 'Lady, we have arrived at the valley of Cluain. But I do not like the gloomy look of it. It seems too deserted. It has a menacing appearance.'

For a moment the woman looked surprised. Then the taut line of her mouth broke into a cynical smile.

'Are you so fearful, Loingsech?' she taunted. 'Are you not a warrior of the Fianna Éireann?'

The young man flushed. 'I merely observe how bare and deserted this valley appears compared with the thick, lush forests that surround this isolated spot. It is as if God has cursed it so that it is devoid of growth.'

'I swear you are fearful, Loingsech,' mocked the woman.

'I am fearful of no living person,' the warrior protested.

'No person living . . . or dead?' she taunted further. 'Have no fear, warrior, the abbey of Cluain should lie only a little way further along this valley track.'

She turned to her companion, sitting in the shadows of the vehicle. 'It is fortuitous that we have stopped here, for it is now time we parted company.'

The figured stirred. It was a young girl, hardly older than her early twenties.

'I am ready, lady.'

The woman nodded slowly. 'You know what you have to do?'

'I should be in Finnbarr's Abbey by tomorrow morning. I am then to rejoin you in Cluain by the end of the week at the latest.'

'Excellent. Go with God.'

The girl bowed her head and climbed down from the carriage unaided. She walked nimbly to the rear of it and untethered the horse. Mounting with the fluid motion of a practised horsewoman, she rode away at a swift trot towards the forest to the north-west, making no farewell gesture. The woman watched her departure, then, satisfied, sank back among cushions that furnished the interior of the coach and called to the driver to move on.

The buildings that they came across a short time later seemed as bleak and deserted as the valley itself. Crumbling blocks of dark, weather-worn limestone were piled in such a way as to create an uneven wall enclosing a half-ruined chapel and, just visible beyond it, several round *bothán*, cabins for habitation. There appeared to be no sign of life, even when the young warrior rode up to the great oak gates and brought out his *stoc*, or trumpet, to blow the customary blast announcing the arrival of an important visitor.

The echoes of the note died away but there was no answer. There was no sound except the angry cacophony of disturbed birds, their calls blending together in a nerve-shattering chorus.

The young warrior moved forward, frowning, and pushed on the gates. They swung open easily at his touch.

He nudged his horse forward a few paces and then halted, suddenly rigid. There was a discernible pause as he stiffened in the saddle, a short bolt of wood protruding from his left shoulder. The horse, surprised and nervous, had jerked its head, twisting the reins from the hand of the injured warrior. With a shrill frightened sound, the horse reared and then turned, uncontrolled, and bounded away

3

with the severely wounded young man clinging to the saddle, blood gushing from his shoulder.

Before the *cairpthech*, the chariot-warrior, could rise to draw his weapon, two more bolts from a hidden crossbow had embedded themselves into his flesh. He looked surprised as he fell, and it did not take an expert eye to see that he was dead before he hit the ground. The horses pulling the carriage reared up in fright as his body bounced over their backs. The driver's cry of alarm was half-choked in his throat as he, too, fell back in his seat. The horses stamped and snorted nervously.

The woman, leaning from the window, stared in bewilderment at the bodies of her fallen entourage; she realised they were beyond helping her now. She reluctantly turned her gaze from them as she became aware of men moving forward to surround the carriage.

A mocking baritone voice called: 'Come and join us, lady.'

Her jaw set determinedly, the woman climbed down from the coach. Her quick eye took in the three men who confronted her. Two of them were aiming curious-looking weapons at her. She remembered that she had seen such weapons before, at Tara, carried by warriors from the Pictii of Alba, known to her people as the Cruithne, accompanying their envoys to her husband's court. They were crossbows, vicious weapons that could be used at fairly close quarters to release their bolts with deadly effect. The third man's features were totally concealed by a mask. His clothes appeared to be of good quality and an ornately worked sword hung in an elaborate scabbard at his side. They belonged to no common warrior or thief.

'Where is Antrí?' she demanded, but her air of authority was somewhat forced. 'This is not how it was arranged!'

'Walk with me, lady,' the masked man replied, indicating the open gates of the abbey. His tone was civil and yet, curiously, held a threatening note.

'Know you that I am Grella, wife to Cenn Fáelad mac Blaithmaic, High King, descendant of the Síl nÁedo Sláine, heir of Niall –'

4

The man gave a cynical laugh and made a gesture of cutting her short with his hand.

'I know you well enough, lady,' he said. 'What other reason would I have for inviting you to be my guest?'

'Who are you?' she demanded, puzzled. 'I seem to know you, but you are not Antrí.'

She glanced at his two armed companions. They were poorly dressed but their clothes seemed to belie their status; they both had well-trimmed hair and beards and carried weapons of quality.

'Thank the powers I am not Antrí,' the man said.

'Your voice is familiar. Where is Antrí? Are you not those sent to meet me?'

'Alas, it is not for me to introduce myself at the moment,' her captor said in an amused tone. 'Suffice to say, I know who you are and you will shortly know who I am. Let me say for the moment that I disapprove of the so-called Abbot Antrí making a separate transaction that betrayed his original agreement.'

He led her through the gates and towards one of the crumbling buildings. He paused before it and pushed open the door. Inside, a man in the brown homespun robes of a religieux was tied to one of the wooden poles that supported the roof. A gag was in his mouth. His wide, frightened eyes stared at them above the gag.

'Antrí!' Grella exclaimed as she recognised the man.

Her captor reached forward to pull the door shut again.

'Your cousin Antrí, who claims to be abbot, has not been very cooperative. No matter. It is you we wanted.'

'Who are you?' she demanded again, this time more hesitantly. 'The men of Éireann use only longbows. Those are Pictish weapons.' She indicated the crossbows. 'You are not Cruithne?'

'Your knowledge is great, lady. But the Saxons also use these weapons. I am surprised you did not mistake us for Saxons.' He seemed to smile as he spoke, as if there were some hidden meaning to his comment.

'What do you want of me?' Grella replied in frustration. 'Why have you imprisoned Abbot Antrí?'

'We can dispense with Abbot Antrí.' Her captor made a dismissive gesture. 'It is your company that we want . . . for a while, at least. As I have requested – walk with me.'

He led her back towards the gates.

She now saw that behind the gates was a line of a dozen bodies, all clad in religious robes. She could see they were all dead. She swallowed nervously.

'What has happened here?' she asked quietly.

Her guide waved a hand in the direction of the bodies. 'Well, I know that Christians are keen to join their God in the Paradise of which they talk so much. You could say that we have just helped to hasten their wish. I'm sure they would all accept that sacrificing their lives in this world will have eased their entry into the next.'

'Who were they? Abbot Antrí's community?' she demanded, her voice rising in fear now. 'Who are you?'

'They are indeed your cousin Antrí's so-called disciples, or should I be more accurate and say that they are his paid followers? Members of the religious they were certainly not, no more than Antrí was an abbot.'

'You have much blood on your hands, whoever you are.' Once more she tried to assert her authority but no longer with much conviction. 'You will pay dearly for it.'

'Oh, come, come, lady. Let us not argue. I am confident that we can come to an alternative accommodation between us. The price you will pay is surely more than I would be faced with.'

'Are you going to kill Antrí?' Her voice dropped to a whisper as she began to comprehend the enormity of her situation.

'Alas, if he were truly an abbot, he might have set a better example to his flock. I am afraid that he and his sheep' – he waved at the bodies again – 'were not good conspirators. He should have been the first to lead them on the path to the next world. In fact, he should have made his own way there but, as it turned out, he tried to make a bargain with me about your fate. You see, lady, I know everything.'

'What do you want of me?' she asked, subdued now she realised just how ruthless this man, whoever he was, could be.

'I've told you. I want only your company, until the time comes when you will make a good confession and make a new arrangement with me about your future.'

He turned and began to issue orders to his men. Others had now joined them. One man had led the carriage through the gates into the abbey compound and was unharnessing the horses. Two others were dealing with the bodies of the driver and the second guard.

'Have your men caught the escaped warrior yet?' the masked leader called to one of the men, who was overseeing the operation.

'The horse bolted and managed to reach the far woods. He was still clinging to it. We have given chase.'

The leader swore viciously. 'I need him found; he must be killed, or your men will be sorry. Make sure none of the bodies is identifiable.'

'But what of the coach?' protested the man. 'It is a good one and it would be sad to see it burnt.'

'But sadder for everyone concerned if it is recognised before we have resolved matters. Burn it.'

The woman attempted to bring her chin up pugnaciously. 'Am I to be killed as well? After all, as wife to the High King, I am more recognisable than the coach.' The fear in her voice eliminated any authority she may have previously held.

Her captor gave a little chuckle. 'Well pointed out, lady. But don't be alarmed. For the moment we are just going for a little ride. Anyway, I don't think you were expecting to be the wife of the High King for much longer. Cousin Antrí was most specific about your plans.'

There was a sudden cry of alarm from one of the men. He was rushing from the hut where she had seen Antrí imprisoned. 'By the Ever Living Ones, my lord, Antrí seems to have loosened his bonds and escaped. Shall we go after him?'

The masked leader swore. 'Am I surrounded by incompetents? Yes, get after him quickly. That parasite knows too much. He is expendable, so make sure he does not leave the valley alive!'

The High King's wife was pale and shivering, but she tried to call forth some dignity even so. 'You will find that this gross insult to the family of the High King will not go unpunished.'

The man turned to her, his voice still filled with amusement. 'Perhaps it is to prevent such an insult that we act in this matter, lady.' Then, while she was still trying to decipher his meaning, he turned and raised his voice: 'Set the fires and let us be away from this place.'

CHAPTER TWO

Three riders paused on the crest of the hill and stared down into the broad river valley before them, screwing up their eyes against the cold air. In spite of a blustery wind, the sky was mainly blue with only patches of brilliant white cloud, woolly domes drifting swiftly in irregular succession across the sky. The leading rider, a woman on a grey-white pony, pulled her thick woollen cape more tightly around her and, as she did so, her long, red-gold hair was caught momentarily by the wind. She was forced to raise a hand to disentangle it and tuck it back under her hood. The second rider, a tall youthful man, leant back on his horse and gazed at the sky.

'The clouds are thickening, lady,' he observed. 'I fear bad weather is approaching.'

The woman turned with a pleasant smile to the speaker, who was clad in the accoutrements of a warrior and wore the traditional golden torc, the neckband of the Nasc Niadh, the Golden Collar, denoting a member of the elite bodyguard to the King of Cashel. Cashel was the principal fortress of the kingdom of Muman, the largest and most south-westerly of the Five Kingdoms of Éireann.

'We will reach the abbey before the rain showers come,' she assured him with confidence. 'It is not far from here.'

The third rider, astride a docile-looking roan cob, was a man in brown religious woollen robes, bearing the tonsure of the Blessed

Peter on his unprotected pate, which showed he followed the rule of Rome rather than that of the churches of the Five Kingdoms. He shivered slightly as the winds caught him.

'How do you know it will rain?' he demanded, slightly petulantly. 'At this time of year it is more likely to snow.'

'Observe the clouds, Eadulf,' the woman replied. 'See the formations? If they continue to change shape, like those approaching from the north, we will see some rain before long. But it is not yet cold enough for snow. It is not until later this month, after the new moon, that the temperature will drop suddenly, heralding the really high winds and the risk of snow falling.'

Eadulf sighed with an almost exaggerated expulsion of his breath. It was clear he was not in a good mood.

The young warrior, Enda, who had been tasked to accompany the couple on their journey, noticed the tension in him and intervened quickly.

'Is this abbey that we seek close by, lady?'

Fidelma of Cashel, sister to Colgú, King of Muman, indicated the wide, lush valley before them.

'The abbey is not so much a building but a large community, sheltering behind a wooden stockade on the top of a small limestone cliff overlooking that river which you see before you.'

'And that river is called . . .?'

'The Sabrann.'

'A strange name,' reflected the warrior. 'But I have never been in this part of the kingdom before.'

'It is an ancient name,' Fidelma explained, 'although the Greek traveller Ptolemy recorded it by the name Dabrona. Traders have long used this river and the inlets it flows into as a great harbour.'

'Well, it looks a peaceful and pleasant countryside,' observed Enda.

Eadulf sniffed, still looking displeased. 'All I see is marsh and swamp and, despite the cold, I have already encountered enough biting insects to last a lifetime. I have no wish for closer acquaintance with any more of them.'

'I thought you had a balm for that,' Fidelma replied cheerfully. 'Honey and apple-cider as I recall . . .'

'I'd rather eliminate the cause than the symptoms,' Eadulf replied curtly. 'Why are we always riding through marshland?'

'I cannot control the geography of this kingdom,' Fidelma replied tartly, responding to the testiness of Eadulf's attitude.

Not for the first time on this trip did Enda, the young warrior, feel he should intercede. Ever since they had left Cashel he had been aware of some curious antagonism between Fidelma and her husband Eadulf. What was worse, it seemed to be increasing.

'It is true, lady, there is a lot of marshland in this part of the kingdom.'

After her momentary irritation had subsided, Fidelma continued in a more controlled fashion: 'This area is not called Corcaigh Mór na Mumhan, the Great Marsh of Muman, for nothing. You will see that the area is made up of many islands intersected by waterways, and even the great river is marshy and prone to flood.'

'Full of the flying insects, no doubt,' Eadulf muttered.

There seemed to be no appeasing his bad temper. If the truth were known, Eadulf was feeling excluded by Fidelma. She had announced that she had been asked to journey to the Abbey of the Blessed Finnbarr in this marshland to discuss some legal matter with the current abbot, Nessán, though she had not been willing to discuss the cause of her mission. Eadulf had heard of the great teaching abbey but had never seen it, so he had promptly decided to accompany her. She had protested, saying she would take the young warrior, Enda, for companionship, and Eadulf had had the distinct feeling that Fidelma did not want him to come but could find no way to refuse. Nothing had been said but he had felt his company was not wanted, which had made him all the more determined to join her. So they had left their son, Alchú, in the care of

Muirgen, the nurse. Fidelma's farewell to the boy had been almost peremptory. That was odd.

Fidelma's reticence about her mission had become a growing frustration to Eadulf as they made their way to the south-west. Her silence was unusual and curious. Fidelma had often explained to Eadulf the intricacies of the law and the tasks she was asked to carry out as a *dálaigh* and legal advisor to her brother. Eadulf had been a hereditary *gerefa*, a magistrate of the laws of his own people of Seaxmund's Ham, in the lands of the South Folk of the kingdom of the East Angles. In the years they had been together, especially as man and wife in accordance with the ancient laws of Fidelma's people, Eadulf had even been trusted with the confidence of her brother, Colgú, the King. Eadulf had frequently assisted Fidelma in solving the mysteries that had made the reputations of both of them; their names were inseparable throughout the Five Kingdoms of Éireann, even in the palace of the High King. So he was increasingly perplexed when she refused to tell him anything about her current task, even when he asked her bluntly. All she would say was that it was a personal undertaking. Her apparent lack of trust in him was what had put him in such a bad mood during the journey.

In spite of the fact that it was Meadhónach Gaimrid, the month designated the 'middle of winter', and in spite of Eadulf's increasing complaints, the journey to the marshlands had been a surprisingly easy and comfortable one. The temperatures had been generally mild, although occasionally, as now when they paused on the hill, a sharp, cold wind turned on them from the north-east. They made their way slowly down the track towards the river, through wood of oak and hazel. As they neared the river banks, they joined a wider and more frequently used path – they could see the ruts showing heavy carts had often passed this way. They even saw a few landing stages along the river, with boats and barges moored by them and other signs that traders and merchants were active here. Fidelma knew it was a long river that eventually emptied into the sea, with an ancient history of encouraging visitors and merchants from many strange lands.

From these landing stages and the few cabins along the river, a gentle incline rose to the limestone ridge above, on which they could see a high wall of wooden stakes, marking the official enclosure of the religious community which was their objective. Fidelma had been to this abbey before and knew that the main buildings were beyond these walls. It was impressive. Fidelma knew that Lóchán, son of Amergin of Maigh Seola, had chosen the site to become a centre where the tenets of the New Faith could be taught to younger generations. Lóchán became a respected teacher of the New Faith, better known under his nickname: 'fair haired' or Finnbarr. He had died fifty years earlier, and his name and teachings had spread throughout the land.

As they guided their horses upwards to the main gates, Fidelma remembered her previous visit, when she had solved the mystery of the vanishing bell that Finnbarr had once used to summon the faithful to prayer in his chapel. The bell had been kept as an icon in the abbey and so its loss had caused great alarm, until Fidelma had been able to restore it to Abbot Nessán, an elderly man even then. It was said that Nessán was so old that he had known Finnbarr personally.

It was Eadulf's first sight of abbey and he was not impressed by it, for he was used to the northern teaching communities of Imleach, Mungairit and Darú, constructed of great cut stones, mainly limestone and even grey granite. This, by contrast, was like any poor village, crudely built from the local trees.

Eadulf suddenly became aware that the gates in the wooden stockade, for such he viewed it, were open and a heavily built man, with dark hair and a sallow complexion, was waiting to greet them. The expression he wore was one of almost petulant suspicion, coupled with bitterness. He was dressed in dyed grey woollen homespun, hands folded before him around a wooden cross that hung from a leather thong around his neck.

'You are welcome, travellers,' he intoned. The words were said without emotion, a ritual only.

They dismounted from their horses and Fidelma responded, assuming the role of spokesman of the party.

'I am Fidelma of Cashel.'

'I am Brother Ruissine, the *rechtaire*, steward to Abbot Nessán. How can I be of service?'

'Abbot Nessán should be expecting me,' Fidelma replied, her tone indicating that she did not appreciate the brusqueness of his greeting.

'Indeed?' Brother Ruissine raised an eyebrow. 'The abbot is resting and no one is allowed to disturb him before the bell rings for the *prain* – that is the evening meal.'

Fidelma's mouth tightened a little and she glanced to the sky.

'Then I hope the bell will ring soon,' she replied drily, causing the steward to blink. 'In the meantime, since darkness will soon be upon us, we require hospitality. We need stables and fodder for our horses, accommodation for Enda, of the King's bodyguard, and hospitality befitting my husband, Eadulf of Seaxmund's Ham, and myself.'

The steward seemed momentarily shocked and then appeared to register for the first time the rank of the new arrival.

'You are all welcome, Fidelma of Cashel,' he said after some hesitation, trying with obvious effort to put more feeling into his words. He turned and signalled to a young man, evidently a stable lad, to come forward to take care of their horses. At another signal, some other attendants approached, with a jug and a linen cloth. 'We observe the customary rituals here, lady,' the steward said, almost apologetically. He parted his lips into an expression that was meant to carry the warmth of a smile.

There followed the traditional washing of the hands and feet of the travellers by the attendants.

'We have adopted many of the rituals of Rome,' explained Brother

Ruissine in an aside to Eadulf. 'The Blessed Finnbarr himself went on pilgrimage there and accepted many of the ways of the Faith that were established during the reforms of the Holy Father Gregory the Great. We still maintain them.'

Once the rituals of hospitality were completed, the steward suggested that Enda should follow the stable lad, who would organise his lodging and food. Then he invited Fidelma and Eadulf to accompany him to the guests' quarters to rest before being summoned to the *prain*. Without further ado, Brother Ruissine conducted them through a series of huts of various sizes. He paused before a very large wooden building.

'This is our *praintech*, our refectory. When you hear the bell sound for the evening meal, come here and make yourselves known to the attendants, who will take you to the appropriate seats.'

Eadulf had noticed that the community housed both men and women.

'I see that this is a *conhospitae*, a mixed house?' he observed.

'We are no different from many of the teaching communities of the Faith,' agreed the steward in an offhand manner. 'However, I have heard there are many who believe in the separation of the sexes. I suppose there will always be such groups, wishing to isolate themselves.'

The steward left them at their hut, but Eadulf found he could not settle – and there was little he could discuss with Fidelma without knowing the purpose of their visit. So he left his wife to rest and decided to look round the community while it was still light. He could feel the growing chill as dusk approached. Now and then he was conscious of the flitting shadows of birds seeking their nocturnal nesting places. The limestone cliffs on which the abbey was built seemed to attract many of them. He noticed the soft continuous sounds of one call: 'druuuu, druuuu . . .', and finally identified the bird as a rock dove, a pigeon that commonly nested in the rocks and cliffs of coastal areas.

He had not explored very far when he again encountered the steward, Brother Ruissine, who now seemed entirely happy to escort him around the meandering buildings. Brother Ruissine explained that there were plans eventually to replace the wooden structures with buildings of stone, but stoneworkers were expensive. He was apparently proud of the abbey and its traditions. He turned out to be a garrulous guide, comprehensively informing Eadulf about the foundation of the abbey and adding that Abbot Nessán was so advanced in years that as a young man he had attended one of Finnbarr's last celebrations of the ritual of the Mass. Only once did he display any sign of serious inquisitiveness about his visitors.

'I was wondering what brings the sister of King Colgú of Cashel to our abbey?' he said, in the middle of pointing out the extensive forests to the south of the river from the vantage point of the abbey wall.

'Surely the abbot has discussed the matter with you, as steward?' Eadulf asked, a little surprised.

'The abbot neglected to inform me of her coming,' Brother Ruissine replied swiftly, as if it was of no consequence. 'It has been a busy time – our scholars have been debating whether we should start observing the Nativity of Christ in the manner of some of the abbeys in Rome.'

'The Nativity?' Eadulf was astonished. 'Even in Rome scholars are in disagreement about the observation. It is more important to the observances of the Faith to commemorate the Lord's execution and resurrection.'

'There has been much debate since the Roman Emperor Lucius Domitius Aurelianus declared that the old Roman pagan festival of the Sol Invictus should be adopted as the birthday of our Lord.'

'I know that idea was accepted at the Council of Tours a hundred years ago. I did not think there was further need for debate. So many old pagan festivals have been adopted to promote the continuation of religious practice.'

'True, it is still not popular. That is the reason for our discussion. Our scholars have considered the arguments made among the early founders of the Faith. A day in the month of Augustus in the Roman calendar, of Pachon in the Egyptian calendar . . . every month of every known calendar has its adherents,' the steward said with a shrug.

'But did not the *Chronolography of Philocatus* says that it was accepted that the twenty-fifth day of the tenth Roman month – as you say the feast of the Sol Invictus – was best regarded as a proper feast day for the Nativitas?'

The steward grimaced tiredly. 'You should have attended the debate, Brother. But what were we saying? Has Sister Fidelma discussed with you the details of her mission here?'

There was something in the tone of the repeated question that made Eadulf frown uneasily. It was clear that the steward knew of Fidelma's religious connections, even though she had introduced herself as Fidelma of Cashel and not as Sister Fidelma.

'Fidelma has left the religious, Brother,' he pointed out. 'As a *dálaigh*, she is now simply a legal advisor to her brother, Colgú, King of Muman.'

Brother Ruissine nodded eagerly. 'Just so, just so, Brother. But she has won fame and reputation as Sister Fidelma and she is known by that honourable title in many corners of the kingdom.'

'And beyond,' Eadulf agreed with a smile.

'Exactly,' rejoined the steward. 'The name of Sister Fidelma . . .' he hesitated and shot a quick smile at Eadulf, 'and, of course, Brother Eadulf the Saxon, are known far and wide.'

'I am an Angle not a Saxon,' Eadulf corrected drily. 'I am from the kingdom of the East Angles.'

'Just so, just so,' agreed the other, hurriedly. 'But the nature of your coming here . . .? I am the steward of the abbey, you know, and should be informed.'

'All I can tell you is that Fidelma has some business to discuss with your abbot,' replied Eadulf sharply, realising the steward had touched on the raw spot that had made him bad tempered ever since leaving Cashel. Fidelma had discussed nothing with him.

The steward hid his disappointment but he also had a discerning eye. 'She did not discuss the reason with you?'

Eadulf decided to counter-attack. 'Why do you ask? Is there something that has happened in the abbey that would lead to an advocate coming to discuss some matters with your abbot? I hardly think the matter of the Nativity is a subject that would concern a lawyer of Fidelma's reputation.'

It was now Brother Ruissine's turn to disclaim any knowledge. 'There is nothing that springs to mind. As I said, I was not even informed that she was visiting the abbey.'

'Yet there is something that worries you about the arrival of a *dálaigh*. I can see that. What would that be?'

Brother Ruissine made a curiously dismissive grimace. 'I am not privy to all the abbot's business,' he acknowledged. 'Fidelma's arrival was simply a surprise to me.'

'Isn't that unusual, since you are *rechtaire* of this abbey?'

There was a long pause before Brother Ruissine sniffed in annoyance. 'It is unusual, but that is the way of it,' he admitted reluctantly.

Eadulf watched as the previously talkative steward turned with a curt nod and hurried away, as if some urgent matter impelled him. For a moment, Eadulf felt his annoyance rise again. He had a suspicion that he had been accused of knowing the secret and refusing to share it. Then he shrugged and made his way back towards their hut.

'If she wants to share things, then she will do so when the time is right,' he muttered to himself as if to justify her silence. Yet he could not help but feel resentment at being left out of her confidence after the many years of their close relationship. He felt a curious anxiety as he remembered the early days when she had rejected his feelings for her, when he had also felt hurt and bewildered.

Fidelma was stirring as he entered the hut and his resolution to wait until she felt like sharing her knowledge vanished in a moment of anger.

'So, is your business with the abbot soon to be concluded?' he demanded gruffly.

'It should not take long,' she assured him, with an annoyed glance.

'And you still cannot tell me what this is all about?'

Fidelma sighed in exasperation. 'Enough questioning, Eadulf. I will tell you when the time comes.'

'When will that be?'

'You will know soon enough.' Fidelma hesitated and gave an apologetic shrug. '*Tempus et locus*, Eadulf,' she observed. 'Time and place. I hope it will be soon but don't press me again.'

'So be it.' Eadulf glowered in surly submission – which was not lost on her and served only to increase her own bad mood.

He tried to stifle his pain and confusion but he felt aggrieved that she was excluding him – for the first time since they had resolved their differences a few years ago, after he and Fidelma had split up following her decision to leave the religious and apply to the Council of Brehons to be Chief Brehon of her brother's kingdom. She had failed in her bid, which was a huge blow to her confidence. It was her brother, Colgú, who had saved their relationship. When an eminent scholar had been murdered in his cell at the abbey of Lios Mór, behind a locked door and a single window unattainable from the outside, Colgú had forced them back together to solve the mystery. And as a result, they had realised that what they had together was more important than their differences. There had been no other secrets between them – until now.

A bell began ringing nearby. Eadulf was almost thankful for the interruption.

'I think that must be the summons to the *praintech*, for the evening meal.' He turned to the door of the hut. Outside, darkness had descended with what seemed unusual rapidity.

Fidelma paused indecisively. She knew Eadulf was hurt by her refusal to share her knowledge with him. It was not her way to maintain such secrecy, but it would be difficult to explain to him the reason. Suppressing a sigh, she followed Eadulf to the abbey refectory in silence.

Members of the community – men and women in ones and twos – were making their way to the communal dining hall. In many ways, the abbey apparently kept to the old customs. At the entrance were two silent attendants; one removed the shoes and sandals of each person passing into the hall and placed them to one side for the owners to retrieve when leaving the refectory. The second attendant sluiced their hands and feet from a jug of cold water and then dried them with a *lámh brat*, a hand cloth. As Fidelma and Eadulf were guests, a third attendant conducted them between the two main tables, where the male religieux sat on one side and the female religieuses sat on the other, to the table placed cross-wise at the top of the dining room. They were followed by the curious glances of the silent seated community members. Their guide showed them to seats at the end of the table. Brother Ruissine was already there with several others, who were obviously the senior members of the community. Eadulf was about to speak in greeting but received a sharp nudge from Fidelma. It was only then that it dawned upon him that the entire dining hall was totally silent. In fact, the silence was almost uncanny. He glanced at Fidelma, his eyes wide in silent query, but found her gaze lowered in concentration.

He surreptitiously examined the others in the hall. Most of the assembly were sitting with bowed heads, deep in contemplation of their own. One man caught Eadulf's attention, as his gaze was focused on the two empty seats at the head of the abbot's table. He was a tall man, judging from the way he sat higher than his companions, and although he was clad in homespun, his robe was black rather than grey or brown and the cowl covered most of his face. But he had drawn the cowl back slightly, as if to observe the members of the refectory more easily, and his profile was partially revealed. The man suddenly caught sight of Eadulf examining him and quickly drew the cowl over his face. Eadulf was puzzled for there had been something familiar about that brief glimpse of the man's features.

The would-be diners seemed to be waiting. There was barely a sound when a nearby door opened and an old man entered. Glancing at the tall religieux, Eadulf saw that his cowled head was turned to where the old man had appeared.

Eadulf turned back to observe the abbot. He was supported on one side by a thick blackthorn staff but on the other side he had the arm of an attractive young girl. She was modestly but richly dressed, and not in religious robes. The elderly abbot was clad in the brown robes of his office, with a silver cross hanging from a chain around his neck. His long hair was white, almost the brilliant colour of snow, and nearly matched the colour of the skin of his gaunt cheeks. His pale blue eyes, whose focus seemed fixed on the middle distance, reflected the light of the brand torches. The only splash of colour on his ancient face was the thin red slash of his lips. The young girl seemed to guide the man forward towards his seat, and the sound of his slow, shuffling steps was punctuated by the hollow rapping of his blackthorn against the stone floor.

Eadulf continued to watch as the girl helped the old man seat himself and placed his stick behind his chair. Then, to Eadulf's surprise, she sat in the chair next to the abbot, thus inserting herself between him and the steward of the abbey. That was unusual and certainly against etiquette. All this had been done in silence for Eadulf now realised what Fidelma had tried to indicate to him: this community must be following the rule that all meals should be carried out without conversation of any sort. He had heard of such strange ascetic communities where this was done.

He was just wondering how the signal to commence the meal would be given when Brother Ruissine rose. His sharp baritone echoed: '*Surgite!*' at which everyone else rose obediently. Then the steward began, '*Benedictus benedicat* . . .' at the end of which the community responded, '*Benedicatur Deo.*' Thus was said the Gratias, then everyone sat down again quietly and dishes of food were handed out by the silent attendants. Eadulf noticed that the main body of the religious helped themselves from platters that were passed along the rows. However, at the abbot's table each person was served separately. The abbot himself was served first, a meal that was obviously prescribed by his age and constitution – a white fish cooked in milk, with a husk of wheaten bread and a beaker of milk. The young girl at his side assisted him with the food, for as Eadulf now saw the old man's hand shook as if with an ague.

When the platters were placed before him, Eadulf could make no complaint about the standard of the cuisine for there were hot dishes of river trout, basted in honey and obviously cooked on a gridiron or spit. This was served on a bed of *biror*, watercress, *cremcamh*, wild garlic, and *foltchep*, leeks. And if that didn't appeal, there were hard-boiled goose eggs with cress, or cold sausage with cornmeal loaves, still warm from the ovens. Evidently the asceticism of the abbey did not extend to frugality with the food, as it did for some communities. To drink there was the traditional *miodh cuill*, hazel mead, or *nenadmin*, a cider made from wild apples. At the end of the main courses, the attendants came round with a bowl of apples and dishes of hazelnuts.

Fidelma, for her part, was aware of Eadulf's unconscious fidgeting throughout most of the meal. She shared his discomfort; they were unused to eating a meal in total silence, as if trying to ignore the fact that there were well over a hundred or more people in the refectory with them. Fidelma had long practised the art of meditation, but even she found it difficult to concentrate, especially with Eadulf so restless beside her. When the steward rose, she greeted with relief his call of '*Resurgemus!*' The company rose and in a tone almost of joy declared: '*Ain oculi eorum in te spirant et tu das eis escam suam in tempore suo. Deo Gratias.*' – 'The eyes of all place hope in thee, O Lord; and thou gives the meat in due season. Thanks be to God.'

But after that, everyone reseated themselves and the young girl helped the abbot to rise, take his staff and in silence they moved slowly together to the door they had entered by. Only when they were through and the door had shut behind them did whispers begin to rise around the room and there was an unbecoming scurry towards the exit. Eadulf was inclined to join the throng but Fidelma hung back, choosing to wait until the crush of those trying to reclaim their shoes had thinned. Suddenly, Eadulf glimpsed the tall figure in the black cowl. He caught his wife's arm.

'Doesn't that tall religieux seem familiar to you?' he asked.

She glanced in the man's direction. 'He could be anyone,' she replied dismissively. Then the man turned and stared over the heads of the fussing brethren, suddenly meeting Fidelma's gaze. He seemed to start in recognition. It was only for a split second, then he turned and disappeared through the doors. Fidelma stood for a moment, thinking. By the time they had retrieved their shoes and found themselves outside the tall man had vanished.

Eadulf, a little red in the face from the jostling exit, turned to her. 'Did you see him? I swear I have seen him before.'

'I know what you mean,' she replied, thoughtfully. 'I cannot be sure, but I believe I saw him at the High King's palace in Tara . . . remember the time we solved the murder of Sechnussach? But in what context was he there?' She frowned as if trying to remember the details.

Brother Ruissine suddenly emerged into the light of the brand torches above the entrance of the *praintech*.

'Brother Ruissine,' Fidelma called, 'you said that the abbot would have time to see me after the evening meal. Can you tell me whether he is able to receive me now?'

The steward halted, hesitated and then said, 'I am on my way to the abbot's chamber now. If you will wait here but a short while, I will see if the abbot is ready to receive you. I know when I mentioned your arrival just before the meal he was most anxious to see you.'

He made to turn but Eadulf interrupted. 'Tell me, Brother Ruissine, who was that young girl who was in attendance to the abbot during the meal? Was it his nurse? She must have some status here to sit between the abbot and yourself.'

The steward turned back with a scowl, although it did not seem to be aimed specifically at Eadulf.

'The abbot needs no nurse,' he replied belligerently. Then he paused slightly. 'The girl is not a member of our abbey. She arrived here yesterday; apparently she is a niece of the abbot. The abbot himself insisted that she be accorded special status.'

'What is her name?' asked Eadulf.

'I believe it is Cairenn of the Eóganacht Raithlind. That is a branch of your family, lady, or so I believe,' he said to Fidelma. 'Now I shall see if the abbot is ready.'

After he had gone, Fidelma frowned at Eadulf. 'You seem unduly interested in that young girl? Why do you ask questions about her?'

Eadulf shrugged. 'It's just that that girl, Cairenn, seems to be closer to the abbot than his steward. She is one of your family. Didn't you know her?'

'The Eóganacht are a large family, as you are well aware.' Fidelma opened her mouth to make some further explanation, then she hesitated. 'It might be explained by the fact that Abbot Nessán himself is of the Eóganacht Raithlind.' Then a memory stirred. 'I do have a feeling that I *have* seen her before, but not in a religious context,' she reflected. 'But where was it?'

'So she is nothing to do with your mission here?' Eadulf asked, almost slyly.

'I can't see how my business with the abbot would affect the young girl.' Fidelma parried his question deftly.

'What matter is so important that you have to come all the way here to see this old abbot?' Eadulf suddenly gave vent to his frustration. 'He looks as though he can hardly remember what day it is, let alone have anything of importance to discuss with you.'

'Do not misinterpret what you see. His intellect is very bright, in spite of the frailty of his body,' Fidelma replied without answering his questions.

Eadulf sighed. 'Anyway, there are religious communities and there are religious communities. This one is oppressive, I must say. It would drive me mad to eat in total silence at every meal. Meals are supposed to be social occasions when one eats, drinks and exchanges news and gossip and debates the finer things of the world. What's the point of a community which does not commune with itself?'

Fidelma smiled thinly, thankful to let the matter of her mission drop. 'I hear that there are followers of Benedict of Nursia who are now seeking to set up communities who will live completely in silence. They will not speak to one another on any occasion. And Benedict is now such an influence in the Roman Church with his rules for religious houses that we may all be eating in silence soon.'

Eadulf was aghast. 'They must be mad!' he exclaimed with vehemence. 'What were we given voices for but to talk, to sing and . . . and I would counter this silent rule with one of the Psalms. "*Et audit clamorem meum* . . ." "I was silent and still; I held my peace to no avail: my distress grew worse; my heart became hot within me. While I mused, the fire burned, and then I spoke . . .'"

Fidelma glanced round at the passing religious and lowered her voice: 'It is perhaps better to speak softly. We would not wish to interfere with local rules.'

As if in contradiction to her words, there came a sudden sound of raised voices nearby; people were shouting. Several people were running, almost in panic, but there seemed no discernible cause.

Brother Ruissine had reappeared. Even in the wavering light of the brand torches, with the flickering light chasing shadows over his features, it was clear that they were distorted. Eadulf could barely make out his expression. But when he paused directly beneath the torch, they could see the shock on his face. His whole body displayed tension and horror. In the background, the sounds of disturbance were growing more intense.

Fidelma examined the steward curiously as the man stood motionless before her as if unable to speak.

'What is it, Brother?' she prompted. 'Is something wrong? Is Abbot Nessán ready to receive me?'

'The abbot will receive no one,' Brother Ruissine finally blurted.

A frown crossed Fidelma's features. 'But it was arranged . . .' she began to protest. 'It is important, very important that I see him.'

'He will receive no one; not any more.'

'What do you mean?'

'Abbot Nessán has just been found dead, lady. He has been strangled with a piece of rope. Someone has murdered him.'

CHAPTER THREE

For a moment or two Fidelma stood completely still, her face showing no change of expression at the news. Eadulf, knowing her so well, realised that she was struggling to control her shock. Then she said:

'Show me to the abbot's chamber, Brother Ruissine.'

The steward looked bewildered. 'I tell you, the abbot has been murdered,' he protested.

'I am a *dálaigh*,' Fidelma pointed out heavily.

The steward hesitated, then shrugged. He turned and led the way, closely followed by Fidelma and Eadulf. The chamber of the abbot was one of the few stone buildings in the complex and was situated immediately behind the refectory. It was a square building made of limestone blocks, two levels connected by a wide oak stairway. The steward led the way to the main door. The noisy crowd around it drew back as he approached and the members of the community stared with puzzled looks at Fidelma and Eadulf.

'Since the abbot has become increasingly infirm his chamber has been on the lower level,' Brother Ruissine explained as they entered.

Two men were in the chamber, bending over what appeared to be a heap of dark clothing on the floor. Only when they moved, to identify the newcomers, was the body of the elderly abbot revealed. One of the men was a squat, portly, moon-faced individual they had seen earlier, seated at the abbot's table. The other was a young, muscular man with angular features and a thin mouth that seemed drawn back into a permanent sneer. The latter frowned as they entered.

'You were told that the abbot is dead, Brother Ruissine,' he said, as if trying to control his annoyance. 'We do not want strangers confusing matters. Why bring them here?'

'Who are you?' Fidelma demanded curtly.

The man clearly did not like her tone and stared back arrogantly. 'I am Brehon Oengarb,' he replied.

Brother Ruissine intervened nervously. 'This is Fidelma of Cashel, Oengarb. This is Oengarb of Locha Léin. He too is a *dálaigh*, making a circuit of this territory, and he often acts as our legal advisor.'

Often lawyer went on circuits, or *cúartaigid*, to deal with legal matters in small isolated places when litigants could not go to the main courts. At the mention of her name, the arrogance seemed to leave the young man.

'I do not think that we have encountered one another in the courts.' Fidelma regarded him coldly. 'Yet your face seems familiar.'

The young man flushed in embarrassment. 'I am only qualified to the level of *clí* so I do not think that we would encounter each other in the courts.'

This meant that he was junior in law to Fidelma, having trained for only six years, as opposed to the eight or nine that Fidelma had trained for to reach the level of *anruth*, which was only one level below the highest degree that the bardic or ecclesiastical colleges could bestow. The young man could hardly claim the title Brehon, although he was a *dálaigh*.

Fidelma nodded curtly and turned to the portly man, noting his *les* or medical bag.

'I presume you are the physician?'

'I am Lúarán, lady. I am the physician of the abbey.'

'What was the cause of the abbot's death?'

'A ligature drawn around the throat,' the man replied, taking from beside the corpse a piece of corded rope. 'This is it.'

Fidelma took it and examined it carefully.

'So the abbot was strangled with this cord? Did it require much strength to perform this deed?'

Lúarán immediately shook his head. 'As you see, the abbot was very elderly and frail. He could hardly move without assistance. He would not have been able to put up much of a struggle against his assailant. A swift twist of the cord round the neck, like a tourniquet, and it would have been over in a few moments. You can see the deep mark of the cord where it has cut into the flesh.'

Fidelma stood aside and motioned to Eadulf. 'I trust you will not mind if Brother Eadulf confirms this?'

Eadulf felt briefly grateful that he was not being excluded from this matter, although it did cross his mind that Fidelma might be seeking to mollify him after her earlier treatment of him. He dropped to one knee beside the body and examined the marks and the ligature, moving aside the neck of the old man's robe and then rolling back the sleeves. There was little bruising to be seen. He looked up.

'Lúarán is correct in his examination. The lack of bruising shows the abbot was surprised by the attack. This means his assailant came up unseen from behind him or, if the assailant was before him, the old man knew and trusted him, turned away and then it was too late.'

Fidelma turned back to Oengarb. 'Have you examined this chamber?'

The young lawyer shook his head in puzzlement.

'What would I be looking for?'

'Perhaps a clue as to why someone should murder the abbot?' There was no censure in her voice. She turned to the steward. 'Is there any known reason why the abbot's life might have been in danger?'

There was a brief silence, then Brother Ruissine shook his head. 'The abbot lived an exemplary life, a pious life, making neither enemies nor creating envy among the community. He sought no temporary wealth. Everyone respected him and honoured him for he was our one living link with our beloved founder, the Blessed Finnbarr, and he was regarded in much the same manner as Finnbarr is regarded. The abbot's health was failing and he needed attendants to help him move from here to there.'

'So I observed,' Fidelma commented. 'I presume that the girl, Cairenn, who helped him to the meal this evening and took him out afterwards, has not been questioned as yet?'

The steward looked at the *dálaigh* and the physician. They both shook their heads at his unspoken question.

'Then I suggest someone fetch her here.'

Brother Ruissine turned and snapped an order to one of the brethren at the door, and he disappeared to find the girl.

'She seemed very caring when she helped him in the refectory,' mused Fidelma.

'I presume she was not here when the body was discovered, yet it is only a brief while since they both left the refectory?'

Brother Ruissine shifted his weight uneasily. 'I suppose she has gone to her quarters. She will be brought here in a moment.'

'You say you can think of no motive for the murder of the abbot. Do you have anything to add?'

The steward started a little at the unexpectedness of this repeated question. Then he said hurriedly: 'I can add nothing to what I have already said.'

'People, least of all abbots, are not murdered without a reason,' Fidelma commented quietly.

'Abbot Nessán was a saintly man. No one would lift a finger against him. Why do you ask?'

'Brother Ruissine, you have said that he had no enemies, that no one was envious of him and all respected him. Yet someone felt the compulsion to end his life,' pointed out Fidelma brutally. 'So there must be a reason. And as leader of this teaching abbey, Nessán is respected among all the churches of the Five Kingdoms. But people do not succeed to such situations without making enemies.'

The resentment in the steward's eyes seemed dangerous for a moment. Then he said: 'If we are to share all we know, perhaps there is something you can tell us?'

Fidelma's brows came together as she stared at the man. 'What can I tell you?'

'I have been steward here for several years, lady. There are few secrets in this place. But then, out of the blue, you – a well-known *dálaigh,* the sister to the King – arrive at the gates of this abbey saying that you have business with the abbot. For the last few days, the abbot was not in his usual relaxed frame of mind. He appeared worried and did not open up when I expressed concern for his uneasiness. Indeed, I would go so far as to say he was afraid and anxious. I did not tell him of your arrival until just before the evening meal and, for the first time ever, he rebuked me, for not announcing your arrival immediately. Then he is murdered. I throw this question at you . . . why did you come here?'

'Why did you not announce my arrival immediately, if he was so anxious?' countered Fidelma belligerently, without answering his question.

The steward seemed surprised at her counter-thrust,

'The abbot had not warned me that he was expecting you,' he replied after a moment or so. 'My task is to run this community as it has always been run, not to read the abbot's thoughts.'

'Why didn't the abbot acknowledge me at the evening meal?'

'Perhaps you would know the answer better than I,' replied Brother Ruissine, his anger rising again.

'I would not ask the question if I knew the answer,' Fidelma replied with equal vigour.

The steward blinked at her forcefulness, surprised that she had not given way to his assertive manner. He was about to open his mouth again when the religieux he had sent to fetch the girl came back, pushing his way irritably through the people still hanging round the entrance. He looked very disturbed.

'Brother Ruissine, the girl is no longer in her chamber and some of her belongings are no longer there . . . except I saw her comb bag was under the bed. The chamber is in disarray as if it had been searched hurriedly or some belongings had been hastily packed for departure and some forgotten.'

Fidelma raised an eyebrow. 'But her comb bag was there? How do you recognise her particular *ciorbholg*?' she asked pointedly.

The *ciorbholg* was a small bag carried by most women in which they kept not only combs but small toiletry articles, such as a mirror and soap.

'I saw her use it when she arrived here,' the man replied with some embarrassment, as if not wanting to admit he had been watching a girl.

Brother Ruissine compressed his mouth in firm disapproval. 'I can vouch that the girl used berry juice to redden her lips and distillations of flowers to form sweet scents. We are not used to such indulgences in the abbey.'

'Where is this comb bag?' Fidelma asked.

'I left it in her chamber.'

Fidelma sighed. 'Very well. We shall go and look at her chamber. Meanwhile, Brother Ruissine, have the community searched for her and bring her to me. I presume some of the brethren will be able to assist you so that the task may not be prolonged?' Without waiting for a response, she turned to the physician, Lúarán. 'Your task, I am afraid, is not the pleasantest one. You can take the body of the abbot to the mortuary and prepare it for burial. If there is any more information you can tell me, please do so.'

The steward looked resentful and Eadulf, who had been a silent onlooker all this time, thought he was going to object at Fidelma taking automatic charge. But the man suddenly shrugged and went off to follow her orders. Outside, they could hear him calling on people by name to instruct them in the tasks. Fidelma turned back to Oengarb as the steward returned.

'Now, though you are the *dálaigh* in charge,' she said with emphasis, 'and I do not want to interfere, perhaps we should go to this girl's chamber. As we go, Brother Ruissine will tell us what is known about her.'

'That is not much. All I know is what you have already been told. She arrived here yesterday and announced herself as a relative to the abbot. This turned out to be correct; the abbot greeted her with great affection.'

'Start with how she came to the abbey,' Fidelma suggested.

Brother Ruissine grimaced. 'She came yesterday, as I said.'

'I meant, how did she arrive. Was it by horse, on foot or in a carriage . . . how?'

'By horse, I think.'

'I don't suppose anyone has checked with the stables to see if the animal is still there?'

Brother Ruissine exchanged a startled look with the young Oengarb; then, with a muttered word, he went hurrying away.

Fidelma turned to the young *dálaigh*. 'Did you observe how the abbot behaved towards her after she arrived?'

'I saw that he seemed to accept her as a confidante. I was told she was of close family to him.'

'Do you know if she came with personal messages from the abbot's family?'

Oengarb paused for a moment and then shook his head. 'I have no knowledge of that.'

He suddenly halted and pointed to one of the many wooden huts. 'I think that is the hut that was assigned to her when she arrived.'

At that moment Brother Ruissine rejoined them, pausing breathlessly before them. 'Her horse is gone,' he admitted. 'The horse master said the beast was there at the evening feed. Now it is gone, saddle and all.'

'So we should now examine her room,' Fidelma said, without commenting on the absence of the horse. She examined the exterior of the hut. 'I suppose it is usual for a young female guest to be given an isolated hut?'

'The abbey is in the middle of construction and the new guests' hostel has yet to be built,' explained Brother Ruissine. 'Therefore it is usual that guests are placed in huts, like you have been. This one is also used as a work hut by the scripter of the abbey, Sister Flaitheamh.'

As they entered, the steward lit an oil lantern by the door. The hut consisted of one room, sparsely furnished. A bed, a table, two chairs and then a second table, a special table of beech wood, which Eadulf recognised as a desk for writing with its maulstick to support the wrist of the writer and tablets called *flesc filidh*, tablets of the poets, and cows horns called *adircí,* to hold ink, and a selection of quills. There were pieces of vellum and some papyrus, and pieces of wood with raised edges into which wax had been poured to make notes on with a stylus called a *graib*, for the wax could be resoftened and used many times. There were also *tiag leabhair*, book satchels, in which books were kept, hung on pegs. It was clearly the room of a *scríbnid*, a scribe.

'I presume all of these items belonged to the scripter?' Eadulf asked, glancing round.

'Everything here belongs to our scripter,' Brother Ruissine confirmed.

'Where is this Sister Flaitheamh?'

'She has gone to Ros Ailithir to collect new inks. One of the scripters there has found that using oak galls, mixed with vinegar or wine, produces an excellent ink and . . .'

'So she was not here when this girl, Cairenn, arrived?' cut in Fidelma.

'No. She left two days ago and will be gone for a week or two.'

'I can't see a comb bag,' Fidelma observed. 'The young brother said he had left it here.'

The steward pointed. 'It may have fallen; it is lying there by the bed.'

'An odd place to leave it,' commented Fidelma. 'Overall it is strange that a girl who, as you say, likes to indulge in paying attention to her looks would leave it behind.' She glanced around. 'Do we know which of these clothes belong to her and which to your scripter?'

'Those robes you see belong to our scripter. She is . . . is of somewhat large build, if you understand what I mean,' explained the steward. 'Cairenn was slightly built.'

'I cannot see anything that would fit a slightly built person,' said Eadulf, who had felt he should make himself useful by looking through the few clothes and cloaks on a side rack. 'If the girl has taken those, why would she have left her comb bag behind?'

Brother Ruissine and Oengarb were frowning, trying to understand what he meant.

'What's in that chest in the corner?' Fidelma asked, pointing.

Both steward and advocate went over to it and Brother Ruissine knelt down to open the lid.

Fidelma took the opportunity to surreptitiously examine the contents of the comb bag, holding it with one hand and feeling the contents inside with the other. Out of the corner of his eye, Eadulf saw her mouth tighten as her fingers closed on something. Brother Ruissine and Oengarb still had their backs to her and Eadulf watched her remove a piece of paper and glance at it before thrusting it quickly into the folds of her robe. Eadulf was surprised when she said nothing but placed the bag on the bed and stood back, looking carefully around elsewhere as Brother Ruissine rose to his feet.

'Nothing there but some old woollen blankets for the winter,' he said, turning to her. 'Those are the property of the scripter.'

Fidelma sighed. Then she spotted something glinting by the bed. She pointed without asking the question. Eadulf bent to examine the glistening spot, touching it with his forefinger.

'It's blood, Fidelma.' He straightened up. 'Blood that has been recently shed.'

Oengarb turned to Fidelma with eyes wide.

'Blood? Then . . . surely that is proof? She must have killed the abbot, come here to gather her things and fled the abbey. She must be the murderer.'

Fidelma was thoughtful. 'You presume it is the abbot's blood. But there is one thing that you have forgotten, Oengarb. Abbot Nessán was garrotted. There was no blood shed and Eadulf observed no wound on the old man.'

Oengarb looked confused. 'I had forgotten that. So what are you saying?'

'I don't think I am saying anything at the moment.' Fidelma smiled tightly. 'I think, however, that you should make sure that the search for this girl within the grounds is carried out thoroughly.'

'I shall find out how the search is progressing,' Brother Ruissine offered and, with Fidelma's acknowledgement, he left.

Fidelma was moving towards the door when she turned to Oengarb as if struck by an afterthought.

'Oengarb – you are qualified to the level of *clí* and that means you have some practice in investigation, do you not?'

The young lawyer shifted his weight. 'I'm not as well qualified as you are, lady,' he said, embarrassed.

'But you are well able to handle this matter of the abbot's death, I am sure of it.'

The man looked puzzled but no more so than Eadulf, who had been trying to work out what she was leading up to. He found it hard to believe that Fidelma would abandon a case like this. He stared at her curiously, wondering what she was not telling him.

'Lady?' It was clear what Oengarb's question was.

'Well, it is obvious that the death of the abbot has no link with the matter that brought me here,' she began.

'Which was?' Oengarb interposed quickly.

Fidelma smiled. 'Just a task for my brother. The King merely wanted to know the number of students that are now attending this abbey, especially the foreign ones.'

Eadulf's jaw clamped shut as Fidelma surprised him yet again. He knew from her reticence on the journey that this was clearly a lie.

Oengarb was bewildered. 'The steward could have given you those figures.'

'Then perhaps you can ask him to give them to me in the morning before we leave?'

'Leave, lady?'

'I see no reason why I should delay since you are qualified and well able to carry out the investigation into the abbot's death.'

Oengarb paused and then smiled, a smile almost of self-satisfaction. 'Well, that is so, lady. I am sure I can carry out this investigation. But are you sure that you want to release the matter to me?'

'I am sure of it,' Fidelma affirmed solemnly. 'My duties now lie elsewhere.'

'Then I will inform Brother Ruissine that, as of now, I have taken over this matter.'

'I will see you and the steward in the morning, at the breaking of the fast.'

Fidelma led the way out of the hut with a speechless Eadulf following. They left the young lawyer to douse the oil lantern. As soon as they had put distance between Oengarb and themselves, Eadulf turned to her with an accusatory manner.

'This is the first time I've seen you become uninterested in the investigation of a murder – and what of the abbot with whom you had such secret business?'

'I am afraid the abbot's death is not as important as the task I was given,' she replied, almost without emotion. 'Oengarb is well able to sort out the details, or those details that affect this situation. But I fear the answers pertinent to my mission are no longer to be found here, so any investigation will be superfluous.'

Eadulf raised his brows. 'You think the girl killed the old man and fled?'

She did not answer but turned towards the stable.

'So are we returning to Cashel in the morning?' Eadulf pressed again.

Eadulf had thought nothing more could surprise him but her next statement made him catch his breath.

'Tomorrow we will have to continue our journey. It will take us south across the river, so we will need the services of a ferryman to take us and our horses across. We still have a long journey ahead of.'

Eadulf tried to gather his thoughts at this unexpected news. 'But your business with the abbot is concluded and . . .?' he began. Then he bit his lip. 'I knew that it was nonsense about seeking the student numbers for Colgú. He has never interested himself in such matters.'

'If you wish to be so precise,' Fidelma cut in, 'then that part of my business involving the abbot is concluded by his death. I have to continue the business elsewhere.'

Eadulf was thoughtful. 'I believe that you are following the girl,' he stated. 'You believe she killed the abbot and you have left Oengarb to continue a fruitless investigation inside the abbey while you give chase to the real culprit. I do not see the logic of it. Why did you not tell Oengarb? He could have raised some men to give chase. The result would have been the same.'

Eadulf waited a moment for her to answer but she did not. She continued to stride towards the stables. Eadulf was almost relieved to see the reassuring figure of Enda, stretched out at ease by the fire of the smithy. There was an air of normality about him compared with the strange behaviour of Fidelma. The smithy had stopped work and was relaxing over a drink with the visitor before the glowing charcoal brazier. Enda saw them approaching and rose to his feet.

'We heard the news about the abbot, lady,' he greeted them. 'Some of the brethren have been here asking if we had seen a girl. Do you need us to join in the search for her?'

'No, Enda. There is a *dálaigh* called Oengarb, who is in charge of the investigation into the abbot's death.' She paused, then said, 'Walk with us a little.' She led him out of earshot of the smithy. 'I came here to ask you to get our horses ready to leave at first light. We are going south across the river. So ask about a ferry, and find one that will take us across the river or even through the islands.'

Eadulf could see by the puzzled look that spread over the young warrior's face that this news confounded him too.

'I would have thought the abbey would be pleased to have you, as a senior *dálaigh*, to help them investigate the matter,' Enda wondered aloud.

Fidelma exhaled sharply. 'It might be better if you kept your thoughts to yourself. I will tell you what we are doing.'

The young warrior took a step back as if she had struck him across the cheek.

'I only . . .' he began.

'Be ready with the horses at first light. Find out about a ferry to take us south of the river.'

With that she twisted on her heel and moved off. Eadulf paused to give Enda an apologetic glance; he raised a shoulder and let it fall as a gesture expressing both surprise and puzzlement.

'Wasn't that uncalled for?' Eadulf asked softly, as he caught up with Fidelma.

'I have been charged with this mission,' she snapped. 'As I recall, you were not invited to come along. It was you who asked to accompany me.'

Eadulf was shocked by her response but did not rise to her sharp tone. 'I hope you have a reason for your behaviour, Fidelma. To be honest, I cannot think of any justification for it.'

'My justification is the desire to fulfil the mission I have been set,' she replied, unmoved.

'A mission you keep secret and share with no one?'

'That is what I am tasked with.'

'I am beginning to believe that you already know why the abbot was murdered, and I want to know why you are now concerned about this girl but not sharing any knowledge about her with Oengarb, the lawyer. I want answers to such question, otherwise I think it behoves me to tell the steward some of what I know. His attitude seems to indicate that all is not as it appears to be.'

They had reached their hut and Fidelma went in first. Inside, she lit some candles and then swung round to face Eadulf, taking a seat on the bed. She glared belligerently at him.

'Shut the door,' she ordered. 'Now, apart from moral delicacies, what makes you think you have anything of worth to tell Brother Ruissine? Why do you think I am concerned about the girl?'

'Because of the paper that you found in the girl's comb bag.'

Fidelma grimaced. 'You are a good observer,' she replied coldly.

'There was a time when you would have complimented me on it and not treated me like a nuisance. Am I not your husband? Or do you still see me as a stranger, a foreigner, just the son of a hereditary *gerefa*, or lawgiver, who dared to wed the sister of an illustrious king of your people?'

The words came tumbling out, the result of the pent-up resentment he had been feeling these last days since Fidelma had been keeping from him whatever it was that had sent her on this quest.

Fidelma's face had whitened; her mouth was a pinched red line.

'You insult yourself, Eadulf, as well as me, if that is how you see our relationship,' she said stiffly.

'Easy to say,' replied Eadulf. His mind was suddenly filled with memories of the fears he had had before their official wedding day. Was it only a little less than four years ago? It seemed longer. True, he had first encountered Fidelma at the great Council of Streoneshalh, or Witebia, the White House, as Abbess Hilda's abbey was called. After some years, having realised their lives seemed inextricably linked, they had decided on the traditional trial marriage in which, under Irish law, they had bound themselves together for a year and a day. During that time, Fidelma had become his *bencharrthach*, 'loved woman', while he had been happy to be her *fer comtha*, with the rights of a husband. It was during this period that their son, Alchú, the 'gentle hound', had been born. Then, at the end of that trial period, they had confirmed their marriage vows at Cashel.

It was a period of unease, for he was well aware that he was a stranger in a strange land who was to marry a princess of the Eóganacht, sister to Colgú, King of Muman and fifty-ninth generation descendant of Eibhear Fionn, who had brought his people to this island. He had talked over his concerns with old Brother Conchobhar of Cashel and confessed he had not envisaged the problems he would have to face in marrying into such a family. He was fearful for he knew that as an outsider he was technically without status, without an honour price that secured a place within the society. True, Colgú and others of the family had welcomed him into their midst, but was that simply for Fidelma's sake? Many others were keen to remind him that he was a foreigner, a Saxon, as they called him, much to his annoyance. He had more recently found himself protesting against this, pointing out that he came from the kingdom of the East Angles. The trouble was that in Fidelma's language the same word, Sagsanach, was applied to both Angles and Saxons. It seemed that these hidden fears about his status had been stirred up now that Fidelma no longer confided in him. His future had begun to seem bleak and dark.

'Easy to say,' he repeated. 'I saw you take the paper from the comb bag. Then you suddenly decided to allow Oengarb to take over the mystery of the abbot's murder and to leave the abbey and head southwards.'

Fidelma's face was immobile for a moment, and then she inclined her head. 'I should never underestimate you, Eadulf. There is truth in what you say.'

'And you are following this girl. What's her name . . . Cairenn?'

Fidelma once again took refuge in silence.

'Am I not permitted to join your thoughts?' Eadulf demanded harshly.

'I am afraid that you cannot join these thoughts,' she returned bluntly.

'Is it because I am a stranger from over the seas that I can't even share the thoughts of my wife?'

Fidelma hesitated. 'That is not how it is,' she replied.

'Then how is it . . . exactly?'

'Are you going to continue to press this matter?' Fidelma said coldly.

Eadulf frowned and then shook his head. 'I need to know what this is about. I shall press it until an answer makes sense, until I see some logic in it,' he affirmed stubbornly.

Fidelma uttered a long, deep sigh. Her shoulders hunched, as if what he said were painful to her. Then she raised her head to meet his challenging gaze with a sorrowful expression.

'You want an answer as to why I cannot tell you?'

'It would help,' Eadulf agreed diffidently.

'I cannot tell you. I have sworn by a sacred oath to tell no one,' she said simply.

chapter four

For several long moments Eadulf stood staring at her, astounded. Of all the answers he had been expecting, this had not been one of them.

'A sacred oath?' His voice dropped to a whisper of astonishment. 'To whom did you make this sacred oath? I don't believe it. Making secret oaths, sacred or not, is not in your nature. To whom would you make a secret oath that would exclude me?'

'It was necessary, Eadulf.' She acknowledged the hurt in his eyes.

'Then explain to me why, even if you can't explain what,' Eadulf insisted.

'I would like to share all my knowledge with you just as much as you wish me to, Eadulf. But all I can tell you is that I have been put under a *geis* not to reveal what I have been told.'

Eadulf was puzzled. 'A *geis*?' He had not heard the word before. 'What is a *geis*?'

She glanced at him in genuine surprise. 'You do not know the term?'

Eadulf shook his head. Fidelma suddenly realised that such an old and sacred term might not have been generally encountered by a stranger to the country, even if, like Eadulf, they had lived in the Five Kingdoms for many years. It was also true that the old ways, the ancient oaths, were changing as the New Faith spread, so it was certainly possible that he had never heard of the old prohibition before.

'It is an injunction that has been placed on me not to reveal the nature of this matter until I am released from the oath. It is a very serious undertaking, which I am honour-bound to observe. Indeed, before the coming of the New Faith, only the Druids could impose the *geis*, and when the Druids began to vanish, those of the royal blood took over the custom. It is the ultimate way to ensure authority.'

Eadulf's eyes widened a little; his expression became a little cynical. 'And this prohibition prevents you speaking of it even to me?'

Her expression softened. 'Even to you,' she conceded.

'And what if you broke it?'

She remained serious. 'In the days of the Old Faith it was said that the breaking of a *geis* merited instant punishment, rejection by society. It was even thought that the old gods and goddesses would cause the death of someone who broke the *geis* – a hideous death. One story goes that when the High King Conaire Mór was placed under a *geis* and broke it, the Mórrígán, the triune goddess of death and battles, appeared to him and told him of his doom. It came to pass that he perished exactly as the goddess had foretold, when his head was severed from his body.'

Eadulf shivered slightly, because he had been raised with tales of the pagan gods and goddesses of his own people, the strange deities who had ruled before the coming of the New Faith and his conversion to it as a youth. Then he pulled himself together.

'That's nonsense,' he told her, though without conviction. 'You have always been too logical to believe in supernatural curses. You have always said you do not believe in evil spirits.'

Fidelma shrugged indifferently. 'Make of it what you will. I merely describe an old tradition that my people still respect. It is still thought that ill fortune will befall whoever breaks the prohibition. It is still the most sacred oath for any person of this land

– so sacred that it is not even allowed to be pronounced before the Brehon courts of law.'

'But you surely don't believe in that sort of thing?'

'Whether I believe in the evil supernatural or not, I do believe in honour, and I am honour-bound by the oath, for it invokes the honour of my family stretching back into the time beyond time.'

'Is this matter somehow connected to your family?' Eadulf asked. His mind turned to the events before they had left Cashel. 'I remember that you did not even discuss anything with your brother, Colgú, before we left.'

Fidelma's eyes flashed dangerously. 'How do you work that out, Eadulf?'

'I have eyes and the ability to observe. I remember what prompted our leaving. Old Brother Conchobhar, the apothecary, came with a message for you. It was after receipt of that message that you decided you had an important matter to discuss with Abbot Nessán. Where did the message come from? It was written on a scrap such as is attached to carrier pigeons. As I say, we left before you even consulted your brother. You did not want me to accompany you, and when you chose Enda to accompany you, you would not even tell him what for, although he is of your brother's elite bodyguard . . .'

'As a *dálaigh* and sister to the King, I have a right to request to be accompanied by a bodyguard,' snapped Fidelma icily.

Eadulf nodded. 'That message caused you much concern. I saw that in your eyes. But you would not speak of it to either of us. It does not need a superior mind to work out that something very important is amiss. That something, it seems, is the very reason why you have come here, and why you did not want me to accompany you. Were you expecting Abbot Nessán to be murdered? Even after that, you are still excluding me and Enda from your confidence.'

'I am under a *geis* not to tell. That still stands, Eadulf,' Fidelma replied, but now her tone was almost apologetic.

'I am trying to understand who made you take this silly oath? You say that only a Druid of the Old Faith or a person of the blood royal could make you accept such a thing.' Eadulf could not keep the sneer from his voice.

For a moment Fidelma's green eyes flashed. 'No one forces me to take an oath – and let me not hear you say the *geis* is silly.'

'It was not your brother, so who else could make you accept this prohibition?'

'I have already explained to you more than I should,' she replied defensively.

'But not enough, for I am your husband. Or don't I have rights?'

'Eadulf.' Her voice was suddenly sad. 'You are my husband and father to our son. But under our laws you do not have total control of me as you would in your country. Let us not go into the rights of husband and wife.'

'I know I have few rights as a foreigner here.' Eadulf's voice was tight at this reminder of his status.

'In the matter of the *geis* you have exactly the same rights as anyone else in the Five Kingdoms,' she countered. 'You cannot demand that the oath be broken.'

'I think,' Eadulf said, thoughtfully, 'if it was not your brother, then there is only one person who could put this *geis* on you.' When she did not respond, he went on reflectively: 'Old Brother Conchobhar keeps a pigeon loft for your brother, for he uses them, as do many others, to communicate with other kings and important princes. The message that troubled you came that way . . . by way of the trained rock doves that old Conchobhar keeps. You are no longer of the religious so the Chief Brehon of Muman has no influence over you. Therefore I suspect it came from none other than the High King himself.'

Fidelma stood up, dismissing the subject. 'We need some rest because we must be stirring at first light.'

'You still mean to cross the river at first light without sharing any information with us? The reason that brought you to this place? No explanation as to why we are pursuing this girl and misdirecting the lawyer Oengarb?'

'I have said that we will cross the river south.' Then it seemed her steadfastness relented a little. 'I'll make you one promise, Eadulf. As soon as I am permitted to tell you, I will.'

'When will that be?' He was not mollified.

'When I am formally released from my oath, or when I have reached the point at which I feel it would be more moral to break it than to maintain it. Perhaps that will be soon, Eadulf. But until then, the *geis* is sacred.'

If the truth were known, she could see no logical reason why she should not tell Eadulf right away, other than her acceptance of the *geis*. But it was a powerful restriction in her culture. It was her respect for the *geis*, as one of the ancient traditions of the Eóganacht, which prevented her from sharing its secrets, even with her husband. It was a taboo, a bond that stretched back into the mists of ancient times, when such prohibitions were not imposed lightly. Anyone transgressing the taboo would be, at worst, subject to rejection by society, placed outside the social order and the law, bringing shame and outlawry. There were many stories about the effects of the *geis,* stories passed down the generations, ancient stories that became legend, such as when Setanta was given the name Cúchulainn – Culann's hound. Having killed the hound that guarded Culann's house, Setanta offered to take on the role of guardian until a new hound was trained, and he was placed under a *geis* never to eat the flesh of a dog. Trapped by his enemies, he was eventually forced to eat dog flesh and for this infringement his own death was sealed.

Fidelma was momentarily tempted to break her *geis* as she gazed upon Eadulf's concerned features but her culture was too powerful an inhibition. She could not do so until she felt she was absolved from the oath. Until then, she alone would know the concerns that brought her here.

She had continued to fret about the prohibition, as she had ever since Brother Conchobhar had handed her the message that had come, as Eadulf had rightly deduced, by carrier pigeon from Cenn Fáelad, son of Blathmac of the Sil nÁedo Sláine, High King of the Five Kingdoms. The message itself had been written in *rúnscríobh*, an ancient cypher, in the hand of Cenn Fáelad himself, so that no one else could read it. She had been surprised that Cenn Fáelad had remembered that she also had knowledge enough to read the cypher. Her old mentor, Brehon Morann, had taught her the art when she studied at his law school in Tara; she had revealed this to Cenn Fáelad while she was solving the mystery of the murder of his brother.

The *geis* had survived even in these days of the New Faith. No member of the royal houses would dare to defy it. Fidelma simply could not yet tell Eadulf about her mission, much as she wished to tell both her travelling companions the truth of what had brought them to the far south of the kingdom.

It is amazing how sleep catches you unawares, even when you think that it will never come, so many thoughts assail your mind and awkward memories come unbidden, interweaving in the darkness until you long, long for daylight so that you can begin the day and escape from them. She knew she had to get up and go to Abbot Nessán's chamber. She found her brother, Colgú, was there and Eadulf. Eadulf was lying dead on the floor, a ligature at his throat, and Colgú was rebuking her for breaking the *geis*. Curiously, a part of her mind was trying to articulate what it was that Aristotle taught: that the images of dreams serve as the start of waking thought and may be prophetic? But, surely, she was not dreaming. This was reality and she had not slept at all. She leapt from the bed, her heart pounding. A few moments passed until she realised she had indeed been sleeping. Eadulf was stirring tetchily beside her.

The grey glimmerings of first light were just showing. She sat, wiped the sweat from her brow and breathed deeply several times, trying to recall the fading memory of the dream. It was Plato that now came to mind. In all people, even the most moral and good, there is a wild beast that peers out at the world when one sleeps. It creates passions and fears. The dream was already floating away into the dark mists, into oblivion, like all dreams. She sighed again, rose and went to splash water on her face. Only then did she notice how quickly the light was growing.

She turned to the bed. Eadulf was making those odd breath-like noises with his mouth and nose, as if reluctant to be dragged from his sleep.

'Come, Eadulf, get up! Enda will be waiting for us.'

By the time they left the hut and walked to the stables Fidelma had forgotten all about the dream and the curious feelings of anxiety it had provoked. Dream memories can be annoyingly short.

Thankfully, the rain of the previous evening had passed and so had the wind from the north. The morning seemed fine; the clouds were again like woolly fleeces but today they were not bunching up but spreading lazily across the sky, with a breeze from the north-east bringing warmer air. Fidelma knew this was weather not to be relied upon – such instability often resulted in showers.

Enda was ready at the stables, waiting patiently with their horses.

'Is all well, Enda?'

The young warrior had not forgotten her irascible temper of the previous evening, even if she had. He rubbed his cheek nervously.

'It is, lady. The horses are fed and watered.'

'Were you able to find a ferry across the river?'

He nodded immediately. 'It is all arranged, lady. The brother of the *echaire*, the master of the stables here, is actually a ferryman. He is called Imchad, and his ferry is large enough to take both us and our horses across. He will meet us on the pier in front of the gates. I agreed a fee of half a *screpall*.'

'That seems fair enough,' Fidelma agreed as she took charge of her pony, Aonbharr, whom she had named after the steed of the old god of the ocean, Manannán mac Lir. Eadulf, who was not a skilful horseman, had his docile cob while Enda's warhorse, a stallion, was a full head taller than either of the others. They walked their horses slowly down to the gates of the abbey, which stood open and where a few merchants were mingling with members of the community, conducting their business. The steward, Brother Ruissine, was there, apparently waiting for them.

He greeted Fidelma. 'I am told you are leaving us already, lady.' There seemed a suspicious tone to his voice. 'I was also told that you needed these figures' – he handed her a small square of papyrus – 'and that this was what you wanted to see the abbot about. It seems a long journey for a matter of so little importance.'

'Nevertheless, that was my business,' Fidelma said. She took the paper from his hand and, without looking at it, put it in her *marsupium*. 'We have other business to attend to, otherwise I would have stayed to help in the matter of Abbot Nessán's murder. However, I am confident that Oengarb will quickly clear it up. It is a sadness that Nessán has met such a brutal end, but there is little I can do now for time is pressing.'

Brother Ruissine glanced at Eadulf and grimaced.

'It seems the girl that you were asking questions about was the very one who killed him. Since she claimed to be a relative of the abbot – they were both Eóganacht Raithlind – we presume it must have been some family feud that prompted her to come here to kill him.'

Fidelma's face did not alter. She nodded solemnly.

'Oengarb told me to pass on to you that he has ordered some men to search the countryside, to see if they can track this girl, Cairenn. And I myself have so instructed a couple of the woodsmen that work at the abbey, who are excellent trackers. I am sure that they will soon overtake her.'

Eadulf, who had barely spoken that morning, his mind still on his wife's explanation of the *geis*, raised his brows interrogatively. 'Then you know the direction in which the girl is heading?'

The steward smiled sourly. 'There is surely only one direction she can go in – that is westward, or south-westward. The girl was of the Cenél nÁeda section of the Eóganacht Raithlind. That was where Abbot Nessán came from, Ráth Rathlind itself.'

Eadulf almost remarked that he was disappointed that the girl was not heading south. He still believed that Fidelma was following the girl. But if she was going west, that was in the wrong direction.

He became aware that Brother Ruissine was still speaking.

'It is obvious that the girl will try to seek sanctuary with her family, among the iron workers of the Cenél nÁeda,' the steward affirmed. 'After such a crime, who else would take her in?'

'That seems logical enough,' Fidelma agreed seriously. 'Well, I wish you and Oengarb success in these endeavours.' Then she hesitated thoughtfully. 'You mentioned that this girl, Cairenn, had arrived recently. The day before yesterday, in fact. I wonder, did she arrive with anyone else?'

Brother Ruissine shook his head at once. 'Why do you ask?'

'There was a religieux in the refectory last night, a tall man in black-dyed robes.'

The steward frowned and then nodded. 'I do recall him. He was just a passing traveller seeking hospitality for a few nights.'

'He arrived separately?'

'I believe so. He came yesterday evening while she arrived in the morning.'

'From which direction did the man come?'

'I have no idea. He arrived at dusk on horseback. His accent was of the northern territories; I would guess he was from Ulaidh. What makes you ask about him?'

'Do you think I might have a word with him before I leave?'

She did not respond to the steward's question. 'It means delaying our departure,' she added in explanation to Eadulf, 'but the man is so familiar that I believe I must have met him and I just want to be sure that I do not cause dishonour by ignoring him.'

Brother Ruissine smiled thinly and shook his head.

'In that case, lady, I am afraid that you are too late.'

'Too late?' she asked sharply. 'What do you mean?'

'He has already left the abbey.'

'Left? At the same time that the girl left, in the middle of the night?'

'He left before dawn this morning. He asked one of the stable lads if he knew any taverns on the road to the Hill of the Yew.'

'That's to the east, isn't it, the township at the estuary of the Great River?' interjected Eadulf. 'Why would he ask a stable boy about that? Isn't it some distance from here?'

'This brother must have heard that the stable lad comes from Eochaill. As you say, it is a long ride, so well worth being prepared to break the journey.'

'Did this brother have a name?'

The steward raised his shoulders and let them fall in a shrug of ignorance.

'We have so many pilgrims passing through that we do not ask them all to give us their names.'

Fidelma gave a deep sigh and turned to her companions. But before she could speak, the steward asked: 'Are you making your way south across the river? That is a difficult and marshy country.'

There was an implied question, but Fidelma treated it as an observation.

'This area is not called the Great Marsh of Muman without reason,' she agreed with a faint smile.

'I'll come with you as far as the ferry,' the steward offered, frowning.

Outside the gates, at the wooden jetty on the river bank, was a large flat-bottom raft. It was, indeed, large enough to take horses and even a fair-sized wagon on its log platform. Enda had made a good choice. A few railings of wood were the ferry's only feature, to afford protection to the passengers, and it was propelled by means of two thick ropes that straddled the broad river. The ferry captain, Imchad, was a large man with a barrel chest and prominent muscles on his stocky frame. He stood patiently, waiting for them to lead their horses onto his craft. He looked a typical ferryman, his weather-beaten skin almost black, and his bright, twinkling eyes seemed so bright that they had almost no colour but reflected the light of the sky.

Brother Ruissine walked with them as they led their horses onto the jetty and the ferrymen helped guide them onto the raft and secure them.

'Well, we bid you good day, Brother.' Fidelma turned to the steward. 'Our thanks for the hospitality of the abbey. Doubtless when I report the news of Abbot Nessán's death to my brother and to Abbot Cuan, who is now Chief Bishop of the kingdom, they will be in touch with you. They will be anxious to hear your decision on who will replace Nessán as your new abbot.'

The steward bowed his head quickly. 'We will communicate any proposal and decision as soon as possible.' The man hesitated and then indicated the far bank. 'If you are going directly south, remember it is a very marshy land, a place of small islands separated by reed-filled waters. Have a care as you travel, for the route can be dangerous. You know that the borderland territory of Ciarraige Cuirche, Cenél nÁeda land, lies that way? It is full of unrest, cattle raiders and robbers.'

If the steward hoped to elicit information in this roundabout way, he was unsuccessful, because there was a shouted order from Imchad and the great raft began to move. The steward was left on the jetty, watching their progress across the flowing waters of the ancient waterway. That the river was fast flowing with deep currents was obvious from the grunts and sweating of the ferrymen as they hauled on the heavy ropes to pull the ferry across from one bank to another. Once, one of the men was forced to take up a large pole in order to push away some branches that were floating downriver and could have damaged the craft.

Imchad smiled broadly when Eadulf winced as the impact was narrowly avoided, though with such dexterity that it was clear that it had been expertly done.

'You should have no fear, Brother,' he observed in amusement. 'Is it not claimed that all you religious are protected by divine powers? What need you fear from a lowly river goddess? Anyway, the old river is calm today. Do you see how she flows like a mill pond with scarcely a ripple or murmur? She'll be like that until she comes through the islands and approaches the open seas beyond.'

Eadulf could not think of a suitable response but Enda, who was carefully examining the new countryside along the river banks, turned to ask: 'Is it far to the sea then? The river seems so beautiful and tranquil here that you could believe there was no sea within miles.'

'Ah!' The ferryman gestured quickly to the south-east with a gnarled hand. 'We are not far from the Great Southern Ocean but the islands form a barrier between the two branches of the great river, and beyond the barrier of the Great Island of Ard Nemed the river empties into what is almost an inland sea. The waters there connect with the large entrance into the mighty ocean but fear not, we are safe here, well protected from the sea.'

Eadulf was still not clear on the local geography and felt Enda was unsure as well. However, he merely asked: 'Ard Nemed? What is that?'

'There are many islands here, many islands to negotiate, but there are none as big as the Great Island. This river divides and one branch flows to the north of the island, the other to the south, towards the inland sea. You could then continue south to the entrance to the Great Southern Ocean, as I have said.'

'Tell me this, my friend.' Eadulf was still confused. 'You call it the Height of Nemed. Who is this Nemed whose island is so great?'

The boatman looked astonished and Enda, who had been listening, explained hurriedly, 'My friend is a stranger in this land.'

Imchad grimaced. 'I thought your accent was that of a stranger,' he said. 'Nemed? The name goes back to the time beyond time.'

Eadulf groaned inwardly but accepted that he was about to hear yet another ancient tale. Why was this land so replete in them? Every question seemed to be answered by the prologue of an old story.

'During the mists of primeval times,' the ferryman was saying, 'it is said, the land of the goddess Éire and her sisters, Banba and Fodhla, was invaded by ancient peoples. Nemed was the person who led the third invasion, setting sail from across some eastern sea with a fleet of forty-four ships. Only one ship made it to these shores, where he battled with the undersea dwellers that we call the Fomorii. They say he came with a beautiful wife called Macha, and to her is credited the naming of Ard Macha in the north, where some claim the New Faith was first taught by Patrick.'

'Which we know to be an untruth,' chimed in Enda cynically. 'Here, in the south, we find many great teachers of the New Faith, even before the time of Patrick the Briton.'

'Just so, young warrior.' Imchan paused for a moment to check the ropes and call on his men to adjust them as the ferry swung a little in midstream. Then he turned back to them. 'Nemed? Oh yes,' he went on, 'he fought the dark lords of the sea but he and his followers finally succumbed and died of the plague. It was a magic plague that the evil gods and goddesses inflicted on them. Nemed had made the Great Island we speak of his fortress and so, when he died, he was buried there and that spot is called Ard Nemed, Nemed's Height. Yes, stranger, it happened in the time beyond time, even before the children of the Gael arrived to claim this land.'

Eadulf hesitated for a moment and it was Enda who asked: 'Does anyone dwell on Nemed's island now?'

'Few people dwell there, mostly farmers and cattle herders. They are of the Cenél nÁeda, a branch of the Eóganacht Raithlind. The island is much in contention,' replied the ferry captain. 'I am surprised you are unaware of it.'

'What do you mean . . . much in contention?' Eadulf had not realised that the Eóganacht Raithlind territory stretched so far east but he knew the family had many sub-divisions.

'The Uí Liatháin often raid the island. They are almost within swimming distance of its eastern end.'

'The Uí Líathain?' queried Eadulf, echoing the name from surprise rather than ignorance.

'A warlike people,' commented the ferryman. 'They claim kinship with the Uí Fidgenti, who are even more warlike.'

Eadulf exchanged a bleak look with Enda.

'I thought their territory was much further north than here,' Enda commented.

'They claim a large territory. Anyway, it is known that Artgal, who is a chieftain of the Cenél nÁeda – that is the people who dwell in these southern marshlands – holds the old fortress at Ard Nemed, in order to dissuade the Uí Liatháin from making their raids on the island.'

'What could be worth raiding on this island?' asked Eadulf. 'You say it is scarcely populated.'

The ferryman stroked his nose thoughtfully.

'Sometimes it is where a territory is rather than what the soil yields that makes it valuable, my friends. Ard Nemed could control all the natural harbours of this part of the kingdom. Who controls Ard Nemed, the Great Island, controls the harbour and the links to many lands. That is worth more to the ambitious man than taking a cow or two or a flock of sheep.'

'Are the Uí Liatháin so ambitious?'

'They have shown themselves to be so. But at the moment they are held at bay.' Imchad smiled. 'Artgal is a worthy prince, a true son of the Eóganacht Ráithlind, whose ancestors were kings at Cashel and who is therefore loyal to Cashel.'

The heavy ferry bumped against the southern shore of the great river. Fidelma, who had been silent during the crossing, led her horse off the boat before turning to the boatman.

'Do you know much about this territory?'

'I do, lady,' Imchad replied gravely. He had been told who Fidelma was – presumably by his brother, the stable master at the abbey, for neither Eadulf nor Enda had mentioned her rank.

'And there are many islands in this area?'

'That is so, lady,' Imchad answered respectfully.

'Are the routes between them good or bad?' she asked.

The man rubbed his chin thoughtfully. 'It is not the best time of the year to be travelling through the territory of the Ciarraige Cuirche. Of course, it depends in which direction you want to go. The tracks to the west are good. Even with last night's rain, you will probably find most of them firm and you will encounter little real marshland until you get to the shores of the River Banna. There is a lot of high ground before the river. South of here it will be marshy, for the winter months increase the marshland. However, some tracks cross the high ground. The worst area is to the east.'

Eadulf stifled a groan, suspecting that it was to the east that she would want to go.

'But I see hills to the east,' Enda pointed out.

'So you do, warrior,' agreed Imchad, the ferryman. 'But I doubt whether you can jump your horses from hill to hilltop. No, my friend, it is by the lowlands, between the hills, that you would have to travel, and, at this time of year, tracks are like muddy rivers. That is why this area is called the Great Marsh.'

Fidelma was looking thoughtful. Then she pointed towards one of several tracks leading south from the river, which entered a thorny-looking winter woodland, with high trees and bushes, some with evergreen foliage, others with gaunt branches denuded of growth.

'Does that track lead south?' she asked.

The ferryman nodded. 'It does, lady.'

'And would that be a safe track to travel on?'

The man grinned. 'If you wanted to go that way,' he began slyly, 'I daresay I might be able to suggest a guide.'

'Who might this guide be and where would he be found?'

The boatman stood motionless for a moment, seeming to examine his left hand with a sharp intensity.

Fidelma grimaced and, feeling inside her *marsupium*, she withdrew some coins, picked one and dropped it into the boatman's hand.

'And who would this guide be?' she asked again, her face expressionless. 'And where would he be found?'

'All you have to do is travel due south, following this stream; it is called the Dark River, although it is not big. It will lead you to a farmstead, named after the stream – Dubh Glas. There the track divides, one branch continuing south, one east and the other west.'

'And where might the guide be found?'

'At the farmstead ask for Tassach. He will help you.'

Fidelma inclined her head in acknowledgment and mounted her pony.

Imchad and his companions stood watching as the party rode away from the wooden jetty. Fidelma was aware of their continued gaze as she led the way between the few rough-built wooden cabins that were dotted on the bank. She noted that several tracks led off in various directions. She motioned with her head towards the southern track and Eadulf and Enda followed her, moving into the bare woodland ahead until they encountered evergreens and the thickening foliage began to spread around them, like an impenetrable and devouring growth.

As Fidelma and her companions entered the tall dark wood, the path narrowed a little. Enda managed to guide his horse alongside Fidelma's grey-white pony, his tall black stallion looming over her.

'Lady, I think it is my duty to go first,' he announced. 'I am, after all, a warrior of the Golden Collar and bodyguard to your family.'

Fidelma frowned a little in annoyance but then realised that it was true. It was not the custom to ride ahead of her brother's bodyguards in such circumstances.

'Very well, Enda, you take the lead and Eadulf and I will ride behind you. We shall keep this small stream on our left-hand side until we find this farmstead, which can't be too far ahead.'

'I wish the countryside were more open, though,' Enda observed, glancing around before nudging his horse into the lead.

Although the thickly growing evergreens enclosed their path as if they were in a narrow tunnel, Fidelma laughed and called, 'Do not tell me, Enda, that you are nervous about riding through dark woods alone?'

Enda did not turn his head. 'If it pleases you to think so, lady,' he replied affably.

Enda had earned his position in the elite bodyguard of the King of Muman. As a boy, long before he had reached the *aimsir togú*, the age of choice, he had decided that he wanted to be a *feinnid*, a professional warrior, and aspired to join the King's bodyguard. He had quickly displayed his abilities to the commanders of the Nasc Niadh, the champions of the Golden Collar. He not only had to be skilled in all manner of arms but also had to display a capability in strategy and planning. Warriors had to be knowledgeable in the arts and philosophy too, for a champion did not merely use brute force on the field of combat. Indeed, it was said that Cormac, the son of Art, when he was High King, had founded three military colleges at Tara for the training of his Fianna, his army's elite. Each ruler of the Five Kingdoms of Éireann had their chosen bodyguard *catha*, or battalions, and each their military training academies.

Enda had swiftly risen to the level of a *curad*, a warrior of valour. It was then but a short step to being accepted to wear the golden collar, or torc. Should the King call a *sluaghadh*, or hosting, in time of war, Enda could command a full *cath*, a battalion three thousand warriors strong. He would not admit it but he was disappointed that there had only once been a war since he had earned the golden collar. That had not been so long ago, when Colgú had been forced to march his battalions to counter the attempted invasion of his kingdom by Fianamal, King of Laigin, using the neutral territory of Osraige into the land of Princess Gelgeis of Éile. The sight of Colgú's hosts had been enough to give pause to the forces of Laigin and their Osraige co-conspirators, and after a few brief skirmishes and the destruction of their fortress of Liath Mór, the invaders had been forced to die or surrender. Not many chose the first option. The intervention of the High King and his Chief Brehon, Sedna, had brought an uneasy peace between Laigin and Muman.

Now, Enda rode confidently ahead and, if the truth were known, he rode proudly as protector of his King's sister and her husband. They had been through several adventures together and often Enda's arms, and sometimes his abilities as a strategist, had stood the three of them in good stead, saving them from many a dangerous situation. In spite of Fidelma's jibe, which was not meant in any seriousness because she had total trust in him, the young warrior sat relaxed on his black warhorse, showing no sign of tension as he led the way. Nonetheless, his watchful gaze swung cautiously from side to side along the path before him. Not that he expected any danger but, until Fidelma felt able to tell him what her mysterious task in this remote corner of the kingdom was, he naturally felt that caution was the watchword.

Enda was confident in his abilities but he was not arrogant. Like all warriors, even those who espoused the New Faith, he preferred to regard his weapons as possessing the spirits of the ancient gods and goddesses. Such old and once sacred names were always given to weapons by the champions of the Golden Collar. He called his elaborately crafted short sword *Fiacail-na-hAnnan*, the Teeth of

Annan, the war goddess. She was said to be the predictor of death
on the battlefield. His javelin was named *Mac-an-Nemain*, after one
of the triune goddesses of war, who created frenzy and havoc among
her enemies on the battlefield. His *lumain*, or stout shield, was
simply *An Cosantoir* – The Protector – named after the ancient
word for the star that the Romans called Mars. Enda used no other
weapons, although some warriors had adopted others, such as a
bow or a battleaxe. In his chosen weapons, Enda felt he was a
master.

Eadulf had brought his docile cob alongside Fidelma, although
there was barely room for the two horses to walk steadily abreast.
Eadulf was sniffing at the air. He could smell that strange stale
odour of rotting vegetation that he associated with marshland, the
low-lying wetlands.

'Well,' he suddenly said, 'like Enda, I will be glad when we have
passed through this area; woods and wetlands do not go well together.
The smell of bogs can be very unpleasant. If you remember, it was
not so long ago I had the misfortune to get lost in marshlands.'

It was true that less than a year ago Eadulf had lost his way in
the southern boglands of Osraige, and had nearly died before he
had managed to find his way out.

'Little chance of being lost here,' Fidelma assured him. 'All we
have to do is follow the stream to the farmstead that the ferryman
told us of and find this man Tassach.'

'Why do we need a guide? Where are we going?' Eadulf was
expecting Fidelma to claim she could not tell him because of her
oath.

'We must eventually turn east to that island that the ferryman
told you of.'

Eadulf was surprised. 'You mean Ard Nemed? I didn't think you
were listening to what was said.'

'I did not want the ferryman to know,' she confided. 'It would
not have been long before our destination was known to all and

sundry, back and forth along the river. I'd rather keep it to myself at the moment.'

'So we must turn east at some point?' Eadulf asked. 'And it is to do with the matter you are pursuing?'

She did not feel the need to answer. It was a logical conclusion. She settled back on her pony, riding at ease like Enda and, like him, she rode with her mind attuned to her surroundings, trying not to think about the task that she had been given and why a *geis* had been laid on her to keep her silent. She noticed a number of wych elm trees, not very tall, that seemed to be giving way to more populous alder, whose brown woody cones would stay on the tree, in spite of the loss of green leaves, throughout the winter. When spring arrived, the seeds would be dispersed. The alder showed they were moving through wetlands, because that was their usual habitat. And there was certainly plenty of moss along the path, and ferns predominated in the little clearings here and there. There were clumps of beech waiting patiently for winter to be gone and their dense leaf canopy to be renewed in brilliant green. She observed that around the base of one or two of the beech trunks, black finger-like projections of fungi were clinging, even the very shape fore-warning that they should not be eaten. There were only few edible fungi that would grow during this winter month. She had already spotted the violet hue of one edible fungus and not far on she saw more, oyster coloured, growing from the bark of a tree. They made a popular dish.

Fidelma was someone who was very conscious of the countryside that she travelled through. One had to be knowledgeable in order to survive, otherwise, in her opinion, you were like a blind man stumbling through the dark. That they were reaching slightly to higher ground was obvious from the increasing number of bare oak trees she could see; they were tall, with longer, straighter trunks and stubby acorns. She knew these trees had to be on firmer soil. Even so, there was plenty of chickweed, and white dead nettles about to remind her that they were close to water, and once she even saw a broad-backed stoat scuttling for its den in a rock crevice. The only birdsong she could differentiate at the moment was the loud, repetitive call of a reed warbler, which was unusual for it had typically disappeared at this time of year.

Her mind returned to her task and she considered the latest development. Why had her unknown adversaries felt the matter to be so serious that the abbot had had to be killed in such a vicious and cruel way? What was it that he knew that caused his death? Cairenn was heading for the Great Island, of course. She was cousin to Artgal as well as to Nessán. And both were distantly related to Fidelma, being Eóganacht. She began to wonder what role the girl had played at the abbey. Events had happened too quickly. Was Cairenn alive or dead; had she truly fled the abbey for her own safety? At least the piece of paper she had left inside had given Fidelma the clue – just the words 'great island' scrawled on it. So why was she making for Ard Nemed and the fortress of Artgal?

Fidelma sighed. She wished she could discuss these matters with Eadulf, or even with Enda. But she knew a *geis* – from no less a person than Cenn Fáelad, the High King – was a sacred prohibition and not to be treated lightly. She had the fearful thought that Artgal's fate might echo that of old Abbot Nessán.

She suddenly felt irritated with herself and told herself there could be no speculation without information. It was her old mantra, but she could not help speculating. She must sit back and enjoy the day for the day's sake until she reached the next stage of her journey, because one could either make the journey easy or hard and she would prefer that the journey be easy, since she knew hardship was not far ahead.

The next thing she knew was that Eadulf, quietly riding at her side, had suddenly turned in the saddle and with a great cry leant forward and thrust against her so hard that she lost her balance and fell sideways from her pony. It was so sudden and so unexpected that her mind was a jumble of confused thoughts even as she landed on the soft moss beside the track. Her pony started nervously, rearing a little, but being blocked in by Enda's stallion in front and Eadulf's cob at the side, it shied before coming down firmly on all its four legs and stood snorting in agitation and shivering in shock. An arrow protruded from the bow of her saddle, on which she had been sitting moments before. A second arrow had sped across the neck of her pony to embed itself in the trunk of a gnarled beech just behind her, and was still vibrating from the impact. For several moments everything was still, as though a deathly silence had fallen across the marshes.

CHAPTER FIVE

A cacophony of sounds filled the air. Fidelma rose to her knees, peering around and trying to shake off the feeling of stunned bewilderment. She was aware of Enda shouting, saw his horse plunging forward and the flashing steel of his blade swinging above his head as he lunged into the undergrowth. Eadulf was yelling for Fidelma to remain on the ground; he had flung himself from his cob and was running after Enda. Thoughts came tumbling into her mind. Someone had shot at them; that much was obvious. An ambush? Of course, an ambush. She had not been expecting it and cursed herself for a fool for not foreseeing it.

There was a scream from somewhere ahead but she could not see. Who was it? Was it Enda? Everything seemed to be moving too quickly for her to take in. Then someone was emerging from the undergrowth onto the path, holding a javelin. Enda had not been using a javelin; he had been using his sword. She gathered herself and tried to rise to meet the danger, and then she recognised Eadulf. He halted and stood breathing heavily, leaning on the javelin for support. There was movement behind him in the thick foliage. He swung round and brought up the javelin defensively. Fidelma balanced herself against the side of her pony, preparing herself to run to help him. Then she saw Enda's black horse moving back onto the path and Enda, sword in hand, who had dismounted and was leading it back to join them. Even in the shadowy light under the canopy of the trees, she realised that there was blood on his blade. He paused to bend and wipe it on the ferns. Then he moved to Eadulf and clapped him on the shoulder, gently removing the javelin from his shaky hand.

'It's over, lady,' Enda called, seeing her standing uncertainly by her pony. 'No danger threatens now.'

Eadulf seemed to recover and ran towards her, hands reaching out to her: 'Are you hurt? Are you all right?'

She forced a smile as she clasped his hands for a moment. 'I am a bit bruised,' she said. 'What happened? An ambush?'

Having reassured himself that she was unhurt, Enda indicated the undergrowth behind him. 'You were shot at,' he said grimly. 'Had it not been for friend Eadulf here one of the arrows might have hit you.'

She could not repress a shudder. 'That much I can deduce.'

'It was a lucky thing,' Eadulf admitted. 'The bowmen had to move aside the undergrowth which concealed them in order to get a clear shot. I saw the movement and could only push you down as they fired. I am sorry if you were hurt.'

'I would have been sorrier had you not,' she admitted. 'What has happened to the attackers?'

'Both dead, lady.' Enda was almost dismissive. 'They did not appear to be warriors, thankfully. From their appearance they seemed more like hunters, or woodsmen. They were armed with bows. I went for one of them with my sword, which gave the second one time to string another arrow. I think he would have managed to hit me while I was despatching the first bowman, but Eadulf seized my javelin from the sheath on my horse. He hurled it at the man and secured a good hit.'

Fidelma's lips compressed in brief annoyance.

'Are both men dead?'

'They are.'

'A pity,' she muttered.

Enda looked surprised. 'Why so, lady?'

'It would have been helpful to know if they were merely robbers or whether their attack had some other purpose.'

Eadulf exchanged a frowning glance with Enda.

'In this sort of woodland, not far from a prosperous abbey and its settlement, one would expect robbers and thieves to haunt the highways, preying on unsuspecting travellers,' the young warrior pointed out. 'Why would they have any other purpose?'

Eadulf stared at Fidelma for a moment. 'Unless they had something to do with Abbot Nessán's murder,' he said quietly.

Enda looked surprised. 'But these men were lying in wait for us. Are you saying their ambush is connected with the abbot's murder?'

'Is this something to do with your mission?' Eadulf demanded.

Fidelma did not respond at first, looking down at the ground. Then she raised her head to meet their gaze. 'I cannot say . . . yet. You know that, Eadulf.'

Eadulf sniffed in annoyance. 'And will you tell us after you have been killed?'

'Sarcasm doesn't become you,' she returned hotly, but she could understand his frustration.

'Perhaps not,' he replied calmly. 'But if you are on a mission that threatens your life, then it would be wise to forewarn us.'

Enda was looking unhappy. 'Why couldn't they be robbers?' he said, trying to keep the peace. 'There are often bands of brigands sheltering in such woods as these.'

'I doubt they were robbers,' Eadulf replied, almost brusquely. 'Look at this track. A track to nowhere, a narrow track meandering through the marshland. What wealthy victims would travel along it? Where would they be travelling to? Robbers would haunt the highways to the west, those leading to the great monasteries and settlements such as Ros Ailithir – which has become a place of pilgrimage as its very name proclaims: the pilgrims' promontory.

That is where robbers would lie in wait for victims, not here. Besides, there are three of us, and a warrior among us. They would have seen Enda's golden collar and known him for a king's champion – and they would know it would not be easy to overcome a trained warrior.'

'But they might have thought their first shots would wound or kill Enda,' Fidelma countered. It was her nature to argue. 'With Enda wounded, they might have thought that we would be easy victims.'

'Except those first arrows were not aimed at Enda,' pointed out Eadulf stubbornly. 'They were aimed at you.'

Enda suddenly understood the point Eadulf was making. 'It's true,' he said, thoughtfully. 'They meant to kill you first, lady, and then deal with friend Eadulf and me afterwards, if they could.'

Once more Fidelma made no direct response. She swung away from them and strode towards the patch of undergrowth where the bodies of the attackers lay.

'Wait, lady!' Enda called in alarm.

'I need to examine the bodies of these would-be assassins as you now describe them,' she declared over her shoulder.

Enda raised his arms in a hopeless gesture before following her, with Eadulf close behind.

The first of the bodies was the one Eadulf had pierced in the chest with the javelin. The man lay on his back just as he had fallen; the bow by his left hand and the arrow by his right showed clearly that he had been hit in the very act of stringing it. As Enda had said, there was nothing remarkable about the man. The face was weather-beaten and rough, with a flat nose and a chin that bristled with an unkempt beard. His clothes were shabby and badly stitched, and the woollen cloak around his shoulders was almost threadbare. They were not dissimilar to the clothes worn by many woodsmen. His leggings were of fur, perhaps rabbit, but also of poor quality. A hat of beaver fur had fallen behind him to reveal coarse and unevenly cut black hair. A leather pouch hung from a *criss*, or belt, of roughly worked hide. A sharp hunter's knife was still thrust in a leather sheath by his side. His quiver had been slung across his shoulders by a thong, and several of the arrows inside had snapped as he fell on it. The man lacked any personal adornment: there was no cheap jewellery, not even a bracelet, as often affected by the poor trying to appear to be of better station. As Fidelma peered down, examining the man, she could see that he was a total stranger to her.

She was about to turn away when a thought occurred to her and she suddenly dropped to one knee and reached for the man's leather pouch. Inside were several copper coins and a single silver piece. The silver piece was unusual enough, for it would take a woodsman some time to earn a silver *screpall*. But there was something else in the pouch, another piece of metal larger than a coin. She gazed at it, turning it over in her hand, and her eyes grew wide with amazement. It was an oblong metal seal, the type cast by a noble house, the type of seal that couriers would carry as identification when they took messages between the nobles of the Five Kingdoms. It was cast in gold, not silver, and the image on it was that of a woman with a solar shield on her right shoulder. Fidelma recognised it as a symbol of the Old Faith. But was it significant? Would a noble family still use this as their seal, and if so, why would a woodsman be carrying it?

After a moment or two, she closed her hand over the seal and, without a word to Eadulf or to Enda, she thrust it into her *marsupium*.

'What is it?' demanded Eadulf.

Fidelma immediately thrust her hand back into the pouch, took out the coins and displayed them, then put them too into the *marsupium*.

'Just some coins,' she said, hoping they had not noticed the seal. 'We'll confiscate them and if we can find someone to come and bury these bodies, we can use them to pay for that trouble,' she added practically.

She paused again and then did a strange thing, or so Eadulf and Enda thought. She took the hands of the dead man in her own and peered closely at them, examining their callused lines, the dirt beneath the nails and the rough, hard skin. There was nothing to indicate they were other than the hands of a rough woodsman. Certainly, they were not the hands of a courier in disguise, or even those of a warrior.

She stood up quickly and walked to the second body. This was the man whom Enda had despatched. The sword slash had rendered the assailant's body an ugly bloody mess. This ambusher seemed very similar to his companion. The thought crossed her mind that they could have been brothers. They both had the same stubby black facial hair, flat nose and badly weathered skin that showed a life of toil out in all weathers. A similar bow and quiver lay abandoned. The only difference was that this man had carried a short sword, which he had unsheathed to defend himself against Enda's attack. Enda had caught the man with the edge of his blade in the neck, which had caused all the bleeding.

Once again, Fidelma stood looking down at the body, observing the rough clothing and unkempt appearance. Then she examined the man's leather pouch – which revealed little except a few copper coins.

'Did these assassins come on foot to this place or are their horses nearby?' she asked, glancing round.

There was an implied rebuke in her tone. Enda flushed as he realised that he should have already found out that very fact. With their own horses secured to some branches to ensure they did not wander, Fidelma and Eadulf sat on a nearby rotting log while Enda quickly made a search of the surrounding woodland. It was pointless trying to take a horse through the undergrowth. Enda, a good tracker, like most warriors of the Golden Collar, could see no sign of horses having brought the would-be assassins to this place. In any case, what would poor woodsmen be doing with horses? He was soon able to ascertain that there were no other horses in the vicinity.

'They must be locals,' said Eadulf as they prepared to remount their own animals. 'Perhaps they were the woodsmen sent after the girl? But then she was said to be heading east, not south.'

Fidelma's face remained impassive. Her thoughts were elsewhere. In fact, she was concentrating on the discovery of the strange emblem the attacker had been carrying. Of course, it was possible that he might simply have stolen it. But it was valuable and he would have soon sold it. Perhaps it was all part of this mystery. It must be. But how? She wished fervently that she could confide her thoughts to Eadulf.

'We shall move on,' she announced quietly.

They continued on down the track that kept parallel with the bubbling stream that Imchad had called Dubh Glas. There was no sign of anyone else passing that way. All was quiet except for the natural sounds of the stream, the rustle of the wind through the undergrowth and the occasional call of a bird or the scampering of pine martens. That they were not far from the sea was evident from the increasing frequency of the querulous cries of scavenger gulls.

Fidelma had relapsed into total silence and so Enda and Eadulf left her alone. Enda had increased his vigilance, though Fidelma had been confident that any danger had passed. His eyes searched from side to side as they passed through the woodland, quickly but intently.

It was not long before the track broadened and eventually spread into a large clearing and they could see, beyond a fringe of trees, cultivated fields. In the centre of the clearing was a small group of buildings: a simple dwelling – a low log cabin – and a group of sheds. On the stream side, a broad bridge had been constructed and beyond it another track opened towards the east. Milling about were a few pigs, some goats, geese, and a few chickens with a large cockerel. They seemed in loose groups, intermingling with one another, seeming unconcerned by any difference in species. A woman was grinding corn in a large stone pestle. From one of the sheds behind the main dwelling came the sound of wood being sawn. The woman, a sturdy-limbed woman with short fair hair, suddenly stopped her pounding as she caught the sound of their approaching horses. She paused and watched their approach with an expression of interest but not of hostility.

'You are safe come and welcome,' she intoned, but she did not put down the short wooden pole that served as her mortar to grind the sheaves of corn.

'Good day, woman,' Enda greeted her formally. They did not dismount. 'Is your man about?'

The woman's eyes narrowed slightly before she answered.

'He is beyond the house, sawing wood,' she said and then, before anyone could move, she raised her voice. They were surprised at the pitch and power of it. 'Tassach!'

The sawing stopped and after a moment a short man appeared, looking every inch the farmer he evidently was. He stood regarding them with mild curiosity before coming forward.

'You are welcome to my house, strangers.'

'Is your name Tassach?' Fidelma asked.

The man nodded, looking slightly taken aback. 'Is it me that you seek, strangers?'

'We do.' Fidelma took the lead once more and dismounted from her horse. 'We have come from the Abbey of Finnbarr.'

By then both the man and his wife had noticed the golden collar around Enda's neck, the cut of Fidelma's clothing and her jewelled emblem, and Eadulf's garb and tonsure.

'You have come down this track from the abbey?' the farmer asked unnecessarily, with a shake of his head. 'This road leads to nowhere of significance, lady. Have you mislaid your way?'

'Not if your name be Tassach, as you have said?'

This time the farmer's glance towards his wife was one of surprise – and something else. It was an indefinable look of unease.

'It is. Why do you seek me?'

'Imchad told us to take this route and gave us your name.'

'Imchad the ferryman? And why would he do that?' The farmer was still suspicious.

'Because we want to reach the Great Island – Ard Nemed,' replied Fidelma. 'I am told the way through the marshes is difficult and the ferryman said you could guide us to where a ferry would be able to cross to the island.'

The farmer was frowning. 'Few people dwell on Ard Nemed these days. Why would you want to go there?'

Fidelma raised a quizzical eyebrow. 'Surely that would be our business.'

'It may well be,' replied Tassach dourly. 'But you came here seeking me to be your guide, so it is surely my business as well.'

There was an uneasy silence until Enda lost his patience. 'Will you guide us – yes or no?'

The farmer actually grinned. 'No,' he replied flatly. Before Enda could give vent to the anger that was welling inside him the man added: 'I am a farmer with a farm to attend to. However, if you are fool enough to seek to cross to the Great Island of Nemed, I will point you in the right direction.'

'Why do you think we are fools to seek out the Great Island?' Eadulf demanded sharply.

'You are a stranger by your accent . . . a Saxon?' queried the farmer.

'An Angle,' corrected Eadulf in a surly tone.

'Because you are a stranger, I will answer your question,' replied the farmer, ignoring the correction. 'There are frequent attacks on the island. Across the short stretch of water that separates it from the mainland both north and east is the territory of the Uí Liatháin, and they lay claim to ownership of the island. They frequently try to enforce their claim by raiding and bloodshed. Why is it necessary to go there and put your life in danger?'

Fidelma was annoyed. 'We have nothing to do with those claims or counterclaims. We merely want to reach Ard Nemed.'

'You treat conflict lightly, lady,' interjected the woman. 'Are you not scared of death?'

'Like all people, I am scared of the process of death,' Fidelma said grimly. 'I am not scared of death itself. It seems that death can visit me here just as much as anywhere else. I presume you are the wife of Tassach?'

The woman thrust out her chin defiantly. 'I am Anglas, wife to Tassach. And you speak in riddles, lady.'

'Why do you feel it is foolish of us not to be concerned about the Uí Liatháin?' asked Enda. 'We know they are considered warlike but no more so than the Uí Fidgenti with whom they claim kinship. They were once deadly enemies of Cashel but have now made their peace. The Uí Liatháin have never challenged the authority of the Eóganacht.'

Anglas sniffed dismissively. 'I know nothing of the concerns of Cashel. But the prince of our people, Artgal, son of our chief, Fe-dá-Lethe, has been sent by his father to restore the fortress on the island, to serve as a warning to the Uí Liatháin that the Cenél nÁeda will not give up the island so easily. These can be frightening times. What if the Uí Liatháin take over Ard Nemed and, not content with that, come sweeping through the marshes to seize the territories of the Eóganacht Raithlind?'

'That will never be so,' Fidelma replied firmly. 'Anyway, this talk makes no difference to our intent. All we seek is a guide to take us to the island.'

The farmer was indifferent. 'But that guide will not be me.'

'Why so?'

'I farm quietly here. I bother no one and no one has so far bothered me. I intend that this state of affairs shall continue.'

'That is fairly said,' conceded Fidelma reluctantly. 'Then we will settle for you to direct us on our journey.'

The farmer smiled, though without humour. 'If you are so intent on going to Ard Nemed, then I will direct you. All you have to do is cross the bridge over the stream there and follow the path straight. It leads directly to the east. There might be muddy stretches and you may have to cross a few strips of water, but none is deep and your horses will keep you dry. Just keep carefully to the track; it is still discernible in spite of the weather and time of year. Do not deviate – the marsh is treacherous on either side. You will soon come to the River Sabrann and find the Great Island on the far side of it.'

Enda was confused. 'But we have already crossed that river and come south.'

'The course of the river is deceptive. Even before the abbey the Sabrann diverts its course into two branches. The north one, that you crossed, flows directly east, and the south one also flows east before making a sharp turn to the south.'

'And so by going east we will come to the Sabrann again?' asked Fidelma.

'You will. On its banks there you will find a settlement called Pasáiste Thiar, the West Passage, because it is considered to mark the western passage of the river. You'll find a small fishing community there. That place has a safe harbour. It is only ten kilometres from here.'

'And what will we find there, besides the fishing community?' Fidelma pressed.

'On the far side of the channel there is the western end of the island, the Great Island, that you seek. All you have to do is cross. I am sure you will find boats enough to transport you.'

'Would one of these fishing folk be able to take us across the water? We would need to take our horses with us.'

Tassach simply shrugged. 'Once you get to the settlement, ask for Fécho. Anyone will tell you who he is. He owns two coastal boats that sail all the waters around the islands. Here are many islands – the Great Island, the Long Island, the Little Island, and the Isle of Foxes. Seek him out; he will take you across to Ard Nemed, for a price – if that is where you must go.' He pointed down the track. 'As I say, the way is simple. That is the path to the settlement and that is where you will find Fécho the boatman.'

'Then we will take it,' Enda said, turning back to his horse. It was clear he was bored by the farmer's eloquence.

Fidelma held up her hand to stay him. 'There is one other matter to be discussed before we depart. Has anyone else come by your farmstead today?'

Tassach's wife gave another sniff. 'As my man has told you, this path leads to nowhere of significance. We can pass many a month without seeing another soul.'

'So you have seen no other strangers here today?'

'No strangers have come here today other than you,' Tassach replied.

'Not two men, who looked like woodsmen,' pressed Fidelma.

It was the woman who answered. 'As we have said, there have been no other folk passing this way,' she said shortly. 'Why do you ask?'

'I am a *dálaigh*; it is my right to ask,' replied Fidelma.

'A *dálaigh*?' Tassach and his wife exchanged a nervous glance.

'You are addressing Fidelma of Cashel,' Enda could not help adding.

It was the first time Fidelma's name had been mentioned and while Fidelma frowned in annoyance at Enda, Anglas's face grew pale.

'The lady Fidelma?' she whispered.

'Sister to your King, Colgú of Cashel,' Enda smiled with satisfaction at the reaction his announcement had caused. Then he added, a little conceitedly, touching his golden collar: 'That is why I wear the symbol of the Nasc Niadh, bodyguard to . . .'

'So no woodsmen, strangers or otherwise, have passed here today?' Fidelma interrupted crossly. Her harshness was not really directed at the couple but was caused by Enda's indiscreet boastfulness.

The couple exchanged another nervous glance.

'No one has passed this way before you,' the farmer finally said slowly. 'Were you expecting to encounter someone?'

Enda could not help seeing the black humour and he did not restrain an outburst of laughter. 'Our encounter with them was the last thing we were expecting.'

'I have no understanding of what you say, warrior.' Tassach was puzzled.

'Two woodsmen tried to ambush us on the way here,' Eadulf explained. 'They paid for their folly.'

Tassach's wife looked nervously about her, as if expecting them to appear. 'Where are they now?'

'Dead,' replied Enda laconically.

The couple looked shocked. 'Who were they?' asked Tassach, after a few moments.

'I think that is what the lady Fidelma was trying to ask.'

Fidelma interrupted with a sigh of exasperation. 'They lay in wait for us on this very track, some four kilometres north of here.'

'We did not see them, lady,' repeated the farmer in a resolute tone. 'And from what you say, they will not pass us now.'

Enda suppressed a guffaw. 'There is truth in that.'

'As my escort tells you, they paid the price for their failure,' Fidelma said. 'They had not observed that he is a warrior of the Nasc Niadh and they did not have the skills to achieve their purpose. Where is the dwelling of your local Brehon?'

Anglas shrugged and glanced at her husband before replying. 'One would probably have to ride back to the abbey from where you have come from to find one. There is no Brehon nearer.'

'Or the lord Artgal might have his Brehon in attendance at Ard Nemed,' suggested Tassach. 'But the abbey would be nearer.'

'We cannot delay our journey,' Fidelma said. 'Do you have a horse here?'

'A horse, lady? No, but I have a good mule. But why? You have horses.'

'As you say, it is a short journey back to the abbey. The two bodies of the assassins must be reported to a Brehon or a priest and buried, and while we do not have the time to delay, you could ride back to the abbey and report the matter.' She reached into her *marsupium* and drew forth the collection of coins she had retrieved from the attackers' bodies and handed them to the farmer. 'This should cover you for the inconvenience and ensure they get buried.'

Tassach gazed at the coins with a bleak expression before nodding slowly. 'You are generous, lady.'

Fidelma turned to her horse. 'Now we will take our leave. Thank you for the directions, and we thank you for undertaking the journey to report back to the abbey about the murdered ambushers.'

With Enda once more in the lead on his warhorse, they made their way across the small plank bridge over the stream, which was not deep, and set off eastwards. The sun was climbing swiftly to its winter zenith, pale and without much heat. However, the day had turned out to be surprisingly mild and the clouds in the sky were not moving at all, showing the threatened winds had not materialised. Although it was not yet midday Fidelma was slightly nervous, wondering how long it would take to reach the riverside settlement and find the ferryman that Tassach had recommended. Tassach had said the place was no great distance but it lay through the marshland, which would slow their progress, and it was the time of year when darkness came with an early rapidity. They had to negotiate transport across this channel to the island and find the fortress of Artgal. She knew it was called the Great Island in reference to its size and wondered whether they would be able to reach the fortress before nightfall. She realised that might be impossible.

She felt that she had better not set her hopes too high. Perhaps it would be sensible to rest in the fishing settlement and, if she could negotiate with Fécho, travel to the island in the morning. She felt uneasy at doing so, her thoughts returning to the attempted ambush. Once more she cursed the *geis* that had been placed on her and forbade her to discuss the situation with Eadulf and Enda. What if her enemies had planned for the possibility that the ambush on the track might fail? What if they had made contingent plans for another attack along the way and she had not forewarned her companions? Her thoughts were turning rapidly.

'Lady!'

It was a low call from Enda. He was pointing to the high evergreens and she saw the leaves were beginning to flutter. There was a wind growing in strength from the north-east and that meant the night would be a chill one. She suppressed a curse. Just as she had been thinking that the day was mild and the threat of wind had ebbed away, the weather had changed. She acknowledged the watchful eyes of Enda and sighed. The main thing now was to pass in safety along this marshland path, rather than thinking ahead about reaching Artgal's fortress. Yes, better to rest in the fishing village this night before negotiating with Fécho the boatman in the morning.

She had been right. The early winter dusk was descending by the time they had passed through the marshes and emerged on the bank of the river. It was cold as well as gloomy when they took what appeared to be a road running alongside the river. Eadulf, who had studied such matters as the laws on roadways, realised it was a *ró-shéit*. The laws classified all manner of roads and stipulated how they had to be maintained, under pain of fines by the local clan and their chieftain. On one side of this road was the dark river and on the other was an artificial ditch, carefully cleared and maintained to keep the path well drained for the passage of wheeled vehicles. Enda looked up and down the road.

'I can see lights to the north, lady,' he said. 'The settlement of fishermen that we seek is probably in that direction.'

'Even if it is not, at least where there are lights there are people, and we can find hospitality from the dark and chill of this evening,' Fidelma agreed.

They turned and made their way north. Night was coming down swiftly now, and the darkness was compounded by thick clouds. The rushing sound of the fast-flowing waters on their right was their guide along the darkening road while the blackness of the woods from which they had emerged showed the now impenetrable western border to their route. The birdsong from this darkness had changed with the ending of the light, and they could heard the plaintive 'hoon hoon' sound of the *ceann cait*, the long-eared owl, surveying its territory before going off to hunt mice or even rats and shrews. Other nocturnal creatures were beginning to stir. They could hear rustling in the undergrowth but could not even see the passing of a shadow.

Thankfully the lights grew nearer and ahead the path rose to high ground, overlooking the almost invisible river on their right. Now they could just make out the black outline of buildings and the whipping flames of several brand torches placed on stakes at strategic points, as well as a glow from what they later found to be two or three braziers in the centre of the complex. Knowing how nervous some of these isolated communities could be, especially in borderlands such as this, Fidelma suggested to Enda that he hail the community as they approached instead of coming on the settlement without warning.

Enda raised his voice.

'Hello, the village!' he shouted as he advanced to the buildings.

There were a few shouts of query and alarm. Fidelma called on her companions to halt at the first of the buildings.

A light moved closer and a voice demanded to know who they were and what their business was.

'We are just strangers seeking hospitality of shelter and food and warmth against the cold of this night,' Fidelma replied.

A figure stepped forward, holding aloft his torch to examine them. They had the impression that many other people had come too, and were surveying them from the shelter of darkness.

'Just strangers?' There was almost a sneer in the man's voice. 'Your comrade cannot hide the sparkle on the golden torc he wears around his neck. Nor am I fool enough not to recognise the emblem of the Nasc Niadh, the Bodyguard to the King of Cashel, when I see it.'

This brought forth an intense whispering in the crowd. Fidelma hoped they would not notice that Enda's hand had fallen defensively to the hilt of his sword in the sheath at his side.

'We are just strangers to your community,' Fidelma answered quickly, but decided there was nothing to be gained by trying to disguise the truth. 'You have good eyes, my friend. I am Fidelma of Cashel, accompanied by my husband, Eadulf of Seaxmund's Ham, and Enda of the Nasc Niadh.'

This was met by excited muttering from the hidden onlookers.

'This is a long way from Cashel,' replied the still suspicious voice.

'No area of the kingdom is a long way from the capital of the kingdom and the palace of Colgú, your King and my brother.' She felt she should remind them of their allegiance, even if distant, to Cashel.

There was a hesitation and more whispering. Then the same voice answered. 'You will forgive our suspicions, lady. We have cause for them. However, come forward. You and your companions are most welcome and our hospitality is yours.'

They moved their horses forward into the centre of the settlement and halted. Quite a few people now dispersed but there were still many who stood watching them: men, woman and several children. A man had come forward to greet them as they dismounted, the same man who had invited them to enter. He examined each of them carefully before nodding, as if accepting their identities.

'We have a small hostel here, lady, but its beds are clean, the food is good and the drink is better. I am Cogadháin, the innkeeper, and you are welcome.'

'Cogadháin? That is a warlike name for one who runs an inn,' Fidelma commented with a smile. Even Eadulf realised the name meant 'hound of war'.

The innkeeper chuckled. 'Well spoken, lady, but I should point out that I am also the *toisech*, the leader, of this community.' He turned to Enda and pointed to a building nearby. 'That is the stable; you may quarter your horses in there. My son, Cogeráin, will help you.' He pointed out a boy holding a lantern. 'Now let me welcome you into my inn, lady, and you, too, Brother . . .?'

'Eadulf of Seaxmund's Ham,' Eadulf answered.

'This is an isolated community,' the innkeeper began as he turned and led the way to the inn door. 'Is it by design that you come here, or are you passing on your way somewhere else?'

'We are passing,' said Fidelma, falling into step with him as Enda took their horses, with the help of the sturdy lad, towards the stables. 'But we are also here in search of someone who we were told would facilitate our journey. We were told that we would find Fécho, a boatman, here.'

Cogadháin halted abruptly and turned. There was suspicion in his voice again. 'Where were you expecting Fécho to transport you to?'

Fidelma nearly told him sharply that that was her business, but she realised that attitude would be non-productive.

'We were hoping that he would hire his boat to cross the river.'

'Is there a problem? This man, Fécho, can be found here, we presume?' Eadulf caught the man's deepening frown.

Cogadháin gazed at him thoughtfully and then nodded. His face, in the shadowy light of the lantern above the tavern door, seemed worried.

'Oh yes, he is here and I will send for him, if you wish it.'

'I do so wish it,' Fidelma confirmed, wondering at the strangeness of the man's manner.

'And we presume that he still runs his boat to take us across the water?' Eadulf added.

'He still runs both his boats in these waters, for he is a coastal trader. But I do not think he will take you across to the Great Island at this time.'

Fidelma frowned. 'Why do you believe that he would refuse us?' she demanded.

The innkeeper scratched his ear thoughtfully. 'I suppose you came on the track from the west and joined the road along the river bank as darkness was falling?'

'We did,' she answered shortly.

'Then you may not have noticed the rising smoke to the east. I suppose the darkness and clouds obscured it from your vision?'

'I have no understanding of what you are talking about.' She was bewildered.

'The rising smoke is on the Great Island,' he said. 'We have been watching the fires and smoke since early morning, lady.'

'What does that indicate?' Fidelma was still puzzled.

'It means that there has been an attack on the island. The only raiders who would do so, who would be capable of attacking our prince, Lord Artgal, who is now with some of his warriors in the fortress of Ard Nemed, are the thrice-cursed Uí Liatháin. All day the fires have burned but we have heard no word from across the river, no word of victor or vanquished. We fear the worst.'

'Are you saying that the Uí Liatháin have launched a major attack on the island?' Eadulf asked in surprise. 'Then why did the people here not go to help your prince?'

Cogadháin shrugged eloquently. 'We have barely a score of able men here and no one who knows the profession of a warrior. We are fisherfolk and traders. What were we expected to do? What more could we do than Artgal and his *catha*, his companies of trained warriors? It looks from the rising smoke of the farmsteads that not even Artgal could hold back the Uí Liatháin.'

chapter six

Fécho was not what they had been expecting when he finally appeared at the inn of Cogadháin. A boatman conjured up an image of someone like Imchad, who had been short and stocky with prominent muscles and weather-beaten skin, browned by the reflected sun on the waters as well as the winds. It conjured an image of a man who was hard, solid and immovable as a rock. Fécho was the very antithesis of this. He was fair skinned, tall, with wispy fair hair, and seemed ill nourished, not muscular at all. He had a solemn expression, a drooping mouth and sad eyes, as if he were in a permanent state of mourning. He spoke so softly that several times Eadulf found himself leaning forward to catch his words.

'It is dangerous, lady,' he replied, after Fidelma had made her request.

'But not impossible?' she pressed.

'Impossible?' The boatman grimaced, and she wondered if she had seen the ghost of humour on his lips but it was gone so quickly she couldn't be sure. 'Isn't it said by the ancients that "impossible" is an unlucky word, for those who utter it find that it is always disproved by their rivals?'

Fidelma acknowledged the man's words with a brief smile.

'So you believe there is no obstacle that cannot be overcome?'

'Not of the sort you are implying,' replied Fécho. 'You want to know if I am prepared to risk my boat to cross to the island in spite of what we have seen, the rising smoke.'

'Would you land us and our horses there in spite of the attacks that the innkeeper has interpreted as the cause of the fires and smoke? Are you prepared to take us across in spite of that?'

Fécho was reflective. 'There would be two conditions. I would land you on the south shore of the island, for the fires seem to have raged on the north side.'

'And the second condition?'

'The price,' the boatman answered readily. Then he added: 'Why would you want to go to the island? Cogadháin, the innkeeper, tells me you are Sister Fidelma. That is perplexing. There's no religious community on Ard Nemed. In fact, I don't think there are any religious there at all. So it seems doubtful that religion takes you there. Yet you travel with a foreign religieux and a warrior of the Golden Collar. I am intrigued.'

'Did Cogadháin not tell you that I am sister to King Colgú of Cashel, and now his legal advisor and no longer of the religious.'

Fécho's eyes widened a fraction and a look of comprehension spread over his features. 'He neglected that fact. So, you are an Eóganacht, as is Prince Artgal. Is that why you go to Ard Nemed?'

'You are fond of making deductions,' observed Fidelma suspiciously.

'As you are, I have heard,' replied Fécho with a smile. 'It seems logical that you are here to see the prince of the Cenél nÁeda. Artgal is known to be at his fortress on the island, attempting to dissuade the Uí Liatháin from attacking it. I conclude that you have come to see Artgal on that matter . . . that is, if he still lives.'

Fidelma frowned. 'You sound pessimistic.'

The boatman stretched in a leisurely way, at the same time gesturing with his thumb towards the east, the direction of the island.

'We know that Prince Artgal has only a hundred warriors with him. Ah, perhaps you have come to negotiate the intervention of warriors from Cashel?'

'Surely Artgal and a hundred warriors are enough to protect the island from these raids?' Enda intervened, annoyed by the boatman's attitude.

'You think that the Uí Liáthain send a bunch of cow herders to attack the settlements on Ard Nemed?' replied Fécho cynically.

Enda was about to reply but Fidelma raised a hand, motioning him to be silent.

'Are you saying that the leader of the Uí Liatháin sent his warriors to attack the island?' she demanded. 'Prince Tolmanach is surely an old man, and has been at peace with all his neighbours for many years.'

Fécho pursed his lips into an incredulous expression. 'News travels slowly. Tolmanach died nine days since. It is his son, Tomaltaid, who rules the Uí Liatháin now. He is a young and ambitious man whose very name suits his character.'

Eadulf looked blank and Fidelma felt obliged to explain. 'The name means "one that goads or threatens",' she explained before turning back to the boatman. 'So you believe this was a concerted attack by the new prince of the Uí Liatháin to claim the island?'

'It seems logical that he would choose this time to secure his position with his own people by expanding their territory with the seizure of Ard Nemed, a place the Uí Liatháin have long claimed as their own.'

Fidelma considered carefully for a moment before asking: 'Is the island so easy to attack?'

'Artgal's fortress is on the southern shore, on cliffs above a cove. I have often used the harbour there when asked to transport goods and people to the fortress. It is an easy landing, and then a track leads up to the high point. That is why it is called Ard Nemed, although the name sometimes applies to all of the Great Island. As I said, if I take you, I would land you there, rather than to the north.'

'I have no problem with that. I would be willing to go to Ard Nemed.'

'To see Artgal, just as I have deduced.' The boatman smiled complacently. 'Well, nothing is impossible, as I have said, lady. But I would counsel caution, especially if it can be seen that the fortress is damaged or destroyed. If so, I will not land. If I am right about Tomaltaid and he has tried attacking the fortress, then it would be dangerous to land.'

'I think you are forgetting that the Uí Liatháin recognise and pay tribute to the King of Cashel,' interrupted Enda sourly. 'They would never harm his sister, for they would know that they would suffer the consequences.'

Fécho gazed lazily up at the young warrior with a languid smile.

'The Uí Liatháin are a law to themselves, young warrior. You should know that. Moreover, they claim kinship with the Ui Fidgenti, so they are not quite the respecters of protocol you might believe them to be. Tomaltaid would attack his own mother if he felt it would give him advantage.'

'I have been in the territory of the Uí Liatháin. I have stayed at Caislean Uí Liatháin, the fortress of Tolmanach, and I was never threatened with danger there,' Fidelma declared.

'Tomaltaid is not the man his father was,' replied Fécho. 'Did you ever encounter him?'

'I did not,' she confessed.

'Then I suggest that this local knowledge might be worthy of your consideration.'

A look of annoyance crossed her face but was gone in a moment. She sighed. 'I always take such information into consideration. Yet it is curious Cashel has received no word of the designs of Tomaltaid. Word of his intent to disturb the peace in this area of the kingdom ought to have reached my brother.'

Fécho looked disconcerted. 'So you know nothing of such designs? But I thought it was this matter that had brought you to this isolated part . . . I can deduce no other reason that would bring the King of Cashel's *dálaigh* here.'

Eadulf looked closely at Fidelma, wondering if this was, in truth, the matter that had brought them here. But why should she be under a sacred oath of secrecy about it?

'You may think as you like, Fécho,' Fidelma replied with a shake of her head. 'However, I can assure you that these raids of the Uí Liatháin are not the cause of my being here. I knew nothing of them until I arrived in this very spot.'

Fécho answered, with a thoughtful look, 'It is logical that Artgal could have sent to Cashel for a *dálaigh* to negotiate with the Uí Liatháin, but I accept what you say, lady. Yet you still wish to be put ashore at the fortress of Artgal . . . that is, if the Uí Liatháin have not destroyed it already?'

The corners of Fidelma's mouth tightened at the scepticism in the boatman's tone.

'I think you would find, if all you say about Tomaltaid is correct, that Cashel would have sent a full battalion of the King's warriors to deal with the Uí Liatháin, not a *dálaigh,* her partner and one warrior.' She paused a moment, then asked with genuine interest, 'Is the passage from here to this cove that you speak of a long and difficult one?'

Fécho smiled and shook his head. 'It is neither long nor difficult, but I would not undertake it before first light tomorrow, lady. If the backing wind blows from the north and the waters are not turbulent, then I think I can promise it will be an easy trip.'

'And your vessel can take all three horses as well as us?'

'I would not offer my services otherwise,' replied the man. 'I have two sturdy coastal vessels and either can carry you and your horses.'

'It's not one of those flat river craft, is it?' Enda intervened. 'I am told this south coast has turbulent tides and I would not like to chance our lives and our horses on a raft should the weather be inclement.'

Fécho chuckled in amusement.

'My vessel is a coastal ship, one that will stand the strongest tides.' He used the word *serrcenn*, which Eadulf recognised as meaning a specially built coastal vessel. 'It carries two *brat*, or sails, and steerage poles and a minimum crew of nine, who know these waters, inlets and rivers as others know the lines on the palms of their hands.'

Enda was still thoughtful. 'That type of vessel has high sides. How will you get the horses on board or, indeed, unload them?'

'You seem to know little of ships, my friend,' Fécho said, with another shake of his head. 'From a jetty, horses can be walked aboard a *serrcenn*. Elsewhere, the side rails of the ship can be opened up to allow them to be walked off the ship. If you are afraid, I will you show you my ship in daylight tomorrow, and thus you will be reassured. You need have no fear about the seaworthiness of my vessel – I have made this journey too many times to sail it in a ship that is not safe. There are many currents around the islands. But the seas that lap these shores and the currents of the rivers are part of me. I know their moods and tricks.'

Enda was not satisfied but decided to let the matter drop.

'Then all that remains is to agree a price,' Fidelma said in a determined tone.

Fécho stretched languidly. 'Three horses and three people to the cove below Ard Nemed? Easily done. But do you wish to return?'

Fidelma shrugged. 'That I do not know . . . yet.'

'Depending on what is found after the Uí Liatháin attack?' he replied with the hint of a smile.

'Amongst other things,' Fidelma agreed solemnly.

Fécho examined Fidelma speculatively. 'Your honour price and that of your companions here must amount to a tidy sum. If anything happens while you are in my charge, then, as owner of the ferry, I would be liable to meet that sum.' He paused and rubbed his chin thoughtfully.

'Remember that as sister to the King the lady Fidelma presumes hospitality of all the people of the kingdom,' protested Enda, outraged at what he thought the man was considering.

Fécho ignored him. 'I would presume that as a *dálaigh*, irrespective of the connection to your brother, you would be classed as an *aire ard* with an honour price of five *cumals*, as one who is skilled in decisions and prepares judgements. You see, I have heard something of your reputation. The warrior is doubtless valued at one *colpach*. But I am not sure of the stranger's value.'

Fidelma was smiling grimly at the accuracy of the ferryman's estimation. Honour prices, or *eneclann*, were set by law; the term's original meaning in ancient times was 'face clearing'. Each member of society had a honour price, which was the basis for all legal compensation against injury, loss and insult and was calculated in proportion to the status of the individual. Because the land was pastoral, with great herds of cattle, values were set against the price of a cow; the value of a milch cow was *séd*, the highest value, while the value of a heifer was *dartaid*, the lowest value. A *cumal* was set at the value of three milch cows, while a *colpach* was a two-year-old heifer, regarded as of more value than an ordinary *dartaid*.

'You appear to have a good eye for evaluating things, Fécho,' she said slowly. 'In regard to the stranger, Eadulf of Seaxmund's Ham, in the land of the South Folk in the kingdom of the East Angles, is also my husband, and his honour price is usually placed at half the value of my own.'

Fécho did not seem impressed. 'It is your honour price I am concerned with.'

'Anyway,' intervened Enda once again, 'do you really think we would be carrying such sums with us to pay whatever ferryman we encounter?'

The boatman laughed sharply. 'I am not such a fool as to think that, my friend. Nor would I expect the combined sum of your honour prices as payment for my services, even as imprecise as you have admitted they might be . . .' He held up his hand as Enda began to protest. 'Yes, warrior, imprecise; for while you seek to go to Ard Nemed, you cannot say that you will stay there nor whether you would need my services to return. In this negotiation that is a difficulty.'

'I would have said a *screpall* would be adequate for the journey.' Enda's voice was sharp. He named one of the two silver coins in use, part of a new coinage development in the Five Kingdoms. The coins were based on weight and the basic unit was the weight of a grain of wheat. The silver *screpall* weighed as much as twenty-four grains of wheat.

Fécho chuckled. 'I would argue that three *screpall* would be a fairer price,' he corrected. 'But it still does not resolve the greater problem: honour price compensation if anything happens.'

'Then it would seem that the problem cannot be resolved,' Fidelma sighed, 'for as Enda has told you, we do not carry such sums.'

'That is so,' Fécho agreed. 'But there is an answer.'

'Which is?' demanded Fidelma.

'I should not have to remind a *dálaigh* that we have an ancient system of loans.'

Eadulf was not certain of the meaning of the word *óin*. Enda explained in a whisper that it was a loan to cover a certain period or specific event. Eadulf could still not understand it completely but apparently Fidelma did, for she called for writing equipment and stretched the parchment before her on the table. The words she wrote promised to Fécho compensation of *enechlann* to answer claims which might be made against him provided he were not to blame, such claims and compensation to be judged by the Chief Brehon of the kingdom. To this, Fidelma added her name and asked the others to add theirs. Then she asked for some wax to melt on the document and set her seal as a *dálaigh*.

With a cheerful grin, the boatman took the document.

'There now,' he said, 'the difficulty is resolved. Don't you believe in the old saying – either find a way or make one?'

Fidelma did not answer his smile. 'Time is gliding by and we should be resting to prepare for the journey tomorrow. When do you expect to depart, Fécho?'

'Is not a journey always best when begun at first light?' The boatman rose, tucking the parchment into his *peasán*, the purse that hung from his belt. 'I will await you at the far end of the settlement, where there is a jetty. That is where my ship is moored.'

When he had departed, Enda sniffed loudly. 'Is he to be trusted, lady?' he asked.

'I think so,' replied Fidelma. 'Just because he is astute on matters of finance and legality is no reason not to trust him.'

'But he seemed overly keen to know your business, who you were meeting with on Ard Nemed and . . .' Enda said suspiciously.

Fidelma smiled. 'I am sure that you and Eadulf are also very keen to know that. Yet I trust you both. And until I can share certain information with you, you will also have to take me on trust. Now, I suggest we get some rest, for who knows what tomorrow will bring.'

The next morning brought a fog. When they left Cogadháin's inn, they found that a heavy sea fog had swirled over the landscape, thicker than any sea mist that Fidelma and Eadulf had ever encountered in their voyaging. The rain had stopped well before midnight and the long clear hours and light winds had, apparently, created the humid conditions in which the water-saturated air had formed the white veil that now hung evocatively over the landscape. They could barely see across the stretch of water that separated the settlement from the looming shadow of the hills of the island. The cold, wet fog seemed to be a living entity, swirling this way and that in the morning breeze.

'Well,' Enda groaned, 'that probably ends our hope of setting sail this morning.'

'We'll find Fécho anyway,' Fidelma insisted. 'Perhaps this fog will start to clear when the sun comes up.'

'A winter fog clearing before midday?' Enda declared in disbelief. 'I cannot see that.'

'It is a sea fog, Enda,' she pointed out mildly, realising the young warrior had little experience of the coast.

'In which direction is this jetty?' interrupted Eadulf. 'I can hardly see more than ten paces ahead.'

'I'll take you there,' a young voice said behind them.

They had not realised that Cogeráin, the son of the innkeeper, was standing behind them, holding their horses.

'I'll take you there,' he repeated. 'I have saddled your horses ready for you.'

Fidelma turned and smiled as she cast a discerning eye over the animals and noted, with appreciation, that they had been well groomed.

'They have been fed and watered, lady,' the boy said nervously, observing her examination.

Fidelma smiled and nodded, reached into her *marsupium*, drew forth a coin and handed it to him. 'I can see they have been well taken care of. Now, which is the way to Fécho's ship?'

Following the innkeeper's son, they walked their horses through the settlement, which was now stirring into life. Fires were being rekindled and torches were being lit, and the smoke was mixing with the fog although to Fidelma's keen eye the the white vapour did not seem as dense as it had been. By the time they had crossed the village and reached the river bank at the far end the fog had thinned to the extent they could see the outlines of the ship.

It was certainly larger than they had been expecting. It had two tall masts, called *crann*, and two *brat*, or sails, furled and lashed on a crossbeam, ready to be hoisted. A small guide sail was ready to be hoisted at the *airrainn*, or prow, which rose higher than the stern. The ship had all the appearance of a large, elongated curragh in design, broad in the central beam. It was made of solid wood, predominantly oak – always a favourite for seagoing ships such as *ler-longa*, the heavy vessels that traded round the coast or across the seas. Masts and spars were always made from tough wood such as ash, which could also withstand heavy onslaught from the elements.

Fidelma could just make out a carved female figurehead at the prow of the vessel, obviously the work of a talented *ersoraidhe*, or woodcarver. Behind that, on the deck, was what looked like a small curragh, a small light boat with a wooden frame, covered by skins. It was obviously used to transport no more than one or two persons at a time from the boat to the shore.

Fécho suddenly emerged from the ship.

'Welcome, lady, welcome to the *Tonn Cliodhna*.'

'To the what?' Eadulf said unthinkingly.

'*Cliodhna's Wave*,' Fidelma said. 'The name of the ship.'

'Cliodhna was a goddess of great beauty in the old times,' explained Fécho to the bemused Eadulf, and pointed to the figurehead. 'She dwelt in Tir Tairngire, the Land of Promise, which was the kingdom of the ocean god Manannán mac Lir. The story goes that the warrior Ciabhán of the Curling Locks went adventuring on the great seas and encountered a terrible storm which swept him to Tir Tairngire. The goddess fell in love with him and together they fled back to the land of mortals at Cúan Dor, not far from here. Coming ashore, the goddess was overcome with tiredness. So that while Ciabhán went inland to hunt for food, she fell asleep on the shore. It is said that the ocean god was so angry that she had fled to the kingdom of mortals he sent a great wave to engulf her and bring her back to his domain, leaving her lover desolate. Thereafter Tonn Cliodhna became known as one of the three Great Waves of Ireland, together with Tonn Rudraige and Tonn Tuaig in the far north. They bring harassment and destruction.'

Eadulf stifled a groan, wondering why there was never a simple answer. It seemed to him that it was part of the culture of this land to answer any question with a long story, and he was not in the mood for it so early on a winter morning.

To Fidelma, however, the storytelling was just a natural part of conversation.

'I would say that *Tonn Cliodhna* is an odd name for your ship,' she pointed out. 'Isn't it a more fitting name for a warship, which does bring harassment and destruction?'

'True enough,' Fécho grinned. 'Although it depends on the meaning you choose. Cliodhna's Wave laps these shores and so does my ship here, bringing trade and people to these areas. Manannán mac Lir, the ocean god, can also be a benevolent presence at times.'

'I hope he is in a benevolent mood, for my horse is named after his great stead that could gallop across oceans,' replied Fidelma.

The man's eyes widened with his smile. 'So you bring the mighty Aonbharr on board? That is a good omen.' He gestured to his ship with a movement of his head. 'Anyway, are you ready to sail with your horses and your companions?'

'You will set sail in this?' interrupted Enda in an astonished tone, waving an arm at the fog.

'The channel is straight until we reach the headland at the south-western end of the island,' replied Fécho, in an almost soothing tone. 'You notice that the fog is less dense than before?'

'I can barely see a few paces before me.'

Fécho shook his head. 'Keep watching, warrior. By the time we get downriver and round the headland we call Whitepoint, the rising wind and temperatures will have dispersed this fog. There is no need for anxiety.'

Eadulf had been feeling some antipathy towards the man since he had first met him the previous evening. He disliked Fécho's amused assurance, his attitude that everyone was an idiot apart from himself. He disliked his easy manner, his familiarity – especially the lack of formality with which he treated Fidelma, sister to his King. Eadulf felt obliged to interject.

'We are putting our lives in your hands, boatman. Remember that one of your passengers is the sister of your King.' He chose the words deliberately, to emphasise that the boatman should remember his rank. 'We see the fog and I think you may appreciate our anxiety at wishing to end our journey on dry land, not dashed against some unseen rock. Yet it is true I am no sailor, so I suppose you have more cause than just confidence for your optimism?'

Fécho regarded him for a moment with no change of expression. 'You are right, Brother Eadulf,' he finally said. 'You are not a sailor. We'll come round the Whitepoint and you'll see the Island of the Fox as clearly before you as if there had never been a fog. We swing eastward before that island and turn north towards the cove where Ard Nemed dominates the passage to the Great Southern Sea.'

When it appeared that he was going to say no more, Eadulf said cuttingly: 'You are asking a lot of us, to put our faith in you.'

'If you don't want to, then put your faith in your God. I swear, Brother Eadulf, for one who claims to serve an omnipotent God, you seem to have little faith in His watchful benevolence over his servants.'

Eadulf frowned irritably. He liked the humour of the man even less since he had tried to better him verbally and found that Fécho could hold his own in banter. Why was he so irritated by this man? Was it just his manner or something else? Eadulf compressed his lips and turned away from the amused gaze of the owner of *Tonn Cliodhna*.

Fidelma, with a glance of annoyance at Eadulf, assured Fécho that they were ready. The nine men in the crew of *Tonn Cliodhna* had been busy unbolting a section of the side of the vessel to allow the horses to step directly from the wooden quay onto the main deck. Fidelma led her grey-white pony on first. It seemed that Fécho had given much thought to carrying horses on his vessel. There were spaces in the centre of the decking, along which ran thick beams of yew with iron rings attached and ropes to lash the horses so that they did not move from their allotted positions. The ship could take six animals in this fashion.

Fécho accompanied her to a forward position and motioned to one of his men to fasten the ropes.

'Are any of your horses skittish beasts?' Fécho suddenly asked, when his man hesitated and glanced at him.

Fidelma raised an eyebrow in query. 'Skittish?'

'Sometimes, if the ship rolls on the waves, a horse can become fretful and lash out with its back hooves,' he explained. 'We often find it advisable to keep a rope to secure the fetlocks. I've known a passenger go to calm his horse in such a condition and get kicked clean overboard. The man died, of course. It's not wise to stand at the rear of a nervous animal.'

Fidelma knew that fact well enough. 'While we are sailing into unknown waters, it would be wise to secure all the horses in that fashion,' she agreed.

It took a while to secure all the horses and Fidelma stood watching the expertise of Fécho's crewmen with approval. It was some time since she had looked at the old texts on laws applying to river and sea travel, and she wondered if there was anything useful she could pick up from the way that Fécho's crew made everything seem so easy. Eadulf and Enda had made their way to a more comfortable spot at the stern, where Fécho himself had gone to take his place at the great tiller with another man. He was called Iffernán and it seemed he was the helmsman. The remaining members of the crew had loosened the spar of the main mast, with the mainsail still furled, but hauled it into position ready to unfurl it when ordered. That order came almost immediately, and two of the men pulled on the ropes. The square sail came down in a tumble and hung moving gently as if some giant's breath were gently blowing against it.

Iffernán took full control of the ship while one of the crew lifted a large pole and began to heave against the quayside, pushing the vessel towards midstream. Here the current of the great river took the craft as if it weighed nothing, and Fidelma felt a shiver as if the timbers had become alive. They seemed to moan and grind beneath her feet as the waters took command, propelling the vessel forward. She turned and made her way towards the stern and realised, with some surprise, that she could now see from stern to the raised prow. Fécho was right: the fog was thinning fast and she could see the banks on either side of the mouth of the river.

'We're in luck, lady,' called Fécho, who stood by Iffernán at the tiller, feet spread apart.

'Luck?' she queried.

'The prevailing wind is from the south-west. When we round Whitepoint and head east, the wind will catch the sail and we'll be at Ard Nemed before you know it.'

She had noticed the breath of wind against her cheek and now she knew the meaning of it. She acknowledged the boatman with a smile. Eadulf and Enda stood by the ship's rail, not looking happy. So she walked across to where they stood.

'The boatman was right. The fog seems to be thinner now and continuing to clear,' she began.

'The fog is thinner, but it is not to my liking,' Enda said quietly.

'What do you mean?' frowned Eadulf.

'With the fog clearing, we could easily be spotted from the shore by the Uí Liatháin, if they now have the upper hand on the island.'

Eadulf found himself in agreement with the warrior. 'We have to put a lot of trust in this man Fécho. And I don't like him.'

Fidelma looked at her companions. 'What is your concern?' she asked softly.

'Only that we are sailing into unknown territory, a territory with warring factions, and we have no trust in this boatman. We just don't like him, that's all.'

'Isn't that just prejudice?' she pointed out.

'Perhaps. But then I am at a disadvantage, not knowing who my enemy might be,' Eadulf replied and turned to start for'ard but Fidelma laid a restraining hand on his arm.

'It's probably to do with what I told you the other night,' Fidelma sighed. 'Believe me, Eadulf, once I am free of this oath, free from the *geis*, I shall tell you. But before then, I can't.'

He remained silent.

'I know you, and Enda, do not like to be excluded from knowledge,' she said. 'I just ask you to be patient and not to take your irritation out on the people whose help we need.'

'My feelings against Fécho are not because of that,' Eadulf almost snapped, surprised to realise that he meant it.

Fidelma waited for a moment or two and then gave a slight shrug, turning to the ship's rail to stare at the passing banks of the island, now clearly discernible through the evaporating fog.

'I think we have a right to be concerned and consider everyone a potential enemy, lady,' pointed out Enda seriously. 'That is natural, since we do not have knowledge of your mission and who our enemies might be.'

Fidelma glanced at him in annoyance. 'You think so?'

'It's been obvious that this matter, this quest of yours, is to do with some personal matter on behalf of your family, lady. This trip to your cousin Artgal seems to prove that.'

'It does?' She gave nothing away by her tone.

The young warrior nodded. 'He is a member of one of the branches of your family whose lineage, like your own, goes all the way back to Conall Corc, who set up his capital at Cashel. Why journey into this inhospitable marshland for any lesser reason than something to do with the honour of the Eóganacht?'

She stared thoughtfully at him for a moment or two before replying.

'I have said this to Eadulf and now I say it to you: I will tell you when the time comes. I will tell you then, and not before.'

Enda grimaced. 'Fair enough, lady. But I think I am right.'

Eadulf did not bother to comment. His expression was almost sulky.

The wind from the south-west was increasing and Fidelma could see that Iffernán, the helmsman, was having to lean against the tiller to keep the ship in the centre of the strong flow of the river. The square mainsail was flapping and cracking sharply as the wind tried to push the vessel over to the eastern bank. Now that the temperature was rising, the wind was also causing the misty white shroud to clear rapidly. They could see both banks of the river in more detail. The river had been widening. Fécho moved to lend his weight against the pull of the wind and the tiller.

In spite of the movement of the ship, the occasional tilt of the decking, Fidelma saw that the horses seemed docile in their stalls – she could think of no other word but stalls to describe the area where they had been secured on the centre deck. The lashing of their back legs was a help but they were certainly well behaved. Fidelma believed that in such matters the welfare of the horses came first. She had grown up with a love of the animals and had been taught to ride almost as a baby. Eadulf felt differently. He was no horseman and if he could travel by any other means, he would do so. It was only recently that he had started to ride regularly on the passive cob she had given him. The only animal she was worried for was Enda's high-spirited warhorse; she knew the stallion would not be happy at being confined on the vessel. But Enda knew his animal and she noted, with approval, that he had gone to whisper to it as the vessel moved against the wind. She saw the horse's ears draw back but Enda was stroking the muzzle as he whispered and the beast stood patiently.

The river was still widening; in fact, it was opening out into a broad stretch of water, although there seemed land all around. She glanced back to Fécho.

The ferryman grinned at her unasked question.

'We are coming to the mouth of the Sabrann, where it empties into the inner sea. Look ahead, lady. Do you see the dark land ahead? That is Inis Sionnach, the Island of the Fox. Did I not promise you that the fog would clear by the time we reached this point and you would see it clearly?'

'I did not doubt your knowledge, Fécho,' she replied, glancing over to where Eadulf stood scowling at the scene. 'Is it not said that every man is a beginner at another man's trade?'

'The old proverb is truly said,' replied Fécho cheerfully. 'We'll commence our turn to the east as soon as we pass that point.' He indicated the left bank. 'That's the Whitepoint, the extreme south-west tip of the great island. With the wind behind us, it will not be long before we see Ard Nemed above the cove where the fortress of Artgal stands.'

Nothing more was said and Fidelma watched appreciatively as Fécho and his crew worked to wear the ship so that it began its slow turn eastwards, and the southwesterly gusts became a backing wind filling the sail. It was done in such a gentle manner that although the ship heeled over a little it did not unduly disturb the horses. Enda had decided to stay with them just in case of any problems, but apart from the tossing of heads, whinnies and stamping of their forelegs, they remained calm. In spite of the strength of the backing wind, the sailing was relatively smooth. Fidelma could feel the subtle increase in the speed of the craft, moving swiftly over the waters. The wind seemed to be clearing the white vapours of the morning before them and the shoreline to the left, the Great Island of Nemed, was becoming more visible.

'Well, there seem to be no fires on this side of the island,' Fécho pointed out with satisfaction.

The comment brought Fidelma back to reality. She had almost forgotten the possibility that the Uí Liatháin might be waiting to trap them. She turned to examine the coastline with interest.

Certainly, so far as she could see, there was no sign of anything disturbing the peace of the landscape, but then there seemed few signs of any habitation along the coast. It was then she realised the *Tonn Cliodhna* seemed to be heading too close to the end of the rocky promontory and glanced in surprise to where Fécho and his helmsman seemed to be struggling with the tiller. It did not take an expert to see they were speeding towards the submerged rocks of the surrounding shoreline.

'Hidden current!' shouted Fécho. 'Difficult to control.'

Eadulf looked around nervously. 'We'll be aground on those rocks soon, and that's if we are lucky. They could rip the bottom out of this ship in a moment.'

'We'll certainly be on the rocks in a moment,' called Fidelma. 'Is there no way we can get back into deep waters?'

Fécho was about to say something when a cry from a crewman at the prow caused them to turn.

A vessel had suddenly appeared, emerging from the shelter of a small, rocky headland, just as Fécho and the helmsman regained control. The tide seemed to toss the *Tonn Cliodhna* about a little and then, by some miracle, they were turning away from the rocky shoreline, the Whitepoint as Fécho called it. The wind was blowing the vessel back into deeper waters, blowing it back into mid-channel – and into the path of the oncoming vessel.

It was a long, low vessel. Its sharp bow was cleaving the waves, tossing white water to either side of its knife-like edge. Although it carried two masts for sails, the sails were furled, and Fidelma's mind registered that sails would be no use against the wind. Yet the approaching vessel was speeding towards them. Then her keen eye noticed the rise and fall of oars, ten oars on each side. Positioned on the upper thwarts of the other ship stood a line of men, armed men. She could see their bows, loosely held. For a moment she was hypnotised by the rhythmic rise and fall of the oars, all working in unison.

Suddenly she felt very cold. Even before Fécho shouted his warning, she realised what the approaching ship was. It was called a *laech lestar*, a 'hero vessel' – a euphemism for a warship.

CHAPTER SEVEN

There was no use putting up any resistance. The war vessel was closing on them too rapidly and it was clear that it was manned by professional *muireach*, mariners able to fight on the sea as others fought on the land. As the fighting ship came closer, Fidelma could see the bows were already strung, arrows in place. Each bowman stood, his feet wide apart, easily balanced against the pitch. A stern voice called: 'Identify yourselves!'

Fécho abandoned the tiller to his companion and moved forward to the starboard rail. 'This is the *Tonn Cliodhna* out of the West Passage. We are well known in these waters. Who are you?'

'I do not know you,' came the unfriendly response. 'What is your business? I see you have horses aboard.'

'We are a coastal ship and we transport passengers to these islands. Who are you? We have never seen your *laech lestar* in these waters before.'

Once again the response was uncompromising. 'What passengers do you carry? I see at least one fine-bred steed. That's a warrior's horse. Do you have warriors on board? Where are you heading?'

'Is it your business?' replied Fécho sharply.

'My ship and weapons make it my business,' the voice stated bluntly.

'We can make little argument with that,' whispered Eadulf, who had come to stand beside Fécho in order to examine the bowmen on the opposing vessel, who still stood immovably with their weapons strung and aimed.

Fécho turned towards Fidelma with a helpless gesture. 'I have tried to get some identification, lady,' he said. 'I do not know this vessel.'

Fidelma moved forward, glancing reassuringly at Fécho. She raised her voice.

'Do I address the captain of the war vessel that impedes my progress?' she shouted across to the vessel, summoning all the authority of her rank.

'I am the commander of this vessel,' came the response, which told her nothing further.

She decided to take a chance. 'I am Fidelma of Cashel. I travel with my companions, Brother Eadulf and Enda, a warrior of the Golden Collar.'

There was a silence for a moment or two. Then the voice answered: 'Do you claim to be Fidelma, sister of Colgú of Cashel?'

'Colgú, King of all Muman,' she replied clearly. 'We wish to land at Ard Nemed.'

'Just you and your companions?'

'And our horses,' she replied, without humour.

There was a further pause before the voice shouted: 'Is the captain of your ship in attendance?'

Fécho moved to the rail again. 'I am.'

'You will head for the cove below the fortress at Ard Nemed. I shall accompany you and, be warned, at any deviation, any attempt to change course, my bowmen will loose their weapons on you and you will be boarded.'

'I was heading for the cove in any event,' muttered Fécho.

He turned back to his companion, Iffernán, at the tiller. Meanwhile, Enda had joined Eadulf and Fidelma at the ship's rail. He was frowning.

'Do you think that they are Uí Liatháin raiders?' he asked.

'They didn't say,' Eadulf replied, with dry humour.

'We shall soon find out.' Fidelma shrugged. 'At least they know who I am – and let us hope that carries some weight and respect with them.'

'If they are the raiders,' Enda pointed out grimly, 'then this escort to Ard Nemed would indicate the island has fallen to them.'

It was a thought that had already occurred to Fidelma but she had not been willing to express it.

Fécho was turning his vessel towards the coast of the Great Island and, with the backing wind still holding, was making fair speed across the choppy waters. The warship seemed to match their course and speed with ease. As the *Tonn Cliodhna* swung around the low tree-covered headland into the cove, Fidelma found it was not as she had imagined it. The long beach certainly curved, scythe-like, from one end to another. It was a long gradual curve with sloping sands. A wooden jetty and fishing boats showed the main occupation of the small settlement that rose from the shoreline, mainly confined to the slopes of the steep hill to where a dark wooden stockade of what was clearly a fair-sized fortress dominated. The fog had totally cleared from this area as it faced due south, and the pale winter sun was bathing the area in soft pink light, creating the illusion of an unusually mild climate. Smaller, wood-covered hills rose on either side, but the trees were without the green adornment of the warmer months.

Fécho and his crew obviously knew the harbour well, and by a piece of dextrous manipulation with the sail, they came up neatly alongside the wooden jetty. By the time they had secured the vessel to it warriors from the warship had already landed and were waiting for them. Some had come forward with drawn swords and stood ready as they disembarked.

A tall man, whose mane of sandy hair and large beard made an estimate of his age impossible, met Fidelma and her companions on the jetty. He wore a burnished silver helmet that was worked with extended birds' wings over the ears and had a plume of blue feather at its peak. He was clearly a warrior of rank and he wore a bright blue cloak over toughened leather armour on a white linen shirt. He carried his weapons, the dirk and short sword, with the confidence of someone who could use them. There was something about his stance and the way he balanced himself that spoke to Fidelma of a seafaring man.

He stood staring at her with bright grey eyes, eyes that seemed to mirror the sea on a winter's day like today.

'Well?' Fidelma demanded angrily as the man stood examining her for longer than was reasonable. 'Do I meet with your approval?'

Suddenly the captain of the warship began to chuckle.

'Red hair, a haughty manner, used to being obeyed without question. Yes, you have the arrogance of the Eóganacht, right enough. You appear to be who you claim to be.'

'And who do you claim to be?' Fidelma asked coldly, trying to stop her rising anger.

'I am Murchú, in the service of Artgal, Prince of the Cenél nÁeda,' the man announced and Fidelma noticed a touch of pride in his tone.

'Murchú?' she replied grimly. 'Well, you bear an appropriate-enough name.' The name meant sea-hound. 'Why am I greeted with this display of hostility? I am Fidelma of Cashel and therefore distant cousin to Artgal, whom you claim to serve?'

'There is no hostility, lady. I am merely obeying orders to stop all shipping approaching this harbour until we have ascertained its purpose. Raiders are a constant menace. I am protecting my lord Artgal.'

'Then I presume we shall be allowed to proceed to see my cousin?' she asked sarcastically. She glanced upwards to the stockade above them. 'I presume he is in the fortress there?'

'Your presumption is correct, lady,' confirmed Murchú. 'I shall take you there once your horses have been disembarked.' He turned to Fécho and issued instructions. The captain of the *Tonn Cliodhna* seemed hesitant.

'I am often at this cove, Murchú,' he said slowly. 'I run my ferry and ship to most of the harbours here and know these settlements like the back of my hand. Yet I do not remember encountering either you or your warship before.'

Murchú frowned with irritation at having his word questioned. 'Come to that,' he answered testily, 'I have not encountered you before this day. However, I have only joined Prince Artgal here recently. My home port is Cionn tSéile, the harbour on the Bandan River, on the western borders of the Cenél mBécc.'

Fécho hesitated, then seemed to decide not to press the point. He turned to Fidelma. 'We'll disembark the horses immediately, lady.'

In fact, this did not take the crew as much time as it had taken them to load the horses onto the ship. Within moments Fidelma's pony, Eadulf's cob and Enda's stallion were all stamping impatiently on the foreshore. Fidelma was left to settle with Fécho. As she did so, the boatman leant forward and said quietly, with a furtive glance at Murchú: 'I wouldn't trust that man if I were you.'

'Why not?' replied Fidelma.

'Because I have lived in the West Passage of the river here all my life. Since I could hold an oar or the sheet of a sail, I have sailed these waters. I have had two coastal vessels for twice nine years; one of these is the *Tonn Cliodhna*. I have sailed to all the islands of the inner seas and all the fishing ports and settlements. I have even made it up the Sabrann as far as the Abbey of Finnbarr itself. And I have never seen that warship or that commander before.'

'But that is understandable if he has only recently come to serve Artgal at Ard Nemed. He explained to you that he had come from the western borders of the Eóganacht Rathlind territory, down by the River Bandan.'

'It is an easy explanation.'

'Very well, but if Artgal is in the fortress above, then he will be able to confirm it.'

'If not . . .?' asked Fécho.

'Then we will soon find out,' Fidelma replied drily.

The owner of the *Tonn Cliodhna* thought for a moment and then shrugged. 'Your lives could be in danger, if they are really Uí Liatháin raiders,' he pointed out.

'Then they are already in danger.'

'I could delay sailing from here until I know all is well.'

Fidelma looked at him speculatively. 'That might be a good thing. Indeed, we might need your ship to leave Ard Nemed. So it would be logical for you to wait until we have found out more.'

Fécho agreed. 'In that case we will wait here until we hear whether you need our services further.'

'Thank you,' Fidelma said. 'Now I see our escort growing restless.'

She turned and made her way to where Eadulf and Enda were already mounted and waiting with the impatient Murchú.

'What took you so long?' demanded a disgruntled Eadulf.

'A little negotiation about the fees,' she said dismissively, swinging up onto Aonbharr.

'These boatmen are all alike,' snapped Murchú. 'All is well so long as you pay. Now, are you ready?'

She confirmed that she was and he turned and led the way, moving slowly through the settlement and up the steep track towards the wooden fort which crowned the hill. The people of the fishing village cast them only brief glances as they went by. They did not seem at all bothered by the warriors moving through their midst, which made Fidelma feel that Fécho's concerns were groundless. If there had been an attack and Murchú's men were part of the Uí Liatháin raid, the people would have shown their antipathy, and there would also have been signs of conflict.

They continued on at a slow walk, up the steep hill, having to lean far forward up the necks of the horses in order to maintain balance. The walls of Artgal's wooden stockade dominated the skyline. The gates stood wide open, but several warriors stood watchfully both at the entrance and along the walls. Murchú led them into the compound and halted, swinging down from his mount. A man came hurrying up to exchange a nervous word, looking at the visitors with a frown. His eyes fell on Fidelma and widened – and he halted before her with obvious obeisance.

'A thousand welcomes, lady.'

The man looked familiar but she could not quite place him. He seemed a breathless, excitable man, with puffy red cheeks, and a look of perpetual worry, glancing this way and that as if never able to concentrate on what was in front of him for fear of other things. She made a guess as to his identity.

'You are steward to Artgal?'

'My name is Corbmac, lady, and I accompanied Lord Artgal to Cashel once to attend a feasting given by your brother. A thousand welcomes to Ard Nemed,' he repeated, obviously pleased to have been recognised. 'Please dismount. You and your companions all.' He signalled to a couple of youths who were obviously stable boys for they came running forward to take charge of the horses. 'I will take you to your cousin at once, lady. When we saw the boats come in, we wondered what ship Murchú was escorting. Who are your companions, lady?'

'This is my husband, Eadulf of Seaxmund's Ham, in the land of the South Folk of the East Angles.' She indicated Eadulf.

'Welcome, welcome,' Corbmac bobbed his head up and down, almost birdlike in his greeting, then turned to Enda. 'You wear the Golden Collar of the bodyguard to the Eóganacht of Cashel.'

'I am Enda,' the young warrior announced solemnly.

'I will take you all straight away to Artgal. He has been expecting you.'

Fidelma halted and stared at the steward as if she had not understood him. 'He has been expecting me?' she echoed.

'Just so, just so.' The steward ignored her surprise and turned towards one of the large buildings across the main courtyard. Fidelma shrugged and accepted that all would be explained when she saw her cousin.

As she walked, Fidelma's eyes quickly examined the building to which she was being led. As in the village below, there was no sign of any recent attack having taken place. She wondered if Fécho, and indeed Cogadháin the innkeeper, who had been the first to speak of fires and attacks at Ard Nemed, had been mistaken. She realised that Corbmac had been standing aside, indicating the open door. She entered and found herself in a feasting hall. True, it was built with skill, but it was of wood and not very imposing, typical of the accommodations of the lesser princes of the kingdom. She found herself coughing a little in the smoke that billowed from the great central fire. She realised how dim and dark the room was. She was about to comment when a figure appeared out of the gloom.

'Cousin Fidelma?' The figure came forward, left hand outstretched in greeting. The other was held in a sling stained with blood.

Even at a glance one could see there was a family relationship between Artgal and Fidelma. His hair had the same red tinge to it, and there was his tallness, together with something about his facial features and the curious grey-green eyes, even the humorous corners of the mouth.

'You have been hurt, cousin,' Fidelma observed. She took his good hand but her eyes dropped to his blood-specked sling.

Artgal grimaced in an offhand manner. 'An Uí Liatháin arrow. A flesh wound only. It could have been worse.'

'Then there *was* an attack here by the Uí Liatháin?' Fidelma declared in surprise. 'I saw no evidence of damage either to the settlement or to the fort.'

'They did not reach this far,' her cousin told her with a grin. 'At least, not alive. When we heard that the raiders had landed in the salt marshes at Ross Liath – that's on the north side of the island – we hastened to teach them a lesson. They attacked yesterday and set alight some of the farms and fishing settlements. We have been expecting such an attack since the old prince, Tolmanach, died. His son, Tomaltaid, is ambitious. We knew he would try to take the island.'

'What happened?'

'As soon as the news came, I mustered some warriors and headed north. The raiders were undisciplined and we drove them back but . . .' He shrugged, gave a wry smile and touched his sling. 'Unfortunately an arrow from one of the departing raiders caught me in the upper arm. It was my fault. I was too confident.'

'Do you have a physician? Has it been looked at?' demanded Fidelma.

'I am here with most of my immediate household, Fidelma. So it has been treated. As I say, it is no more than a flesh wound.'

'And where are the Uí Liatháin now?'

'They have fled back to their own territory across the river . . . for the time being.'

'I did not know this warfare existed. Does my brother know?'

'It is not exactly warfare, cousin. There have always been cattle raids across this territory, and the Uí Liatháin have always claimed it was once theirs and should be again. Tolmanach at Caislean Liatháin used to distance himself from the raiders, even from any such claims. Not so young Tomaltaid. He is ambitious to the point that he has hired *amasae*. We captured some of them. One is a northerner, by his manner of speech.'

Eadulf had recently learnt that *amasae* were mercenary warriors, who sold their swords to whoever paid them.

'That is a bad sign,' admitted Fidelma.

Artgal gave a nod. 'The Uí Liatháin are bad enough without

bringing others along on their raids.' He paused and then smiled apologetically. 'But where are my manners? Where is the protocol of hospitality? Let me greet you and your companions properly, Fidelma. We have a feast to prepare and after that we must talk of the business that brings you here.'

Fidelma frowned. 'Yes, I was told you have been expecting me. How so?'

'Later, cousin, later. First things first. Now, I recognise Eadulf . . .'

Artgal greeted each of them and seemed to brighten with the ritual of being the perfect host. He waved them all to be seated and ordered his steward to arrange drinks. He then gave orders for food to be prepared for everyone, adding that Corbmac should ensure the needs of the crew of the vessel that had brought his guests were seen to as well.

Fidelma was troubled but kept silent while her companions were being distracted by the attendants with a choice of dishes. It seemed an interminable age before she was able to broach the subject again and she leant towards Artgal. 'How is it possible that you expected me?' she insisted in a lowered voice.

Artgal glanced round as if ensuring they could not be overheard, then he motioned her to follow him. He led the way to a corner of the hall that gave entrance to his private chamber. This was no more than a small room with walls built of polished yew wood. Had there been four people in it, it would have been crowded. There were no windows and the walls were hung with skins and tapestries. There was one ornately carved chair, which was occupied by Artgal, a table and two simple chairs. Fidelma sat in one of these. The only light in this enclosed space came from an oil lantern in a metal container, hanging from the centre of the ceiling. It also provided heat.

Argali sat back and spoke without preamble. 'Yesterday, while we were driving back the raiders, I was surprised to find my cousin Cairenn hiding from them. She had come from the Abbey of Finnbarr and crossed to the island to see me before continuing to a rendez-vous at Cluain. She was forced to seek a hiding place from the raiders. My men came across her that morning and brought her to me.'

'So Cairenn did come here?'

'She did. She's a clever girl. You must remember her?'

Fidelma shook her head. 'I saw her at the abbey but I did not recognise her.'

Artgal shrugged and said: 'She remembers you. She was a great-niece of old Abbot Nessán and became a companion to Princess Grella of the Uí Liatháin of Eochaill.'

Fidelma started and there was sudden tension in her body. 'Grella, who is now the wife of the High King?' she almost whispered.

'Some years ago, when Grella married Cenn Fáelad of the Uí Néill, Cairenn went with her to Tara to be her friend and companion.'

Fidelma frowned reflectively. 'I begin to see a little light now.'

Her cousin looked puzzled. 'To see light?'

'Did Cairenn tell you what happened at Finnbarr's Abbey?' she asked, ignoring his question.

'She said that old Nessán had been murdered and that you were there. She also said she had to leave the abbey in secret as some suspected she was involved in the murder. Before she left, she placed a message for you in the hope you would follow to Ard Nemed.'

'She did.' Fidelma nodded in agreement. 'Is that why you were expecting me?'

'That is so. I hoped that you would not come by the northern route, otherwise you would have encountered the Uí Liatháin raiders just as she did.'

'What did she tell you about what she was doing at Finnbarr's Abbey?'

'Nothing much. Only that she went there to see our cousin Abbot Nessán. She refused to say anything except that she insisted that she did not kill him and that she was running from the real murderer. What is it all about?'

'I cannot say. I suspect that she is telling the truth about not killing Nessán and that she is innocent. I am following her to find the real murderer,' Fidelma replied. 'Where is she? Why does she not join us?'

'Simple,' Artgal said with a shrug. 'She is no longer here at Ard Nemed.'

Fidelma tried to hide her surprise. 'She has left?'

Artgal leant forward and shrugged again. 'I would keep Fécho and his ship here until you are ready to leave.'

She stared at him uncertainly. 'Why?'

'You will have need of his ship to take you further, if you are following Cairenn.'

'Where has she gone?'

'She left the island almost immediately in a small fishing craft. She travels east to meet up with the lady Grella at Cluain.'

Once again Fidelma was disconcerted at the news. 'So Grella is not in Tara?'

'She is in Uí Liatháin territory, to the east,' Artgal confirmed. 'That is where Cairenn said she would go. She persuaded a fisherman to take her across to the Uí Liatháin mainland. What I am trying to say is, if you went to follow her, I cannot spare Murchú and his ship. The only other warship I had at my command was burnt during the Uí Liatháin attack on the north shore.'

Fidelma was frowning. 'You appear to know many things that I do not. What is Grella doing in Cluain?'

'All I know is what Cairenn told me, and she did not say.'

'So what did she tell you?'

'She told me that she had accompanied the lady Grella to Uí Liatháin territory, where Grella was to visit the Abbot of Cluain. That's in the south. Apparently, her cousin is abbot there.'

'I thought that the abbey there had been abandoned half a century ago?' queried Fidelma in surprise.

'So I thought, too, but Cairenn said that Grella had told her she would stay there while Cairenn went to see her great-uncle. He had some information for her. When she had done that, she was to rejoin Grella in Cluain.'

'What was this information about?'

'I've no idea. If it involved Grella, then it might have been something to do with the Uí Liatháin. Her family were minor nobles in Eochaill.'

Fidelma frowned. 'Cairenn did not elaborate on why she was sent to see Abbot Nessán?

'She either did not know or was not willing to tell. She was anxious to be on her way, to get back to Grella. So it did not seem important to pursue the matter.'

'She was to join Grella at Cluain, you say? Why did she come here then? From Finnbarr's Abbey she could have taken the northern route on the mainland rather than cross to this island and then have to recross to the mainland. Why leave me the message identifying this island?'

'Because she believed that you would follow her here before you followed her to the east. Perhaps she wanted you to avoid the dangerous northern route,' suggested Artgal.

'But Grella is of the Uí Liatháin, as you say, and Cluain is in their territory. So I can't see the problem.'

Artgal raised his hands in a helpless gesture. 'Unless there is some difficulty among Grella's family?'

Fidelma sighed. 'I do not believe Cairenn killed Nessán. If she did, or if she was an unwilling participant in his murder, I think there must be more to it. There is something strange about this.'

'But why was the abbot killed? After all, he was a relative of Cairenn.'

Fidelma felt she could answer that question, in part. 'It seemed that he had some information for me. Someone did not want him to reveal it. My suspicion is, if I am right that Cairenn is innocent, that whoever killed Nessán laid the blame on her by design. She had to flee the abbey immediately. I am not sure whether she even knew who the killer was, otherwise she might have indicated that to me when she left her message. But then why tell me to come here and not to go straight to Cluain?'

Artgal shifted uncomfortably. 'I nearly forgot. She did ask me to tell you what Abbot Nessán's dying words were.'

'Which were?' She tried to keep her irritation from her voice.

'I was to tell you to beware of the *roth na grían* – the solar wheel.'

Fidelma looked blank.

'It's a symbol of the old religion,' Artgal said.

'That much I know . . .' Fidelma took her comb bag and drew out the seal she had taken from the dead woodsman. She held it out to Artgal.

'It means nothing to me,' he said. 'Isn't it the sun goddess Étain who stands holding the solar wheel?'

'I don't care who it is, I want to know what it means,' Fidelma said petulantly, replacing the seal in her bag.

'Let me tell you this,' Artgal went on. 'When we attacked the Uí Liatháin this morning there was a religieux with them. Could he have been from the abbey?'

'Who was he?'

Artgal shrugged. 'That I do not know. One of my men pointed him out to me just as the raiders were crossing the river back to their own side. He was a tall man in a black robe; his features were covered by a cowl.'

Fidelma gave a soft sigh, murmuring aloud, 'So Cairenn is the companion to Grella, wife of the High King? And Cairenn is of the Eóganacht Raithlind.'

Artgal stared at her for a moment or two, and when she did not elaborate, he leant forward earnestly. 'What has this to do with the matter? I think you should explain.'

Fidelma shrugged. 'That is just it, Artgal. I cannot.'

'Cannot or will not?'

'I am under a *geis* not to.'

Artgal made a whistling sound through his teeth, 'A *geis*? Then I will ask no more. Anyway, you and your companions are surely tired. Let us continue the feasting and then it will be time to rest.'

'You were right; we should follow Cairenn eastward. I will need to negotiate passage with Fécho.'

'I will send word for him to join us and you may give him instruction.'

Fidelma was quiet for a moment or two, then said bluntly: 'I have to ask you a question.'

'Another question – and I cannot ask you anything of what this is all about because of your *geis*!' Artgal replied with dry humour.

'It is a question whose answer might rebound on the honour of our family,' she replied seriously. 'On the honour of the Eóganacht.'

'Ask away. I am intrigued. But I will hold my peace, because of your *geis*.'

'I have heard that many years ago the Eóganacht and the Uí Néill vied with one another for the High Kingship. Is that so?'

'Have you suddenly become a student of history?'

'Let us say the fact intrigues me. Am I right?'

'Easy enough to answer that. Crimthann mac Fidaig, the brother of Conall Corc, was the last Eóganacht to govern from Tara.'

'That must have been at least three or four centuries ago.'

'It was. Then the sister of Crimthann, an Eóganacht princess no less, became enamoured of an Uí Néill prince. She murdered her brother so that her husband could claim the throne of Tara. She did not last long as the lover of the new High King. Since then, the Eóganacht have left the Uí Néill to squabble over Tara among themselves, while they built up their own kingdom from Cashel, strong and independent.'

'Have you ever heard of anyone in the many branches of our

family who regretted that the Eóganacht abandoned the right to claim the High Kingship?' asked Fidelma. 'Is there anyone who makes reference to the ancient edict given by Amairgin, the first Druid, that the island should be divided between the children of Eibhir Fionn, ancestor of the Eóganacht, and Eremon, the ancestor of the Uí Néill?'

Artgal looked astounded. 'What a question!' he exclaimed. 'I doubt even the learned scholars of today would have heard of the edict of Amairgin.'

'So there is no one among the various branches of our family who would like to see an Eóganacht rule again at Tara? None who is restless and resentful that during these centuries it has been either the northern Uí Néill or their relatives, the southern Uí Néill, who have claimed the High Kingship of Tara? None who is resentful that the Eóganacht have been excluded? After all, tradition has it that we were the first to land on this island and should rightfully rule it.'

'Legend is a great thing but it has no bearing on today's reality, Fidelma,' her cousin replied.

'It can be a motive nevertheless,' she said slowly, as if reluctant to abandon the matter.

'The only rumour that I have heard is that some of the Uí Néill are as displeased with the High King Cenn Fáelad as they were with his brother Sechnussach, and you know well what happened to him.'

'I was involved in solving the matter of his murder,' acknowledged Fidelma.

'Indeed. You and Eadulf prevented mayhem among the Five Kingdoms, when you were called to Tara at the time the High King was assassinated. That was only the other year. So, in spite of your *geis*, are you hinting that we are facing another plot?' He suddenly stopped and thought. 'You really suspect a conspiracy among members of our family?' Having voiced the thought, he stared at her in disbelief.

Fidelma thought she might have gone too far and was about to change the subject when Artgal's eyes lit up. He was not a stupid man.

'You are not only saying that there is some plot to oust the Uí Néill at Tara which might involve our family – but what is at the back of your mind is the fact that the only person with a reasonable chance of being chosen High King under the law is . . .'

'My brother,' Fidelma acknowledged softly. 'I can assure you that the Eóganacht Cashel are innocent of any involvement to seize the High Kingship by murder. My brother has no ambition to take that title.'

Artgal inclined his head. 'But someone has clearly suggested that possibility to you, suggested that the family is involved in this matter? If not true, rumours travel swifter than horses.'

'As you said, Artgal, Crimthann mac Fidaig was the last Eóganacht to take the High Kingship four centuries ago – and what good did it do him? Poisoned by his own sister to secure the High Kingship for her lover Niall from the northern clans. Thereafter, we have left the claim to his descendants, the Uí Néill. Muman is as large a kingdom as we want.'

Her mouth closed in a determined line. There was an uneasy silence.

'But Grella of the Uí Liatháin is wife to Cenn Fáelad, of the Síl nÁedo Sláine,' pointed out Artgal. 'Her closest companion is the girl, Cairenn. Cairenn is of the Eóganacht Raithlinn. She is sent by Grella to see her relative the abbot. The abbot is found dead. Is this all coincidence?'

'Meaning?' Fidelma was troubled.

'I am wondering who has placed you under this *geis*, this sacred oath?'

'I am a *dálaigh*, whoever my family is. My primary oath is to the law of the Fénechus and to the truth of its justice.'

'That is well and good, but you might have choices to face when

121

you find yourself in the territory of the Uí Liatháin at Cluain; that is, if you are determined to follow Cairenn there. Before then, I would advise you to think carefully about your *geis* and the person who placed it on you.'

'What do you mean?'

'In Uí Liatháin territory, you may well be in danger and therefore you should warn your companions, so that they can be prepared. They should be watchful for danger from any likely source connected with your mission.'

Fidelma sniffed dismissively. 'That's just it. What likely source of danger? I was hoping that Abbot Nessán would have been able to provide me with some relevant information. Are you sure that Cairenn said no more about what she was doing at the abbey or what Nessán told her?'

'All she told me, as I said, was that she had been sent by her mistress to the abbot as he had information for her.' He paused as if a thought had come into his head. 'One other thing I forgot. Grella told Cairenn that Abbot Nessán had sent her a message by means of carrier pigeon. It was that message that took her from Tara to Cluain.'

Fidelma was reflective. 'I knew that Nessán corresponded by carrier pigeon with the High King's steward, as indeed he did with my brother and others. Old Brother Conchobhar at Cashel is in charge of the rock doves. There is quite a fashion now for using them, particularly for sending messages over long distances. But unless we know what is in these messages or behind them, it is hardly knowing anything at all.'

Artgal gave an eloquent shrug. 'I cannot help you further. There is much to speculate about. Does this mean that the Uí Liatháin bear responsibility for the murder of Nessán, or is there something sinister happening within our family? Where did you get the idea that our family are in a conspiracy to overthrow an Uí Néill High King?'

Fidelma compressed her lips. 'I repeat, again, I am under a *geis*.'

'That seems contrary, for someone such as yourself who is a *dálaigh*.'

Fidelma shrugged. 'I have always said, no speculation without information. But there is little enough information and much to speculate on. Anyway, I am presuming that Fécho's ship will be allowed to transport me into the territory of the Uí Liatháin?'

'As I said, we have only Murchú's ship here now for our protection if there is another Uí Liatháin attack. We cannot spare it to protect your passage. Fécho knows all the settlements and harbours in these islands and even along the Uí Liatháin shores.'

Fidelma inclined her head. 'I am happy to trust the passage to him.'

'His trust, so I have heard, is only to those who pay him. I doubt he has any other allegiance.'

Fidelma smiled tightly. 'Well, I certainly know he is very precise about payment and its legalities. If he can land me somewhere near Cluain, that will be sufficient.'

'It is in a valley inland, so you will have to get your horses back on board. However, I don't think it is an arduous journey from the nearest landing place.

Fidelma was thoughtful for a while and then she gave a long sigh.

'Well, there is little more to be achieved today. I will persuade Fécho to undertake to transport us tomorrow morning. These winter days grow dark too quickly and we have been travelling since first light . . . or as light as it could get with the thick sea fog that greeted us.'

'Those fogs and mists are rare among these islands and on this coast. Anyway, you and your companions will be my guests this evening. I can offer you little support other than that.'

Fidelma pursed her lips wryly. 'And that support will have to be measured, Artgal, especially if we are to leave early in the morning.

I hear you have a reputation for importing wines from Armorica, across the water.'

Artgal laughed. 'Little Britain as it is now being called, since the mass migration of the Britons to that place. But you are wise as ever, cousin. We too must be constantly vigilant now, watchful for any further raids from our Uí Liatháin neighbours.'

A short time later, she was giving her request to the ship owner. Fécho did not look happy.

'What exactly do you want me to do, lady?'

'It is simple enough. I want you to take me and my companions, with our horses, from here to a landing place from which we can proceed to the place called Cluain.'

'The old abbey?'

'Exactly. Do you know it?'

'There's nothing there. It has been deserted these fifty years or more.'

'Nevertheless, that is where I want to go. Just set us ashore nearby.'

Fécho shook his head slowly. 'It means another fee and since there are now new dangers involved, with the Uí Liatháin raiders . . .' He let his words trail off.

'Of course,' acknowledged Fidelma, trying to hide her smile. 'You will not lose by transporting the sister of your King.' The emphasis of her words held a message for the boatman.

'I am neither afraid nor concerned about just payment, if that is what you are thinking,' he snapped, his voice suddenly haughty. 'I have lived in close proximity with the Uí Liatháin all my life. I have friends and trading contacts among them. Why should I be scared?'

'Then there is no problem.'

'The problem is who you are,' he replied, almost bitterly. 'I can understand why the sister of the King wanted passage to come to see her cousin, Lord Artgal, but now . . . why does she want to go into Ui Liatháin territory?'

'In case you have forgotten,' she said coldly, 'the territory of the Uí Liatháin is as much part of my brother's kingdom as any other territory of the princes. I am also a *dálaigh* and entitled to travel through that territory in my legal role. It is my intention to cross the territory of the southern Uí Liatháin and join An Abhainn Mhór, the Great River, along which I can return to Cashel via the great abbey of Lios Mór. That is a quicker route than going back the way we have come.'

Fécho hesitated for a moment. Fidelma hoped her explanation sounded reasonable; in fact, it was a partial truth because, if all went well, that was the route she intended to follow, rather than return to Finnbarr's Abbey.

The owner of the *Tonn Cliodhna* gave a sigh, hesitated only a moment and nodded. 'But the payment to transport you to a landing point from which you can get to Cluain will be twice as much. Don't forget, it is into Uí Liatháin territory that you are going.'

'I thought that you said you had friends among them, having traded these waters?' she asked cynically.

He shrugged indifferently. 'That I do. But you would be surprised how quickly, in time of war, your friends can desert you.'

'So you think that these raids constitute a war?' she asked with quick interest. 'Why is that?'

'Raids, war,' Fécho said in disgust. 'For those who die in them, it matters not by which word the conflict is described. They remain dead. Besides, if your rank were known, as I said, you and your companions would make good hostages for the raiders; they could obtain what they want without recourse to further battle.'

'Then, Fécho, we shall have to ensure that my rank remains unspoken if we encounter any Uí Liatháin raiders, shan't we?'

Fécho hesitated once more and then gave a gesture which seemed to signify agreement. 'Very well . . . if you agree the price.'

'Where would you put me ashore?' she countered.

'Do you know the territory?' he asked in surprise.

'Not this area of it. But I shall be trusting you.'

'I will have to put you ashore where there is a small harbour, so that we may disembark the horses without injury. There is such a place, a sheltered inlet with a landing stage, opposite the south-eastern point of this island. There is habitation there but a small population, generally isolated from the rest of the country. It's just a fishing settlement, where I have traded before. It's known as the Promontory of Tialláin; Tialláin is chieftain of that settlement. He is a man not to be trusted but there is no reason why he should bother you. I can assure you that it is a safe place to land.'

'Very well, Fécho. Your terms are agreed. We will join you at first light tomorrow. The sooner we are on our way the better.'

'That will be fine, lady. Is that warship to follow us?' He jerked his head in the direction of Murchú's ship, anchored not far away.

'Murchú's ship remains here, which is why I am hiring your vessel to transport us.'

Fécho sniffed indifferently. 'I don't like it, or its captain.'

'My cousin vouches for Murchú and his ship.'

Fécho was not impressed. 'You are not in Cashel now, so who vouches for Artgal, lady? There are curious happenings in this part of the world. I have never known the air so filled with suspicion.'

CHAPTER EIGHT

'What on earth is that?' called Eadulf, leaning forward over the bow of the *Tonn Cliodhna*. He was staring beyond the carved figurehead of the goddess towards the approaching shore.

The land before them was mainly wooded, tall oaks mingled with hazel trees coming almost to the shoreline. However, there appeared a large inlet, into which Fécho was directing Iffernán, the helmsman. They had covered the distance across the channel from Ard Nemed, a little over a kilometre, slowly, battling some fierce contrary winds, which had torn the sails and forced them to put into another cove to make repairs. Now, with the sun at its zenith, they were finally approaching their destination.

Even from some distance, Eadulf could see the inlet, which was narrowing into the month of a small river, and ahead, on the southern side of the river, evidence of habitation: several large wooden buildings and a landing stage. Yet it was not this that had seized his attention.

What had caught his eye was the dark outline of a grey stone construction, not very tall – perhaps two metres in height – which stood to one side of the inlet, rising from the waters.

'What sort of monument is that?' he asked again.

Beside him, Enda glanced to where Eadulf was staring and shrugged.

'They call them dolmens, friend Eadulf,' he replied. 'Portal stones, I suppose.'

'I've seen plenty of dolmans in this land, Enda,' Eadulf replied. 'I meant, what does it signify?'

One of Fécho's crewmen, who was standing nearby, ready with his *sluasat*, a special type of oar, to stave the ship off any threatening rocks and guide it into the inlet should it be necessary, turned with a sour expression.

'The warrior is right, stranger. It is a portal monument from the time before time. It warns you that you are entering the territory of the Uí Liatháin.'

'Warns us?' Enda asked irritably.

The crewman seemed amused. 'Although this is still part of Colgú's kingdom, warrior, it is also a foreign country. You are entering the land of the "grey people", for that is the meaning of their name. Grey by name and grey by nature.'

Enda shifted his weight and his hand automatically closed on his sword hilt.

'Then perhaps it is time that they were persuaded to show some respect to their King and those who represent him,' he replied sharply.

Fidelma, who had come across the deck to look at the shore, overheard what he was saying and shot him a disapproving glance.

'That is not our purpose here, Enda,' she rebuked, turning and moving back to where Fécho watched the approach of the landing stage. 'I have never entered Uí Liatháin from this direction and certainly not this far south,' she told him. 'I always came on horseback from the north and was usually accorded the hospitality of Tolmanach at his fortress in the north of the territory.'

'Caislean Uí Liatháin is a long way north,' the boatman agreed. 'Even Tomaltaid, the new prince, might find it difficult to rule these people. This is the southern half of his land, and they are a strange people, these southerners. They claim they are related to the Uí

Fidgenti. They do not even obey their own princes, and they certainly do not acknowledge the authority of the King at Cashel.'

Fidelma raised her brows in an expression of concern. 'Then what sort of territory are we coming to?'

'This land is called Achadh Fhada, the Long Field, and all the land in between here and the Hill of the Yew Wood, the settlement of Eochaill, where you find the estuary of the great river Abhainn Dubh, is southern Uí Liatháin territory ruled by a noble called Glaisne. He is a ruthless man, by all accounts. One who prefers to rule by fear instead of law.' He grimaced. 'Did you know that the wife of the High King, the lady Grella, is a princess of these people and distant cousin to Glaisne?'

She did not reply directly but asked: 'And you say this is called the Long Field?'

'Yes, the territory around this inlet and beyond,' confirmed Fécho, indicating it with one hand. 'It is a fertile land and perhaps the most peaceful corner of the territory. I trade goods for their wheat and barley, and they have ample livestock here. Just south of this inlet . . .' He pointed to the wooded land on their right. 'That is called the Promontory of Tialláin, Ros Tialláin. He is the local chieftain whom I spoke to you about.'

Enda came to join them, intersted in what the captain had to say.

'Tialláin respects only two things . . . power and financial reward,' Fécho added.

Enda opened his mouth, about to remark that Tialláin ought to respect Fidelma, but she had motioned him to silence.

'How long will it take us to ride to Cluain from here?' she asked.

Fécho frowned. 'You still insist on riding through this territory to Cluain?'

'We want to see the Abbey of Cluain before we continue on to the estuary of the Great River, as I told you.'

Fécho shook his head. 'And as I told you, there is nothing there, lady. That place has long been deserted. The Blessed Colmán mac

Léine, who made it his principal abbey, died nearly a hundred years ago. I tried to convince you last night that it is abandoned. There are only ruins there.'

'How do you know that for a fact?' Fidelma pressed.

'Oh . . . I have heard it said. I have never ventured so far east beyond Ros Tialláin – never would,' replied Fécho, looking serious. 'So far as I know, the old abbey was abandoned long ago. Why would you want to go there?'

Fidelma looked up and found that Eadulf and Enda were also waiting for her response. She could feel their ill-concealed curiosity. Once more she wished that she could break the *geis* and tell them everything.

'We intend to ride to Eochaill, the Hill of the Yew, anyway,' she said tersely. 'Then we can make our way north up the Great River to Lios Mhór and then home to Cashel.' She turned back to Fécho. 'So you have never been to Cluain?'

Fécho shrugged. 'I know it is east of here. Perhaps there is a trail that the locals would know. For myself, lady, I am content to keep to the waters around the Great Island. I have no need to see what lies beyond. With the shortening days, however, I suggest that you delay your departure from here until tomorrow morning.' He turned and realised the waters had quickened and his attention was needed to help guide the vessel to the landing jetty.

They knew that their approach had been spotted because they heard the traditional long warning blast of a *stoc,* a bugle. But the woods around the settlement were so thick they could not see anyone apart from a few people on the jetty, watching their approach. They had no doubt their arrival was being cautiously evaluated, in case they were hostile. However, as they got closer to the jetty where the trees thinned, they could see movement along the right bank. Fécho's ship had obviously been recognised – the *stocaire* sounded three short rapid blasts, indicating the newcomers were friends. Though the portal stone still held an aura of menace, they could now observe, stretching up the bank from the jetty, a circle of domestic buildings. Unusually for a southern seaport, there was no high wooden stockade around the settlement to protect the inhabitants from sea raiders. Some interested spectators were now making their way down to the jetty, while others seemed to be carrying on with their pursuits, indifferent to the new arrivals.

Eadulf examined the place named Tialláin's promontory without enthusiasm. Enda seemed to agree with his assessment for he turned to Fidelma.

'I know you can't tell us of your purpose here, but if we are to return to Cashel it is an easy journey back on the mainland. As Fécho indicates, and as we saw at Ard Nemed, the stories about the lawlessness of this land of the grey people seem true enough.'

Fidelma drew her brows together in annoyance. 'We are here because the task that I have been given has not yet been fulfilled,' she replied shortly.

'But we still have no understanding of what that task is,' the young warrior complained, exasperated. 'My task is to protect you and friend Eadulf here. How am I to do that, if I know not what I am protecting you from?'

Fidelma's face darkened but before she could reply Eadulf cut in with a forced smile.

'I am sure that Fidelma will be able to tell you soon,' he assured the warrior. 'But perhaps this is not the best place to do so?' He nodded at the curious onlookers standing nearby, who seemed to include a number of armed men.

'Enda, I can assure you, and Eadulf, that before we leave Cluain you shall know the details of the task I have been asked to fulfil. Unfortunately, we must reach Cluain first; after that, we can continue east to An Abhainn Mhór, the Great River.'

'And what do you expect to find at this place called Cluain?' pressed Eadulf.

'Expect? When you pursue the unknown, you expect nothing or

much trouble,' she returned irritably. 'Enough. You will know when the time comes. Once we have disembarked, we should find an inn where we can refresh ourselves. If, as Fécho has said, we would not reach Cluain before nightfall, then we will have to stay here. Curse these midwinter days – they are not the best of times to travel. Hardly has the day begun than night closes in.'

Eadulf suppressed a sigh of resignation. They had indeed already been on a long and exhausting journey to this point. He, too, would have preferred the days to be longer, so they could complete their journey in a more relaxed fashion.

They were aware now of the growing noise of people crowding on the quayside to help make the ship secure and shout questions to Fécho and his crew. Apparently the *Tonn Cliodhna* was well known in this little haven. Once again, Fidelma had to admire the dexterity with which Fécho and his crew were able to berth the ship. Again, and with the minimum of fuss, the side panel of the ship was unbolted, the horses untied and led across the jetty to firm land.

Fidelma asked the boat owner: 'Is there a *burden*, an inn, where we can stay here?'

Fécho pointed to the hill overlooking the harbour and a substantial log building on the steep slopes.

'There is an inn there. It's a good place and has a stable for the horses.'

'Then we shall stay there and continue our journey tomorrow.'

'Well, lady,' Fécho said almost with regret, 'I wish you well in your curious journeying. It will surely take you a long time to reach Cashel on the route you have chosen. Still, good luck – and I am here for a while, for I intend to see whether there is a cargo I can pick up. So if you change your mind and need to return the way you have come, let me know.'

'Thank you for your offer, Fécho,' replied Fidelma solemnly. 'But we ride on to the Hill of the Yew as soon as possible.'

While Fidelma and Fécho settled the matter of the fee and the boat owner was released from the responsibility of the honour prices of the King's sister and her entourage, Enda and Eadulf began leading their horses up the path towards the inn. None of the locals seemed particularly interested in them; no one challenged them or even greeted them, apart from with the occasional nod.

Fidelma finally left the jetty, with a nod of farewell to Fécho, and began to follow Eadulf and Enda up to the inn.

The inn was built on a small platean, protected on the side where the hill rose steeply again by a line of beech trees.

'Ah, at least this walk will help get our land legs back,' Enda said spiritedly.

'I must admit,' Eadulf replied, following him, 'that I would prefer not to board another ship for a long, long while. A couple of times I thought we were in trouble. Yesterday when the currents started to drive us towards that headland and then this morning when the winds tore our sails.'

Enda chuckled. 'Don't tell me, friend Eadulf, that you would prefer to be on horseback?'

Eadulf was not put out by this joke at his expense.

'I would rather not be travelling at all but seated before a log fire somewhere, contemplating the world with a mug of mead.'

They led their horses to the long, low-built wooden building and secured them to a wooden rail. As no one was about, they left their belongings still packed up on the horses and went to the door of the inn.

The tavern appeared to be empty, but a welcoming fire crackled in a stone hearth to one side. The place was plainly furnished with a number of benches, a table and cupboards, and the smell of newly brewed beer perfumed the air. It was dark but warm and they felt comfortably enveloped as they stepped inside, in spite of the acrid fumes of the fire.

'Well, it seems you will have your wish at least, friend Eadulf,'

Enda said. 'A log fire, warmth – all we need is a mug of mead.'

'You wish for drinks, strangers?' A hollow voice caused them to start, so unexpected was it.

They had not seen the tavern keeper enter. He seemed to have simply emerged from a dark corner of the room beyond some cupboards. He did not look at all what one expected of a tavern keeper, being bent and cadaverous with dark eyes, sunken cheeks and an unusually solemn air.

Enda turned round and, giving the man a quick appraisal, said: 'If you are the keeper of this tavern, my friend, yes; we do want some drinks, and perhaps some food. I presume you have such items?'

'This is a *bruden*, a public hostel, for free lodging and entertainment,' replied the man in a voice that carried neither warmth nor interest. 'It is classed as a *brugaid cedach*, although that in itself is an embellishment of the truth, but our chieftain likes to maintain that we are able to meet all manner of guests and to serve them three types of meat when called upon. So we have plenty of meats, cooked and uncooked. We also have plenty of beverages, ready to drink.'

Fidelma regarded the man with some amusement at this monotone recital. She glanced about the inn. 'So, this is a *brugaid cedach*?' she asked, unable to hide her laughter.

The mournful expression did not leave the innkeeper's face. 'It is, as I have said.'

'Then we will take mugs of your mead first, *brugh-fer*,' Fidelma replied, trying to keep her features serious as she addressed him as 'hosteller'. 'And then we will discuss what manner of food you serve.'

The man stared at her, hesitating, then looked at Enda. The warrior sighed impatiently.

'Well, man? I presume you do have mead to serve us?' he asked sarcastically.

The thin man seemed to catch himself and nodded, turned and walked off at a leisurely pace to get their drinks.

The three travellers took seats near the fire.

'I thought a *brugaid cedach* was a big public hostel?' Eadulf queried, looking round the narrow room.

'It is the lowest grade of public hostel,' confirmed Fidelma. 'Even so, it is supposed to have room for one hundred guests and to be ready at all times to receive them and serve them food and drink. The fires should always be lit and the cauldrons for cooking should never be taken from the hearth.'

'The man did confess that the description of this place was a little overambitious,' pointed out Enda cheerfully.

'Overambitious?' Eadulf chuckled. 'I doubt whether this place will meet the needs of three of us, let alone a hundred guests.'

They were just relaxing after the journey when the door of the inn burst open and two men appeared, swords in hand, followed by a third man. He carried no weapon.

'Do not move, strangers!' One of the men brandished his sword threateningly as he shouted this order.

Fidelma and her companions were stunned into inaction.

The unarmed man stepped forward. His features were hard to describe, neither young nor elderly. He had a mop of unkempt black hair merging into a thick, straggly beard. His eyes were dark and small, with an unfathomable malignant quality about them. He was of medium height but well built, and even without the silver chain of office at his neck one would realise he was someone of importance. The quality of his clothes also differentiated him from his two companions.

'What is the meaning of this?' demanded Enda, beginning to rise, his hand slipping towards his sword hilt.

'Move another fraction and you will be dead,' the man who had shouted the first order now said, his voice cold and without emotion.

A darting movement of his eyes as he said this caused Enda to look over to where the innkeeper had disappeared. Another man now stood there with a bow in his hands, an arrow already strung and pointing at them. Enda shrugged and placed his hands on the table before him.

'This is an outrage,' he said. 'Do you know to whom you speak?'

The leader stood a step forward and seemed to examine Fidelma for a moment.

'I speak with Fidelma of Cashel, sometimes known as Sister Fidelma, sister to Colgú of the Eóganacht,' he replied, to their surprise.

It was Enda who recovered first. 'Colgú, King of Muman, of *all* Muman, to whom your prince, Tomaltaid of the Uí Liatháin, must pay tribute,' he stated.

For the first time the leader of the newcomers gave a lopsided smile. 'Tomaltaid? The name seems vaguely familiar . . . The prince of the Uí Liatháin? Didn't someone recently claim such a title?' There was sarcasm in his voice. Then he turned to Enda and said sharply, 'Tomaltaid's word has no authority in this territory, warrior. We are of the southern Uí Liatháin. We have no overlord, not even Glaisne of Eochaill.'

'Then titles apart,' Fidelma spoke for the first time, and coldly, 'I am a *dálaigh*, qualified to the degree of *anruth*, and thus you will know my authority. I presume you recognise the law, if not your princes?'

This seemed to cause the man even more amusement.

'A lawyer? I tremble! Princes may come and go but lawyers go on for ever. Indeed, I do fear lawyers. Gadra, show my authority under the law that I respect.'

One of the men at his side took a step forward and raised his sword, pointing it at Fidelma's breast. Fidelma did not even blink. Her face was tightly controlled. It was Eadulf who gave a gasp and started to reach out, as if to attack the man.

A push from Enda knocked Eadulf back onto his seat a moment

before an arrow sped by his head and embedded itself into the wall behind him. He felt its breath on his cheek.

'Stop!' commanded the leader. The bowman in the doorway halted in the act of stringing a second arrow to his bow. The man called Gadra took a step back, and brought his sword back to the defensive position. 'I would advise no more stupid movements, for your companions' own health.' The leader addressed himself directly to Fidelma.

'May I remind you that you started this stupidity?' she replied icily, as if unperturbed by his threats.

'A point I will accept for the moment, lawyer,' the man acknowledged drily. 'Now, what are you doing in my territory?'

'Your territory?' Fidelma queried with a cynical smile. 'I thought this was the territory of the Uí Liatháin, and yet you tell me that you do not recognise Tomaltaid's authority. So tell me where I am mistaken?'

'You are in the territory of Tialláin,' the man Gadra said proudly, glancing obsequiously at his leader.

Fidelma sighed. 'That much I know, for I am told this is called the Promontory of Tialláin, a minor chieftain among the Uí Liatháin, if that is not to give him too much honour – for he controls only this little harbour, no more than a jetty by a stream.'

There was a moment of tension. Gadra looked to his leader, as if expecting an order, but the moment passed and the leader gave a forced chuckle.

'You speak bravely, lawyer.'

'I speak as I must, Tialláin,' she replied. 'I presume you are the *bó-aire* of this harbour? Or do you claim a higher rank?'

The black beard and hair disguised the man's facial features but his body language seemed to indicate controlled anger.

'I will ask the questions, lawyer,' he snapped. 'What are you doing here?'

Fidelma made a point of glancing around as if in bemusement.

'Here? Why, we were waiting for the *brugh-fer* to serve us the drinks we ordered. He seems to be a little tardy in fulfilling his duties.'

'Why did you land here? Where are you going and for what purpose?'

'Oh,' Fidelma replied easily, 'we do not intend to stay here, as much as we are impressed by the welcome and your hospitality.'

'I am still waiting for an answer!' the man almost shouted.

Eadulf eyed Fidelma nervously, hoping that she had not pushed the man's patience to its limit.

'After we have a meal and a night's rest, we intend to ride on to the Hill of the Yew. I am told that from there we might find a boat to transport us to Lios Mór . . .'

'I know where An Abhainn Mhór leads,' interrupted the man sharply. 'And I suppose that it is just by chance that your path to the Hill of the Yew will take you through Cluain?'

For the first time Fidelma hesitated, but only for a moment. 'I have heard of Cluain,' she said in a measured tone. She hoped that Eadulf and Enda would not remark on the fact that she had mentioned Cluain was important. 'I am told it is just a ruined abbey, deserted for many years. Do you reckon that is the best path to the Great River? Is there a more direct route from here?'

'What do you seek at Cluain?' Tialláin demanded, ignoring her questions.

'Seek?' Fidelma was back in control. 'Why, only the path to the Hill of the Yew.'

Enda was clearly puzzled by the exchange and sat frowning, while Eadulf was worried by the antagonism shown by Tialláin.

'It is pointless to lie to me, lawyer. I know the truth as to why you seek Cluain.'

'Then you know more than I do, Tialláin, so perhaps you will enlighten us?'

'I know why you have landed here,' he repeated.

Fidelma gave an exaggerated shrug. 'Then you have no need to ask these questions and waste my time and yours.'

'You are trying to catch up with the girl, Cairenn. I know the plot that you are both involved in.'

Eadulf felt Fidelma's body suddenly tense next to him. Her shock was palpable. He, too, was surprised to hear the name of the girl who had been accused of murdering the old abbot at Finnbarr's Abbey. He wished that Fidelma had been able to tell him what she knew instead of keeping this stupid sacred oath. If he knew what her mission was about, he would be able to act accordingly and not inadvertently betray her.

'Of course, you will claim that you do not know Cairenn.' Tialláin was smiling sarcastically. 'There is a hue and cry for her by the folk of Finnbarr's Abbey. She is said to have murdered Abbot Nessán.' Tialláin's tiny eyes had narrowed so that they could hardly be seen.

Fidelma remained silent. Tialláin exploded in irritation. 'You know that I speak of one of your own – the girl is a member of the Eóganacht Raithlind, a cousin to Artgal, who thinks he has a right to rule Ard Nemed, across the water there.'

'Indeed?' Fidelma tried to sound mildly perplexed. 'I do not know her. Our family is large and widespread.'

'She was the companion and confidante of Grella, wife to the High King, Cenn Fáelad. Grella of the Uí Liatháin.'

The look of genuine surprise on the faces of Eadulf and Enda seem to distract Tialláin for a moment, allowing Fidelma time to reassume her expression of bewildered innocence.

'What was she doing in the abbey?' she said, as if she had little understanding of what he was saying. 'Truly, Tialláin, your knowledge and your behaviour are alarming and I have no comprehension of it. You say that I have some involvement with this girl. Why would that be? Do you think I am employed by the abbey to follow her? Why should she be passing in this direction anyway?'

Tialláin gave a grunt of exasperation. 'I said nothing of the sort, lawyer. You are trying to play games with me.'

'I am trying to understand what games you are playing.' Fidelma was confident now that the man was puzzled.

'No games. I know that Grella, wife to the High King, was at Cluain and heard that her bodyguard was killed.'

Now Fidelma was really shocked and there was little hiding it.

'So how does this girl Cairenn fit into all this?' Eadulf's question was so obviously sincere that Tialláin hesitated a moment before responding.

'Enough of your games! I know them too well. And until I am assured that you pose no danger to me, you and your companions will remain here as my guests.'

It was Enda who now spoke. 'I think you should reconsider your suggestion, Tialláin. May I remind you that Fidelma is sister to King Colgú of Cashel, to whom the princes of the Uí Liatháin pay tribute; moreover, Fidelma is a lawyer. You may disregard and disrespect your own prince but be warned that the King of Cashel's warriors are a not inconsiderable force. Does not the lady Fidelma's rank impress you enough that she should be treated with courtesy?'

Tialláin ignored him. 'Gadra, take charge of the woman,' he instructed, coldly. 'You will find the accommodation frugal, lady. I am afraid the place of confinement was not built with a female lawyer or a princess in mind.'

Gadra grabbed Fidelma's comb bag and *marsupium* and handed them to one of the bowmen. He deftly patted her clothing, searching for any hidden weapon. Then he took Enda's weapons and Eadulf's knife and bag and gave them to the bowman, too.

'What shall I do with these?' the man asked Tialláin, indicating the confiscated items.

'Take them and put them with the horses; they can go to the stable yard until I decide what to do with them.' The man left on his errand.

'What about my companions? What do you intend to do?' demanded Fidelma as Gadra waved his sword at the door to show she should precede him.

Tialláin stroked his beard for a moment as if trying to make up his mind.

'We could kill them,' he said reflectively. 'But I suppose it would be a waste of effort and of value. We will hold them until the Saxon raider puts into our harbour. He may give us a tidy sum for all of you . . . *Don't*!'

The last was a shouted order as Enda lunged forward. The arrow struck him in the upper arm before he had even raised his hand.

'Stop!' It was Fidelma. 'We submit, Tialláin. Call off your bowman. Do not harm my companions further.'

Tialláin called: 'Keep them covered, Gadra. I will remove the lawyer myself. You, woman, come with me, and move slowly and without blocking the aim of my bowman – because if either of your companions moves, he will shoot whether you are in the way or not.'

'Very well.' Her voice was tight. 'Enda, how is your wound?'

Enda was standing, one hand clasped to his bleeding upper arm, from which the arrow still protruded. The warrior grimaced sourly. 'A scratch, lady. I have had worse in practice fights.'

'Can Brother Eadulf attend to his wound?' she demanded of Tialláin.

'Enough of your orders, lawyer,' snapped Tialláin. 'Leave them and come with me.'

'But Eadulf has studied the healing arts at Tuaim Brecain. He can attend to the wound,' she said, unmoved by his threatening tone.

Tialláin hesitated and then snapped to his man, 'Gadra, let the Saxon tend the wound but keep a careful eye upon him. I'll send in a couple of the other men to help. Then make sure these two are placed where they can do no further harm. Now, lawyer, come with me and not a further word lest I lose my temper entirely.'

With an apologetic glance at her companions, Fidelma followed Tialláin to the door. He moved aside, drawing a short sword, and allowed her to exit first. As she hesitated before going through the doorway, he seemed to smile behind his beard.

'I have heard that you were known to excel at the *troidsciagaid*, the unarmed combat that is taught to the religious before they go on missions to strange lands. Do not try anything . . . I will not hesitate to use this weapon.'

Fidelma said nothing but left the inn.

Outside, she saw more of what were obviously Tialláin's men, one of them leading their horses away. Two armed men joined the chieftain, who ordered another two to go to Gadra inside the inn.

'I hope you know what you are doing,' she remarked to Tialláin, as he indicated that she should go before him along a path around the hillside.

'I know well enough,' he replied curtly. 'Go towards that stone building beyond those trees.'

She saw, beyond a circle of yew and hawthorns, a grey building. It was distinguished from all the wooden structures she had seen by being built of limestone blocks. She moved slowly towards it.

'Do I have your word that my companions will not be harmed?'

Triallán made a derisive sound. 'I have said they will not be harmed by me. That is enough. Now get a move on.'

As Fidelma looked around the little copse that surrounded the stone building, she caught a glimpse of a figure standing watching at some little distance. It was then things became clearer: the figure was none other than Fécho.

'So Fécho is involved in whatever you are up to?' she asked brightly.

'You may be too clever for your own good, lawyer,' was the unhelpful reply.

'I was wondering how you came to know who I and my companions were,' she said. 'I hope the boatman was more honest with you than he was with me.'

This caused Tialláin to halt uncertainly.

'What do you mean?'

Fidelma paused and smiled. 'Just that a person who can lie to one can also lie to another. Fécho works for profit not for causes, isn't that right?'

'What do you know about causes?' sneered the man.

'Only that some people sacrifice themselves for a belief while others do so merely for profit. Fécho, I judge, is one of the latter, and as such, his truth can be changeable, depending how large the profit.'

Tialláin smiled in turn. 'He might have told you that I, too, work for profit. Fécho has been trading among these harbours for many years. I have known him a long time.'

Fidelma grimaced sourly. 'Then you know what I mean.'

She saw the troubled look in Tialláin's dark eyes and knew her remark had struck home.

The chieftain shook his head. 'He would not lie to me. He knows my vengeance has a long hand and that it is merciless.'

'More so than your own new prince, Tomaltaid, who seems to be asserting the power that you would now deny? I'd have a care about Fécho's loyalty. And Tomaltaid might come to question your allegiance soon.'

'I owe no more allegiance to him than to Glaisne!'

'Then perhaps it will be my brother, King of Muman, who will come with his army.' Fidelma smiled grimly. 'Have a care, Tialláin.'

The man hesitated and then shook himself like an angry dog. 'Enough of this! Move on, sharply now.'

His two men closed in threateningly. Fidelma turned and walked on towards the limestone building. It was a large rectangle with no windows, at least none that she could see from the angle they approached it. There were large double doors of what she thought were oak, studded with iron nails. She noticed that wide tracks led up to these doors, as if the building were used as a stable or storage barn. As they came closer, Fidelma saw that it rose to a double storey with a small square tower in one corner. It seemed indeed to be a large store house; in fact, as she now observed, the wide track led from the double oak doors all the way down to the harbour below. There were traces of wagons being frequently used along this path.

One of Tialláin's men went forward and produced a great key to unlock the doors, and held them open. It was dark inside and they paused while the man struck a flint and tinder to ignite a small oil lamp. Fidelma confirmed there were no windows in the building and that it was mostly given over to storage. She noticed an open door, which must lead to the tower that she had seen from outside. At the far end of the building, she saw, a part was partitioned off by a stone wall in which there were set more heavy oak doors. This interior wall rose only to a single storey and the enclosure was roofed by a sloping series of heavy timber boards.

Tialláin halted and indicated one of the doors.

'Here you will stay, lawyer, until you tell me what you know or until I decide that you have nothing that I need.'

'What about my companions?'

'I have already told you what I shall do. I am acquainted with the captain of a Saxon ship that has business along this coast. He is due here within a day or two. An Eóganacht princess will make a fine hostage for him to take to his home port, and a warrior of the Golden Collar will make a fine slave. And no one in this kingdom will lament the departure of your Saxon husband. They might even be grateful for it.'

'That's where you are wrong, Tialláin,' she replied coldly. 'And I think you will suffer for your mistake.'

'But I will not suffer as much as you,' the chieftain replied, nodding to his men.

Fidelma found herself being roughly manhandled through one of the doors and into the darkened room behind.

She blinked in the darkness. 'Can you at least provide me with a candle?' she demanded.

'Giving orders to the last?' sneered Tialláin. Then he suddenly laughed. 'Why not? Give her a light,' he said to one of his men. 'Give her a light so that she may see there is no means of escape.'

One of the men gave her the small, flickering oil lamp with a cynical smile. 'It won't last you long but long enough for you to see there is no escape from your imprisonment,' he said, echoing his chieftain's words.

With that, she was pushed inside and the door swung shut with a bang. She heard the key rasp in the lock. She turned with a sigh. The place was dank and smelled of wet hay. Piles of straw were everywhere, some rotting. There was no other furniture, and no light apart from the small lamp she had been given. She held it high and peered around carefully.

It was during this examination that she saw what appeared to be a pile of clothes under the straw in one corner. She moved forward. There came a groan, and she realised that the clothes covered a body. She bent and removed the straw. The body lay face down but Fidelma noticed the rise and fall of the shoulders and heard the gasping breaths. She put the lamp down and knelt beside the body, using all her strength to turn it over. It was a young girl. She had auburn hair and, even with the bruises and cuts on her cheeks, Fidelma could tell she was remarkably attractive. Fidelma had last seen her in the Abbey of Finnbarr a few days ago.

'Cairenn!' she exclaimed.

CHAPTER NINE

E adulf was examining the wound in Enda's arm.

'I'll have to pull the arrow out,' he announced.

'That's all right, friend Eadulf,' muttered Enda. 'I don't think it has gone in far.'

Eadulf turned to the man called Gadra. 'I need my *les*,' he said. It was the medicine bag carried by all physicians. Since Eadulf had studied the healing arts, even though he had not qualified and was unable to carry an *echlais*, the symbolic whip which was the emblem of a qualified doctor, he had developed the habit of carrying his medical bag. In fact, it had been useful on more than one occasion, especially in some of the investigations he had undertaken with Fidelma.

Gadra stared at him, confused.

'My medical bag, man! It's on my horse. Do you want this man to bleed to death?'

Gadra hesitated a moment more, then shrugged and turned to one of the men who had just joined him. 'Get the bag,' he instructed.

'Sit in that chair, Enda,' Eadulf told him. When the warrior had sat down, Eadulf bent to look at the arrow. He glanced towards the bowman who had remained behind to cover them. 'Let me see your arrows,' he snapped.

The bowman looked uncertain and turned questioningly to Gadra.

Gadra shrugged and motioned to the bowman to give him an

arrow. 'The Saxon is hardly likely to overwhelm us with one arrow and no bow,' he grinned.

Eadulf saw that it was a crude arrow without a flint or metal head, just a long willow stick that had been whittled into a point at one end.

'It means it went in cleanly in one piece and can come out that way,' Eadulf murmured. 'Bring me a mug of *corma*.'

Once more Gadra stared at him in bemusement.

'*Corma*,' Eadulf repeated impatiently. 'I need the alcohol to cleanse the wound!'

Gadra called for the innkeeper and gave the order. The *corma* appeared at the same time the man returned with Eadulf's medical bag. Eadulf poured some of the alcohol around the point where the arrow tip had penetrated. Then he handed the rest to Enda. 'Drink,' he instructed. Enda took a large swallow. He was just setting down the mug when Eadulf grasped the shaft of the arrow and pulled.

The invective that came from Enda's lips was not surprising.

Eadulf was peering at the arm. 'Good,' he smiled. 'It looks like a clean wound anyway. Is there some of that *corma* left?'

'I needed it,' muttered Enda, looking at the empty mug.

'I wasn't thinking of you but of the wound,' Eadulf replied and turned to the *brugh-fer*. 'Get this refilled.' The man glanced at Gadra, who shrugged again. When the *corma* appeared, Eadulf once more poured some of it over the wound and gave the rest to Enda, who drank it back in one swallow.

Eadulf was peering into his *les*. 'Now, a salve to prevent infection and ease the tenderness. Then I'll bind it up with linen strips.'

There was silence while they watched Eadulf at work. The puncture mark the arrow had left was not large, with more of a bruise around it than an open wound. Eadulf spent some time applying his treatment and binding up the arm.

'Nice and tight and no infection,' he said with satisfaction. 'It should heal soon, especially after the bruising becomes less tender.'

He packed the things back in his medical bag and then looked questioningly at the man called Gadra.

'So what do you intend to do with us?'

Gadra seemed perplexed by the way Eadulf had assumed authority. He did not answer for a moment, then remembered Tialláin's orders.

'You will remain here until a decision is reached.'

Eadulf smiled and sat down.

'In that case the *brugh-fer* can bring us drinks and the good meal that we were about to order when you interrupted us.'

'On your feet, Saxon,' Gadra shouted, apparently realising he should try to regain authority.

'Angle,' interrupted Eadulf casually. 'I am from the kingdom of the East Angles.'

Gadra swore, conscious that he had almost been mesmerised into complying with Eadulf's wishes. 'I do not care if you come from Magh Da Chéo . . .'

'Oh, I don't think it would do for a Christian to come from the Plain of Mists,' chided Eadulf, recognising one of the names for the pagan Otherworld.

'Silence!' Gadra turned to the scrawny *brugh-fer*. 'I presume that you have a *talam* here for storage?'

A *talam* was a large underground chamber, a storage cellar, common in large buildings like this. The innkeeper pointed to a trapdoor in the middle of the floor without comment.

'Can it be locked?' demanded Gadra.

'You can see there it has a bolt to secure it.'

'And there is no other way out once the trapdoor is secure?'

'None.'

'Raise the trapdoor.'

The man did so and Gadra took a pace forward to look down. There was a flight of wooden steps descending into darkness. He smiled and turned back to Eadulf and Enda.

'Get down there, the both of you.'

'Oh, can't we take anything to drink or eat with us?' Eadulf asked. 'We are starving.'

'Get down!' Gadra shouted in fury.

'It's dark. What about a stub of candle? Surely you can give us that?'

Gadra struck Eadulf across the cheek with the flat of his sword. It did not cut but made a nasty red weal on his cheek.

'Have a care, friend Eadulf,' Enda muttered. 'These people do not seem possessed of a sense of humour.'

Eadulf took his *les* and moved to the trapdoor in the floor. If the truth were known, he had been goading the man so that he would not notice Eadulf pick up the bag. Eadulf knew there were things inside that would be of use. While Eadulf was going down into the *talam*, Enda was subjected to a quick search for any other weapons he might have had. His sword and hunting knife had already been removed. Then he was pushed down after Eadulf. The trapdoor, pulled by its own weight, crashed shut above them.

The underground chamber was large and one could almost stand up in it. In fact, they did not need a light for the wooden planks of the floor of the inn – the roof of the cellar – were uneven and light permeated through the gaps between the boards so that they could see well enough. They stood for a few moments looking about them in the gloom. Sacks and boxes were piled up everywhere. There was certainly no other means of exit than the trapdoor. That was going to be difficult. Even if they could prise it open, they would emerge into the middle of the inn.

'What now, friend Eadulf?' Enda sighed. 'There is no way out of here without being seen.'

'Don't give up so soon, Enda,' Eadulf replied. 'Remember what Hannibal said – *aut viam inveniam aut faciam*? I'll either find a way or make one.'

Enda sniffed dolefully.

'I don't know who Hannibal was,' he said sourly.

'As a warrior, you should know who he was,' Eadulf advised. 'He was the great general of Carthage who nearly defeated Rome.'

'Ah,' Enda sighed, sounding cynical. 'Nearly? Much sadness in that word "nearly". It is not much of an achievement in life to nearly do something.'

'Cairenn!' Fidelma whispered urgently, bending over the body of the girl. 'Cairenn! Can you hear me?'

The girl stirred with a groan, turning her head slightly on the bed of damp straw and blinking a little in the fluttering light of the oil lamp that Fidelma held over her.

Fidelma hesitated, then placed the light to one side. She had spotted a water barrel. She reached for the small square of linen she always carried tucked into her *criss*, or belt. Then she moved to the barrel and immersed it in the brackish water. Returning, she wiped the girl's face. With the blood wiped away, the bruises and abrasions were not as shocking as they had at first appeared. The girl was slowly coming round.

'Who are you?' she finally asked, after Fidelma had found a mug and brought water to wet the girl's lips, advising her not to drink for the water might be contaminated.

'I am Fidelma of Cashel,' she replied, holding the lamp so the girl could see her face.

'Ah! So you followed me from Finnbarr's Abbey?'

The answer was obvious, so Fidelma did not reply. Instead she asked, 'What happened? Who did this to you?'

Ciarran eased herself up on the straw. She seemed to quickly recover from her ordeal and take in her situation.

'He was called Tialláin by his men.'

Fidelma compressed her lips. 'How did you come to this place?'

'You saw how I came to flee the abbey. I could not talk to you but I left you a clue in my room. I presume you went to Artgal?'

'Artgal confirmed you had been there but said you were heading to Cluain. So we followed you here – but I have no understanding of why you have laid this trail for me to follow.'

'Let me start in this way. I did not murder Abbot Nessán. I am companion to the High King's wife, Grella. We came to Cluain together, where I left her and, on her instruction, went to see my cousin Nessán, who, I was told, had certain information for me to take back to Grella.'

'So you were making your way back to Cluain when this happened?'

'I was taken prisoner by the people here.'

'Tell me, first, how you arrived with Grella at Cluain initially?'

'To be accurate, I left the lady Grella at the entrance to the valley in which Cluain lies. Apparently Abbot Antrí is also a cousin to Grella. She was to stay at the abbey of Cluain while I went to see my great-uncle Nessán.'

'Why did you and Grella leave Tara?'

'Grella told me she had received a secret message from Abbot Nessán, telling her that there was a plot by the Eóganacht to assassinate her husband, the High King, Cenn Fáelad, and provoke a war. She said she had been instructed to seek refuge with her cousin Abbot Antrí at Cluain and send me to see Nessán, who would then tell me all the details of the conspiracy.'

'And did he?' Fidelma asked, thinking that the story seemed a curious one.

The girl shook her head. 'When I arrived at the abbey, old Nessán was bewildered. When I told him of the message Grella had received, he said that he had sent no message. He told me that *you* had sent a message telling him that you were coming to see him on behalf of the High King, and said that he would wait until you arrived before he discussed the matter with me. I knew something was wrong but I did not know what.'

'I had a message from the High King, asking me to go to the abbot,' Fidelma said. 'I was placed under a *geis* not to discuss it.'

The girl frowned. 'A *geis* from the High King?'

Fidelma went on: 'Tara keeps pigeons that are trained to fly to certain places, just as the Greeks and Romans have done – still do. Messages travel fast these days.'

'Nessán was always fond of keeping rock doves,' replied Cairenn. 'That was how he alerted Grella. She said he had written the note in the old language in Ogam script as he could not openly send details of the plot, but he was worried that it could be read by any scholar. So I did not question the wisdom of going to see him in person.'

'Someone read the messages and therein is probably the motive for his murder,' Fidelma commented. 'So what happened when you arrived at the abbey?'

'I think he was worried. He had an argument with his steward, Brother Ruissine, about why he had not been informed immediately when you arrived. After the meal, he told me to go and find you. So I left him and went in search of you. I saw you in deep conversation with Brother Ruissine and went back to tell Nessán. He was lying on the floor with a cord around his neck but he was not dead.'

'You removed the cord?'

'I did. He managed to whisper a few words before he gasped his last breath and died. I heard Brother Ruissine at the door and I panicked and left. After that, there was uproar. People were calling that the abbot had been murdered and I heard people searching for me. I went back to my room to get some belongings, for I feared I would be accused.'

'Why leave me the note with the name of the Great Island on it?'

'Abbot Nessán seemed to trust you. I knew you would think it odd that I left my *ciorbholg* behind and therefore you would search it. I have heard of your methods as a *dálaigh*. I thought I could leave further word with my cousin Artgal on my way to meet Grella.'

'What were those dying words of Nessán?'

'As I told Artgal. He said to beware of the solar wheel. I don't know what that means. Anyway, I took my horse and left the abbey in darkness. No one saw me.'

'Are you sure?'

'It was dark,' continued the girl. 'I followed the track to the east, intending to make my way to Ard Nemed and leave a message with Artgal for you.' She suddenly glanced at the lamp. 'The lamp is running out of fuel,' she pointed out practically. 'Should you not extinguish it to conserve the oil?'

Fidelma shrugged. 'If I put it out, I have no means to ignite it again. I don't have a tinder box. So tell me, what happened?'

'I found myself on the north shore of the Great Island. I knew Artgal had his fortress on the southern shore. I had landed, exhausted and tired, crawled into an abandoned *bothán* and fell asleep. When I awoke, I heard the sounds of conflict. A group of warriors had halted nearby; I recognised them as Uí Liatháin by their emblems. To my surprise, one of them used my name . . . and instructed the others that I must be prevented from reaching Artgal.'

Fidelma's eyes widened. 'He specifically said your name and that of Artgal?' she pressed.

'I was fearful,' Cairenn said, confirming it with a nod of her head. 'I hid myself as best I could and then when I thought it safe I emerged, determined to make my way south. After a short while, I was surrounded by warriors. They took me to their commander – to my relief, I saw it was my cousin Artgal. They had just driven off the Uí Liatháin and some prisoners had been taken. Artgal had been wounded.'

'I heard this account from Artgal. So what made you leave the safety of his fortress and chance your life to cross to this place?'

'My purpose was to meet Grella at Cluain, as we had arranged, and to tell her what Abbot Nessán had said. I found a fisherman who was willing to bring me to this shore in his small boat and was put ashore not far from here. But luck was against me. I had not gone far when Tiallain's thugs seized me and brought me here. Even before I gave him my name, he seemed to know who I was – and my purpose. I was shocked and alarmed.'

Fidelma was thoughtful. 'He knew you as the personal attendant of Grella?'

'He knew me as Cairenn of the Cenél nÁedo, of the Eóganacht Raithlind,' she confirmed. 'That dumbfounded me, and he seemed to have no respect for Grella, even though she was a princess of the Uí Liatháinn. Then he told me news that shocked and frightened me.'

The pause was tantalising and Fidelma had to restrain herself from shouting at the girl to urge her to explain.

'What news?' she demanded.

'According to Tiallain, the lady Grella's carriage was waylaid in Cluain.'

Fidelma was silent for a moment as she considered this. 'The wife of the High King was waylaid?' She repeated it slowly, as a question.

'Abducted,' explained the girl. 'The wife of the High King has been abducted.'

'Tiallain told me her bodyguard had been killed. Did he claim to have had a role in this?'

'I am not sure. He knew about it, but from the way he spoke it was as if he had heard about it rather than played an active part. Either way, he did not seem to care.'

'That does not surprise me – he seems a man of no morals. So Tiallain knew about this event at Cluain. Did he have any other information – such as who had carried out this deed, or why?'

'He made a curious remark about Saxons being cunning lovers. That's all.'

Fidelma was completely bewildered. 'Saxons? What do you think he meant by that?'

The girl hesitated and then shook her head.

'I have no idea. It sounded like some old saying, one I have never heard before. Is not your husband a Saxon?'

'My husband,' corrected Fidelma softly, 'is an Angle not a Saxon.'

'Isn't that the same?'

'Apparently not,' Fidelma replied with an affectionate smile. 'And I certainly would not call him a cunning lover.'

There was a sudden flicker and hiss as the oil lamp went out. For some time they sat in the dark. Their eyes slowly adjusted, and Fidelma realised that a faint light permeated the building through cracks and chinks so that it was not completely dark but filled with a soft, grey gloom. Fidelma considered her situation. She could do little other than accept it, though it was not in her nature to submit without trying to find an alternative first.

However, the girl brought her attention back to the puzzle.

'Do you know what is behind all this?' she demanded.

'I am placed under a *geis* by the High King. I was not allowed to tell anyone until I spoke to Nessán. I could reveal nothing, not even to my companions, who were captured with me. But since you are involved in this, you probably know more than I do.'

'You have companions with you?'

'My husband, Eadulf, and Enda, of my brother's bodyguard, were with me.'

Cairren sighed. 'I am still confused. I do not begin to understand what has happened. Do you know what Tialláin has in mind for us?'

'No more than you do,' Fidelma said. 'I suppose that will depend on his involvement in this conspiracy – whatever it is. I presume the root of it is the kidnapping of the wife of the High King . . . but for why? What is the purpose of abducting her?'

'Abbot Nessán denied sending her the message, as I told you. It was that message that brought her back to the Uí Liatháin territory. So who would send a false message to lure her here and then abduct her? Perhaps to coerce the High King into doing something?'

'A possibility,' acknowledged Fidelma. 'But we don't have enough information. If the false message was to lure Grella to Cluain, then sending you to see Nessán was equally false.'

'Perhaps it was to separate us,' replied the girl. 'I was a friend to Grella when she was just a princess of the Uí Liatháin. When she married, I went with her as her companion to Tara.'

Fidelma was still puzzled. 'And I do not understand why Abbot Nessán would not send his message directly to Cenn Fáelad, the High King. After all, the High King has his own carrier pigeons. Why send word to Grella? And why instruct Grella to leave Tara, if the assassination plot was against her husband?'

From her silence it seemed the girl had not considered that before. Then she said: 'It might be that Abbot Nessán thought the message more likely to fall into the wrong hands if addressed to Cenn Fáelad. Perhaps he assumed that no one would notice if the message came to Grella?'

'A good logic except, of course, Abbot Nessán denied sending the message to Grella.'

'Then who . . .?'

'Did it not strike you as curious that, having received a message warning her that her husband was about to be assassinated, Grella got into a carriage and headed south, away from her husband and from Tara?'

There was another pause and then the girl replied: 'Perhaps she was anxious to get the full facts before she accused anyone to her husband?'

'Perhaps, but I was told that she did tell him. The High King's message to me mentioned that she had alerted him. That's why he sent me to Abbot Nessán, to learn the facts.'

'I don't understand.'

'Grella had warned her husband – but you did not know that? She sent a note before she left Tara telling him that she had heard of a plot, and she specifically said the Eóganacht were involved. She wanted time to see Abbot Nessán and find out the truth.'

'She wanted to see Nessán . . . then why send me?' The girl was clearly bewildered.

'The Cenél nÁedo are of the Eóganacht Raithlind,' Fidelma pointed out heavily. 'Grella, you say, was instructed to send you to see Nessán – and you were close by when he died.'

The girl gasped. 'Do you mean she sent me there on purpose so that I would be a suspect?'

'Not necessarily. If Grella has been abducted, it could be that she, too, was a victim in this matter. If she was lured here by a false message and manipulated into sending you so the Eóganacht were blamed . . . that would make some sense.'

'I can only tell the truth as it is known to me,' the girl said, sounding exhausted. 'I merely followed the instructions Grella gave me.'

'And she thought those instructions came from Abbot Nessán. But then wouldn't she wonder why Abbot Nessán would send her to seek refuge in Cluain?'

'Part of the conspiracy to lure Grella to a place where she would be abducted?'

'It sounds too complicated. If the aim of the conspiracy is to assassinate Cenn Fáelad and seize the High Kingship, then it is far too complicated.'

'But it does look as though the message to Grella and its instructions were faked. And Grella fell for them.'

Fidelma nodded, frowning a little. 'One thing more, though. When you heard the abbot was murdered, why did you not wait and try to see me?'

'I told you – I did not know what to do, I was confused. I panicked because I heard my name being summoned. I was afraid and felt I had to report to Grella.'

'You could have appealed to me as a *dálaigh*,' pointed out Fidelma. 'And there were enough suspicious circumstances for me to question things and offer you legal protection.'

'I was merely a messenger from the lady Grella. I had no experience of such things as murder. As I say, I panicked and fled. Because Abbot Nessán trusted you, I did leave you a clue as to where I was going, but I did not want to reveal that Grella was at Cluain.'

'Well, I found the message. But someone wanted to ensure you would be blamed and did not escape. On the road south, across the river, we were ambushed – but I think that they were waiting for you, in case you went in that direction. One of them carried a seal with the emblem of the solar wheel.'

Fidelma could sense the girl's fear. 'We left the two attackers dead,' she went on. 'You had gone along the eastern branch of the river to the Great Island and those warriors were waiting for you there as well. I believe the conspirators – whoever they are – intended you to be blamed for the murder of the abbot.'

'And now we have been captured by Tialláin,' concluded the girl bitterly.

'There are many questions that arise,' Fidelma said thoughtfully. 'However, to keep things simple, let us consider what facts we know. There is a plot to assassinate the High King Cenn Fáelad. Or is there? A message is sent to his wife with certain instructions. It purports to come from Abbot Nessán. But does it? The abbot denies all knowledge to you. You are to be blamed for his murder; Grella is abducted. Is this all a plot to kidnap her? If so, why is it so complicated? It seems as incomprehensible as ever. I thought that all had been peaceful in Tara since Cenn Fáelad took the sovereignty?'

'Peaceful, yes,' the girl replied. 'But there is a resentful undertow, drawing support away from the High King, because of who my lady's family were. There were whispers that the Eóganacht were trying to reclaim the line of the High Kingship.'

'But that is ridiculous. Grella is of the Uí Liatháin. And anyway, no Eóganacht has wanted the High Kingship in four centuries. There are certainly no such aspirations in Cashel.'

'In which case, is it possible that whoever abducted Grella meant to eliminate her influence at Tara?' suggested Cairenn.

'I would have thought, being of the Uí Liatháin, she would have had little influence in any argument between the Uí Néill over the High Kingship.'

'And it is the High King who is to be assassinated, not the lady Grella. I swear, this is all bewildering,' the girl said in a helpless tone.

'Bewildering indeed,' Fidelma sighed. 'I would suggest we better devote our intentions to removing ourselves from this place, instead of just wasting our efforts on seeking an explanation for how we came here. How do you feel now?'

Cairenn raised a hand to her head. 'My head still throbs. It is never good to be slapped around by a coward of a man.'

'Have you been able to explore this store room since you were locked in?'

The girl grimaced. 'I was as you found me, Fidelma, unconscious, and so not in the best of conditions to begin any exploration.'

'I am sorry.' Fidelma was irritated at her thoughtlessness.

'I am now recovered enough, however, to start. How are we to inspect the place when we have no lamp?'

'We have eyes and there is a little light, so we are not entirely blind.' Fidelma stood up and reached forward to help the girl to her feet. 'Also we have our hands free to explore. So I think we should start as best we can.'

'What are you doing, friend Eadulf?' called Enda, as Eadulf bent over his medical bag and started rummaging around in it.

'Looking for a way out of this confinement,' answered Eadulf.

He stood up, holding a candle stub. 'I remembered I had this in my bag. And so I hoped those idiots did not remove the means of igniting it?'

'Do not worry,' answered Enda. 'The fools left me my *tenlach teined*.'

Every warrior carried kindling gear in a *firbolg*: flint, steel and tinder to produce the spark to make fire. They were trained to do this even in the dark. Indeed, warriors prided themselves on their ability to light a fire in a remarkably short time.

With the candle lit, Eadulf began to explore their prison with growing disappointment.

'It is not good, is it, friend Eadulf?' Enda said, pointing out the obvious.

Eadulf sighed in frustration. 'It does seem that they were right. The only way in or out is through the trapdoor above us. As I recall, there was only one iron bolt fixing it, and the door itself was pulled up by an iron ring that was not fixed. Perhaps if we could find a way of loosening the bolt, a good thrust of your broad shoulders could snap it open.'

'True enough,' grinned Enda. 'The trapdoor would fly open and up we would come . . . into the inn, among all the locals having a drink. How long would we last?'

Eadulf made a wry expression with his mouth.

'You are saying that there is not much prospect of escape?'

'I am saying that there is no prospect at the moment. We have no weapons, even if we could burst into the inn and surprise them. Furthermore –'

'What's that?' Eadulf suddenly interrupted as a new sound caught his ears.

It was the faint sound of a bugle being blown. It came in several short blasts.

'That signals another ship coming into the harbour below,' Eadulf guessed. 'Remember, a *stoc* was sounded when Fécho's ship entered?'

Enda shook his head. 'I don't think it was the same. This sounded more urgent, like a call to arms.'

Eadulf raised an eyebrow in surprise.

'You mean someone is attacking this place?'

'Maybe, maybe not. But someone is approaching to whom, it is felt, the people need to show a defensive posture.'

Eadulf shook his head. 'I can't say I understand the difference.' He brightened. 'Maybe it is Fidelma's cousin, Artgal, who has heard of our predicament?'

'How would Artgal know we were in trouble?' Enda was dismissive. 'Anyway, whoever is approaching, friend or foe, Tialláin appears to be making sure his people are ready in case it should be the latter.'

They could hear some movements now. Shouts, orders, acknowl-edgements, and then the sound of the *stoc*, the bugle, died away and there came the echoing sound of several goatskin drums being beaten quickly but rhythmically, in a loud rolling motion. Then all went quiet.

'I'd give anything to see what is happening,' muttered Eadulf.

'Then let us try your suggestion,' Enda suddenly said.

'My suggestion?' Eadulf was astonished.

'Don't you realise? Whatever has happened, everyone will have gone down to the harbour to witness it. The tavern is quiet above; it is probably empty.'

Without waiting for a reply, the young warrior went to the short flight of steps and braced himself, back and shoulders firmly placed against the underside of the trapdoor, his head down. His knees bent to take the strain; he reached out to clutch the support that the slim wooden beams afforded. Enda breathed deeply and began to push upwards.

Wood groaned against wood, and there was a slight give. The trap door was raised a little against the pressure of the single bolt.

Eadulf began to see hope. 'This trapdoor was never meant to hold prisoners,' he exclaimed excitedly. 'It was only intended as a covering for a food store. Try again, Enda. Try again.'

Once more the warrior braced himself, his face reddening, muscles bulging as he exerted his strength again. This time the boards gave even more. He felt that he had prised up the screws holding the bolt a little. Sweat began to stream from his face and his breaths became shorter. Eadulf was impatient, but he tried not to goad the warrior to greater exertion before he had recovered. Moments passed, and then Enda braced himself again. With a wild shout, the warrior pushed his shoulders once more against the trapdoor. Slowly he ascended the steps backwards until he was in the main room of the inn and could let the wooden boards crash to the floor.

Enda turned round quickly and surveyed the empty tavern with satisfaction. He looked down at Eadulf and grinned.

'Come on up, friend Eadulf. No one is here, just as I suspected.'

For a few moments, they stood nervously, looking around. There was no sign of anyone else – nor of their confiscated weapons and belongings.

Some distance away the drums were still pounding, and they could even hear pipes being played. Orders were being called and people were moving here and there.

'I wonder what is going on?' murmured Enda.

'Whatever it is, it sounds like some friends of Tialláin have arrived below. That does not bode well for us,' Eadulf replied. 'Let's get away from here and assess the situation.'

'We cannot desert the lady Fidelma,' protested Enda.

'Did I say that we should desert her? Let's first find out what is happening and then try to find where they have taken her. Watch out for any weapons we can use.'

He suddenly realised that Enda's wound had begun to bleed again, soaking his shirt.

'I'll have to dress that wound again,' he said, shouldering his medical bag. 'I'll do it as soon as we have a moment.' He led the way across the tavern to the back door.

They went through a deserted kitchen and out into a garden that obviously served the inn, for it contained all manner of edible plants.

Nearby was the stable yard and to their surprise they saw their horses tethered there, standing patiently, complete with saddlebags and weapons.

Eadulf hesitated but Enda pulled at his sleeve. 'We had better not chance taking the horses until we have discovered where they have put the lady Fidelma. It will be easier to go on foot. Once they see the horses are gone, they will be looking for us. They will know we have escaped and follow. And we cannot abandon the lady Fidelma.'

'But we will never have a better opportunity to retrieve the horses,' protested Eadulf.

'If they have trackers, and I am sure they do, they will soon follow. Better stay and see if we are able to effect a rescue of the lady Fidelma first.'

Enda turned and began to lead the way from the stable yard into an area of thick bushes and undergrowth with several trees on rising ground, the only place suitable for concealment for the moment. The rise overlooked the inlet and harbour below.

'Let's hide ourselves here for a moment,' Enda muttered, 'where we should have a good view over the harbour. We can see who has arrived and we might see what we can do to find the lady Fidelma.'

Eadulf placed himself beside Enda behind some rocks. The view below was extraordinary.

It was easy to spot the *Tonn Cliodhna*, with its furled sails, secured next to the jetty. He could almost think he saw Fécho strutting angrily up and down.

But then he realised that a second ship was tying up alongside Fécho's vessel, a sleek and much larger ship. The sails were still being furled: broad squares of white canvas with blood-red stripes on them. Voices were shouting as ropes were secured, and drums still beat a wild, rapid rhythm. The local people were crowding around the newcomer at the landing place below.

Eadulf stared down for a moment. Then he exclaimed, in barely a whisper: 'My God!'

Enda turned to stare at him in bewilderment. 'You recognise that ship, friend Eadulf? I have not seen its like before. What manner of ship is it?'

'It is a ship that I had hoped never to see in these waters.' Eadulf's voice was no more than a soft breath.

'What do you mean?'

'That, my friend Enda, is a Saxon warship.'

CHAPTER TEN

'What is that?' Cairenn asked, frowning, as the sounds of the *stoc* came to their ears.

Fidelma rose to her feet and went to stand by the door, listening.

'Someone or something important has arrived. That was similar to the trumpet that announced the arrival of Fécho's ship. I can hear the noise of people gathering in the harbour.' She had placed her ear close to the wood, trying to detect any sounds that would give her a clue to what was happening outside.

'Nothing that can be of help to us then,' Cairenn sighed. 'It is probably just another merchant vessel.'

Fidelma turned back and stared up at the darkness of the wooden roof. 'Perhaps one of those boards might be loose or could be prised up,' she said thoughtfully.

Cairenn made a sound that was meant to be a cynical laugh as she looked up, too. 'How are you going to get up there to reach them?'

Fidelma looked quickly around.

'Those boxes.' She pointed to the dark shapes. 'It would only need two of them balanced on top of each other.'

'Fine, if they will hold our weight. They are just storage boxes and their wood seems thin and rotten. We'd probably fall through the moment we climbed up.'

'We won't know until we try.'

'If we do manage to climb up, how long do you suppose it would take to explore the roof boards by that means, pushing the boxes into position to explore just a small area each time?'

'Where there is a will . . .'

'And then,' went on the girl remorselessly, 'if by some miracle, we find a loose board and manage to loosen it and its neighbours to make a hole big enough to pass through onto the roof, what then?'

Fidelma then remembered that the roof of the storehouse would lead them only into the bigger storehouse, where they would be presented with the same problem. And the next roof would be entirely beyond reach.

Fidelma could not help but take out her disappointment on the girl. 'You have a quality of defeatism about you, Cairenn. Anything is better than sitting here. We don't know what the conditions are like outside. We only know that if we get out of this small room, we might find a way out.'

The girl shrugged. 'It would take stronger folk than us to find a way out.'

'I had thought, Cairenn, judging by your escape from the abbey, that you had more tenacity about you.'

'Tenacity? I did well to get so far. But I do not believe in wasting time and effort on something that can't succeed.'

'And you can guarantee this lack of success that you predict?' snapped Fidelma.

'It is obvious,' the girl said dismissively.

'I was always taught to suspect the obvious – *semper credunt appertus est*. The obvious way might be the only way.'

The girl seemed about to reply when there came the noise of people entering the building.

Fidelma backed away from the door and joined Cairenn. Almost immediately they heard the rasp of a key as it grated in the rusty lock.

The door of the small storeroom creaked and swung open. A lantern lit the room, and behind it they could see several shadowy figures.

'Come with us,' a sharp voice ordered.

Cairenn moved closer to Fidelma, as if seeking protection.

'Where are you taking us?' demanded Fidelma.

'You'll find out soon enough,' replied the leader of the group in a threatening tone. She could see the flash of light on his unsheathed sword.

Another of the men laughed. 'You might as well tell her, Matudán. It seems you women are in luck. Our Saxon friend has just arrived in harbour. The Saxons will take you both off our hands once a price is agreed with Tialláin.'

The girl beside her gave an inarticulate sound, a sob of horror. Indeed, cold fear seeped through Fidelma's body as the man's words sank in.

'You cannot do that . . .' Cairenn protested.

'But it is easily done,' said the leader with malevolence. 'Now – move!' The sword point flashed dangerously.

Fidelma and Cairenn moved slowly from the storeroom into the larger building. Four of Tialláin's men closed around them, smiling and making ribald speculation about what the Saxons would do to the women on the voyage back to their own land.

The Saxon ship was impressive. Eadulf and Enda stared down from their hiding place at its sleek lines. It was thirty metres in length and its great masts dwarfed Fécho's ship beside it. They could see the crew fastening the furled sails and going about other tasks on deck. Eadulf counted the rowlocks along the side he could see. There were fifteen of them. That meant at least thirty rowers. He also saw several Saxon warriors on board, in full armour and with rounded shields slung on their backs. A banner fluttered briefly at the stern of the vessel. As he saw the device, Eadulf gasped in astonishment for the second time. Enda glanced at him, puzzled.

'What is it?'

'That's the banner of Cenwealh,' muttered Eadulf, almost in disbelief.

'Who?'

'He is King of the Gewisse, the West Saxons,' replied Eadulf grimly, shaking his head. 'He became King of the Gewisse when I was still a child – he must be very old by now. But what would a ship belonging to him be doing in these waters?'

'I've no idea who the Gewisse are but I have heard that the Saxons trade in slaves, and it is not unknown for them to make slaving raids along this coast.' Enda was worried. 'Do your people really own slaves, friend Eadulf?'

'I am afraid so. When my ancestors, the Angles, and the Saxons and Jutes first arrived in Britain and began to carve out their separate kingdoms on the island, they made slaves of the Britons; the *welisc*, foreigners, as they called them. The word was interchangeable for slave. Slaves are still kept now, but our laws do recognise them as having certain rights. Although they have no *wergild* – something like your honour price system – if a slave is killed, then the value has to be paid as compensation. But these Saxons don't appear to be raiding. They are being greeted as friends.'

'Certainly, they have not come in stealth,' agreed Enda. 'But I have never heard of Saxons coming this far west along our coast before.'

Eadulf suddenly pointed. 'Look! There's Tialláin walking down to the jetty, and there is Fécho. They seem to be very friendly with one another.'

'And just as friendly with the Saxon captain,' noted Enda angrily.

As they watched, a tall man left the Saxon ship, crossing Fécho's vessel to reach the jetty. He hailed Tialláin with an outstretched hand, like an old friend. Laughter echoed up to them as the greetings were exchanged.

'Traitorous dog!' muttered Enda.

'Obviously the Gewisse are no strangers to this harbour. It looks as if they do regular business with Tialláin.'

'But what business?' demanded Enda.

With two men in front and the other two behind, Fidelma and Cairenn were ordered to march down the hill towards the jetty. Fidelma's mind was working rapidly. She had once seen how slaves were put in iron manacles on board such ships, when she was attending the great council at Streonshalh. Once aboard and secured like that, there would be little hope of escape. She realised that she had to act and act quickly.

The only hope was her knowledge of ancient unarmed combat, the battle through defence, *troid sciathagid*. It was taught to the missionaries sent abroad to pagan lands so that they could defend themselves without recourse to arms, and thus preserve the New Faith's teaching that violence was an evil to be avoided. It was also part of the training of young warriors and had been used in the time before the New Faith. Fidelma, observing their guards, was sure that none of them had warrior training. Therefore, it was the best option open to her.

She suddenly pivoted on one foot, raising the other so that as she swung it caught the man on her left with force in the area below his solar plexus. He screamed in agony. At the same time, Fidelma shouted to Cairenn: 'Run!' Then she turned on the surprised man on her right and as he hesitated, she caught at his right arm and seemed to throw herself backwards, pulling him forward in such a way that he tumbled directly over her. Then she sprang back onto her feet and twirled round in a fighting crouch.

Taking advantage of the bewilderment of the two men behind, Cairenn had obeyed Fidelma's shout and was racing beyond them, bounding away like a doe, this way and that, running for the woods beyond.

One man was still cursing and groaning on the ground. Fidelma seized the sword of the second, aiming a kick at his jaw which sent him sprawling backwards, apparently knocking him out. But the other two had recovered their wits and came at her, spacing themselves out and approaching from separate sides. Eyes narrowed – she was admittedly no sword fighter – Fidelma cast the weapon at one of the two, forcing him to raise his own sword to deflect the flying blade. The impact caused him to stagger back a pace or two, giving her time to leap forward under the parry of the second man and grasp his beard in a painful tug, setting her shoulder against his midriff and using the man's own momentum to pull him over onto the ground.

She was about to take to flight after the now-vanished Cairenn when an arrow struck the ground in front of her.

'The next one is in your back!' shouted a voice.

She turned to see Gadra smiling at her, with raised bow and a second arrow already strung. He was shaking his head in admiration.

'Get up, you scum,' he said, addressing the guards, who were trying to struggle up from where they had fallen. 'By the ancient gods, here is a pretty sight. Four men defeated by a mere woman. Who are you, lady? Scáthach, the teacher of heroes?'

According to the old tales, Scáthach was a legendary female warrior who had taught the ancient heroes like Cúchullain, Connla and Fionn. No one could defeat her.

Fidelma actually laughed and motioned towards the angry men.

'You compare these to real warriors? It does not need a Shade from the Otherworld to teach them the art of fighting. A kitchen attendant taking out the rubbish could defeat them just as well.'

'Stop!'

Gadra's cry halted his angry men in their reaction to her insult. At his command, they stood glowering at her, shamed by their defeat.

'You may be right, lady,' replied Gadra dourly, 'but you are still a prisoner. Now, you will march down the hill to the jetty . . . unless you prefer to remain here with an arrow in you.'

Fidelma knew the man was not saying it for effect. There was a cruel look in his eyes and his thin red lips parted slightly, as if in anticipation of her refusing his order.

'What of the other wench, Gadra?' muttered one of his men.

'We can find her later. Let's ensure this one is taken to Tialláin.' Gadra's eyes did not leave Fidelma as he stood almost willing her to make a wrong move. She shrugged and started down the path, wondering if Cairenn had managed to find a hiding place.

Eadulf heard a stumbling through the undergrowth and sprang up, ready to fight at first, then changing position to catch the young girl as she burst out of the bushes and straight into his arms. She opened her mouth but before she could utter the scream he grabbed her, his hand closing over her mouth to stifle the sound.

Enda rose and grabbed the girl's wildly beating fists.

'It's the girl, Cairenn!' gasped Eadulf, recognising her. 'The girl who fled from the abbey.' Then, sharply, to the girl he snapped, 'Be silent or you'll have Tialláin's men here. We mean you no harm.'

They waited, the girl unable to move, constrained in Enda's arms, her breast heaving. They stood listening for a while but, curiously, there seemed no sound of pursuit.

Then Eadulf said: 'Are you escaping from Tialláin? So are we. If we release you, you will not scream?'

The girl nodded. He removed his hand from her mouth, and she coughed to clear her throat and breathe more deeply.

'I saw you in the abbey. You are the lady Fidelma's companions,' Cairenn acknowledged. 'She said that you were prisoners.'

'We escaped . . .' began Eadulf. Then, in surprise: 'You have seen her? Where is she?'

'We were locked up together. Then, just now, we were being taken down to the harbour. The lady Fidelma attacked the guards and told me to run. I did so. They must have killed or taken her.'

'Killed?' Eadulf was aghast. It was Enda who urgently suggested they had better get further into cover before they were seen. They resumed their position looking over the inlet. Eadulf forgot his Christian conversion and let out some curses in the name of the old god Woden. His anger was born of the shock of hearing that Fidelma could be dead.

'We were being taken to the jetty,' Cairenn repeated. 'They said we would be sold to a Saxon slaver.'

Enda inclined his head towards the harbour. 'There is a Saxon ship just arrived down there,' he confirmed. Then he strained forward, as something had caught his eye. 'There, friend Eadulf; look! Some men are walking down the path to the harbour . . . and the lady Fidelma is with them. She was not killed.'

Eadulf gave a groan, halfway between relief and fear: relief that she was not dead; fear of what it meant to be delivered to a Saxon slaver . . .

Cairenn strained forward as well. 'They must be taking her to that ship,' she said, declaring the obvious.

'Would Tialláin really sell the daughter of his King to a Saxon slaver?' Enda was shocked.

The girl sniffed cynically. 'It seems that he would do anything to obtain riches.'

'Do you know him?' Eadulf asked, puzzled. 'What are you doing here anyway? I saw you at the abbey. Who are you?'

'Fidelma did not tell you?' Cairenn reflected his bewilderment.

'Tell me what?'

'I am Cairenn, personal attendant to Grella, wife of the High King, Cenn Fáelad.'

Eadulf and Enda both stared at her in astonishment.

'And so what are you doing here? Why were you at Finnbarr's Abbey? Fidelma did not believe that you murdered Abbott Nessán.'

'In that she was right.'

'Then what is happening? We do not understand.'

'If you have no understanding, then I cannot help you. If you needed to know, Fidelma would have told you,' the girl replied firmly.

Eadulf gave an angry hiss. His fear of what might be happening to Fidelma was overcoming his restraint. 'If you won't tell us then . . . I have had enough of this business of a *geis*!'

Enda placed a hand on Eadulf's shoulder and shook his head. 'The main thing we need to know is how we can rescue the lady Fidelma, friend Eadulf. Everything else can be explained later.' He turned to the girl. 'Only one question do we need answered by you. Whatever this matter is, and it is true that we do not know, are you with Fidelma or against her?'

'I am of the Eóganacht Raithlind.' There was some pride in the girl's voice. 'Since the lady Fidelma is the sister of the King at Cashel and a *dálaigh*, pursuing truth and justice, I am with her.'

Enda turned to Eadulf. 'Then there is only one way that we might rescue the lady Fidelma.'

When Gadra marched Fidelma down onto the jetty to confront Tialláin and explain the situation, he was met with a storm of abuse. His four men were despatched immediately to find Cairenn and to ensure that the other prisoners were still safe in the *talam*, the cellar of the inn. Fidelma found herself confronted not only by the belligerent coarse features of Tialláin but also by the amused, appraising look of a tall, handsome, blond-haired, clean-shaven man, whose dress showed him to be someone of importance. He seemed to be the captain of the Saxon longship that had tied up alongside Fécho's boat. She saw Fécho standing some distance away, his helpless body language making a stark contrast to his usual self-confidence.

'Well, well, didn't I tell you that she was a wily one.' Tialláin was smiling at the Saxon as Gadra finished the sorry tale of how he had been delayed. 'But she is attractive, and should command a good price among your people. After all, her brother is King of Muman.'

The Saxon started at this reference. He moved closer to examine Fidelma's features. His cold sea-grey eyes bore into her. Another man joined them. He was short, with dark hair and beard, and tanned by weeks at sea.

'Is it worth burdening ourselves with another prisoner, lord?' the man muttered in his own language.

The Saxon captain shook his head. 'This one is a king's sister. That might help us, Beorhtric. And since my woman's companion has been got rid of, she will need a good servant – who better than one of her own people?'

Fidelma found she could understand much of the Saxon's speech from what she had learnt from Eadulf, for the exchange was in his native tongue, but she couldn't really grasp the meaning of the exchange. The Saxon captain was appraising her closely.

'You are a long way from home, Saxon,' she told him haughtily, summoning her scant knowledge of the language. 'And at the moment you are still in the kingdom of my brother.'

The Saxon stared at her in surprise for a moment, and then threw back his head and gave a loud guffaw.

'By Beldaeg, son of Woden, father of the Gewisse! She speaks our language. Better yet, better yet. Well, lady, since we meet on the soil of your brother's kingdom, allow me to present myself as Aescwine, Prince of the Gewisse, and once the old sot who rules us, Cenwealh, is taken off to the Hall of Heroes, I shall be their King. You will enjoy a special place in my fortress.'

'If you should live so long, Aescwine,' Fidelma replied coldly. 'It is a long voyage that you have ahead of you.'

'And you are just the hostage we need to ensure a safe passage from whatever warships your brother may send to prevent us arriving safely at our home port. Anyway, soon your brother will have his hands full, when the successor of Cenn Fáelad invades his territory.'

Fidelma's eyes widened. 'The successor of the High King?' she whispered. 'What do you know of Cenn Fáelad's successor?'

The man called Aescwine chuckled loudly before replying: 'Let us say that I am intimate with him.'

Fidelma compressed her lips. Maybe she should not have been so quick to reveal her identity, but no sooner had she had this thought than she realised that Fécho would have been able reveal everything about her. She saw him still trying to make himself inconspicuous further along the jetty.

'We have a negotiation to begin,' broke in Tialláin impatiently. 'I want an exceptional slave price for her.'

'And don't forget my fee,' Gadra added anxiously to his chieftain.

'You said there were others captured with her,' Aescwine said. 'Did you not tell me there was a Saxon religieux and a warrior? And I was relying on you to hold or eliminate that girl called Cairenn.'

'Once my men have found the girl –' Tialláin began to reply.

'Once?' sneered Aescwine. 'I expected her dead long before this.'

'My men will have her shortly,' replied Tialláin. 'She can't have gone far.'

'You fool! She should be dead already. Why isn't she dead?'

'But you promised a good price for the prisoners,' whined the chieftain. Tialláin was no exception to the rule that most bullies, once challenged, become whinging sycophants. Just as he spoke, one of his men came hurrying back. He looked anxious and whispered nervously to Gadra.

'There is no sign of the girl.' Gadra passed on the message to Tialláin. 'And the *talam* at the inn is empty. The woman's companions are gone!'

Fidelma felt a surge of relief at this news, while Tialláin exploded into a tirade of profanities.

Aescwine's handsome features still bore an amused smile. He appeared to have understood the exchange, which had been in the local language. It was then that Fidelma became aware of a tall man, clad in religious robes, who had suddenly emerged onto the deck of the Saxon ship. He had a cowl that covered his head, but he was clean shaven, and from the little of his features that she could see, he did not look at all Saxon. He looked very familiar, but she could not recall, in that highly charged moment, where she had seen him before. He managed to keep his face turned away from those on the jetty. He waved to Beorhtric, who went to him immediately and stood submissively while the man whispered to him urgently. Beorhtric nodded, and then returned to whisper to Aescwine. The Saxon captain surveyed Tialláin coolly.

'Well, the prisoners are your problem, not mine,' he announced lightly. 'I'll settle for this one.' He pointed at Fidelma.

'But you'll get a good price for the others.' Tialláin was almost pleading. 'You can kill the girl if you want, but you'll be mad if you do. She will fetch a good price – why waste it? Wait and we will soon recapture all of them. They cannot have gone far.'

Saying this, Tialláin turned and started to issue orders to Gadra. But Aescwine was shaking his head.

'Do you know what signal fires are, Tialláin?' he asked conversationally, as if asking about the weather. 'I intend to sail immediately. I have already taken on board the supplies you were kind enough to give me. Now I'll take this hostage.'

Tialláin was confused. 'What do you mean, signal fires?'

The Saxon turned and pointed to the north-west, across the water.

'You know this coast. What lies in that direction?'

Tialláin frowned. 'Why, the Great Island.'

'I understand there is a fortress on it?'

'Ard Nemed is the fortress of Artgal of the Cenél nÁeda. Yes, I see smoke rising from the fort . . . a signal fire.'

'And if I told you that that smoke started to rise after my ship entered this inland sea, what would you make of it?'

'But Artgal has only one warship. He is in no position to launch an attack here.'

'Probably not.' Aescwine smiled thinly. 'But the longer I stay here, the greater the chance that any warship may catch up with me. I cannot waste time doing battle. It will delay me, and that might give time for other ships along the coast to be alerted. So, I will take what I have and be gone.'

Fécho came forward, having overheard this discussion. He interrupted the exchange in a tone close to panic. 'If a warship is on the way here, let me set sail first. I don't want my ship destroyed.'

Aescwine did not bother to reply. Tialláin also ignored Fécho and raised his arms in a helpless gesture. 'Then give me what you owe me for the stores and the woman,' he said to the Saxon. 'I'll need a good price.'

'There will be no bargaining.' Aescwine turned and raised his arm. There was a sharp command from Beorhtric to those on board the Saxon ship. The warriors lining the sides of the vessel had dropped their shields. Those on the jetty were now staring at a row of Saxons holding short but deadly crossbows.

Aescwine spoke to Fidelma in his own language. 'Get on board, lady,' he instructed. 'It will not be long before we reach the land of the Gewisse.

Fidelma cast a hopeful look around, but there was no sign of Eadulf or Enda, or even of Cairenn. No sign of any impending rescue.

'Taking a last look at your brother's kingdom, lady?' Aescwine asked sardonically.

'You'll find that I am not that sentimental, so-called Prince of the Gewisse,' she replied. 'Your voyage may turn out to be a very short one.'

Aescwine indicated that she should precede him across to the Saxon vessel. As they boarded, a member of the crew came forward and roughly pushed her to a covered place at the stern, just below a high deck, not quite a cabin. There was another prisoner there, a man bound to a bench. Fidelma was pushed to the bench opposite and expertly tied to her seat with her back against the side of the ship.

She could hear Tialláin calling down curses on the Saxon captain and still demanding a good price.

Then Aescwine shouted something to the man called Beorhtric. From her position, Fidelma could see the Gewisse warriors at the rail of the ship aiming their crossbows at those on the jetty. Beorhtric shouted an order. There was a hiss of crossbows being discharged, then came screams and cries as a mass of bolts were released towards the shore. Fidelma wondered how many had been hit.

Aescwine was still smiling as he began to issue orders for ropes to be untied and the oars to be unshipped to guide the boat out of the inlet. Then she heard Beorhtric shout again and the release of the crossbow. She could hear the sounds of more bolts impacting. Only when there was space to manoeuvre was the order to release the sail given, and members of the crew went scrambling up the mast. Then, with an angry cracking sound, the great sails came down and were quickly secured in place by strong ropes. The prow of the vessel was veering round to point to the open sea.

She was aware that Aescwine had walked over to look down on his prisoners. She glanced up defiantly at him. He was wearing the same mocking smile on his handsome face.

'And so we set sail, lady, and with fair weather it shall not be long before we pick up our important guests. Then it is a short journey to the land of the Gewisse. So rest well and pray for a swift wind in our sails.'

'If I am to rest well, Saxon,' Fidelma retorted defiantly, 'then perhaps you would remove the bonds that hold me for we will never rest trussed up like chickens for the market.'

Aescwine threw back his head and laughed. It seemed a habit of his, a full belly laugh but one that was for show, with little genuine warmth in it.

'Don't take me for a fool, lady,' he replied shortly before turning away.

Eadulf, Enda and Cairenn had witnessed what had happened on the jetty with horror. They had seen the brief argument and they had seen the Saxon warriors let loose a fusillade of bolts from their crossbows. Tialláin had been the first to go down while Fécho and his crew had dived behind the bales on the jetty. They saw Gadra with a wound in his leg and several others lying prone, either dead or injured. The rest of Tialláin's men seemed to be running hither and thither in confusion, looking for shelter. The few women of the settlement set up a great cry of lamentation and fear. But Eadulf's greatest concern was that Fidelma had been pushed onto the Saxon ship, and now it was pulling out of the inlet and heading for the open sea.

Enda was thinking rapidly. He turned quickly to Cairenn. 'I presume you can ride? Do you know this country?'

The girl frowned: 'I can ride – and I know a little of the country, for I used to come to this coast with Grella as her companion before she married.'

'Tialláin's men are preoccupied. Our horses are tethered behind the inn. Do you know where it is?' She nodded and he went on: 'They are still saddled. Take the cob, he is docile but strong. If you can, lead the others and leave here quickly. No arguments,' he said urgently, as the girl seemed about to protest. Then he paused, and realised that Eadulf was still automatically carrying his *les*. He pointed to it. 'Here, place that in one of the saddlebags.'

She took it, still looking bewildered.

'You say that you know this country?' Enda demanded of the girl. 'Do you know some place along the route where you could leave the horses or that we could meet once we free Fidelma?'

'Grella once showed me a fishing village on the coast, due south from here. It is called Baile an Stratha, the Settlement of the Strand. I can go there and wait for you with the horses.'

'Good,' Enda replied. 'We will meet you there.'

'But,' the girl interrupted, 'I have my own duty to fulfil. If you are not there in three days, then I shall continue on to Cluain, where I was to meet Grella.'

'Agreed,' Enda said impatiently. 'Baile an Stratha. We shall find the village. But now – go; go quickly.'

He glanced back down to the inlet. The Saxon ship was slowly moving away from the jetty. 'We must hurry if we are to free Fidelma,' he told Eadulf.

'Free Fidelma?' Eadulf was looking bewildered – but Enda was already bounding down the hill like a mountain goat, darting here and there for if he lost pace he would surely fall over but his speed kept him upright.

'Are you mad?' shouted Eadulf. But there was nothing to do but follow. 'What are you going to do? Swim after her?'

There was no answer as their momentum took them, threading their way through the trees and bushes, down the steep incline towards the small harbour. Only when they reached a level patch and paused for breath could Enda gasp: 'We must follow the Saxon ship.'

'Follow the ship?' Eadulf gasped back. 'In what? There's only the *Tonn Cliodhna* and Fécho is not likely to help us.'

'Fécho has not heard the offer I intend to make him.' Enda smiled grimly, finally slowing his pace as they came to the harbour. 'That is, if he is still alive after the Saxon demonstrated his gratitude to Tiallián.'

'This is madness, Enda.'

'When there is no alternative but to be mad, then one must be mad,' replied the young warrior.

They had reached some outhouses alongside the landing stage and the groans and cries of the wounded were plentiful. Without hesitation Enda led the way onto the jetty. A body lay in their path. It was one of Tialláin's men. A bolt had pierced his forehead. He lay on his back, one arm flung back and his sword thrown a short distance away.

'Grab that!' Enda cried, indicating the sword.

Eadulf needed no encouragement. He picked up the sword, then saw the hunting knife at the man's belt and secured that also.

'Enda!' he called.

Enda turned and Eadulf tossed the sword to him hilt first. Enda caught it deftly and turned back along the jetty. He spotted his objective.

Fécho was crawling out from behind the bales and before he knew what was happening, Enda was on him, the sword at his throat.

'Stay still!' he hissed.

Fécho blinked rapidly, still dazed by the Saxons' attack but suddenly appreciative of his current situation. He looked at Eadulf and began to plead with him.

'Brother, do not let him harm me. You are a man of the New Faith. You cannot allow –'

Eadulf cut him short. 'You will have heard that Christians are supposed to obey a commandment not to kill,' he said evenly. 'Know that I did not convert to this New Faith until long into my maturity. Until then I worshipped Woden and the gods of blood and honour. I have difficulty in remembering the prohibition about killing at times of stress. This is certainly such a time, so you will obey Enda. Quickly!'

Fécho continued to plead. 'It wasn't anything to do with me. I did not betray you; it was Tialláin who was in touch with the Saxon. I didn't sell the lady Fidelma to them. I didn't—'

'Shut up!' Enda snapped. He pressed the edge of the sword close to Fécho's throat. 'Where are your crew?'

'My crew?' The man was bewildered.

The blade pressed closer.

'You have one chance to live,' hissed Enda. 'You are going to set sail on the *Tonn Cliodhna* in pursuit of that Saxon ship.'

'I am *what*?' His last word was an exclamation.

'Where is your crew?'

As the blade pressed closer, Fécho began to call some names. One by one, first Iffernán and then more of the embarrassed sailors emerged from their shelters and shuffled forward. Eadulf realised just how vulnerable he and Enda were, but the young warrior brandished his sword at Fécho.

'Your men will obey now – no tricks, understand?'

'You will obey him,' Fécho called, echoing Enda's words.

'Tell your crew to board your vessel and get it ready to sail,' ordered Enda.

Fécho repeated the instruction. Puzzled and unwilling, they did as they were told. Around them, Tialláin's men seemed at a loss what to do now their leader was dead, and there were several wounded to attend to. A woman was bending over Gadra's wounded leg and he was too busy to notice what was happening. No one made any effort to impede Fécho's crew.

On board, with the crew preparing to set sail and Eadulf keeping a watch on them, Enda could turn his full attention to Fécho and Iffernán.

'You will both take the tiller,' he instructed.

'Then what?' Fécho demanded, a little more truculently now he felt himself out of immediate danger.

Enda met his gaze with malice in his expression.

'Once out of the inlet, you will steer south to the open sea, after the Saxon ship.'

Fécho raised his eyebrows.

'This is not a *ler-longa*, a seagoing vessel,' he protested. 'It is certainly not a fighting vessel.'

'It is a large coastal ship,' acknowledged Enda. 'You told us so several times. The Saxon, once out of the passage and around the southern headland, must head eastwards along the coast if they want to reach the land of the Gewisse. I intend that they will not get as far as the seas between Éireann and Britain.'

Fécho frowned, still bewildered. 'How are you going to prevent it?' he asked.

'You have already demonstrated your sailing ability against a warship. Remember?' the young warrior pointed out.

'But the warship captured us.'

'That was when the warship was chasing us, not when you were chasing a warship,' replied Eadulf. 'Do you know the Uí Liatháin coastline, as far as Eochaill and the mouth of the Great River that leads up to Lios Mór?'

'I have traded as far as Eochaill,' Fécho admitted reluctantly.

'Then you know the waters beyond the headland?'

The man did not reply for a minute. 'You are mad, Saxon. Your anger has made you mad.'

'I told you before, I am an Angle,' replied Eadulf evenly. 'And as for anger, you have not seen anger in me yet. You would not want to.'

'And so you have a plan to prevent that Saxon ship, twice the size of this one, whose crew is who knows how many times the size of mine,' replied Fécho, gaining something of his old cynicism. 'And you have one professional warrior with you and he is wounded in the upper arm. Can you remember how many deadly crossbow men Aescwine had on board?'

'Aescwine?' Eadulf started at the name. 'Is that the name of the Saxon leader?'

'I overheard him when he introduced himself to the lady Fidelma,' explained Fécho.

'The ship bears the pennants of Cenwealh of the Gewisse,' Eadulf said thoughtfully.

'It is the name by which Tailáin addressed him and . . . I heard

Tialláin say he had been expecting him as he had goods to trade.'

Eadulf smiled without humour. 'Tell me, Fécho: do you want to live?'

The boatman saw the dangerous malevolence in Eadulf's eyes. 'I do,' he said simply.

'And would you hope not to be dragged as a prisoner before the Chief Brehon and face retribution for what you have allowed happen this day to the sister of your King?'

Fécho swallowed and shook his head violently.

'I did nothing. I swear I did not know that Tialláin was going to capture and trade the lady Fidelma to a Saxon slaver. It was nothing to do with me. It was Tialláin alone.'

'Even so, someone was responsible for bringing us into the territory of Tialláin. They could have landed us anywhere on this coast, from where we could have reached Cluain.'

'What do you want of me?' Fécho said through gritted teeth.

'Surely it is what you want for yourself,' smiled Eadulf ruthlessly. 'Perhaps there is a way that you might continue to live; perhaps there is even a way you might escape punishment . . .'

'But you and your warrior friend are asking me to attack a Saxon warship twice my size and with what?' Fécho's voice was almost a wail.

'At the moment, all I am asking is for you to follow the ship. I think this Aescwine will be too busy heading away from this land to turn and attack us.'

Fécho was not convinced. 'You are presenting a case between death and death!'

Eadulf shook his head. 'What I am presenting to you is a choice between certain death and the possibility of death.' His voice was flat. 'Which do you want?'

Fécho hesitated for a moment, aware that they were floundering at the mouth of the inlet. Then he shouted to his crew.

'Wear ship. We are turning south!'

The carved head of the goddess, Cliodhna, at the prow of the ship, began to swing southwards, turning with the wind filling the sail towards the open seas.

chapter eleven

F idelma gently tested the strength of the bonds that secured her wrists. The ropes were tight and had obviously been tied by an expert. She sighed and relaxed back, realising that she was being observed by the other prisoner confined in the covered stern of the Saxon ship. He was a short man with a look of life having been led in the open air. He was of swarthy appearance, with black hair and beard and dark eyes. His clothes indicated that he pursued some kind of rural work. There was something about him that reminded her of a young tethered colt, waiting to be released into action, although he was well beyond middle age. As she raised her eyes to his and met his gaze, his features broke into a lopsided smile.

'The man who secured these bonds was no newcomer to the art,' the man ventured.

Fidelma found herself giving an answering smile. 'That is true,' she replied. 'I suppose that you have checked your bonds, too?'

'I have,' replied the man. 'Yet even if the bonds were loose, we would stand little chance against those Pictish crossbows.'

'Pictish? What makes you say Pictish?'

'These Saxons carry crossbows that bear the design used by the Pictii of Alba. Most Saxons use the designs that the Romans used.'

Fidelma was thoughtful for a moment and then asked: 'So you know about such things?'

'I am a *saer*, lady, a carpenter and maker of bows – from the long bow to the crossbow. I was once bow-maker to Cathal Cú-cen-máthair, who was King when your brother became his heir apparent.'

'So you know me?' Fidelma asked.

The man contrived to shrug even with his bonds. 'Oh yes. I recognise you, lady. I worked at Cashel for a time.'

'And what is your name?'

'Áed Caille, lady.'

Fidelma grinned. 'That is an appropriate name for one of your profession.' The name meant 'fire of the woods'.

'My father was also a *saer*.'

'How did these Saxons capture you?'

'I was out cutting wood by the Hill of the Yew when they landed. I had no time to hide.'

'They landed and attacked Eochaill?' Fidelma was surprised.

'The place was undefended, so it was hardly an attack.'

'Undefended? Is there not a fortress there, the fortress of an Uí Liatháin chieftain?'

'The chieftain and his warriors had just left. The Saxon leader took me for interrogation.'

'Interrogation about what?'

'Their leader behaved curiously. It was as if he were expecting someone to meet him on the quayside at Eochaill. This ship tied up and the warriors made a protective cordon around it. But they did not attack, nor did anyone attack them. After a while, I was taken a prisoner and the leader asked me where Glaisne was.'

'Glaisne?' Fidelma frowned.

'The chieftain of the southern Uí Liatháin; that is his fortress at Eochaill. I told him that Glaisne and his warriors had left – I knew that for I had seen them. They left the fortress as soon as the Saxon ship came into the estuary.'

'That sounds as though they fled from the Saxons,' Fidelma commented disapprovingly.

The bow-maker shrugged. 'Perhaps they had no choice. They were protecting the lady Grella.'

Fidelma took a moment to control her surprise. 'The *lady Grella*?' she demanded. 'Was she at the fortress?'

'I recognised her from my time as bow-maker, when she visited Cashel on her way to her wedding in Tara,' the man replied easily. 'You know she was a princess of the Uí Liatháin before she married an Uí Néill. So the lord Glaisne is related to her.'

Áed Caille did not seem to notice Fidelma's controlled astonishment.

'Then I presume that Grella was Glaisne's guest? How did you come to see them leaving the fort?'

'It is as I have said. I was on my way to cut willow when Glaisne, with the lady Grella and some of his warriors, came riding from the fortress, passed me on the road at a canter and made off. Just after that I saw the Saxon ship tying up at the quay and soon after that they took me prisoner.'

'When did all this happen?'

'Three days ago.'

'I don't suppose it was known where they were heading?'

Áed Caille shook his head. 'I think they were heading west, maybe towards Cluain. Cluain is where Glaisne's cousin Antrí is supposed to be re-establishing the old abbey. Maybe they went there to seek sanctuary from the Saxon raid? I would not think Glaisne would seek refuge with his brother.'

'His brother?'

'He has a twin called Éladach, but they are as alike as the bear and the deer. They do not have a good relationship. Éladach an Gréicis he is called.'

'Éladach the Greek?' asked Fidelma in bewilderment.

'It is because he is fanatical for the Eastern Faith. He has a band of followers, a small community called Doirín somewhere in the forests near Cluain.'

'You said the Eastern Faith. What do you mean?'

'Éladach recognises the Bishop of Constantinople as Father of the Church, not the Bishop of Rome. So the Faith is already splitting, as people follow different rites, doctrines, even the language – Greek in the East and Latin in the West. There was a council at Chalcedon twenty years ago that proclaimed the Bishop of Constantinople equal to the Bishop of Rome.'

Fidelma frowned. 'Well, Greek was the first language of the Faith, wasn't it? We still use it in the rituals of our churches here.'

'There is a schism coming in the Faith, even though we call it the New Faith. In any organisation men set up, there are always divisions.'

'You say that this Éladach adheres to Greek rites; how so?'

'It is said that he spent time among the people of Greece before returning here, and he is very pious. That's why Glaisne would not seek refuge with his brother, even in the face of a Saxon raid. Glaisne is not a prince one admires, and his cousin Antrí is even worse.'

'If this was not a raid, what was the purpose?' Fidelma asked, changing the subject. 'You said it was if the Saxons were waiting for someone.' She suddenly remembered the tall man in the dark religious robes who had seemed to give instructions. 'When did the tall religious come on board? The man who wears a cowl and is dressed in black.'

The bow-maker shrugged but it was obvious from his expression that Fidelma had started a chain of thought in his mind.

'I did not notice him when I was captured. We stayed at the jetty, guarded by the Saxon warriors, until early the next morning, when we set sail. That was when I noticed that man had joined us.'

'Who is he? Do you know?'

'Only that he is no Saxon. When he speaks, he does so with the accent of the north. But what matter? Our fate is now bound to this ship wherever it goes . . . literally,' he said with a feeble laugh, trying to indicate his bonds.

Fidelma was not in the mood for humour. 'I am not prepared to accept that fate,' she said sharply, then another thought struck her. 'You say that the Saxon asked about Glaisne. Was the name of the lady Grella also mentioned?'

The bow-maker thought for a moment, then shrugged indifferently. 'Now you mention it, I was asked what guests were at the fortress. I told them nothing but I wondered why I was asked?'

'You say the Saxon ship waited at the jetty all night?'

'I presume it was waiting for the morning tide.'

Fidelma sighed. Had Aescwine landed specifically to abduct Grella and been disappointed, because Glaisne had taken her to safety? She tried to make herself comfortable. Good slaves were valuable in the Gewisse culture, but it was not a happy prospect. She glanced around and looked back at her fellow prisoner. 'We will have to be on the watch for an opportunity to escape.'

'Show me a path of escape and I shall be happy to follow it,' the bow-maker replied with a dry laugh. 'There are thirty crewmen on this ship that I can count. Thirty who man the oars and deal with the sail. Then there are at least a dozen warriors, who can also man the oars when they are not needed to use their crossbows. So that is forty or so Saxons warriors against two bound prisoners – in case you have not noticed.'

'I can count, Áed,' she said, trying not to sound sarcastic. 'Have you observed anything useful about how this ship is run?'

The bow-maker frowned. 'In what way? You mean, how do the Saxons work their ship?'

'Just so.'

'How would that help us?'

'All knowledge is helpful at some point.'

'Then . . . they are content to let the wind do most of the work. The ship is fast; it drives well before the wind. The men handle the sail well. The captain seems to have a good eye and some knowledge of the Uí Liatháin coast. The second in command – I think his name is Beorhtric – is also a good sailor. They were able to avoid two of our warships that were at anchor in the Great River. They gave chase once we were spotted coming out into the estuary and I watched in agony how the Saxon gave them the slip. They thought he would turn east for home but he avoided them by turning west, hiding in an inlet. By the time they realised the ruse, it was too late for them to turn and follow.'

Fidelma's brow wrinkled for a moment. 'But that presents an interesting possibility. Those ships might still be waiting as we sail back past the estuary. This ship still has to sail east to their country.'

'That encounter was a couple of days ago. The Saxon hides now and then in coves along the coast. The warships have probably given up looking for him.'

'Where does he get his knowledge of these waters? The tall man in black? You said he was not a Saxon?'

'Well, he is not an Uí Liatháin.' Áed shrugged. 'However, it is possible.'

'But also, from what you say, this Aescwine is a good sailing master?'

'That is a fact. He is a good sailor. I say so, even though I hate to admit good of these people. And when the winds are contrary and it is too much effort to tack, he can simply order the sails lowered and rely on his oarsmen to make headway.'

'You say there is never more than half the crew attending the oars?' Fidelma asked thoughtfully.

'I don't understand.'

'He never has to use all his men to tend to the oars? That means there are always warriors who constantly watch us prisoners?'

Áed understood what she was getting at and smiled briefly. 'There is no need to watch us. There are enough warriors to overwhelm us even if, by some miracle, we escaped and had weapons to confront them.'

Fidelma sighed and sat back. 'At least I know the worst of the situation. Now one has to find the best.'

Áed chuckled. 'You are an optimist, lady.'

Fidelma grimaced: '*Est locus ad optimo interpretatio semper.*'

'What does that mean?' queried the bow-maker.

'There is always room for the best interpretation. If you are not an optimist, then there is no future.' As she sat back, she suddenly saw the tall religieux emerge from a cabin-like construction near the prow. He was talking urgently to Aescwine. Fidelma tensed for a moment as memory came back and she realised abruptly where she had seen him before.

One of the Saxon seamen was standing nearby. She paused, trying to summon what fluency she had with Eadulf's tongue.

'Who is that religieux? The tall man with the black robes and the cowl? I am sure I have seen him in Finnbarr's Abbey.'

The Saxon seaman just ignored her.

Suddenly one of the crew, from a position halfway up the main mast, gave a shout. He was pointing towards the stern of the ship.

Aescwine came hurrying back and climbed with agility to the deck that formed the roof under which they sat. He was quickly joined by Beorhtric, his second in command. Something was happening astern – Fidelma could hear some loud exchanges among the Saxons, but she could not interpret exactly what was being said. She was aware of the creaking of the tiller and the movement of the vessel, which was veering slightly off its course due east towards a more south-easterly direction. There were more shouted instructions from Beorhtric and the seamen began adjusting the larger mainsail.

'What is happening?' Fidelma shouted at one of the Saxon sailors, but once again she was ignored.

She cursed the fact that she and the other prisoner were cooped up without any view of what was going on behind them.

'Something has disturbed them,' Áed suggested. 'They've seen something they don't like behind us.'

'That much is for sure,' agreed Fidelma, 'but what? Could those warships of which you spoke have sailed down the coast and managed to come up behind this vessel?'

'It's possible but not probable,' Áed reflected.

'What disturbs them then?'

'Whatever it is, they are changing course to run from it. There's one problem: there's been a change in the direction of the wind. Didn't you notice the way the sails were barely filled before they ordered the change? Now they fill, but not in the right direction. The wind is now against us. That might be to our advantage.'

'To our advantage?' frowned Fidelma.

'I mean to the advantage of us prisoners.'

Fécho, on board the *Tonn Cliodhna*, was also disturbed. He was leaning against the side rail watching his ship's sail being buffeted by the contrary winds.

'I can hardly hold her on this course,' he called to Eadulf, raising his voice to be heard. 'We've had a good run with the wind behind us but it's veered and is contrary to us now. This is a coastal vessel, not built for the deeper seas. It won't stand this weather for long.'

Eadulf, whose eyes had been on the distant black speck of the Saxon ship, reluctantly turned his attention to the captain. He was aware of the dangerously tipping deck as angry white waves began to strike at the sides of their vessel.

'Maybe the wind will just die away,' he called back.

The boatman seemed to give a cynical laugh but the sound was lost in a gust of wind.

'The wind has veered so it is blowing against us.'

'But what is bad for us is surely also bad for the Saxons? Look! Haven't they changed their course?'

'True enough. But they have a bank of oars to help them. Can you see that headland in front of us, those shadows in the distance? They are heading out to sea to try to pass that headland. If they are able to round it, then they can lay close inshore and turn to follow the coast on a north-easterly course. The headline will shelter them for a while as it sticks out into the Southern Sea a full kilometre. Of course, they need luck. There are hidden rocks which break the tides. But once round the headland, they will be safe enough – from us and from the contrary wind.'

Eadulf examined the dark, rocky coastline. 'Is there nothing beyond that will stop or slow them?' he pressed.

Fécho shrugged. 'There is a promontory fort a short distance beyond but Glaisne ceased to place warriors in it a long time ago. They might encounter warships sailing out of the estuary of the Great River, from Eochaill, but if the Saxon captain knows the coast, he will steer a course out of sight of land.'

'So we must stop them before they reach the headland,' cried Eadulf in desperation.

Enda had made his way back to where Eadulf was standing next to Fécho. The warrior used as many handholds as he could. His face was grim.

'This does not look good, friend Eadulf,' he called. 'One of the men told me we should put in closer to shore until the wind abates.'

'True enough,' Fécho shouted. 'I've said that we can't hold this course much longer. We'll have to get the sail down, before the contrary winds rip it to shreds.'

Eadulf stood in frustrated indecision. He was no sailor but even he realised that the ship was veering dangerously and with its shallow bottom, built mainly for deep rivers and calm inner seas, he saw the danger of it capsizing. It was an agonising decision.

'Very well,' he shouted to Fécho. 'Do as you must.'

Fécho needed no other prompting. He began shouting orders to Iffernán, the helmsman, and relaying orders to his crew. They began slackening the mainsail and the ship began to turn, helped now by the wind. It was not long, however, before the wind slackened, almost to nothing. Seeing Eadulf's puzzled look, Fécho explained.

'The big cliffs there, the headland, have blocked the south-west wind that we were encountering full on. So now we are in calmer waters but still not out of danger.'

'The black cliffs of the coast here certainly do not look like they provide safe anchorage,' observed Enda.

'True enough. We call that point the Place of the Grey Rocks but behind is a small anchorage called Gaibhlín, the Little Fork in the Cliffs. We can shelter there. We need to steer carefully for this whole coastline is full of rocks – some you can see but others are hidden.'

One of the crew was now able to climb up to loosen a rope that was blocking the complete lowering of the mainsail. Eadulf, not being wise to such things, had not even noticed that the sail had been positioned precariously on the masthead. The sailor seemed to be looking towards where they had last seen the Saxon vessel. Now he came shinning down the mast and made his way to Fécho.

'The Saxon did not make it round the headland, skipper,' he reported.

Eadulf went cold as he overheard the man. 'Do you mean the Saxon ship has foundered?' he demanded.

'No, but they have been driven back into the shelter of the cliffs. Not even their oars could pull them around the point of the headland.'

New hope surged in Eadulf's mind. 'Does that mean they won't be able to move until the winds die down or change?'

'That is so,' agreed Fécho without enthusiasm. 'And what applies to them also applies to us. Winds are contrary things, blowing from one direction at one moment and then from another the next. Who knows how long the wind will keep them from moving in the right direction?'

'Maybe we can close on him?' Enda suggested.

Fécho shrugged sceptically. 'Then what? Ask the Saxons politely to release their prisoner? There are many armed warriors on that ship – I can see only one warrior on this ship and he is wounded.'

Eadulf was well aware that Enda's arrow wound had started to ooze blood.

'It does not hurt,' Enda said at once. 'I can manage.'

Eadulf compressed his lips. He glanced at the dark rocky cliffs that they were now sailing parallel to. They seemed to be passing through a narrow passage between the rocky cliffs on one side and some rocks, just hidden under the white frothing waves, on the other.

'Is there a sheltered spot further on?' he asked. 'Anywhere that would place us closer to the Saxons without being observed by them?'

Fécho, carefully watching the passage of his ship between the rocks, did not reply at first. Eadulf realised it was no time to distract the man. Enda leant forward and said softly: 'I think it is lucky that this ship does not have a deep draught or those rocks would have ripped out our bottom before now.' It was a diplomatic way of telling Eadulf to be quiet until Fécho was able to stop concentrating.

After some time, Fécho looked at them and gave a rueful smile.

'We are out of the worst,' he said with a sigh. 'All we have to do now is keep away from that rocky shore.' Then he paused and examined Eadulf for a moment. 'There is a spot which might serve us. As you see, the coastline here forms a sharp forty-five-degree angle with the headland. Right in the corner of the angle is a sandy cove which provides a sheltered spot to heave to in. If the weather is clear, we can probably observe the Saxon ship from there if they attempt to take shelter anywhere along the cliffs.'

'Where is this cove?' asked Enda.

'Not far ahead, just beyond that point on our port side.' Fécho pointed forward. 'It's called Baile an Stratha; as the name suggests, it is low flat land by a river, with a few cabins there. Its curious position makes it a good shelter.'

Enda shot an astonished glance at Eadulf. 'Baile an Stratha? That's where –?' he began.

'Can you send one of your men to the masthead to see if there is any further sign of the Saxon ship?' Eadulf interrupted sharply.

Fécho raised his eyebrows. He turned and gave the order to the sailor who had originally reported the movements of the Saxon vessel. The man was certainly agile – he made his way easily up the mast and it was not long before he was back.

'Their ship has managed to turn under the shelter of the cliffs. They've been blown quite a way from the point of the headland. It looks as though they are putting into a sheltered cove not so far from here. I know that place. It's just a deep sheltered inlet between two large rocky cliffs,' he reported.

Fécho was reflective. 'I think I remember that place. It's a good spot to shelter and wait the turning of the wind and tide if one is attempting to round the headland.'

'Is it a place where they can land ashore?' Eadulf asked anxiously.

'I am afraid not. The cliffs are precipitous. So you can't approach the Saxon ship from the shore.'

'How close can we approach it from the sea without being spotted?'

Fécho looked surprised. He paused and studied the winds for a moment. 'We might be able to get to the next bay under these conditions.'

Eadulf suddenly turned to Enda. 'Can you swim?'

The warrior raised his brows. 'You mean, in these seas? I grew up swimming in the calm waters of the river and the lakes. Just look at the waters here.'

'The sea is fairly sheltered here but still choppy,' Fécho intervened. 'There are hidden tides and currents along a rocky coast, and strong undertows.' He regarded Eadulf with amusement. 'Are you still expecting us to attack a Saxon warship with a few men armed with a few knives?' he sneered.

'I am not,' Eadulf retorted. 'All I want is for you to get me to a place within swimming distance of the vessel.'

Now the boatman's face really showed astonishment.

'Then you are mad! Are you saying that if I get you to the next bay, you will try to swim to Saxon vessel and then . . . do what? Ask them to hand over their prisoner, the lady Fidelma?'

'Something like that,' admitted Eadulf, 'except that I won't be asking them.'

Enda was shaking his head. 'Friend Eadulf, I admire your courage but . . .' he pointed to the waters around them. 'These aren't the waters of some calm lake or even the flowing waters of a river.'

'I am fully aware of what they are, Enda,' Eadulf said grimly before turning back to the owner of the *Tonn Cliodhna*. 'Fécho, can you do what I ask?'

Fécho regarded him almost with pity.

'Drop you at a point within swimming distance?' he mused. 'How good a swimmer are you and can you deal with waters such as these?'

'That is for me to find out. I have swum great distances before.' He was thinking of the time he and Fidelma had had to jump overboard when the merchant ship they had been travelling on, returning from the great church council at Autun, had been attacked off the coast of Morbihan and they had swum to a distant island for safety. It was then he discovered that Fidelma was a brilliant swimmer, learning to swim almost as soon as she could take her first footsteps in the rushing waters of the local river near Cashel. Eadulf was not a bad swimmer, but he knew she was far better. He hesitated and then repeated: 'Can you bring me within swimming distance of the Saxon warship?'

'I can probably put this ship into a tiny sheltered inlet almost next to where the Saxon is. It's not far.'

'Not far? How far is that?'

'The closest I can go in is forty *forach*.'

It sounded quite a distance to Eadulf as he tried to work it out in measurements that he was familiar with.

He estimated that even if the water was not too rough it would still be a long swim.

'Do you think you could make it?' Fécho asked.

'Even if you did,' Enda said, 'then what? You are hardly likely to overpower the crew single-handed.'

'I do not intend to try to overpower anyone,' Eadulf replied. 'If I could get on board unobserved, then I might find a way of releasing Fidelma before they realise it and we could swim for it. She is a strong swimmer, I know.'

'Friend Eadulf, I don't think this is a good plan.'

'I am open to a better one.'

Enda glanced at Fécho and shrugged. 'As of this time, I can think of no plan at all.'

'Then it is settled,' Eadulf said. 'If there is no plan but one, then it is the only plan.'

'Do you know anything about these Saxon ships?' demanded Fécho. 'Do you know their strengths and weaknesses? Do you even know the best way to get on board undetected?'

'I am an Angle from the Ham of Seaxmund, which is near the coast. I have seen many such ships in our harbours and have even been aboard them. I am no stranger to their construction.'

Fécho looked impressed. 'You will need a distraction when you climb aboard. These Saxons are not stupid.'

'I agree.' Eadulf gave an ironic smile. 'If my knowledge is worth anything, I would say that the captain of their vessel could only anchor there by using a drogue.'

'A what?'

'It is an anchor like a drag, a funnel-shaped sea anchor which is towed behind the vessel to keep it from drifting too far. It also gives some stability,' explained Eadulf. 'On the other hand, in these waters, they might have heavy anchors of metal to keep it fast.'

'What has that to do with trying to board the vessel and rescue the lady Fidelma?' demanded Enda.

'I am thinking how to use it to cause a distraction.'

Neither Fécho nor Enda understood what he meant, and he did not enlighten them.

'The ship is not tossing as much as it was,' Fidelma observed.

Áed Caille raised his head. 'Aescwine must have been able to bring it under the shelter of the cliffs beyond Leath-ard, a height they call Gentle Hill. I can see where we are now by the shape of the cliffs up there.'

From where he was tethered, he could see over Fidelma's shoulder to the cliff face beyond.

'I don't suppose there is any hope of the Saxons being seen?' she asked.

'This headland is pretty isolated. There is a fortress on the promontory at the other side but that has long been deserted.'

'Isn't it dangerous to ride out the winds here?'

Áed Caille shrugged. 'Not if this Aescwine is the seaman he must be in order to have brought this craft all the way along our coast from the land of the Saxons.'

'Why do you say that?'

'He will have either put a drogue out, as some of our *ler-longa* do, the seagoing ships, or heavy weights with flukes, of the type that the Romans and the Greeks use. What are they called . . .?'

'Ah, yes,' Fidelma agreed. 'Anchors. Well, in this instance I hope Aescwine is a good sailor.'

She was remembering how, years before, the ship she and Eadulf had been on had been caught in a storm and foundered off the coast of the kingdom of Dyfed among the Britons. Then, as the memory stirred, she realised that she had been on sinking ships several times. Once, coming back from her mission to Rome, her vessel had been heading to Massilia when a storm had appeared out of nowhere – a sail ripped, a spar cracked and the ship was driven onto some rocks but, thankfully, the captain had managed to get into the port of

Genua before it sank. Then, after leaving the port of Naoned, years later, when she and Eadulf had attended the notorious Synod of Autun, they were attacked by brigands and had to leap overboard and swim for their lives to an island.

Perhaps if she had been free she might have risked leaping from this vessel and striking out towards the rocky shore. Once again she tried, surreptitiously, to test her strength against the bonds around her wrists. It was a forlorn hope. They were still bound tight. So rather than waste time brooding or even filling it with the traditional *dercad*, the ancient form of meditation which so often helped calm her extraneous thoughts, she decided to learn what other information she could from the bow-maker.

'I grew up on the banks of the Great River and learnt my art from my father and his father.'

'But you said you went to Cashel?'

'As I told you, I went as bow-maker to King Cathal, your cousin.'

'How did that happen?'

'I worked for several of the Eóganacht princes.'

'Including the Eóganacht Raithlind?' Fidelma was delighted that the path to where she wanted to get to was so easy.

'That is so. I was bow-maker to Bécc, who died a decade ago. Artgal of the Cenél nÁeda, whose fortress is on the Great Island, is his grandson.'

Fidelma knew that well enough but did not comment. She allowed him to continue: 'I was working at Cashel when Grella stayed there on her journey to marry Cenn Fáelad, son of Blathmac. That was before your brother was King. In those days no one dreamt that Cenn Fáelad would become High King.'

Fidelma had to agree. First Cenn Fáelad's grandfather, Áed Sláine, had died violently as a result of a blood feud within his family. Then his father, Blathmac, and his uncle Diarmait, inaugurated as joint kings at Tara, had both died from the Yellow Plague. Then Cenn Fáelad's brother Sechnussach, who had ruled wisely and well for six years or more, had been murdered in his own bed. It seemed that this Uí Néill branch had been cursed in maintaining their kingship at Tara.

'So you easily recognised Grella riding out of Eochaill before the Saxons landed?'

'That is so. When the Saxon ship was sighted, her cousin Glaisne must have decided it was better not to fight. He had only half a dozen men with him. That must be why he headed west towards Cluain.'

'Who accompanied her, apart from Glaisne and his warriors?'

'Who accompanied her?' Áed seemed puzzled by the question and repeated it.

'You would hardly expect the wife of the High King not to have attendants to accompany her? Some members of her personal household.'

'You mean women?'

'That is precisely who I mean.' Fidelma smiled thinly

'I really didn't see. No, there were no women. Just Glaisne and his warriors.'

'And you are certain it was the lady Grella accompanying this noble Glaisne?'

Áed stared at her for a moment, puzzled. 'I was close enough to recognise her and she was accompanied only by Glaisne and his warriors,' he said slowly.

'Did she seem to be going with them willingly?'

'Willingly? But she is wife to the High King. Who would order her to do anything against her will? Besides which, Glaisne is of her own family.'

Fidelma was thoughtful. 'Has Grella been a guest of Glaisne before?'

'Lady, I am only a poor bow-maker. What would I know of such things as who is a guest to whom?'

'A final question, Áed. You are absolutely sure Glaisne and Grella were going in the direction of Cluain?'

At that moment, a shadow fell across them. Fidelma raised her head to find the cruel features of Aescwine staring at them with a curious expression.

'Grella?' he suddenly said to the bow-maker. 'You mention the lady Grella? So she was at Eochaill?'

'I told you Glaisne had fled his fortress when you came into the estuary,' Áed replied with spirit. 'I said he had a lady with him.'

Aescwine let out a curse. 'You were saying just now that she returned west to Cluain?'

Only Fidelma seemed to pick up on the use of the word 'returned'.

The Saxon was clearly trying to control his anger. 'Now you appear to have a lot more information than you gave me before. Where is Grella?'

Fidelma stared at the Saxon raider, astonished by the anger in his tone. She and Áed Caille sat silently, regarding the man. His whole expression in body and face had changed, as if he were trying to control himself. It was a dramatic contrast to the arrogant, self-controlled captain of the raiding Saxon vessel of a few moments ago.

'Where is she?' he repeated harshly. 'Tell me or I will throw you over the side!'

'I said I saw her riding with Glaisne towards the west,' protested Áed. 'Cluain is certainly in that direction.' Aescwine raised his hand to strike the bound body of the bow-maker.

'What does a *díberg* know of the High King's wife?' Fidelma intervened sharply in her own tongue. Then, seeing he did not understand, she tried to repeat it in Saxon but she could not think of a word for 'sea marauder'. She repeated herself using the Latin word: 'What does a Gewisse marauder know of the High King's lady?'

Aescwine paused, then lowered his raised hand. He seemed to make an effort to control his temper. Then his lips twisted as if in a smile, but there was no humour in it.

'If I am not told what I want to know, then one of you will be tossed over the side, still bound. Perhaps you will answer me now. Where is Grella?'

chapter twelve

F écho pointed to the western sky.
    'It will be dark shortly. I strongly urge you to reconsider this madness. It is the moon of Meadhónach, the middle of winter, and it is obscured by clouds so there is precious little light. The water is freezing. You could be dead of the cold before you even reach the Saxon vessel. Even if you survive the swim into the next cove, you will not find the ship in the darkness unless they have lights on deck.'

The man was speaking logic and Eadulf knew it. Nevertheless, his concern for Fidelma seemed to override that.

'What if the Saxons set sail in the night?' he demanded. 'We will never find them again.'

'They won't,' Fécho assured him. 'No sailor in his right mind would try to sail out of these coves and inlets in darkness.'

'How can you be so certain? The wind will probably blow the clouds away and the sky will provide a good map to steer a ship by.'

'The winds that have brought clouds across the face of the moon will leave much of that map obscured,' replied Fécho. 'I know. Besides which, I do not think the Saxon will weigh anchor before first light so that he can be sure of his position. This is a rocky and deceptive shore and I don't think, as good a sailor as he seems, that he will chance it.'

'Then I must still leave here in darkness to get to the vessel at first light or before,' pointed out Eadulf.

Iffernán, Fécho's helmsman, had been listening to the conversation with some interest. Now he called to Fécho and whispered urgently in his ear. Fécho nodded rapidly. Then he said: 'Go and examine it. We'll have the last of the light soon and if repairs are needed, now is the time to do them.' The man hurried for'ard to the ship's storage.

The owner of the *Tonn Cliodhna* then turned to Eadulf with a grim smile.

'Have you ever handled a *grotán*?' he asked.

Eadulf looked blank, not having heard the word before.

Enda, at his side, said: 'I have.' He turned to Eadulf. 'It is a one-paddle *cliab*, a coracle.'

'You mean one of those basket boats that you punt about on rivers?' Eadulf queried.

'Not exactly,' replied Fécho. 'But I think you have the idea.'

'I've been in one but never handled it. Why do you ask?'

'Iffernán reminded me that he has been repairing the one we have stored aboard. Sometimes a harbour is too shallow for the *Tonn Cliodhna* to get close to. It either means wading ashore or using the *grotán* . . . the coracle. Iffernán suggests that if it is seaworthy it would save you an icy swim in the morning.'

Eadulf was frowning. He had no liking for the idea, but then he had been prepared to attempt the swim in the freezing waters.

'I could handle the coracle,' interposed Enda. 'If Eadulf tells me the plan he has, I could carry it out.'

'I must be the one to go,' Eadulf insisted with a shake of his head. 'I know the weakness of the Saxon ships. Besides, you are wounded.'

'The wound does not trouble me. And you have never handled a coracle in any type of water, let alone an open sea,' protested Enda. 'I know how to handle these craft – because they sit on the water and not in it, they can easily be carried by current and wind – so, if you aim to cross these waters, then best let me handle it.'

They saw that Iffernán and one other of the crew had brought the ungainly looking craft to an open place on deck. It was a small basket-shaped affair, not more than a tall man's length across, with two light wooden planks for seats. Eadulf moved forward to look more closely. He saw that the boat's willow frame formed a flexible skeleton, to which a cow-hide covering had been sewn. Black wood tar coated the hide, making it watertight.

Enda looked down at it, frowning.

'It was only meant for rivers, or a short stretch of inland water,' explained Iffernán, 'but I vouch it is watertight. There is one flat-plank paddle.'

'That settles it,' Enda announced. 'I must go.'

Eadulf thrust out his chin but then, realising the limits of his capabilities, he let out a resigned sigh. 'If you insist, then the two of us must go.'

'But—' began Enda.

'The two of us,' Eadulf said with emphasis.

There was a silence. Then: 'So be it,' Enda conceded.

'I'll use these last moments of light to double-check the boat,' offered Iffernán, 'but I think it is as well built as any such craft.'

Fécho had been listening to the exchange and offered the benefit of his professional seamanship. 'Well, if you are both agreed, I suggest that you go just before first light so that you can get to the Saxon vessel before Aescwine starts to think of setting sail. It is no use going in the black of the night. Seeing that the *grotán* has no depth to worry about, you can keep to the shelter of the rocks for most of the way. Just avoid the sharp ones here and there that will rip the bottom out.'

Eadulf acknowledged the advice before asking: 'Do you have any really sharp knives – or even better, a *rodhb.*'

Eadulf knew a *rodhb* was one of two names for a carpenter's saw, one which had sharp teeth along its blade.

Fécho was puzzled for a moment and then he chuckled. 'You mean to saw your way into the Saxon ship? Surely you would be better with a *biail*, the axe for chopping wood or felling trees?'

'The saw is what is needed not an axe,' Eadulf replied firmly, his face still serious, 'but two good sharp knives would also be useful.'

'Well, you have the sword you persuaded me to start this voyage with,' smiled Fécho, having apparently regained his sense of irony.

'And you have the knife you picked up from Tialláin's man on the jetty,' Enda reminded him.

'I want something strong with a blade sharp enough to cut a ship's rope,' Eadulf explained.

Fécho pursed his lips and whistled softly as he suddenly understood what Eadulf had in mind.

'The cutting of the anchor ropes will be your distraction?' he asked slowly.

When Eadulf confirmed it, Fécho frowned: 'It could be dangerous, even if you succeed. Don't forget the tide will be coming in at that time of the morning. And whether low or high, the tides on this part of the coast are not your friend.'

'There seems no other way,' Eadulf replied. 'With the anchor cut, hopefully the crew will have to man the oars and all their concentration and effort will be on keeping the ship from running onto the rocks. While everyone is occupied by that, I go up over the side, find Fidelma and get back down to the coracle.'

Fécho was still sceptical. 'You mean to escape with three in the coracle? It barely has room for the two of you.'

'Better than nothing,' Eadulf replied. 'Anyway, I can try to hang on to the side and swim, while Enda paddles with Fidelma on board. It has to be attempted.'

'And we are to wait here until you return?'

'I am trusting you to wait for us. Enda and I will head for the

Saxon ship just before first light and, with luck, we should be back on board while the Saxons are still floundering.'

Fécho retained his cynical expression. 'In the old days, we would have said: what man plans, unless he is loved by the gods, they will oppose.'

Eadulf was still pagan enough to shiver slightly.

'We are in their hands,' he said simply.

'I know nothing,' Áed Caille said, looking up at the menacing form of Aescwine as he demanded yet again to know where Grella was. 'All I saw, as I have told you, was the High King's wife in the company of Glaisne, riding westward.'

'You told the woman something more,' replied the Saxon, indicating Fidelma.

'What more could I tell her? Grella rode westward with the lord Glaisne of Eochaill.'

Aescwine let out violent curse. 'So she was in Eochaill the whole time?'

'I don't know,' replied the bow-maker. 'The whole time of what? All I know is what I saw.'

'But you knew enough to recognise the wife of your High King?' sneered Aescwine. 'How is a churl from this part of your country able to recognise the wife of the High King of Tara?'

'Churl?' Áed did not understand the Saxon word *ceorl*.

Fidelma smiled grimly. 'He calls you the equivalent of a *fiudhir*,' she explained, naming the lowest of the non-freeman class under Brehon law.

This brought Áed's head up angrily.

'Tell him I am a *saer*, a *ceile*, and my honour price is equivalent to the price of two milch cows.'

Aescwine appeared to have no difficulty in understanding the language and the interruption seemed to calm him down. It was clear he had thought more on what Áed had said.

'She was in the fortress at Eochaill after all,' he mused. 'And I was sent on a fruitless errand to that treacherous scum Tialláin. I should have known better. I should have known they would not have trusted that old thief with any dealings in this matter.'

'What dealings would those be?' Fidelma asked innocently. 'Who would not trust him?'

Aescwine's eyes narrowed. 'I should try not to be clever, Fidelma.'

Fidelma shrugged. 'I'll try not to be,' she responded drily. She shifted uncomfortably to emphasise that she was still tied up. 'What use would the knowledge be to me anyway, while I am in this position? How could I rush away to reveal your secrets when we are bound for the land of the Gewisse?'

'I am glad you accept that fact,' Aescwine replied, his customary amused tone returning. 'The high winds have delayed our departure – which, it seems, is a good thing because now I learn I narrowly missed my quarry. So I have a new option to consider.'

Fidelma gazed at him thoughtfully. 'Grella is your quarry?'

He appeared not to have heard her, because he was staring at the bow-maker. 'They rode westward, towards Cluain? So Glaisne is taking her back to Cluain. By the teeth of Woden, is he now playing some game of his own?'

Aescwine probably realised that he had said too much and turned away abruptly. In the gathering gloom, Fidelma watched him with curiosity as he made his way through the oarsmen and resting warriors towards the prow of the ship. She saw a figure stir. It was the tall man with the dark cowl. He and Aescwine bent towards one another in deep and animated conversation.

Darkness had overtaken the vessel and although the winds were gentle in the shelter of the inlet, the ship continued to rise and fall with the rhythm of the white-capped waves. Lamps had been lit at the bow and the stern and Fidelma, who had done plenty of sea travelling, felt the vessel tug against the constraining ropes that indicated that sea anchors had been cast both fore and aft.

Fidelma leant back against the side of the ship, her mind filled with a turmoil of thoughts.

Why would Grella be the quarry of a Saxon marauder? How did such a marauder know of the geography of this part of the Five Kingdoms? Was he being advised by the tall, dark-mantled religieux? And who was he? Obviously, the first possibility was that the wife of the High King was being abducted for ransom. Was this the plot that Abbot Nessán had heard about? Who else was involved? Certainly not a member of her family, she was sure. This tall religieux, who Áed Caille reported spoke with a northern accent, might well have been the abbot's murderer. But why? And what did Aescwine mean when he said he had to consider 'new options' now that he believed Glaisne had taken Grella to Cluain?

She wished she could have had just a brief moment with Abbot Nessán before he had been killed. Had Cairenn told her the complete truth when she'd said that Nessán had refused to say anything until Fidelma arrived? And then . . . then, of course, it had been too late to say.

She suddenly scowled angrily. She had also forgotten one thing. The whole crux of this matter was an attempt to assassinate the High King and the claim that it was the princes of the south-west, the Eóganacht, who were behind the conspiracy. So why this abduction of Grella, the High King's wife? What was the Saxon marauder and his ship doing in these waters? Had she missed something vital? She gave an inward groan and if it had been possible she would have raised her hands in despair. That she couldn't merely increased her frustration. What was she doing anyway, wasting time trying to piece together all these thoughts? She was a prisoner on the ship of the Saxon marauder. She was being transported to the kingdom of the Gewisse. What could she do to stop a conspiracy to assassinate the High King?

The darkness was full of sounds: closest, the troubled breathing of her fellow prisoner, fallen asleep through plain exhaustion. Then there was the whispering of the waves, and the slap of the larger ones against the side of the vessel as it bobbed up and down. The sibilant wind in the rigging, the occasional mumble of conversation among those sailors who remained on watch, the rustle and swish of a hundred other sounds that pervaded the silence of the night as the ship rode at anchor. The flickering of the oil lamps made a tangible accompaniment to the motion of the vessel. The crash of the waves upon the hull seemed to intensify, almost drowning out the other sounds, or at least putting them into perspective, muting them. Suddenly she felt that all the sounds were conspiring against her and she wanted to cry out and cover her ears.

'Are you all right, lady?' Áed's concerned voice came from the darkness.

Fidelma caught herself, realising she had been moaning softly as she slipped into an uncomfortable state of fretful sleep.

Fidelma tried to ease her position against the hardwood planking of the ship.

'I am sorry, Áed. Did I disturb you?'

'I think you were dreaming a little, lady,' the bow-maker replied gently.

'I think I was,' she admitted.

'You realise they have brought us nothing to drink, let alone eat, since we were captured?'

It was only when he mentioned it that she realised how dry her mouth was. She could bear the lack of food but lack of water was something else; it was dangerous. She saw the shadow of a warrior leaning over the rail nearby. He had been placed next to their shelter at the stern, presumably to keep an eye on the prisoners.

She tried to lick her dry lips, which was difficult because of the sea salt drying on them.

'Seaman!' she called. 'We need water.'

The shadow did not move. She was about to call again when she realised the man probably did not speak her language. She tried to think of a translation into Saxon.

'*Garwiga!*' She settled on the word for 'warrior'. '*Garwiga*, we need water before we die. Please, water!'

This time the shadow stirred and moved slowly towards them.

'Water, is it? Are you not surrounded by water?' he sneered in the darkness.

Fidelma sought to make her tone commanding. 'Do I have to call for your prince, Aescwine? He will not be best pleased if you allow his prisoners to die, especially considering the price he intends to get for us in the markets of the Gewisse.'

The man hesitated and then swore. They heard him call something, and then a voice replied from some distance away. The man turned, muttering, and said something. Fidelma understood enough to know the first man had asked his comrade to bring the lamp close so that he could attend to the water.

There was much grumbling but the light was brought by a second man, addressed by his impatient comrade as Osulf, who dipped a wooden ladle into a barrel nearby. He ladled out the water to each of the two prisoners in turn. At last Fidelma had drunk her fill and she sat back, thanking the man, even calling him by name. He frowned for a moment, then replaced the ladle on the small barrel and left, taking the lamp. The prisoners were once more enveloped in darkness. Fidelma sighed and leant back.

'Thank you, lady.' Áed's voice came out of the shadows opposite.

'I am afraid there is little to thank me for,' she replied. 'I fear that I have merely increased your danger.'

'How so?'

'Had I not started asking you about Grella, Aescwine would not have overheard. Now I am worried about his future plans.'

'I have no understanding of all this, lady.'

Fidelma smiled ruefully in the darkness. 'He knows that Glaisne has taken her to Cluain. He'll be heading there next.'

'Not in this ship. Cluain is inland. He'll have to find a safe anchorage. Anyway, how could a Saxon have known that Grella was visiting the land of the Uí Liatháin? Is that why he was making the raid on Eochaill, in order to abduct her?'

'He said that she was his quarry,' Fidelma pointed out. 'Therefore he must have gone to Eochaill for that purpose. But Glaisne is somehow involved in this matter. How? What manner of man is this Glaisne? I seem to remember that he is not well liked.'

There was a pause while the bow-maker thought.

'He is not well liked by most of the people. Some think that his brother, Éladach, might have made the better prince of the southern Uí Liatháin. Glaisne demands tribute, and is ruthless when he does not get it. He only supports those who are loyal to him without question. Antrí is his lickspittle.'

Fidelma was about to point out that the Saxon had been surprised by Glaisne's actions. What made him wonder aloud whether Glaisne was playing some game of his own? What game was Glaisne supposed to be playing? And with whom? She wished Eadulf was here and they could . . . She paused. With horror, she realised that she had given very little thought to Eadulf or to Enda since her capture. Now her mind began revolving with anguished questions. Had Tialláin's men survived the massacre and, if so, what had happened to Eadulf and Enda? Had they been recaptured? She knew that Tialláin had been killed in front of her and Gadra badly wounded. Would the survivors have turned on Eadulf and Enda, and killed them? Could they have escaped? She groaned inwardly at her self-ishness for not thinking of them before now. Then logic forced its way into her mind. What could she have done anyway – a prisoner on the marauder's ship, anchored heaven knew where? How would that help Eadulf? How would that help Enda?

Then there was Cairenn. Had she been able to escape and, if so, where to?

She sighed deeply, so deeply that Áed asked again: 'Are you all right, lady?'

'As right as I can be,' she said testily, then relented. 'Sorry, Áed. I was just thinking about my husband, Eadulf, and the warrior who was accompanying us.'

'Were they with you when you were captured?'

'They were at first,' she said. 'But they were not taken by Aescwine. I last saw them in the inn where we were captured by Tialláin, and while we were on the jetty I heard they had escaped.'

'Then there might be hope for them,' the bow-maker replied. 'Perhaps they can seek help?'

'Who would they seek help from in that place?' Fidelma replied bitterly. 'Anyway, I am going to try to sleep.'

She felt the concept of sleep might be easier for him to understand than if she had told him she hoped to retreat into the *dercad*, the act of meditation that she used to soothe irritations and calm any fears that came rioting into the mind. It was a way of achieving *sitcháin*, a state of peace. Fidelma also felt it best not to identify what she was doing because many Christians denounced the practice because it had been used by the Druids, those of the Old Faith; it was said that the Blessed Patrick had expressly forbidden its use. But then, many things had been forbidden that were positive and good in the Old Faith. She remembered how aghast she had been when she read that Blessed Patrick had burnt 180 books because they had been written by Druids. That had been boasted of by Bennin mac Sesenen, the Irish prince who had become one of the first followers of Patrick and adoped the Latin name Benignus. The same Benignus had been appointed secretary to the nine-man commission appointed by the High King Laoghaire that had sat for three years to amend the laws of the Fenechus so that they did not say anything contrary to the New Faith.

Rather than clearing her mind with the *dercad*, it was with these thoughts that Fidelma, rocked by the bobbing waves, drifted into a deep, troubled sleep.

CHAPTER THIRTEEN

'There's going to be a thick sea mist this morning,' Fécho greeted them cheerfully, 'although it won't be as thick as the fog we encountered the other day. Anyway, I was right about the cloud obscuring the night sky, preventing the Saxon ship from sailing before dawn.'

Eadulf had already noticed that he could not see the figurehead on the prow of the *Tonn Cliodhna* from the stern. The white wispy mist, with its salty taste on his face and tongue, swirled about but not violently. It was clear that there was a wind beginning to stir.

'It is indeed thick,' Enda muttered, joining them. The ship's owner moved away to the side of the vessel to peer seaward.

'Perhaps that is a good thing?' Eadulf suggested cautiously.

'It will make our approach to the Saxon ship more difficult,' the young warrior pointed out.

'But it surely helps us in another way. It will obscure our approach to any watchers on the Saxon ship until we are upon it.'

Enda snorted. 'That is if we are able to come upon it and do not miss our way in the mist.'

Fécho had turned back to them, having examined how the sea was running, and overheard the exchange.

'There's a dawn breeze getting up and that will soon blow this mist away,' he observed. 'So you will not miss the ship. Just make sure you stay away from the shallow rocks. As I said, the coracle sits on the waves but that does not mean it is impervious to any sharp rock hidden just beneath them.'

'I'll have a care,' Enda reassured him.

'How is the wound?' asked Eadulf.

'It's no problem, friend Eadulf. Do not worry about me,' replied the warrior.

Fécho and Iffernán had already supervised the launching of the coracle, or *grotán*, from the side of the ship. It now sat bobbing on the water, waiting for them.

Eadulf went to the side and looked down at the small, fragile craft. He seemed to square his shoulders and then turned to Fécho: 'If we have not returned by midday, then you are released from your task.'

Enda had already lowered himself into the coracle and was waiting patiently, paddle in hand. It took a few moments for Eadulf to negotiate himself into the tiny boat. Then they were disappearing into the chilly embrace of the sea mist. So close to the water were they that Eadulf felt the choppy waves were not indifferent but somehow watching for the slightest mistake on their part, waiting to embrace them in their freezing froth-strewn arms.

Eadulf was glad the poor light and the sea mist hid his hands, for he held the seat on either side of him with such a grip that the white knuckles would have shown his nervousness; indeed, his fear. He had been a fool earlier to think that he could have undertaken the swim to the Saxon ship. But the current method of travel was not too far above swimming. He moved his feet carefully so that they did not touch the sharp tools that had been placed in the bottom of the coracle at his request and looked towards the silent figure of Enda, bent against his paddle. He could not see the warrior's face, for he was sitting behind him, but he could guess at the determined set of Enda's features and his fixed gaze as he pushed the boat into the blankness of the mist.

'Is it hard work?' Eadulf asked nervously, still thinking of Enda's wound.

'Hard enough with the waves and tide trying to push us in the direction of the cliffs,' came the response, through gritted teeth. 'But I can manage.'

Eadulf realised that through the uneven mist, like smoke blowing in the wind, he could just glimpse the rocky face of the cliffs to his left. Now and then he could see that they were narrowly passing rocks that pierced the sea like sharp pinnacles, around which the water bubbled and sighed with sibilant greed. But for the most part, they journeyed with only the sound of the waves and, now and then, the cries of gulls and guillemots announcing the clearing of the mist.

'From what Fécho said,' Enda called over his shoulder, 'we should be passing the rocky point and able to sight the Saxon vessel shortly.'

'Well, the mist is still not cleared but we can see further than before,' Eadulf observed quietly. 'At least Fécho was right that the mist has kept the vessel from escaping to the sea.'

'Therefore it should be somewhere in front of us,' replied Enda. 'Keep a sharp lookout.' He moved the bobbing coracle cautiously forward, his eyes on the now-lessening intensity of the mist.

It was Eadulf who suddenly pointed.

'It's there! Directly ahead of us.'

A gust of wind suddenly whisked aside the white curtain and they found themselves within metres of the Saxon ship. For a moment, Eadulf felt naked. His mouth was dry, the lips parted against the continual spray of salt from the waves. He glanced up at the vessel. He could see none of the crew or warriors on guard duty at the rail.

He tapped Enda on the shoulder. 'Make for the bow anchor first,' he whispered.

The warrior did not reply but bent to his paddle.

It took a few moments of paddling before they came under the high prow of the ship, with its beast-like carved head. A thick rope

ran taut from the vessel into the sea. Eadulf caught hold of it as
Enda brought the coracle in close. It was a stout rope of braided
fibres, called *haenep* in his own language. It was very strong.

'This secures the first anchor,' whispered Eadulf. 'Hold us close
by and I'll try to saw through it.'

Enda grasped the rope above the point where Eadulf indicated
he would attempt to cut it, as high as he could without endangering
them. Eadulf took up the saw from the bottom of the coracle. He
glanced swiftly upwards to check that they were still unobserved.
The mist was clearing rapidly now. He reached forward and began
to use the saw against the tautness of the rope. To his relief, the
teeth did not make much noise and that which the saw did make
was lost in the rustling breath of the waves. It seemed an eternity
until he had severed most of the strands. Then he saw the remaining
ones begin to snap.

'Let go, Enda.' Eadulf almost raised his voice in his excitement.
'It will go of its own accord. We must try to get to the stern.'

Enda released the rope and grabbed the paddle. The waves caused
the coracle to knock against the side of the ship and bump its way
along towards the stern before he regained control, but because the
little craft was of light basketwork and hide they made no alarming
noise to give them away. The for'ard rope was creaking. They could
hear someone moving up above, a voice raised slightly. The for'ard
rope snapped. Then they were at the stern and Eadulf could see the
line connecting the ship to the stern anchor.

His face fell as Enda brought the coracle towards it.

The stern anchor was fastened with an iron chain.

'What do we do now, friend Eadulf?' muttered the young warrior.

'Maybe the severance of the front anchor will be enough distraction,' replied Eadulf, though with little hope. 'Anyway, hold the
coracle steady here. I am going to shin up the chain and see if I
can find Fidelma.' So saying, he reached for the knife which lay by
the sword in the bottom of the boat and thrust it through his belt.

Enda was about to oppose the idea but Eadulf had already seized the anchor chain and was climbing up it with an agility that surprised the younger man. Enda was used to the rigours of the military training that a warrior of the Golden Collar had to endure. He had always thought of Eadulf as a person of intellectual rather than physical pursuits and had not realised that Eadulf prided himself on keeping his body in good shape.

Hand over hand, it did not take Eadulf long to reach the railing of the ship, where the anchor chain was attached. He climbed over the rail and paused, looking around. There was no one to be seen on the raised deck where he stood. The tiller had been secured with ropes. The pitching movement of the bows was more obvious now, and there was shouting and people were rushing to the prow of the ship.

Eadulf prayed that Fidelma was not being held prisoner in the for'ard part of the vessel, which was now swarming with men leaning over the bows to see what was wrong. He jumped down the short flight of steps to the main deck and turned back to the covered area. The long fighting knife was ready in his hands. As he turned to face the occupants of the recess, the first person he saw, staring at him in amazement, with white face and wide eyes, was Fidelma.

'Eadulf!' She tried to stifle the cry.

Eadulf did not waste words. 'Are you bound?' he demanded.

She held out her wrists and he severed the bonds in a moment.

'Cut his bonds,' she ordered, pointing. 'Áed must come with us.'

Eadulf knew it was pointless to argue and did as she asked. There was a sudden angry howl as they were spotted and he realised the only thing they could do was jump into the water. Some of the crew were already moving, either to intercept them or to reclaim their weapons.

'Over the side,' yelled Eadulf to Fidelma. 'Swim for it. Make for Enda in the coracle astern.'

He almost threw Fidelma over the rail and jumped after her. He did not spare a thought for the man she called Áed. There was no time to think before he hit the cold water and plunged into blackness. The shock of the cold almost knocked him out. When he broke the surface, he saw the dark outline of Enda in the coracle, paddling away from the anchor chain. Fidelma was swimming towards him. Eadulf began to strike out after them.

He was aware of shouts from the Saxon ship and he turned on his side to look back, treading water as he examined the condition of the ship. There was no mistaking that it was in trouble. Though still anchored firmly by the stern, its bow was swinging with the incoming tide. He presumed the crew were struggling to stop the vessel foundering on the rocky coastline. To gain control, they would have to haul in the stern anchor while, at the same time, trying to steer the bow that was being buffeted this way and that. He became aware then of splashing objects close by and realised the danger he was in – the splashing objects were crossbow bolts, aimed by the few warriors who stood at the rail. Their aim was not good because of the irregular movements of the ship, but they were dangerous enough.

Eadulf trod water for a few more seconds, his mind working rapidly. He wondered who the other prisoner was, and peered about. The mist was almost clear now. He could see Fidelma hanging on to the side of the coracle, and Enda holding it steady with the paddle. Near him, there was a head bobbing in the water, whether a man or one of the seals that frequented the waters along the coast Eadulf did not know. He struck out for the coracle.

Coming up alongside Fidelma, he shouted to Enda: 'We must try to get as far away from the Saxon ship as possible.' He called to Fidelma, 'Can't you climb into the coracle?'

'It would capsize at once,' Fidelma shouted back.

He noticed another head next to him. It was the man, Áed, treading water. 'We'll have to swim for those rocks,' he called. 'If we get there before the Saxons have a chance to regain control of their ship, we'll have a chance.'

'But that's a steep and rocky shoreline,' shouted Enda, trying to make himself heard above the noise of the waves pounding on the surrounding rocks.

'Trust me!' replied the man. 'I know this coast. Folk collect edible seaweeds along that shore, as well as gulls' eggs from the cliffs. There is a small path there.'

'Paddle for the shoreline, Enda!' Fidelma called. 'We'll keep close so that no one gets separated.'

Enda struck out with a will. The tide was with them, driving them towards the rocky shore, but it was still not easy. The rocks were slimy from algae and covered with long green strands of eel grass, which disguised their sharpness. They were made even sharper by the barnacles, chitons and other invertebrates that clustered on them. Now and then Eadulf shuddered as he was touched by something he could not identify, such as a mucus-covered fish with spiked dorsal fin that darted out from behind the rocks. Though the varied marine life made the going difficult for the swimmers, one thing in their favour was the fact that Aescwine and his men seemed to have their hands full trying to regain control of their ship. They had not the time nor the means to deal with the escaped prisoners.

Suddenly, Enda was standing up and turning to help Fidelma to her feet. Behind him was a narrow ledge, a stretch of hard rock that was fairly flat and without too much slippery greenery making it impossible to stand on. Eadulf waited a moment to catch his breath and then he found a strong hand helping him. It was Áed beside him. The man was grinning.

'I told you that there was a way here,' he said. 'Look at that . . . along there.'

He was pointing to a bed of purple and brown plant life.

'Seaweed?' hazarded Eadulf, as he climbed onto the ledge with Fidelma and Enda.

'*Fithrech*,' nodded Áed. 'What some call *dulse*. It's good eaten raw. I told you the local lads come down here and harvest it, along with the little rock plant *carraigín*.'

Eadulf snorted in annoyance, almost forgetting that the man had guided them to a temporary safety at least.

'I am more concerned how far we can get along this path and away from our Saxon friends.'

Fidelma was still in a state of utter astonishment. 'How did you get to the ship anyway? You surely did not come all the way after us in a coracle.'

It was Enda who quickly explained with a few words.

'So you are saying that the *Tonn Cliodhna* is hove to a little way along this coast?' she questioned. 'But didn't Fécho betray us to Tialláin?'

'I suppose you could call him a victim of circumstances,' Eadulf replied. 'You see –'

Áed interrupted: 'I suggest that we save all explanations for later. The Saxon, Aescwine, seems seaman enough to get his ship under control – if you have a ship, let's go along the coast and find it. The sooner we reach a friendly harbour the better.'

'This narrow ledge . . . how far does it go?' demanded Enda.

'I believe we can get round those rocks to the next inlet,' replied Áed.

'Can we carry the coracle?' Enda asked. It was not a matter of weight, for one person could carry it easily. Enda meant was there room to transport it along the path. He realised that the boat might be useful again.

Áed paused, seeming to understand what was on the warrior's mind. 'If it becomes difficult, we can probably balance the boat on our shoulders and carry it above the rocks.'

It was in that fashion they proceeded. Fidelma and Eadulf led the way and Enda and Áed followed, taking the first turn to carry the coracle. They were all soaked, even Enda, who had been saturated by sea spray as he sat precariously in the coracle – and there was still blood on his shoulder. Eadulf knew the wound should be dressed again.

As they reached a point where the ledge took them out of sight of the Saxon ship, Eadulf could not help but take a quick look back. It was obvious that Aescwine was, indeed, a good seaman. The big ship was already under oars. He saw their rise and fall as the rays of the early sun flashed on the wet blades. The stern anchor had been pulled up and the bow was pointing out of the inlet towards the open sea.

Eadulf found himself considering the problem of what Aescwine would decide to do next? He hoped the Saxon would cut his losses and sail away around the great headland which had previously thwarted his efforts to turn east for home. Yet Eadulf feared he might decide to come after them. He could still turn back and try to catch them, in which case he would come across Fécho's ship and, in spite of all Eadulf's braggadocio when he had forced Fécho to give chase, he now realised that Fécho had little hope of defence.

Another thought occurred to Eadulf. How long would Fécho wait for them? Indeed, would he wait for them? Could they even trust Fécho? Eadulf's mouth sat in a grim line as he considered the matter. Thus far the owner of the *Tonn Cliodhna* had not been the most trustworthy of allies. He had seemed overly friendly with Tialláin, before the man's untimely death. He had also had to be persuaded to chase Aescwine in his ship. What else was there about him that Eadulf did not know?

It suddenly struck him that he did not know anything. He had almost forgotten that he and Enda did not even know what they were doing in this country in the first place. Fidelma had not broken her oath; she had revealed nothing about her mission to them. Eadulf ground his teeth; it was painful but he felt like biting against bone in his frustration. Now was the time for her to tell him what all this was about. Now! Well, as soon as they were safely aboard the *Tonn Cliodhna.*

Yet another thought burst into his mind. How were they all to get aboard Fécho's ship? The coracle would not hold all of them. That was assuming Fécho cared whether they came aboard or not; if he had waited for them; if the Saxon ship was not nearby; if Fécho was not otherwise engaged by the attentions of Aescwine . . .

He paused and tried to stop the whirlpool of thoughts. He wished that he had Fidelma's curious meditative ability – what was it called? The *dercad*? Her way of causing the tumult of thoughts to be still.

'Enda!'

Eadulf started. It was Fidelma who had called to the warrior and they paused.

'How far do you estimate that we have to go?' she asked.

'If Fécho is still in the inlet where we left him, just beyond that rocky promontory.' Enda indicated where he meant with a nod of his head.

Fidelma glanced round with a wry expression. 'I hope you are right, Enda. Staying soaked through on a midwinter day is a sure way to meet death from cold and ill.'

'Better that way, lady,' muttered Áed, 'than the future Aescwine had planned for us.'

Fidelma was examining Enda's shoulder. 'You are bleeding,' she said.

'Eadulf will see to it as soon as we are back on board,' Enda assured her.

They continued on in silence for a while until, climbing through a small slippery passage between the rocks, they came on a wide inlet. At the mouth of the inlet, sheltered by a rocky headland, a ship rode at anchor.

'So Fécho has waited for us,' Enda cried enthusiastically to Eadulf. There was relief in his voice.

'It's a long way across deep waters from here to Fécho's ship,' pointed out Eadulf pessimistically. 'How can we all get out there?

I don't think he'll be able to pick us up from here because there is no way he can manoeuvre close to these rocks.'

Enda was confident. He and Áed put down the coracle. 'I'll row out to him. I will first take the lady Fidelma with me, then I'll come back for you, and then Áed . . . we can manage. Perhaps Fécho will be able to move a little closer to make the run a little less arduous.'

There was not much else to be said. It was a fairly slow business. However, once Fidelma and Enda were safely aboard, the men on the *Tonn Cliodhna* unfurled the sail and managed to guide the shallow-bottomed craft close into the shore, fending the ship off any dangerous rocks using the long poles. It was Iffernán who returned in the coracle. More expert at handling it, he was able to hold it steady against the rocky shelf so that both men could carefully climb in, positioning themselves to give Iffernán room enough to manipulate the paddle. Eadulf's heart was in his mouth as the coracle pushed off, for with the added weight it had become so low in the water that he was sure it would be swamped and sink.

Somehow, the bobbing craft remained afloat, even when Iffernán turned it, and with his back bent to the task of paddling it was hardly any time before the coracle was bumping alongside the *Tonn Cliodhna* and they were being hauled on board.

Fidelma was already changing into dry clothes in the sheltered stern area, a curtained section used as a cabin and for storage, though Fécho had only been able to provide her with seaman's clothing. For the rest, Fécho was handing round a jug of *corma*, the strong barley alcohol.

Immediately, Eadulf voiced his worries.

'Any sign of the Saxon ship?'

'Not so far,' Fécho said with a shake of his head. 'Should there be?'

Eadulf briefly described their escape.

'The last I saw of them, they were heading out to sea. If they had turned in this direction, they would have reached here by now.'

'You think the Saxon would chase us?' asked Fécho.

'It probably would be best to put some distance between Aescwine and this ship in case he does,' Enda said.

It was unnecessary advice, for the moment they had come aboard Fécho had ordered his men to start manoeuvring to the mouth of the inlet and Iffernán was already at the tiller, keeping a careful watch on the winds for the right moment to hoist full sail.

'What then?' Fécho asked. 'Where do you want to be taken? Back to Ard Nemed?'

'You spoke of that place Baile an Stratha earlier,' Eadulf said. 'Land us there.'

Fécho looked surprised.

'A good thought, friend Eadulf,' smiled Enda. He was sitting on the deck, leaning against the side of the ship, trying to take his shirt off to uncover his wound. 'At least we might get our horses and things back.'

Eadulf grinned at Fécho's bewilderment and he bent to examine Enda's wound. It did not look infected but, asking for fresh water, he cleaned it as best he could and bound it with dry linen strips, which Fécho provided. Then he smiled at Enda. 'I suggest we get out of these sodden rags and put on something warm and dry before we are visited by the fevers.'

At that moment Fidelma emerged, clad in seaman's clothes, looking refreshed in spite of her recent experiences. Eadulf followed Enda and Áed to the curtained-off area to change. It was, of course, far easier to fit Eadulf, Enda and Áed with dry clothing than it had been to find something suitable for Fidelma.

As they returned to Fécho, standing with Fidelma and Iffernán at the tiller, the ship began to heel a little, bending into the wind, indicating that they were turning out of the rocky inlet with the coastline on their right.

Fidelma was regarding Eadulf with curiosity.

'Fécho tells me that you want us to be landed at a place called Baile an Stratha. Why there?' she asked.

'It is a sandy cove just north of here, in the angle of the cliffs before you turn due west for the inner sea to Ard Nemed,' he replied.

Fidelma frowned. 'I did not ask where it was but why,' she said irritably.

Eadulf gestured her to accompany him to the far side of the ship, out of the hearing of Fécho and the others.

'Well now,' Fidelma said, 'is there some secret?'

'Until you release yourself from your *geis* and tell me what we are up against,' Eadulf said slowly, 'then I do not know what is secret from whom. However, I will tell you. The girl, Cairenn, said she would wait for us, with our horses and bags, at that very place.'

Fidelma stared at him for a moment in bewilderment. Then a look of understanding came into her eyes.

'Cairenn! When did you see her last?'

'After she escaped when you attacked the guards,' he replied. 'Enda and I decided to chase Aescwine, so we told her to get our horses and take them away from the settlement, and find a place not that far away where we would meet up with her later. She knew the village.'

'You expect her to be at this place where you have asked to be put ashore?'

'It was the girl who named the spot. She said that she would take the horses and wait for us there for three days. If we had not joined her by then, she would leave the horses there and go on to Cluain.'

'Cluain?' Fidelma frowned at the name. Everything seemed to end at Cluain.

'Well,' urged Eadulf, 'do we go to Baile an Stratha or not?'

Fidelma thought briefly. 'It seems we have no choice,' she replied.

'Not if we want a chance to get back our horses and baggage,' Eadulf said. 'Anyway, surely it is now time for you to tell Enda and me what this is all about? I don't mind being drowned, or shot at with Gewisse crossbows, or imprisoned by strange Uí Liatháin ruffians, but I would like to know why.'

Fidelma gave a reluctant sigh. 'I will tell you as soon as we are in Baile an Stratha. It would be wrong to say anything until we can be sure that the ears that hear what has to be said are those that can keep a secret.'

She glanced meaningfully towards Fécho.

'You don't think he can be trusted?'

'Only to a certain point. He could have warned us about Tialláin.'

'He did say that the man was someone to be wary of.' Eadulf found himself almost defensive. 'Anyway, until we reach Baile an Stratha, you are insisting this sacred oath still applies?' He could not help using a condemning tone.

'It still applies,' Fidelma answered as if with cheerful equanimity.

'Does that secrecy apply to an explanation about Áed?' Eadulf suddenly asked. 'Why were you so keen to have him rescued? Who is he?'

'A bow-maker from Eochaill. That's easy enough. He knows something about this business that I am engaged in. That's why I wanted him along.'

'And I have to wait to hear about that business?' Eadulf asked sourly.

'Aescwine, the Saxon prince, was very interested in what Áed saw at Eochaill – someone special riding in the direction of Cluain.'

'Cluain?' Eadulf shook his head. 'I am sick to death of hearing about Cluain. You still intend to go there?'

She smiled and inclined her head. 'You have a quick mind, Eadulf. I will explain soon, very soon. Please accept that.'

'I'll accept it. But let us hope you never have to take another such oath again.'

'Such is not my intention,' Fidelma solemnly assured him.

The winds were fine and the tide was at its peak when they came into the bay with its long white sandy shore. In fact, the seas were very calm now and the bay contained several small fishing craft. That was good since Fidelma and her companions were reluctant to make any further attempts to swim, which might have been the only other method of getting ashore apart from the coracle. Eadulf declared it would still be too soon if he never saw another coracle in his life. Fécho signalled one of the small boats and negotiated a fee for it to take Fidelma, Eadulf, Enda and Áed ashore.

The problem was that neither Fidelma nor her companions had any means of payment since their capture by Tialláin and their adventures with Aescwine. They had nothing – unless Cairenn had indeed brought their horses to this very spot. However, Fécho conceded that the word of an Eóganacht princess, sister to the King, was good enough security and even returned some of the money she had already given him, in case they needed it ashore. Fidelma promised to return it with interest, slightly amazed at the boatman's change of attitude.

When they said farewell to Fécho and his crew, they felt – in spite of their suspicions – they had known him for a long time rather than just the crowded few days they had been aboard the *Tonn Cliodhna*. Anyway, they parted in friendship and went down over the side into the small fishing boat. By the time they were approaching the sandy shore, Fécho's ship was already out of sight beyond the rocky coastline towards the east. Eadulf had a curious moment of feeling deserted and vulnerable; then he sniffed in contempt at his own emotions.

The fishing settlement to the west of the sandy beach was hardly more than half a dozen rough dwellings, and all seemed deserted. They presumed that it was because most of the fisherfolk were out on the waters, but it was strange that there were few women about. When Eadulf asked, one of the fishermen on the shore grinned and pointed to the pale sun appearing from behind the white billowing clouds. Eadulf saw that it was near its zenith and needed to ask no more – he understood that most of the fishermen's wives would be preparing food for the evening. Nevertheless, he had been hoping for a glimpse of Cairenn watching for them. She and others would surely have seen Fécho's boat come into the bay and transfer its passengers to the smaller vessel to come ashore. With a sinking feeling, Eadulf realised that he could see no sign of any horses grazing in the vicinity. Did that mean that he and Enda had been misled by the girl?

Fidelma asked the fisherman: 'Is there an inn or hostel here?'

The weather-beaten man squinted at her. He seemed amused by the fact that she was dressed in rough boatman's clothing but didn't think her worthy of reply. With a frown, Enda stepped forward. He might have changed out of his water-soaked clothing, which would have indicated he was of some rank, but he still wore the golden torc of the Nasc Niadh. As he towered over the disrespectful fisherman, his shirt collar flapped back, revealing the shining metal. The man obviously recognised it for it had an immediate effect on him. He raised a hand to his brow in salutation.

'Just because the lady Fidelma has been immersed in the sea and lost her clothing,' Enda said harshly, 'there is no excuse for disrespect to the sister of your King.'

'Forgive me, lord, I did not know,' stuttered the man. 'The . . . the lady Fidelma, you say?

'Fidelma of Cashel,' confirmed Enda. 'Now respond to her question.'

'Lady,' the man was almost bowing, 'we boast no inn nor hostel here. Sometimes, when merchants visit, old Mother Báine, in that cabin up there, offers food and beds. I will take you to her, for she is an aunt of mine – she is related to most of us in this community.'

'Very well.' Fidelma decided to say no more and save her questions for the man's aunt.

In fact, 'old Mother Báine' seemed to correspond to her relative's description in only one particular. She was certainly white of hair, as her name suggested. But she was apparently neither a mother nor older than middle age. She met them frowning but on hearing the fisherman's introduction, as he drew her attention to the golden torc at Enda's neck, her features spread into a broad smile of welcome.

'Have you had an accident at sea? A shipwreck? There, there,' she tutted, gazing at their clothing. 'A nasty experience, no doubt, lady. Nasty, indeed.'

Fidelma did not expand on the details.

'Needless to say, such a misfortune leaves us impoverished but be assured my brother, Colgú of Cashel, will ensure that you shall not lack for giving hospitality.'

'Think nothing of it, lady. The pleasure is with me and mine to offer the hospitality as it is required by custom and law.'

Eadulf startled them then, for he had been examining the surroundings carefully.

'It might well be that you do not have to wait for reimbursement of your hospitality, Báine.'

All eyes turned to him in surprise.

'Tell me,' he continued, 'to whom does that curious Gaulish-looking pony belong?'

The woman frowned. 'Gaulish? I don't understand . . . oh, you mean the grey-white pony? Yes, it is an unusual beast.'

'It is, indeed. I noticed it in the field behind your cabin. To whom does it belong?' Eadulf repeated.

'Why, a young girl came riding into this settlement only yesterday, with not only that pony but two others also. She said she would be met by her companions. There were bags on all three horses. I have them stored.'

'The other animals were a roan cob, docile of nature, and a spirited black stallion?' Enda pressed excitedly.

'They were, indeed.' The woman was astounded.

'And they are safe?'

'Safe in the far field by those trees. How did you know this?'

'We are the companions she was waiting for,' Fidelma replied, relieved. 'And the bags that you say you have stored? They are ours.'

'I stored them, just as the young girl asked me to. My, and they belong to you? The girl did say that she would be waiting a few days for some friends who were supposed to join her, and that the horses belonged to them.'

'They are our horses,' Fidelma confirmed.

'The horses are all well, well looked after?' intervened Enda, voicing his main concern.

'As far as we have been able. Looking after such fine animals costs much,' the woman added, with a hint of complaint in her voice.

'If all is as you said, you will be well compensated,' Enda replied. 'You said the bags were stored by you with care.'

'Indeed, even a comb bag, which was carelessly slung on the pony,' Báine affirmed.

'So where is the girl now?' Fidelma asked. 'Where is Cairenn? I didn't see her on the beach or as we came through the settlement.'

The woman looked awkward for a moment, then said: 'She left yesterday.'

'Left?' Eadulf was surprised. 'Where did she go? How? The three days she was to wait here are not gone.'

The woman responded immediately. 'She left on horseback.'

'But you said all three horses are still here.'

'So they are. Yesterday afternoon, the girl, she went to the beach. I heard some noises and went to the door to look down the hill. That was when I saw her leave.'

'What?' prompted Eadulf. 'I don't understand.'

'Half a dozen riders came down the valley to the beach. They were strangers to me, armed men. They saw her and went straight to her and surrounded her. The next thing I heard was the girl scream. Then one of them hoisted her up on his horse and all six went riding back from where they had come. They rode very fast.'

Eadulf's jaw was set firmly. 'Which way did they go? Was it towards Ros Tialláin?'

'Oh no, in the other direction entirely, north-east towards the distant hills.'

'What lies in that direction?' Fidelma asked slowly, suspecting she already knew the answer.

'There's little enough by way of habitation these days, since Cluain has been deserted these many years.'

CHAPTER FOURTEEN

'Cluain?' Eadulf gave a sharp sigh. 'Always Cluain.'

'There's nothing there now,' the woman repeated. 'The abbey has long since been abandoned.'

'So I have heard,' Fidelma said heavily. 'But hasn't it been newly inhabited? Hasn't a religious community decided to re-establish it . . .? They are led by an abbot called Antrí.'

The woman answered with a cynical laugh.

'You don't mean Antrí the cousin of Glaisne, our so-called prince?' She astounded everyone by making as if to spit on the ground. 'Even the Devil himself would turn him away at the portals of Hell as too evil for the place! He's no religieux, just a thug with blood on his hands.'

'The girl was taken in that direction yesterday, you say?' Fidelma pressed.

'It was just after midday,' affirmed Báine. 'God help her if they are Antrí's men.'

Fidelma glanced at the sky, which was overcast with dark, scudding clouds, trying to assess the time of day.

'Lady,' muttered Enda nervously, watching the expression on her face, 'we are all tired and need some rest and food – it has been a long night.'

Fidelma drew her gaze reluctantly back to her companions. Enda had read her thoughts; she had been wondering whether to ride on immediately. 'Very well, food and rest first.' She turned to Báine. 'Will you see to that?' When she had gone, Fidelma added: 'Tomorrow we will start after them. I will rely on your tracking ability, Enda.'

'And what of me, lady?' demanded Áed, whom they had tended to ignore since landed. 'Cluain would be my destination also for that is on the way to Eochaill, my home.'

'Then you will come with us, especially as you seem to know that area,' she replied.

'But I have no horse.'

'If there is not another horse to be found, then, Enda, you will have to ride double with our bow-maker friend.' She turned to the fisherman who had brought them to the cottage and who was still waiting. 'Do you know anyone who has a spare horse, or even a mule?'

The man, eager to be helpful, indicated that he knew someone who had a strong ass that he would willingly hire.

'Can you ride an ass, bow-maker?' Fidelma asked. When he answered in the affirmative, she instructed him to go with the fisherman and make the arrangements. 'Don't worry,' she added to the fisherman. 'Assure the owner of the ass that he will be compensated by me.'

'Before we do anything further,' Eadulf said when they were alone, surprising her by sounding quite belligerent, 'don't you think it is now time to release yourself from this oath of yours and tell us why we are risking our lives?'

Fidelma did not reply immediately but took a chair by the fire, indicating to Eadulf and Enda that they should find seats close to her. She glanced towards the door, beyond which they could hear Báine preparing a meal.

'I am renouncing the *geis*, the sacred oath,' Fidelma told them quietly, trying to modulate the emotion in her voice. 'It is not a matter that I take lightly. I have given it much thought because a *geis* can be more binding than the law itself. But I am resolved that withholding the truth, as I know it, from you both is now more dangerous and obstructive to justice than sharing the secret. If, later, I am judged to be wrong, then I am prepared to accept the consequences.'

Enda was looking suitably awed. 'We learn all about the importance of the *geis* in the story of the High King Conaire Mór, who broke all the nine *geisi* that were imposed on him and having broken them was himself killed.'

'It is a solemn matter,' Fidelma went on slowly, 'but I am persuaded that the law is more important than to uphold this sacred injunction. In this case, justice outweighs everything.'

There was a silence. Eadulf and Enda waited expectantly.

'The matter began with news of a plot to assassinate Cenn Fáelad –'

'The High King?' gasped Enda. 'His brother Sechnussach was only recently assassinated. You and Eadulf were responsible for bringing his murderer to justice.'

'That is why Cenn Fáelad has trusted me and no one else in this. That is why he placed me under a sacred oath not to reveal anything until I could investigate the matter.'

'The High King was responsible for making you swear this sacred oath?' Eadulf sounded almost relieved that his suspicion had been right.

'I knew it would be difficult to keep a secret from you and from Enda. But I had to undertake it as there was a suspicion that a member of my own family was involved. So who would plan such an assassination and why would it bring me this far south? If those who killed Sechnussach are responsible for an attempt on the life of his brother, then they would surely be Uí Néill. And so what are we doing here, among the Uí Liatháin?'

The look on Eadulf's and Enda's faces was indescribable.

'You mean . . . you mean that your brother is accused?' gasped

Enda. 'Impossible! But as King of Cashel, he is the only legitimate claimant in your family. Only a descendant of Eber Fionn could claim the High Kingship, as it was ordained by Amairgin when the Children of the Gael first came to these shores.'

Eadulf was uninformed about such matters but Fidelma was answering Enda, clearly troubled. 'I do not believe my brother is involved,' she said firmly. 'But, at the moment, I cannot discount anything. That was why the *geis* was so important.'

'Perhaps you should start your story from the beginning?' Eadulf suggested. 'I know nothing of these things so perhaps it would help me understand at the same time as helping you to clear your mind and put things in order. I know you have been suppressing your thoughts, keeping them to yourself these last days.'

Fidelma paused for a moment, glanced at him appreciatively and then nodded slowly.

'You know that old Brother Conchobhar, the apothecary at Cashel, keeps the rock doves for my brother.'

Eadulf knew that well – he had always been intrigued by the method of communicating quickly by carrier pigeon.

'Before we left Cashel, Conchobhar came to you with a message,' he recalled. 'Was it from Cenn Fáelad?'

'It was from Cenn Fáelad,' she confirmed. 'The message was written in the *berla file*, the ancient tongue that few people know. It first placed me under a *geis* not to reveal anything. It told me that Grella, his wife, had left Tara to go south to stay with her cousin. Before leaving, she had written a message revealing that there was a plot to assassinate him.'

Eadulf frowned immediately. 'Sent her husband a message with this news? Why didn't she just go to tell him?'

'Let me tell the story first and we will consider these matters later,' Fidelma replied. 'As the High King explained, Grella said she had received the news also by pigeon directly from old Abbot Nessán of Finnbarr's Abbey . . .'

'Nessán himself is a member of your own family,' pointed out Enda, ignoring Fidelma's request. 'He is of the Eóganacht Raithlind; a distant branch, but Eóganacht nevertheless.'

Quickly she described how, according to her information, Grella had been instructed to come to Uí Liatháin territory, to stay with a cousin called Antrí, who was supposed to be abbot at Cluain. How she was told to send her companion, Cairenn, to see Nessán, who would then give her the details. And how Nessán had denied sending the message before he had been murdered. She outlined what Cairenn had told her.

'Already I am finding this story curious,' Eadulf muttered. 'It is not logical.'

'Cenn Fáelad sent a message to me asking me to see Abbot Nessán, for he trusted me to learn the truth. He excused his wife's actions, believing Grella was being manipulated by her fear for his life. He felt it might be a ruse to draw her out of Tara.'

'So that's how you recognised the importance of Cairenn in this matter?' Eadulf observed. 'That's how you knew that we must follow her?'

'So why didn't Grella go to see Nessán herself? Why send Cairenn?' Enda asked.

'Grella told him that the presence of the wife of the High King would alert the conspirators but Cairenn's visit would be considered normal. Nessán was her uncle.'

'So Cairenn is also of a distant branch of the Eóganacht?' Eadulf frowned.

'And if there was an Eóganacht conspiracy . . .?' Enda said excitedly, leaving the question incomplete.

Fidelma said, 'I think you are coming to the conclusion that I drew. Cairenn was used as a cat's paw –'

'A what?' Eadulf had not come across the term *cait o crobh* before.

'A cat's paw, a person used unwittingly or unwillingly by another to accomplish the other's purpose,' explained Fidelma. 'She was sent there so that she would be suspected when Abbot Nessán was murdered. But Cairenn escaped immediately, knowing every moment in the abbey was dangerous after the old abbot had been killed. Even after she escaped, the killer or killers thought that it would be easy to track her down and eliminate her. We were ambushed by mistake on the road south. Cairenn barely escaped another ambush when crossing to the Great Island, Ard Nemed.'

Eadulf was shaking his head. 'This is quite a conspiracy, if your theories work out. Abbot Nessán was killed to prevent him talking?'

'I'll make things even more complicated for you.' Fidelma smiled thinly. 'Do you remember the tall religieux at the abbey who left early the next morning?'

'The one in black robes who kept his face covered by his cowl?' Eadulf asked.

'He was on Aescwine's ship and seemed to have a position of authority. Áed heard him speak and he sounded as someone from the north . . . someone from Uí Néill territory.'

Her words caused Eadulf to gasp in his astonishment.

'But what would a northern religieux be doing on a Gewisse raiding ship? And why would he murder the abbot if . . .'

Fidelma raised her hand to silence the questions to which she had no answers. 'It is pointless to speculate. There are too many questions and not enough answers. There are only a few other pieces of information. What is the involvement of the Saxon, Aescwine, who was seeking Grella? Áed Caille said his ship had landed at Eochaill. Just before that, Áed saw Grella, in the company of a local prince called Glaisne, a cousin of the mysterious Antrí, flee from the fortress there and head westward . . . to Cluain.'

There was a silence. 'Now you have totally lost me,' confessed Eadulf. 'I thought Cairenn had already left Grella at Cluain before she went to see Abbot Nessán. So what was Grella doing in Eochaill, having to flee from the Saxon ship? And how did the religieux, whom we saw at Finnbarr's Abbey before the old abbot was murdered, suddenly appear on the Saxon's ship?'

'All good questions,' Fidelma agreed grimly. 'One thing more . . . Cairenn, when we were prisoners together, said that Tialláin had told her that Grella had been abducted and the rest of her party killed.'

A silence fell as they tried to make some sense of what they knew. Finally, Eadulf stirred. 'Do you have any idea who, among the Eóganacht, would contemplate an assassination of the High King, or the kidnapping of his wife? I thought the High Kingdom was confined to the Uí Néills of the north?'

It was Enda who answered him.

'Until a few hundred years ago the Eóganacht and the Uí Néill could, and did, both claim the inheritance of the High Kingship, in accordance to the decree issued by Amairgin the Druid in the time beyond time. I recall that the sister of the last Eóganacht to be High King had married Niall mac Echach Mugmedóin, a northern prince. She had her brother murdered so that her husband could seize the High Kingship. That was when the Eóganacht ceased to claim their right to the High Kingship; the descendants of Niall have retained it in their family ever since.'

Fidelma nodded slowly. 'I suppose a lot of the princes of Muman might support my brother if he declared an interest in resuming that role, although he would now have to contend with the other provincial kings. But only the kings of Ulaidh have armies of the size that my brother could command.' Her voice was flat, resigned, as she stated the obvious. 'The warfare that might ensue from the declaration of such a claim would destroy the Five Kingdoms. My brother would never contemplate the prospect.'

'Your brother is not the only Eóganacht prince, lady,' Enda pointed out. 'Finnbarr's Abbey is in the territory of the Eóganacht Raithlind and Nessán was of that branch. But are there not also the Eóganacht Áine, the Airthir Chliach, the Glendamnach, the Locha Léin? Don't forget even the Uí Fidgenti claim to be Eóganacht, as descendants of Cormac Cas, the brother of Eóghan. Indeed, these very people of the Uí Liatháin are said to be of the same blood as the Uí Fidgenti.'

Fidelma sighed and raised her arms helplessly. 'I know, I know. The same thoughts have whirled incessantly in my mind during these last days. I confess, for the first time I am confused and can see no way to proceed with all these disjointed facts.'

'But somewhere, as you have always said, all streams and rivers come from one source,' offered Eadulf. 'Cluain keeps reoccurring wherever we turn.'

'So, our only path is to go to Cluain,' Enda said. 'That is simple.'

Fidelma smiled softly for she had already decided that their path led inevitably to Cluain.

'I agree,' she said, as if reluctantly. 'Yet a place does not solve a mystery. Only people do. When I think of Cairenn, I find that the story darkens. Grella and Cairenn had set out from Tara with the purpose of visiting Abbot Nessán, according to Cenn Fáelad. Grella announced that she would first stay with her cousin, this curious Abbot Antrí of Cluain. You have heard from people like Báine here that he is no religieux. Before they reach Cluain, Grella tells Cairenn to go on to see Nessán on her behalf and then come back to join her there. They part company: Cairenn to see Nessán and Grella to stay with Antrí and . . .'

'You said that you felt Cairenn was sent there as a . . . a cat's claw?' ventured Eadulf.

'Cat's paw,' she corrected.

'But Grella sent her there,' Eadulf said.

'Grella was then abducted. So it seems that she had been misdirected. Was it all a ruse just to get her to Cluain and abduct her?'

'But why bring her all the way from Tara to here to do that?' Eadulf asked. 'It seems so complicated.'

'What seemed to upset the plan is Grella sending a note to Cenn

Fáelad to tell him she was coming south,' pointed out Fidelma. 'She sounds a woman with a good head. Being unsure of how things stood among the Uí Liatháin, Grella decided to send Cairenn to the abbey – and the girl was accused of the murder instead of Grella, the intended suspect. When that plan went wrong, the conspirators kidnapped Grella.'

Fidelma fell silent, reflecting on this possibility, not really happy with the theory.

'No, Grella was told to send Cairenn to Finbarr's Abbey. I think we need to know more about this Antrí, the cousin of Grella. After all, Cluain is said to have been deserted for nearly fifty years. Why would Grella be sent to seek refuge in a deserted abbey?'

Báine came into the room to replenish the jug of cider and overheard this last. Fidelma turned to her.

'You told us something of the man called Antrí, cousin of Glaisne, who I am told is ruler of the southern Uí Liatháin. Tell me more about him.'

The woman gave a deprecating sniff. 'Antrí is not a person who is spoken well of in these parts, any more than his cousin Glaisne is. Thugs, the both of them.'

'Yet Glaisne is cousin to Grella, wife of the High King?' Fidelma voiced this as a question.

'People cannot help their relatives.'

'And Antrí? You say he is not a religieux?'

'He is a thief, pure and simple,' replied the woman. 'He is Glaisne's lackey, a flunkey who carries out all the tasks his cousin finds too distasteful to perform himself,' explained Báine sourly. 'It is hard to tell which one is the more ambitious or the more evil. Take my advice: steer clear of them and, if they are at Cluain, avoid the place.'

Fidelma sighed softly. 'It all seems so confusing. But you know the lady Grella is from that same family?'

The woman nodded pleasantly. 'Who does not? She escaped a

vicious brood when she left this territory to travel north to be married to Cenn Fáelad. He was a young, handsome prince, so we were told. Now he is High King.'

'Then the lady Grella is not close to her relatives?'

Báine shrugged. 'I wouldn't know about that, lady. I suspect there are bad pups in every bitch's litter. Glaisne and Antrí are the worst of them. I have never seen her, for she grew up in Eochaill and the furthest I have been is across the bay you see before you. All I know is that she is best living in the north away from that family. Now, excuse me, while I go and finish preparing your meal.'

There was a short silence after she left the room. Then Eadulf tried to sum up their conclusion. 'So if Cairenn was captured yesterday and taken in the direction of Cluain . . . that is not good. It seems that whoever has taken her must be the same people who have abducted Grella. Yet we are told Grella was seen with Glaisne, her own cousin, leaving Eochaill for the direction of Cluain but days after Cairenn left her at Cluain. It just doesn't make sense.'

Fidelma agreed with him. 'This is why we must go to Cluain and look for answers.'

Enda coughed softly and shifted his weight in his chair. He was frowning.

'I do not like it, lady. It appears we are going into the wolf's lair, but there are just the three of us.'

'I am a *dálaigh* and sister to the King,' pointed out Fidelma. Then she caught the smile on Eadulf's face and started to chuckle, much to Enda's astonishment.

'That has not helped me, or you, lately, has it?' she admitted wryly. 'There seems little respect for the law and its officers here.'

'In any case,' Enda pointed out, 'I am the only warrior among you and not in perfect fighting shape. So, how do we overcome a band of armed warriors, of the type that abducted Cairenn, if they be waiting at Cluain?'

'By stratagem,' replied Fidelma calmly.

'But now I have access to my *les*,' Eadulf said, rising, 'I need to re-examine that wound of yours, Enda, and redress it.'

He had just finished when Áed reappeared, smiling. 'Well, I have the hire of a good ass. So I can accompany you. When will we leave?'

'Tomorrow.' Fidelma did not elaborate further as Báine entered with platters of mackerel, some of the local edible seaweed and barley cakes, with flagons of cold ale. The consumption of the food quickly stopped any discussion among them. None of them had eaten properly for a long time and they each did more than justice to the fare set before them. There was no complaint when Báine brought another large dish of barley cakes, this time with honey from her own hives.

The food had a soporific effect and, although they all felt sleep approaching rapidly, Fidelma insisted that they must first examine the bags that Cairenn had brought on the horses. Báine had placed them in an unoccupied section of her guest quarters, and they were relieved to find that everything was there. Now Fidelma could change out of her sailor's garments into something suitable. She was particularly grateful to retrieve her comb bag, which carried not only her toiletries but also some gold and silver, hidden away as a precaution to cover unexpected expenses on her travels. Importantly, the golden seal with the figure of the woman and solar wheel was still there too.

When they had been captured in the inn at Ros Tialláin, Gadra had stripped them of their weapons and possessions and had these piled on their horses at the back of the inn, ready to take them elsewhere. Their disposal had been interrupted by events and so, thankfully, Eadulf and Enda found their belongings undisturbed. Enda's favourite sword, shield and javelin were hanging there next to his riding cloak and saddle bag; even his hunting knife, a gift from his friend and commander of the Nasc Niadh, Gormán, was there. Having these items restored to them seemed to put new confidence in everyone. The only things missing were Fidelma's riding cloak and the one belonging to Eadulf. Fidelma mentioned that they would need to find something to replace them for one could not travel far without such protection in midwinter. Báine promised that she would do what she could.

By the time Fidelma had finished speaking with Báine and returned to her companions she found them all succumbed to exhaustion and fast asleep. It was only a few moments before she, too, was in a deep slumber.

It must have been light for some time when Fidelma opened her eyes to the cold, grey, winter morning. She lay blinking in confusion for a moment until memories came scudding into her mind. She must have been more exhausted than she had imagined. The regular rise and fall of Eadulf's breath told her that he was still sound asleep. In a corner, Enda was also curled up, oblivious to the sounds of the new morning. Now the crow of a cockerel and the protesting clucking of chickens joined the various harmonies of the sea birds. She rose and went to wash, as was the custom, and when she returned to the room, Eadulf and Enda were beginning to stir.

She went into the main room, where Mother Báine was preparing the morning meal, and wished her a good morning. After the pleasantries, Fidelma looked out across the bay and confirmed that it was not a bad morning for midwinter. The clouds were sparse, though the areas of blue between them were pale and the sun seemed to hang limply without much colour. A thought suddenly occurred to Fidelma. She had seen only Eadulf and Enda in the guest room.

'Where is the man called Áed?' she asked. 'Is he up already?'

Báine shrugged but seemed worried. 'I wondered whether to mention it, lady, because I thought he must have arranged it with you.'

'Arranged what?'

'He has gone.'

'Gone?'

'As I say, I wasn't sure if it had been arranged. That is why I said nothing. He was up at first light. I heard him take the ass from the yard and so I rose and watched him make his way to the north-east.'

Fidelma stared at her for a moment or two. She did not have to ask what lay in that direction.

'Yes, lady,' Báine seemed to read her thoughts. 'He rode towards Cluain, in the same direction as those men took the young girl the other day.'

'He left without saying anything or leaving a note?'

'He said not a word to me, lady. That's why I thought you had agreed his departure.'

Eadulf entered and paused, feeling the strained atmosphere before he saw the sombre look on Fidelma's face.

'What is it?' he demanded.

'Áed appears to have set off without us,' she replied simply.

Eadulf did not seem surprised. 'Was he so important? His contribution was only that he had seen Grella being escorted from Eochaill. I expect that he was grateful for his rescue from the Saxon and that is as far as it goes.'

'I am sure he knew something about the abduction of Grella,' she insisted.

'Did he leave any explanation of his departure?' Eadulf sat down and helped himself to a mug of Báine's cider.

They looked towards Báine, who was shaking her head. 'Not a word did he say to me.' Then a look of bitterness spread over her features. 'I hope he did not think his bed and food would come free and that he would be able to make off with the ass as well?'

'I have said that I will guarantee all that,' Fidelma assured her sharply. 'You will not lose for helping the sister of your King.'

The woman muttered something under her breath and returned to her kitchen.

'Well, it seems as if you have lost money on the ass,' Eadulf said ruefully, as Báine left the room. 'Lucky he didn't ride off on one of our horses. In which direction did he go?'

'He went in the direction of Cluain,' she told him.

Eadulf pursed his lips in a soundless whistle. 'So everything winds up in Cluain? Why Cluain?"

At that moment Enda entered to join them for breakfast and was quickly told what had happened. He seemed philosophical.

'Perhaps the man simply wanted to get back to his family after his experience with the Saxon raider. He just seized the opportunity to get a free ride back to wherever it is he came from.'

'The bow-maker knows something more of this business,' Fidelma repeated bitterly. 'I was a fool not to question him more rigorously yesterday, but we were all exhausted from the experience with Aescwine.'

'I'd still like to know what Grella was doing at Glaisne's fortress just before the Saxons landed,' Eadulf said. 'Besides, Tialláin told Cairenn that she had been abducted at Cluain. So how did she come to be free in Eochaill and riding back towards Cluain some days later?'

'As we planned last night, after we have finished here, we will ride for Cluain. As it is a long ride, I suggest you eat sparingly,' she said reprovingly, watching them tuck into the cold meats, cheese and barley bread. 'It does not do well to ride distances when the stomach is overfilled.'

They had nearly finished the meal when the fisherman who had brought them to Báine's house entered. He wore a worried expression and seemed relieved to see them.

'I've just been speaking to some fishermen from along the coast – they sighted a warship. The talk is that this ship has been sailing up and down the coast without challenge.'

'What manner of warship?' Fidelma demanded immediately.

The fisherman shrugged. 'Surely a warship is a warship?' he asked uncertainly.

Fidelma stood up with a determined expression and thought for

a moment before declaring: 'We must continue our journey immediately. Until we know who is friend or enemy, it is best to ensure
we stay safe.'

'Enemy? Why would it be an enemy?' asked the fisherman.

'What direction was it sailing from?' Enda suddenly asked.

'Direction? Why from the east, I think.'

Eadulf frowned. 'The Saxon ship?'

The fisherman's eyes widened. 'Saxons? Why would they be in
these waters?'

'Maybe it is that Cenél nÁeda warship,' Enda said, unthinkingly.
'After all, Artgal might want to make reprisals for the Uí Liatháin
raid on the Great Island.'

Fidelma frowned angrily at his tactlessness.

'Where was this ship last seen?' she interrupted. 'Are you sure
it is a warship and not a coastal merchant?'

'Fishermen know the difference,' affirmed the man, annoyed. 'It
was seen coming this way, but with this morning's contrary winds
it won't be here until well after noon.'

'From east or west,' Fidelma said firmly, 'we must continue our
journey.'

As they rode away from the small fishing village, Fidelma looked
back over the grey seas. She could just make out the sail of the
familiar-looking warship heading into the bay. It was causing
consternation among the villagers. Already, the people of the settlement were rushing hither and thither, collecting animals and valu-
ables. Many were heading towards the distant hills.

Fidelma kept her horse alongside Eadulf's as they put distance
between themselves and the village.

'I wanted to ask you about this man Aescwine,' she said. 'He
calls himself a prince. Do you know of him? He told me he would
be King of his people when the current King died.'

'I recognised the banner on his ship at Tialláin's harbour,' Eadulf
nodded. 'I told Enda as much. He is of the Gewisse.'

'Tell me what you know.'

'The Gewisse are also called the Saxons of the West. Aescwine's ship carried the banner of their King Cenwealh, who has made the Gewisse territory into a powerful kingdom. For most of his life, Cenwealh was a pagan; only after he converted to the New Faith and adopted the rule of Rome did he became powerful. He drove the Britons from the north-west of his territory and established his summer fortress there. He has renamed the captured territory Sumersaeton. But Cenwealh is elderly now and no longer strong.'

'So, is Aescwine his son?'

'Not so,' replied Eadulf. 'He is a young man who has been trying to make a name for himself as a warrior but he lives under the shadow of his father, Cenfus, a prince who also claims the right to inherit the kingdom of the Gewisse.'

'Is that what he is doing raiding our coast? Does he think to achieve his reputation by attacking undefended villages?'

Eadulf pulled a wry expression. 'It might be a reason why he was keen to take Grella hostage, or – indeed – you. He could parade you before the Gewisse and claim to have performed great deeds to capture you. That would enhance his reputation among his people and even impress the other Saxon kingdoms.'

'Wouldn't he be condemned by his own King for such behaviour?'

'Cenwealh? He is no longer strong enough to keep his rebellious princes in order. Aescwine appointed himself as an envoy to Tara.'

Fidelma's eyes widened in disbelief. 'This Aescwine was an envoy at the High King's court?'

'He was. I heard tales that he was well favoured by the ladies there.'

Fidelma screwed up her face in mock distaste. 'That explains how he knew some of our language. It might explain what he is doing with the northern religieux. But I can't see how these things fit in with the plot against Cenn Fáelad and the abduction of Grella.'

'I can see no connection at all,' Enda commented.

'Nor I,' agreed Eadulf. 'As well you know, many sons of the noble Saxon houses have been sent to the courts of the Irish kings in the traditional manner of hostages, or to escape from blood feuds among their own people, or even to learn the Faith.'

'And this Aescwine was sent as envoy from this people you call the Gewisse?'

'A very powerful Saxon people,' confirmed Eadulf.

Fidelma was thoughtful for a moment. 'Then there is a possibility that if Aescwine spent time at Tara he might be involved in an assassination plot?'

Eadulf was dismissive. 'But he is a foreigner, Fidelma. As you have often quoted Cicero – *cui bono*? To whom the benefit? What would a foreigner gain from such a plot? I know the limitations your laws place on foreigners; there seems no reason for him to get involved in the dynastic politics of the High King.'

'There are other means by which he might gain,' reflected Fidelma. 'He wants to make a name for himself, you say?'

'True. But how would killing Cenn Fáelad aid him in his ambition to be ruler of the Gewisse? His position under Cenwealh's patronage is assured.'

'There must be a link.' Fidelma was stubborn.

'Wouldn't it weaken the High King's position if the Saxon was supposed to abduct Grella? Pressure could be brought on him to obtain her release.'

Fidelma inclined her head appreciatively. 'There is something in that,' she agreed. 'But it might also give the Uí Néill a cause to rally round in his support.'

'I can't understand the involvement of Abbot Nessán. Why choose him as the person who sent the message to Grella,' protested Enda.

'The old abbot was influential in this kingdom. But you forget that he denied that he had done so to Cairenn. Anyone can tie a message to the leg of a carrier pigeon. That would mean someone who had access to Abbot Nessán's pigeons,' Eadulf pointed out.

'There is another aspect,' Fidelma said suddenly.

'Which is?'

'Are you forgetting that Nessán was an Eóganacht of the Raithlind branch and the whole plot is supposed to be an attempt by the Eóganacht to oust the High King? We have not entirely eliminated someone in my family from the conspiracy.' She was unhappy when she said it but, nevertheless, it was her duty as a *dálaigh* to point it out.

After that a silence fell between them and, as the track became easier, they coaxed their horses into a canter. Although the clouds were changing formation, becoming almost a mackerel sky, as fishermen called the patterning of the grey wisps, the temperature was not as low as previously. There had not even been a frost that morning. The hills were not high, perhaps averaging less than a hundred metres or so. For the most part it was fairly rich pastoral land, though some woodlands were evident and tiny streams and small rivers proliferated across the landscape. Here and there they saw sheep grazing on the hillsides and even herds of cattle sheltering from chilly winds in the valleys between. They had asked the way to Cluain twice from local shepherds and had travelled over eight kilometres before an elderly man gave them the information that they wanted.

He was typical of the type Eadulf immediately thought of as a shepherd, white haired and long bearded, a thin, wiry man with bright blue eyes and a hook nose. His skin showed white around his open collar, but this contrasted with the face, which was weather tanned from a life working in the hills. A dog of mixed breeds sat a little way away from him, watching the newcomers with intent eyes as if ready to spring into action at a word of command.

'Cluain, is it?' he echoed reflectively. 'Just in the next valley – but there is nothing there these days. I suppose you think that there is still a religious community there? No longer. It is all deserted since the time of my father's father.'

'We already know that Colmán's community was abandoned over fifty years ago,' Fidelma told him with a smile.

'Ah, then perhaps you search for Antrí? He has gone as well, in spite of all his boasting.' The man suddenly spat on the ground. 'Good riddance to him, I say.'

'You know this Antrí?' Fidelma asked.

'Calls himself an abbot. Abbot Antrí,' the shepherd said in sour amusement. 'He arrived only a short while ago. He brought with him some folk who, he said, would form a new abbey community. They were no more than thieves and brigands, hired toughs.'

'Didn't the local people protest about this?'

'What local people? There are only a few of us. We would not go near the place, especially when word had it that they brought the Yellow Plague back to the country again and that they all died. Yes, all of them died.'

'When was this?'

The old man shrugged. 'Why, less than a week ago, I suppose. A friend from the farmstead over by the hazel wood across the valley passed this way and told me that the place had been deserted again. We thought there was some disease there that caused them to quit . . .'

'What makes you say that?' Fidelma asked with a frown.

'Well, my friend said that when he passed they had been burning the bodies of those who died. The stench was awful, like roasted pork he said.'

Fidelma's features were an expressionless mask. 'Burning bodies? Did he see this?'

The old man shook his head. 'Only the smoke and the fumes and the smell were left. It was enough.'

'I was told that Antrí was related to your prince.'

'Not that that is any recommendation. God's curse on him. May his house rot!' shouted the shepherd. 'There is a man that the evil ones would flee from for he would do thrice the evil to them as they would to him.'

Fidelma was impressed. 'You speak of Glaisne? Why don't you like him?'

'He demands tribute at every opportunity, and those who do not give him full measure he has taken out and beaten for what he calls disloyalty and impudence. Wasn't my own brother stripped and flogged by him for being a month late in payment?'

'Those actions are totally against the law,' Fidelma protested automatically.

'We are in the country of the southern Uí Liatháin, lady,' Enda pointed out drily. 'They probably do things differently here.'

'The law of the Fenechus applies everywhere in the Five Kingdoms,' snapped Fidelma in pedantic anger before she picked up Enda's irony. Then she grimaced and turned back to the shepherd. 'Tell me more about this prince, Glaisne.'

'What more is there to tell? They tell me he has a twin brother who has a community not far distant from here. I have never seen him.'

Fidelma raised her brows slightly. 'Is this the man called Éladach, who is also something of a religieux?'

'I would not know. I have no interest in such matters. I stay up here in these hills and avoid local lords and abbots with their pretensions and their demands.'

'You are very free with your opinions about people you have not seen and do not know,' pointed out Fidelma.

'Lady, I keep to my isolated life. My dog and the sheep are my main company, except for the occasional passer-by. I hear their news. I know what I am told. Sometimes it is better not to hear news, for is it not said that no news is better than bad news and bad news is always the quickest to travel?'

They left the shepherd to his solitary contemplation of his sheep grazing across the hillside.

Enda glanced at Eadulf, looking decidedly uncomfortable.

'I don't like the sound of burning bodies,' he finally said. 'I remember how it was a few years ago when the entire world fell victim to the Yellow Plague. Why would they burn bodies, unless it is the plague returned?'

Memories of the Yellow Plague, the Buidhe Conall, were still sharp in their minds. It had devastated not only the Five Kingdoms but had visited all the kingdoms of the Britons, the Angles and Saxons. It was said that it had come out of the east, from far-off Byzantium, and rampaged throughout what had been the old empire of the Romans. People had expired from its feverish embrace. It spared neither kings, nobles, bishops nor commoner or serfs.

'There have been no reports of the Yellow Plague for some years,' Eadulf reassured him. 'I know that religious communities do burn bodies when there are a lot of unexpected deaths. Just as bodies are burnt after a battle, as no one is able to bury the dead in such numbers.'

Enda seized on the point. 'If there had been some battle here, then news would surely have come to the Nasc Niadh.'

They rode on in silence, ascending a hill that was not steep but whose summit supplied a clear view of the long bare valley beyond. It was a curious-looking place, a rocky vale cleared in the middle of afforested hills.

'That must be the community of Cluain.' Fidelma was pointing to a group of buildings, surrounded by a rough stone wall.

Enda, whose sharp tracker eyes were surveying the buildings, breathed in sharply.

'There is smoke still rising from it. It must have been a large fire.'

It was true. There was a pall of black smoke hanging almost motionless over the centre of the complex. Eadulf's reaction was to sniff at the air but, of course, with the winds blowing, and the fire having smouldered for some days, he could detect nothing of the shepherd's roast pork. Even the thought made him shiver with distaste. He tried to think of something else.

'Why is it called Cluain? It looks nothing like a meadow,' he said, more for something to say than interest.

'Well, it looks an unpleasant valley sure enough,' Fidelma replied examining the area. 'It is curious how there are woods at either end as well as high on the hills but not actually in the valley. Why did Colmán choose to set up his community there? I suppose there is tranquillity in its bare, rocky vista.'

Enda snorted derisively. 'Tranquillity is not what has been experienced here recently, not with those burning bodies.'

Eadulf suddenly pointed. 'What are those black holes in the side of the hills high up over there . . . just under the tree line?'

'They look like caves to me,' Enda offered.

'Come on.' Fidelma suddenly urged her horse forward down the hillside. 'It's no use sitting here speculating on what we cannot fully appreciate.'

She led the way down into the valley. As they moved along it, Eadulf could see the rising hills were of limestone and presumed the caves must extend into those rocks. A stream flowed through the valley floor, which seemed covered in stunted blackthorn, its impenetrable nature, with cruel thorns and rough, black-brown branches, undisguised in its winter nudity. As they came close to the crumbling wall of limestone blocks, they realised the valley was not quite as sparse of growth as it had at first seemed. There were no oaks, but a few yew trees and some willow presented a shady woodland rather than the 'meadow' of the local name.

'At least no one will starve here,' Enda called, pointing to the proliferation of fungus along the path.

'Examine them closely,' Fidelma advised, in a meticulous mood. 'Most fungus you see in this sort of area will not be good for eating. They do not grow at this time of year – instead you find crampballs, and those are dead man's fingers.'

Eadulf shivered slightly. 'Speaking of which, have you noticed there are no bird sounds along this valley?'

Fidelma had but did not say so. 'And what do you make of that?' she countered.

'With those bodies, burnt or not, I would have thought some scavengers would have been about. Birds and mammals.'

'It's not a nice place, lady,' Enda commented, glancing apprehensively around. 'There is an aura about it that makes me feel cold.'

Fidelma smiled. 'It is only people who create auras, Enda. Look!' She pointed. 'We are coming up to the gates of the enclosure.'

An oppressive silence hung over them as they halted before the rotting wooden gates set in the stone walls. The gates hung slightly ajar, moving gently with the rustling wind.

'Well, what are we waiting for?' Fidelma urged after a few minutes.

Enda shook himself as if he felt cold. He reached forward from his horse and pushed at the swinging gate. It moved backwards, opening into the central compound. Instinctively, Enda drew his sword as he urged his horse in. He had gone only a short distance when he stopped. Fidelma and Eadulf followed and halted alongside him. It was clear why he had stopped. The acrid smell of smoke was strong now, rising from the blackened pile before them. There was something else, something which Eadulf had been prepared for by the shepherd's tale.

It was, indeed, the sweet smell of burnt pork; except it was not pork.

Eadulf turned away in disgust and as he did so his eyes fell on another burnt pile. This one was no longer smoking. Even though it was almost totally destroyed, he could see it was the burnt-out remains of a carriage and that it had been quite ornate and unusual. Part of the side panel of the door was undamaged enough for him to make out part of an engraving on it.

'Look!' He called their attention to it. 'How did this unusual carriage come to be here, in this deserted religious community?'

Fidelma drew a sharp breath as she examined the half-destroyed side panel. For a while she said nothing but stood staring at the almost obliterated emblem.

'The Red Hand of the Uí Néill!' she finally said in a hollow tone. 'This is the symbol of the family of the High Kings. This was Grella's carriage.'

CHAPTER FIFTEEN

'At least we know she did not perish in it,' Eadulf pointed out, after a few moments' examination. 'Áed sighted her at Eochaill after whatever happened here.'

'If we can trust Áed,' Enda observed sceptically.

'No reason not to trust him simply because he seized the opportunity to take the ass and leave for home,' Eadulf replied.

Enda was gazing with distaste at the smouldering pile behind them. They were clearly bodies and now the odours were strong and nauseating. The pyre had not completely destroyed everything. Some scorched fastenings for clothing and other pieces of metal were among the remains, and there was a lot of scorched leather: sandals and a few boots of half-tanned hide. One particular item fascinated Enda, who poked at it with the tip of his sword.

'Why do you find that interesting?' Fidelma asked, noticing his scrutiny.

'It's not the usual *cuaróg*, the boots worn by our warriors,' he pointed out, indicating his own footwear. 'This is called a *búatais*.'

'And so?' prompted Fidelma.

'I doubt if an *cuardnaidhe*, a boot-maker, from these parts made it.'

Fidelma was a little impatient. 'I wish you would make your point more clearly.'

Enda was apologetic. 'These are the type of boots that Saxons use.'

'How do you know?' she demanded.

'I have seen enough of them on the feet of Saxon warriors when they have accompanied their emissaries to Cashel,' Enda replied.

Fidelma turned to Eadulf. 'Is this Saxon?'

Eadulf regarded the burnt remains and gave a nod. 'Enda has a good eye,' he confirmed. 'The work is of Saxon origin. You can still see there are seven folds of hide in the sole and there is a wooden block sewn around with hide as a lift for the heel.'

Fidelma stared at the object thoughtfully. 'But a boot does not present evidence of the wearer. We should not read anything more than possibility into this. There are many Saxon students at the ecclesiastical colleges these days.'

'Not wearing military boots,' Enda replied drily. 'I wonder if Aescwine sent his men here?'

'We are encountering a lot of Saxon involvement in this mystery.'

'If one of these bodies was a warrior accompanying Grella,' Eadulf went on, 'then who is to say that he was not of Tara? There is enough interchange between Tara and the kingdoms of the Angles and Saxon kingdoms, especially after Oswiu declared support for the Roman Church against the Irish churches at the Council of Streonshalh. There are many refugees, nobles seeking protection from the murderous intentions of their relatives. It is quite likely that such clothing might be worn by natives as well as –'

'I have considered it,' Fidelma cut in. 'Perhaps I am prejudiced by my encounter with Aescwine. However, I want to know why his ship is in these waters and how he is familiar with Grella's name.'

'That could be for any one of many reasons.'

It was Enda who brought them back to the subject in hand. 'We can say with certainty that Grella's coach was here; that means a coachman and perhaps her guard were killed here. So it seems Tialláin was right about Grella being abducted. Did Cairenn tell you what their escort consisted of, lady?'

It was a question that hadn't occurred to Fidelma during her short incarceration with Grella's companion.

'If Grella did not meet her end here,' went on Enda, 'but was at Eochaill, why were all these bodies burnt? There must be a dozen here.'

'Good questions, but we cannot answer them just standing here,' Fidelma said sharply, to disguise her annoyance that she had not thought of them.

'Perhaps some information can be gleaned,' Eadulf said, turning to the pile of fire-blackened corpses. 'Look, the heat has not been so intense for those poor fellows who were at the bottom of this funeral pyre.'

He took a piece of cloth from his *firbolg*, the man-bag that he carried like a satchel for his personal possessions, and tied it around the lower half of his face. Then he moved closer to the pile and began to peer closely at the bodies. He turned to Enda: 'Can you find or cut me a stout stick?'

The warrior went off to search and soon returned with a suitable piece of wood. Eadulf took it and began to poke cautiously among the pyre. Even Fidelma, used to all sorts of violent death that beset the world in which she lived, had to steel herself to look on as he turned over the remains. It took him some time, poking this way and that.

'Find anything?' Enda asked after a while.

Eadulf shook his head. 'Nothing that makes sense. I would say that most of these bodies were of the religious: I see remains of wooden beads, some crucifixes and the fragments of robes rather than pieces of armour. There are some partially tanned burnt hide sandals as well. However, there are a couple of interesting bodies. There is the one you found with the *búatais*, the warrior's boot – by the way, I found its companion. However . . .'

'However?' queried Fidelma.

'There is something even more significant than Saxon boots.'

'Significant? In what way?'

'This one had the remains of a crossbow bolt in the chest, so deep that the fire hardly touched it.'

'A bolt?' queried Enda. 'Do you mean like those used by Aescwine's men?'

'Hard to tell who fired a crossbow by the finding of a bolt,' said Eadulf.

'Well, it is not a weapon of choice among the warriors of Muman,' Enda countered.

'But, again, is not unknown,' Fidelma pointed out. 'It seems likely that the Saxons are involved, because they use the weapon. But it is not evidence. It's a distasteful task, Eadulf, but would you see whether there are any other such bolts?'

Using the stick to move the burnt remains, Eadulf spent a little time in closer examination. He surveyed the blackened skulls with a critical eye. Fidelma motioned to Enda and they left Eadulf to his inspection. Enda looked after the horses while Fidelma did some exploring but there was hardly anything left in the deserted buildings; most of them were in a dilapidated state anyway, and it was easy to see that there was nothing worth examining there. There were signs that some buildings had been recently used, but nothing to connect the use of the buildings with the mound of destroyed humanity in the courtyard.

Enda spent some time studying the tracks around the buildings.

'Anything?' asked Fidelma shortly.

'Plenty of horses were here. There are, of course, the remains of the coach' – he nodded to the burnt-out vehicle with the remains of the Red Hand emblem on it – 'doubtless that coach came here and halted before the gates. I saw some wood on the gates splashed with blood that had dried. I would go so far as to say that there were several horses that were already here and when they left, some of the horses were carrying more weight than they had brought. You can see that by the deeper indentation of their hooves.'

Enda had a deserved reputation as an expert tracker among the warriors of King Colgú's bodyguard.

'The addition of the weight would be caused by . . .?' queried Fidelma, knowing full well the answer.

'Some of the horses could have been double mounted or have been carrying extra baggage,' Enda confirmed. 'I would say that the horses carrying the extra weight were only two or three at most, so I would hazard a guess and say they were carrying an extra rider and baggage.'

Fidelma grimaced. 'You mean the occupant of the burnt-out coach and her baggage?' she said, thinking of Grella.

'More than likely.'

'It does seem a logical deduction, especially as she was seen alive subsequently,' she agreed.

Eadulf called to them and they returned to the pile of burnt corpses. He was a little white faced and stood leaning on the stick that Enda had provided.

'I now realise that I should be thankful that I spent that time in Tuaim Brecain studying the healing arts,' he said, 'for it has given me an eye for the clues that a human leaves behind after death.'

'Which are . . . in this case?' prompted Fidelma.

'To summarise, most of the bodies, some twelve in all, were clad in religious robes. The remains of their clothes and sandals and a few other items all confirm that. What is more, they were all dead before those who had killed them started this immolation.'

'How do you know that?' demanded Fidelma.

'Easy enough when one looks closely. When a body shows signs of a smashed skull, or a sword thrust into the neck, for which the bone is often the witness, and these wound patterns are repeated, then one can say that they were all killed with sword thrusts to the neck or the head.'

Fidelma regarded the remains sombrely. 'So the majority of corpses were dressed in religious robes and all were murdered? Is that what you are saying?'

'I am also saying that our friend, the shepherd, was probably right. They were all young, muscular from what I could see. A few of those bodies better preserved from the fire showed old wounds, healed wounds. Unusual, if they were religious. There were only two exceptions.'

'What exceptions?'

'Firstly, the warrior wearing the Saxon-style *búatais*. He also wore items made of hard material: belt buckles, a knife, jewellery and . . .' Eadulf paused and turned to Enda. 'Although the body-guard of the kings of Muman are called Warriors of the Golden Collar, the Nasc Niadh, is it the custom of all warriors to wear distinctive torcs of gold?'

'Of course,' Enda said immediately. 'Each torc is of a different pattern, depicting which group the warrior belongs to. The High King's men, the Fianna, usually have roundels on the ends of their collars where they fit, whereas, as you well know, we carry the heads of wolves on our torcs. The torc has a magical signifi-cance . . .' He glanced at Fidelma, seeming suddenly awkward. 'At least, so it was said in the days of the old religion.'

'Are you saying that you found such a torc?' asked Fidelma quickly.

'No, but I found a mark on the neck of one of the bodies that could only have been made by wearing such an item over a long period. The torc had been removed. Thankfully, the neck was not entirely burnt and the mark was clear. This body also wore untanned leather boots.'

'So what you are saying is that among the bodies you could identify at least one professional warrior?'

'That would be my deduction,' Eadulf affirmed. 'And, of course, there was the body of the coachman.'

He indicated another body that had been burnt almost down to the skeleton but, oddly, the lower arms had been left almost intact due to the way the body had lain in the pyre.

Fidelma's eyebrows were raised. 'How do you identify that as the body of a coachman? By what power do you deduce that?'

Eadulf actually smiled complacently. 'What does a coachman, one who drives a team of horses, wear around his wrists?'

'Jewellery?' volunteered Enda curiously.

Eadulf shook his head and his smile broadened a little. 'The driver has to hold the leather reins. Sometimes, for better control, they wrap the reins around their wrists. To protect the flesh on their wrists, they often wear cuffs of stiff leather, often pieces of semi-tanned hide. I think they are called *muinchille*. They go around the wrist so that drivers can turn the reins without injury to themselves. If you look, this corpse had such cuffs on both wrists and, because of the nature of the material, they were singed but not burnt, so protecting the lower arms. Thus this poor man was obviously the driver of that coach.' He nodded towards the remains of the vehicle.

Fidelma shot Eadulf one of her rare looks of admiration.

'So,' she said, 'we are putting together a picture. Grella came here in her coach. She was driven by a coachman and accompanied, it seems, by at least one bodyguard . . . If we ever catch up with Cairenn, she can confirm the details of who remained in the party when she left them to go on to the abbey. Were they all killed?'

'I found the bolts in the remains of the warrior and the coachman,' replied Eadulf. 'I would say that they were.'

'So all the party, except for Grella herself, were killed. The bodies were put with these others, who were dressed as religious, and burnt. We know that Grella was later seen alive with Glaisne of Eochaill. So was Glaisne the assassin or did he rescue her?'

Eadulf was thoughtful. 'The questions arises: why were those men killed? If Grella was abducted, then the reason for her coachmen and escort being killed is obvious. But what about the men dressed as religious? We know that the man Antrí claimed to be an abbot, falsely it seems, and some men came here with him supposedly to reopen this abbey. So what was their real purpose and what had it to do with Grella? Who were they and why were they here and why were they killed?'

'And, more important,' Fidelma sighed heavily, 'what bearing does all this have on the conspiracy to kill the High King, Cenn Fáelad?'

They fell silent for a while before Eadulf brought them back to the reality of their current position. 'There is a stream passing not far away. I feel I should go and clean the touch and odours of the dead from my body even though the winter temperature is not conducive to bathing.'

'Very well,' acknowledged Fidelma, glancing up at the sky. It was now heavy with grey winter clouds, edged in white. 'I would say it is well past the sun's zenith, if we could ever see the sun. We should also be thinking of a meal, but in a more conducive atmosphere.'

'I could agree to that,' Enda smiled. 'But I suggest that we bathe first, as friend Eadulf suggests.'

Eadulf looked slightly pale. 'I can't see how one can contemplate eating a meal after . . . after that.'

Fidelma laid a hand on his arm in sympathy. 'Yet it is no use making ourselves ill because of it. We have seen much death, you and I, Eadulf. This is just more evil, but we have to be strong enough to overcome it. We owe it to those people who lie here to find out why they met their end in this manner. To do this, we must maintain our strength.'

Eadulf knew that she was right.

'We might find a place on the other side of the stream, towards the valley entrance, where there are more trees and undergrowth. Along there where I saw the entrances to those caves.' Enda pointed. 'That would be a good place to bathe, rest and discuss what next we should do.'

They left the putrid smells of the former abbey stockade and followed Enda to the spot he had indicated. It did not take long to reach a suitable spot, by a small protective entrance to one of the limestones caves on a stone-covered knoll overlooking the stream. Fidelma suggested that she take the horses to water and feed them while the men had a bathe in the stream. Then she would bathe while Enda went in search of some food.

While Eadulf and Enda went off to the stream, Fidelma also found reasonably dry wood, to use as kindling with dry grasses. She dug a small pit in the soil with the blade of her knife. In it, she was able to kindle a good fire. Neither Eadulf nor Enda prolonged their immersion in the stream because it was icy cold, and while Eadulf understood the importance of washing after his search of the bodies, it was far too chilly to take a long time over it. He had even found a piece of *sléic*, soap, in his *firbolg* and, with it, he thoroughly scrubbed his hands and arms where he had picked up pieces of the bodies to examine them. Now he felt better, although he was still made uncomfortable and almost nauseous by the memories.

Eadulf went to help Fidelma while Enda went off to hunt. They collected water from where it cascaded down the rocky hillside before feeding the stream below. Soon Enda rejoined them, with a woebegone expression. He carried a sack.

Eadulf tried to regain his usual humorous attitude.

'That's a small sack, friend,' he said with forced joviality. 'Do I presume that you have brought no deer for our meal? Not even a well-fatted hind? Even the fawn of the fallow deer should have been an easy task for a hunter with your reputation.'

Enda screwed up his face in mock anger. 'Let us see how well you could hunt in these woods bereft of deer. Why, even the wolves huddled together for warmth and are clearly starving. I thought I might relent my prejudice against them and invite them to join our fire.'

'So what have you got for the fire?' Fidelma asked, interrupting their banter.

'Just a couple of *gráineóg*,' Enda said, dropping his sack.

Eadulf sniffed in disgust. 'Hedgehog? How do you expect us to eat those creatures with all their yellow-tipped spines? Anyway, I thought they hibernated in the winter.' He was secretly pleased, for he certainly had no appetite to eat anything substantial, in spite of Fidelma's admonition.

'Do you say that you don't know how to roast hedgehog?' Enda scoffed.

Actually, that part was true. Eadulf had never prepared and cooked the meat but had only eaten it when it had been prepared by others.

'I leave such things to mighty hunters such as yourself,' he replied solemnly.

'Eadulf does have a point,' Fidelma remarked. 'The creatures do hibernate during this period. So how did you find them?'

'Finding not even a hare or rabbit in the vicinity, I was looking for some birds' eggs in case there was nothing else. I did find some wild garlic, and *lus bhríd*, dandelions. I was passing a small cave behind some bushes where there might be birds' nests. I glanced in and saw that some hedgehogs had made their burrow there for the winter days. So I . . .'

Fidelma raised a hand. 'I don't want to know how you despatched the creatures. So let's get to the other question that Eadulf raised: how are you going to cook them – because I have no experience of doing so.'

Enda shook his head at them. 'It is a sad day when people cannot cook a simple meal. Very well. I will teach you how to prepare baked hedgehog. Can you make that fire base deeper into the soil and get it really hot with more wood? Do we have a pan to boil the *lus cainnen* in and *meacon*? It is better if they are boiled.'

'Where are you expecting to get those from?' demanded Eadulf in astonishment, for these were onions and parsnip.

Enda chuckled and produced them from his bag, along with the wild garlic and dandelions.

'I found them near where the hedgehogs were. I suspect that the old religious community there,' he nodded back along the valley towards the deserted abbey, 'once kept a herb garden and these plants escaped after it was deserted and started to seed themselves. They were growing wild.'

Fidelma meanwhile had begun expanding the little pit she had made the fire in and was adding more wood to get it really hot.

Enda left the vegetables and herbs with her and then took his bag down to the bank of the stream. Eadulf watched him closely and was surprised to see him place the carcasses in the mud and proceed to spread a thick covering all over the spiky coats. Enda brought the mud-encased carcasses back to the fire, which he examined approvingly. He put the creatures into the base of the fire, spreading the glowing embers all over them and piling more wood on top so that they were fully covered by the hot ashes.

'It will take a little while but soon we will have good meat,' he remarked with satisfaction.

'But you have not removed the spikes or the skin,' Eadulf protested. 'All you have done is enclose them in mud.'

'When the mud bakes, it will harden, and then we can break it open in such a way that it will tear off the spikes and coat, revealing the meat underneath,' the warrior explained, almost condescendingly. 'Then you can eat it. Unfortunately, this method precludes seasoning the meat, but if Lady Fidelma will prepare the vegetables and season them with the wild garlic, they will give an added flavour. You can heat the tin of water on top of the fire.'

Eadulf shook his head. 'Where did you learn such methods?' he asked curiously.

The young warrior chuckled. 'Easy to explain, friend Eadulf. You learn this means of cooking while out on campaign, when there is often no time to get a hare or rabbit, let alone shoot a deer. Many a battle has been won on the cooked carcass of a mole, badger or even a vole. More often than not, a battle is won on such small carcasses as the hedgehog.'

Fidelma screwed up her nose with an expression of distaste. 'Probably many a battle has been lost for the same reasons,' she said. Cooking was not one of her accomplishments and, while she enjoyed food, she certainly did not admit to any interest in the fine art of preparing it.

The cooking took a while but eventually Enda portioned out the meal onto broad leaves that he gathered from nearby plants. It was true what he had said, for when he broke open the mud, which ripped away the spikes and skin, there was succulent white meat underneath. It was not as white as chicken but nowhere as dark as rabbit or other such creatures.

Eadulf found it quite sweet and certainly very edible. Once the vegetables and herbs were added, he found himself thinking that no dish had ever tasted as tender and luscious. The warrior showed his companions that by crushing the edible flakes of meat into manageable pieces and mixing them with the blanched wild garlic the flavour was enormously enhanced. Fidelma seemed to relent her concerns about the crude meal and even voiced her appreciation of Enda's cooking.

After they had eaten, Eadulf collected some ice-cold water from the small waterfall that fed the stream for them to drink. An uneasy silence fell between them. It seemed that each of them was occupied by their own thoughts. Certainly, Fidelma was trying to understand the mystery. She felt relieved that she had cast aside any guilt about breaking the *geis* that had bound her at the outset. She felt that Cenn Fáelad would have absolved her oath, if he knew the difficulties she would encounter. But try as she might she could find no logical path to follow. What disturbed her most was the curious connection with Aescwine the Saxon. Was it by chance that his ship lurked in the coastal waters here and that he seemed to be in pursuit of Grella? Yet anything else seemed too ridiculous to contemplate.

There were so many questions. Why had Antrí's men been slaughtered at Cluain? Who by? Glaisne? But Antrí was surely Glaisne's man? Why had Grella been kidnapped, when the conspiracy was against her husband? He was in Tara and surely well guarded. Why had the attack on his wife happened in the territory of her family? And what was the role of her companion, Cairenn? Was there really a plot being organised by a member of the Eóganacht? That was truly unimaginable.

'We are going to have to find Grella and Cairenn,' she announced. She had meant to say it to herself as her thoughts resolved into the only conclusion for action, but it came out aloud without her realising it. Her companions glanced quickly at her.

'We thought that was exactly what we were doing,' Eadulf pointed out with a frown. 'The problem is . . . how are we going to find them?'

She looked at him blankly for a moment before she realised that she had spoken aloud and he was answering.

'How are we going to achieve it?' she echoed. After a moment's thought she said firmly: 'Grella was last seen riding in this direction from Eochaill with this cousin, Glaisne. If we find him, then we shall find her.'

'What we need,' Eadulf suggested, 'is someone who knows this territory.'

'Áed said that Glaisne had a brother who had a community somewhere near here,' she said.

'We should have kept a more careful watch on that bow-maker,' Enda sighed.

'That does not help resolve the question now,' Fidelma replied. 'When you looked at the tracks in the abbey complex, how clear were they?'

'Fairly clear so far as the muddy ground allowed,' Enda replied. 'We followed them to the stream here.'

'Could we follow them further?'

'I am not sure how far we could, but it is worth trying. But they are old and we do not know if they were made before or after Grella was in Eochaill.'

Fidelma stood up abruptly. 'Then we will follow and see if they initially went there. Wherever they went, we will have to follow and try to pick up a newer trail from there. With these winter days so short, we should not delay. Let us see how far we can get.'

From the entrance to the grim valley, the woods grew thicker but the track followed the winding stream. Enda began to lead them eastwards through the valley. The track was hardly more than a *tuagróta*, a farm track, fairly narrow and muddy because it was not maintained, and Eadulf wondered how Grella's ornate coach had managed to negotiate it in the first place. He called to Fidelma, riding just ahead and behind Enda.

'Have you noticed how small this track is?'

Fidelma had already realised the point he was going to make and could not help disappointing him.

'You think it is strange that Grella's coach could have come along it? The way is too difficult.'

'More than that,' he replied. 'If that girl, Cairenn, told you correctly, then she as well as Grella must have had knowledge of the existence of this route.'

'How so?' Fidelma asked.

'You said that she told you that they came to the mouth of this valley, that Grella asked her to go on to Finnbarr's Abbey to hear what Abbot Nessán had to say and then return to meet her here. They had brought a spare horse with them and so Cairenn took it and rode off, leaving Grella to go to the abbey to meet her relative – Antrí. So Grella knew the existence of this obscure trackway, as did Cairenn. How would that be? They had not been in this territory for some years, living in Tara. I also thought it odd that she also knew about that village, Baile an Stratha, as a place to meet.'

'A good thought,' Fidelma agreed. 'However, there could be an explanation. People do retain memories from younger days. It is conceivable that she even visited this place before she left for Tara.'

'Anything is conceivable, I suppose,' muttered Eadulf, somewhat hurt that his speculations had been so easily explained away.

'The point that I think needs explanation,' Fidelma was continuing, 'is why the wife of the High King came to this remote corner at all. Of all the places she could have chosen, why here? If she meant to question Nessán at Finnbarr's Abbey, why remain here? Why not stay closer to Nessán's abbey?'

They were suddenly aware that Enda had halted his horse and was searching the ground around him. He turned with a disappointed expression on his features.

'The trail ends here, lady,' he called. 'They must have taken themselves into the stream.'

'Not crossed it?' Fidelma asked.

'There is no sign they left it. So they probably used it to disguise their tracks. The riding is easy on the bank, so it was not for easy progress. We might follow the stream, because they would have to eventually emerge from it somewhere along its route.'

'Why would they feel the necessity to disguise their tracks?' asked Eadulf. 'Who would be pursuing them? They would certainly not expect anyone like us to follow them.'

Enda turned and began guiding his horse into midstream. The waters were shallow and came only above the horses' fetlocks. However, any indentations in the soft muddy bottom would have been washed away by the flow of the waters and there was no hope of tracking previous movement.

They moved slowly on, eyes moving from side to side to try to spot any place where the riders had felt it safe to emerge.

Suddenly Enda halted and pointed wordlessly. Just ahead, on the northern side of the stream, was a shallow, muddy bank. Hoofmarks could clearly be seen emerging from the water. Some of them had barely dried, showing a recent passage.

'Why leave the stream here?' questioned Eadulf, looking around. 'There is nowhere to go except to those caves. That cliff-like hill blocks any path in that direction and the close-growing trees and bushes form a horseshoe which would prevent movement either side. To move from here, you would have to go back into the stream.'

It was true that beyond the scrub and denuded willows the hill rose very steeply, and some way up they could see several cave entrances. But there seemed to be no tracks going in that direction. It was too steep.

'But as you can see for yourself, friend Eadulf,' replied Enda quietly, 'the tracks of the animal leave here.'

'You speak in the singular?' Fidelma picked on the syntax.

'Because only one animal left the stream at this point. Look at the tracks.' Enda was suddenly still and lowered his voice. 'I think we are being observed, lady. There is movement in those trees along there.'

They sat still on their horses, peering cautiously forward into the undergrowth and the shadows of the copse of willows. There was, indeed, movement and now they could hear the snap of dead branches breaking. Obviously, their observer was not unduly concerned about hiding his presence.

With some suddenness, the 'observer' appeared from the bushes and stood on the bank of the stream, looking at them with mournful eyes.

'It's an ass!' Enda cried, letting out a loud laugh.

It was then they noticed that the grey-coated ass was saddled. At once Enda had drawn his sword and was peering round warily. But there was nothing but winter silence in the woods around them. He moved his horse forward to the bank, keeping watchful eyes on the undergrowth. Nothing stirred. He glanced back at Fidelma and Eadulf with a motion of his hand, indicating they should remain silent and be vigilant. Then he swung off his horse and went to the patiently waiting ass. He stroked its muzzle with one hand, whispering softly to it in order to reassure it. Then he made a quick examination of it. He must have seen something, for Fidelma and Eadulf saw him lean forward and place his hand on the saddle, then look at his hand. They heard him stifle an exclamation.

He turned back to them. 'I think the rider must be injured or dead,' he said quietly. 'There is blood on the saddle.'

CHAPTER SIXTEEN

They all dismounted and crowded around the patient ass to examine the bloodstains. There seemed nothing on the beast to give a clue as to whom its rider had been. The blood on the saddle was fairly fresh.

'That means the rider can't have gone far,' Eadulf pointed out. 'There must be signs nearby.'

Fidelma agreed to make a search of the undergrowth. The search did not take them very long. They found a body almost immediately, barely hidden in the undergrowth. They recognised him at once, though his clothes were dishevelled, torn and dirty as well as blood stained.

'It's the bow-maker,' Enda said, with a long sigh.

There was no need to ask how the man had met his end. The crossbow bolt was still embedded in his chest, the blood saturating the clothing around it. There was also a heavy welt that had broken the skin and caused some bleeding across the forehead.

They stared at the body of Áed Caille for a while in silence.

It was Enda who noticed that there was something clutched in the dead man's hand. It was a piece of torn cloth, and something else. Eadulf bent down and began to ease it out of Áed's grasp.

'He has not long been dead,' he observed. 'The hands have not stiffened in death and the blood is not entirely dried.'

He removed the item and held it up. 'It looks like a piece of gold.'

Fidelma shook her head. 'It's a seal . . . a gold seal,' she said.

Eadulf frowned. 'How do you know? You have barely looked at it.'

For an answer, Fidelma reached in her comb bag and brought out the seal she had taken from their would-be assassin, with the replica of a woman holding a solar wheel on her right shoulder. She held them both for her companions' inspection.

Enda sighed. 'What does it mean? Is it a cult of some sort?'

Fidelma stared at him for a moment and then her features broke into a smile.

'A symbol of a group – yes. I believe that you may well have hit upon it. It is something to do with this matter. The seals are usually carried by couriers as identification. But identification of what? We were not ambushed by those two men at Dubh Glas abbey by mistake. I think Áed was similarly targeted.'

'But why?'

'Let us consider the "how" first. He was obviously shot while seated on his ass, probably just as he emerged from the stream. He fell and probably crawled to the cover of those bushes before he died. Look!'

She moved forward and picked up a second bolt, almost hidden by the foliage.

'The killer must have tried to make sure by releasing a second bolt from his crossbow but missed. Then the killer or an accomplice came forward to check whether Áed was dead. He bent down and Áed, even dying, managed to grasp the man. He tore away that piece of cloth, perhaps part of a *firbolg* or purse, and with it came the seal. Then Áed was struck across the forehead and was probably dead moments later.'

Enda was staring at the corpse thoughtfully. 'Who would have killed the bow-maker and left the gold seal behind?'

'The killer probably did not realise the seal had come away with the torn cloth. We'd better have another look around.'

'You mean the killer might still be nearby?' Eadulf asked.

'And if he is not, we might find the spot where he fired from and see if we can pick up any tracks.'

'We must be on our guard,' Enda reminded them, glancing around. 'The hill protects us like a horse shoe. So the shot could only have come from across the stream.'

Eadulf looked down at the corpse. He suddenly shook his head, glancing up at the cliff. 'You are wrong. If Áed was emerging from the stream, he would be facing forward. The bolt hit him in the chest so it had to have been fired from the hill above us. See the way the bolt protrudes at an angle? It was not fired from a point below or level. Remember, Áed was sitting on the ass. We need to look for a point above.'

Fidelma stared up at the hill that rose from the trees and undergrowth. It was fairly bare terrain with only two black holes, like expressionless eyes, indicating caves in the hillside.

'The caves are high enough. But horses could not reach them. So whoever killed the bow-maker would have had to climb up there.'

'If so, lady, we are easy targets,' Enda said nervously.

'If the killer was there and wanted to kill us, he would have done so before now,' Fidelma pointed out. 'If he is there, I don't think he has identified us as his enemy.'

'What next then, lady?' asked Enda. 'Do we go on as before, go on following the stream? I would advise that we should not stop here to bury Áed's corpse. If we stay longer, we will have to spend the night here.'

Fidelma was hesitant, and continued to gaze at the caves above.

'We will go on,' she decided. 'I think the killer has already departed. If he has not, then he means us no immediate harm. We will go. Our first duty is press on and find out what happened to Grella . . . remember, the High King's life depends on our resolution.'

'Not to mention the life of the girl, Cairenn,' Eadulf added. 'She was honest with us, at least. She said that she would take the horses to Baile an Stratha and she did so; the horses were there with all our bags, and not even a gold piece was missing. And she waited for us as she said she would, until she was herself abducted.'

Fidelma's expression was sombre. 'I had not forgotten, Eadulf.'

They decided to leave the corpse of Áed as they had found it and remounted. But Eadulf took the reins of the ass and secured them to his saddle before they moved off once more along the route of the stream. This time Enda was more alert, his eyes seeking out any possible place for an ambush. They were not sure how far they had travelled before they noticed that the light was diminishing fast and the heavy grey winter clouds were thickening.

'I suppose we should think about stopping soon and finding shelter.' Fidelma sounded reluctant but it was no use going on until dark when they did not know the countryside.

'We're coming to a clearing ahead,' Enda replied. 'There seems to be a flat stony patch next to the stream, and some sort of rocky overhang; maybe it's a cave. That would be ideal, or do you want to try to continue further before nightfall?'

Fidelma considered only for a moment before replying. 'We'd better take this opportunity; we might never find another suitable place.'

They emerged from the stream onto a flat stony shore. It was remarkably similar to the previous place they had stopped as the hills followed a similar pattern along the path of the stream. This little inlet, too, was backed by a rocky rise with woodland on either side. It seemed quite sheltered and certainly out of the way of the winds. They had not yet dismounted when Enda raised a forefinger to his lips, indicating they should be silent. Then he was taking up his longbow with a slow cautiousness; he drew an arrow and strung it. They did not see what had caused his alarm, but he was not taking cover or making any sudden movements. He was aiming towards the stream and suddenly, with a hum, he loosed his arrow. Almost before it had left the bow he had sprung from his horse and was running, as if after its flight, with a drawn sword.

They turned to look after him, ready for any defensive action.

There was a strange cry and they saw Enda's sword come up and swing down. They saw something long and brown thrashing in the water. Blood was spurting everywhere. They watched, mesmerised, as Enda slashed down with his weapon. The animal was some ninety centimetres in length with a tail almost as long. Its brown fur was contrasted by a white bib running from under the jaw to its chest. Enda turned triumphantly to them, holding the carcass by the fur of its neck.

'This will last us a few days, at least,' he said with satisfaction. 'The meat of the *doburchú* is regarded as a great delicacy,' he added – Eadulf was staring at the dead furry creature with an expression somewhere between distaste and sorrow.

Eadulf searched his memory for a translation of the term. He knew the name meant 'water hound' but what was the equivalent in his language? 'You've killed an otter?' he finally said, recognising the water mammal by the shape of its body and its webbed feet rather than the name.

Enda regarded his quarry with contentment. 'That's a fine pelt. The skin is highly prized, equal to that of the deer and fox.'

'Are you sure it is edible?' Eadulf demanded, not having eaten otter before, to his memory.

'Of course,' Fidelma confirmed. 'As Enda said, it is regarded as a great dish among our people.'

'Indeed, lady,' Enda agreed. 'I claim its liver.'

Fidelma, seeing Eadulf's surprise, explained. 'Hunters often claim the liver as a prize. I would have thought with your knowledge of the healing arts that you would have heard of the curative properties of an otter's liver. It helps heal burns and scalds and other hurts.'

Seeing that Eadulf was unconvinced, she pursed her lips reprovingly.

'You will not last long in the country unless you are prepared to eat the food that the country provides you with.'

'I understood otters were sacred creatures and regarded as such in terms of religious symbolism?' Eadulf replied as he dismounted from his cob and led it with the ass to tether them to a nearby tree.

'Not exactly,' Fidelma corrected him. 'The storytellers have it that the mother of the king and warrior Lugaid mac Con Roí, who killed the great champion Cúchullain, was impregnated by an otter. And, of course, Cuirithir, the lover of Liadain, was also known as Dobharachon, the son of the otter. To our ancients, being born from an otter's seed was something special.'

Fidelma had also dismounted and was looking around the area. It was certainly suitable for a night's encampment.

'Will you collect some wood, Eadulf? I'll see to the horses' feed and Enda can light the fire. He is better at working up a blaze with flint and tinder than I am, and I admit that he is also better at skinning and preparing meat than I am.'

Enda smiled. 'That is all right, lady. Leave such tasks to the experienced.'

The fire started to snap and crackle as the flames engulfed the dry wood. Enda stood back and admired his handiwork. Most warriors, during their training, were instructed on how to make a fire quickly. Each carried in their *firbolg*, or man-bag, flint, steel and kindle, the means to start what was known as 'hand-fire'. Warriors would pride themselves on how quickly they could produce a fire when out on campaign, or a *slúagad* or 'hosting', as it was called. He had already skinned the otter with a deftness that impressed Eadulf. He placed the skin to dry and jointed the carcass, cutting it into manageable pieces, and removed the stomach as well as the offal, which he put to one side, separating the liver and kidneys. He selected some branches of willow and cut three pieces of suitable length, and made the ends pointed in preparation for cooking.

The sky was darkening now but, thankfully, the fire produced a good enough light and some warmth. As one who had travelled much, Fidelma always carried in her baggage at least two candles. Called *innlis*, the poorer sort were made with wicks of peeled rushes that had been dipped in meat grease, usually the natural fat of cattle or sheep. In more noble households, bees' wax was used. Fidelma set these aside – she did not light them as the fire provided enough light.

They were sitting down waiting impatiently for the meat to roast when a sound came to their ears, from the cave behind them. It was a strange groan, like someone in pain. They froze. Fidelma quietly rebuked herself. Before doing anything else she should have explored the area carefully, especially the cave, which she had assumed was deserted.

'Enda,' she whispered, 'can you move slowly away from the light of the fire and reach your bow? Eadulf, you stay in front of the fire but be ready to move when I say so.'

Eadulf said nothing and the warrior replied by rising slowly and moving to one side. They heard nothing until he whispered from the shadows close by: 'Ready, lady.'

Fidelma came to her feet languidly, reached forward to where she had placed the *innlis* and lit one. Then she turned and moved leisurely to one side – the opposite side to where she knew Enda was. She balanced the candle on a low branch. Eadulf realised she was using it as a distraction because she then moved into the cover of the trees, leaving the candle burning there. He knew she was heading for the cave entrance from the left side while he was sure Enda was moving up to the right side. Eadulf knew his task was to stay seated in the light of the fire in case whoever – or whatever – was in the cave was watching.

A moment later he heard Fidelma give a shout to surprise the inhabitant of the cave and the sounds of Enda and Fidelma springing into the entrance to overcome their quarry. Eadulf swiftly moved to one side out of the light of the fire and stared up. There followed a short silence, then Eadulf heard a pitiful groan.

Fidelma's voice called down. 'Eadulf, bring the *innlis*!'

He need no second bidding but grabbed the candle from where she had left it burning on the branch and hurried towards the shallow cave entrance.

Its light revealed his companions bending over what appeared to be the body of a man. Then he realised the man was alive and groaning in pain.

'Bring the candle nearer,' instructed Fidelma.

Eadulf moved forward. He was surprised to see the man was young and wore a golden circlet around his neck. His clothing, such as Eadulf could see, was of good quality, though it was ripped and dirty. Blood stained his shirt, which could be clearly seen because the leather jerkin that had covered it was almost in ribbons, as if it had been slashed with a blade. The face, handsome and clean shaven, was deathly pale and, even in the flickering candle light, Eadulf saw it was covered in an unhealthy sweat. The lips were flecked with blood and the eyes were closed. A groan now and then escaped the throat, like an inarticulate exhalation of breath.

'Who is he?' asked Enda, having put aside his bow and quiver. 'Is he the person who killed Áed?'

'There's no sign of a crossbow,' Fidelma pointed out. 'And it seems unlikely that, in this condition, he could have shot Áed from a height in the other inlet and then, abandoning his crossbow, climbed down, made his way here and climbed up to this cave. No, I do not think this is the killer of the bow-maker.'

'Maybe he is someone from the abbey, who escaped the slaughter?' Eadulf suggested. 'He could have crawled here to hide. He was probably unconscious and we would not have known of him until he groaned aloud in pain.'

'You had better examine him, Eadulf. But I think it may be too late,' Fidelma said sadly. 'He looks like a young noble.'

Enda moved aside so that Eadulf could take his place by the wounded man.

'I'll bring some water,' he said as he left the cave.

The candle was placed on a rocky shelf nearby and the next thing Eadulf noticed by its light was dark bloodstains around the man's shoulder. He tried to ease the man over on his side to examine the source of the wound. Then he saw the telltale part of a broken wooden bolt embedded under the left shoulder blade. It did not take him long to examine the man so far as his knowledge allowed. He glanced up at Fidelma and shook his head.

'Another victim of a crossbow bolt,' he told her reluctantly. 'The bolt did not kill him so he was also struck by swords. He has lost too much blood and the wounds are infected. I don't think there is much I can do.'

Enda returned bearing an *uter*, a leather water bag, which he had freshly filled from the stream.

'Shall I fetch your *les*, friend Eadulf?' he asked, referring to the little medical bag that Eadulf always carried with him.

Eadulf took the water bag and shook his head. 'It will not be necessary,' he said flatly. They both understood his meaning.

After Enda had left, Fidelma glanced at Eadulf, who was busy bathing the man's face and lips with the cold water.

'How long?' she asked.

Eadulf hunched one shoulder and let it fall. 'Not long.'

'Can you extract that bolt from his shoulder?'

'If I did, we would not have to wait at all.' He paused. 'At the moment it is acting like a plug to the flow of blood. Even so, not long.'

The cold water seemed to be having some effect on the man for suddenly he opened his eyes wide and groaned. The dark eyes were wide and staring. Fidelma and Eadulf were not sure if the man was seeing anything. He convulsed for a moment and tried to twist away from them.

'Keep calm, keep calm,' Fidelma urged softly. 'You are among friends. No one is going to hurt you.'

The man fell back and Eadulf trickled water over his dry lips and he lapped almost eagerly at the drops. The eyes closed again.

'Can you speak?' Fidelma asked. 'Can you tell us who you are?'

The mouth began to work and Eadulf let a few more drops of water onto the lips and dry tongue.

'Escaped,' came the groaning word. 'Tried to kill . . . killed others.'

'What is your name?'

There was a long pause. Then the young man seemed to gather his strength.

'Loingsech of the Fianna. I was . . . was bodyguard to the lady Grella . . .'

Fidelma let out a gasp of surprise and moved closer to him. 'Can you tell us what happened?' she demanded, perhaps a little too curtly.

'Plan for refuge . . . refuge at Cluain. Plan betrayed.' He paused and tried to swallow. Eadulf reached forward and moistened his lips again. The young man went on. 'Lady's cousin not there . . . strange men tried to kill me . . . think they killed others and took Lady Grella . . . I escaped into woods. Hid for several days. They found me but escaped . . . wounded me badly . . . but I killed them.'

'Who were they? Glaisne's men?'

'No . . . Glaisne . . . Fínsnechta's man. Antrí his man.'

Fidelma leant even more closely forward. 'Fínsnechta?'

The young man was trying to summon his last strength.

'They supposed to be safe in . . . in . . . Cause war with Eóganacht. Cenn Fáelad would lose . . . Fínsnechta's plan.'

'What plan?' she urged, trying to race against time with death.

'Grella's lover . . . whole thing betrayed . . . too late . . .'

The dying warrior was fading in and out of consciousness now.

'Did Glaisne abduct her?' pressed Fidelma. 'Who betrayed Grella?'

The eyes opened for a moment but they were unfocused. There was a long exhalation of breath, a harsh rattling sound. Eadulf had heard that sound before. He knew what it portended.

Fidelma was staring at the man, trying to make sense of what she had heard. She shook him roughly, as if trying to bring him back to consciousness. Eadulf reached forward and placed his hand on her wrist. 'He's dead, Fidelma,' he said softly.

They left the young man in the cave and, taking the candle, went back to join Enda, by the fire. They no longer seemed to have an appetite. They sat before the fire silently.

It was a long while before Eadulf finally broke the silence.

'I am not sure I understand anything now. Who is Fínsnechta?'

Fidelma was looking moodily into the flames. 'I think he is the key. Fínsnechta, son of Dúnchad,' she replied in a heavy tone. 'He is first cousin to Cenn Fáelad. If my guess is correct, he is the tall religious who was at Finnbarr's Abbey and the person I saw on Aescwine's boat.'

'So he was involved in the kidnapping of his cousin's wife?' Eadulf asked in astonishment.

Fidelma shook her head. 'I can't say for sure. There are little clues floating through the mists, each cloud bearing information. But like a mist, each one seems substantial at first but when you try to make it fit, it dissolves.'

Eadulf leant forward 'If Fínsnechta was involved in the plot to overthrow his cousin, then perhaps he would have also arranged to get his wife, Grella, kidnapped. Maybe he paid Aescwine to abduct her?'

'A possibility,' conceded Fidelma. 'But I am not convinced.'

Eadulf thought for a moment and then said: 'Fínsnechta would have had the opportunity to meet Aescwine to arrange the matter at Tara. But there seems no logic in it.'

'Perhaps it is a prelude to an invasion of the Five Kingdoms by the Saxons?' Enda suddenly suggested.

Eadulf sat back and stared at Enda in surprise.

'But that would make no sense, unless we are dealing with two different stories. What benefits accrue to the Saxons if the High King here is overthrown? I can't see any,' he confessed with an apologetic look at Enda. 'It was a good theory,' he added to the now irritated warrior, 'but I can't see why the Saxons would raid or try to conquer any part of Ireland.'

'Why not?'

'Because the Five Kingdoms have long been a sanctuary to Britons fleeing the conquests of the Saxons – and even Angles and Saxons fleeing from their ambitious relatives. Remember that the person who is a refugee today is a king in their own country tomorrow.'

'But Enda does make a good point in reminding us again of Aescwine's presence in this particular territory. Perhaps we should consider why it would not have been easier to abduct Grella at Tara or along the eastern coast rather than here,' Fidelma said.

'What if the overthrow of the High King might provide the Saxons with an opportunity to invade?' Enda persisted. 'What if Aescwine was merely scouting to gather information?'

'Information about what?' demanded Eadulf.

'About our weaknesses,' Enda suggested. 'Information necessary to take over the country.'

Eadulf chuckled cynically. 'You know well that there is a strong cohesion among your people. There may be five kingdoms, but they have a High King to whom the provincial kings make acknowledgment and pay tribute. The High King has his Fianna, his army, and each provincial king has his own army. There is a single law system which governs all five kingdoms, and the language, while it has its dialects, still has an almost universal form so that no part of the land is totally separate. This country is unified compared to the eleven separate kingdoms of the Angles and the Saxons. Each of these kingdoms makes alliances against others, each one tries to claim the magical title of the Bretwalda: the ruler of the Britons.

Of course, this is rejected by the Britons who are strong enough to still defend those kingdoms that remain to them. It is still not clear whether the Britons could rise up and drive the Angles and Saxons back into the sea whence they came – remember it was only two centuries ago that they arrived in Britain.'

Fidelma was smiling. 'You might have made my point for me, Eadulf. You say this island of the Five Kingdoms is strong enough to face any invasion from the Saxons?'

'I believe it is.'

'Then think of your own history. When the Romans left Britain and the native British princes rose again and a central prince was given the title Vortigern, the Overlord, who would have thought that his mistake was inviting your ancestors to help him fight off the raids of the Pictii?' mused Fidelma. 'That mistake resulted in Angles, Saxons and Jutes arriving in Britain and, within these last two centuries, taking control of nearly half of the island.'

'That's a good point, lady,' murmured Enda.

Eadulf shook his head. 'But that's different,' he began, then found himself struggling to explain why it was so. 'I don't think there is such cohesion among the Angles and Saxons that they would ever want to invade the Five Kingdoms. Why, many of our people, nobles and commoners, have come to this land for the sake of religious studies or to live a more ascetic life in the New Faith. Your people have welcomed them without fear of bad intentions. Conversely, you have sent missionaries to my people, teaching them not only religion but other learning and literacy. Even I was converted and taught by the Irish teachers of the East Angles – teachers like Fursa and his brothers. Look at the marriages among your people and mine . . . just like our own marriage, Fidelma. Isn't there a son of Oswiu and the Uí Néill princess Fín living among the Northern Uí Néill, content just to write poems and sagas?'

'Flann Fín, the poet?' Fidelma nodded in confirmation. 'Yes, I have heard of him.'

'His given name is Alfrith and he is Oswiu's son,' added Eadulf. 'And who knows? Under the laws of our people, he may one day go back to become King of Northumbria.'

'You make a very passionate argument that we should not fear the Angles and Saxons,' remarked Enda wryly. 'I note, with respect, that you do not make it entirely on the basis that your people do not wish to invade our island as they did the island of Britain. You make it on the basis that they do not feel strongly enough.'

'Maybe it is the same thing,' Eadulf grunted in annoyance.

Fidelma decided to intervene. 'Tell us more about this man Aescwine, Eadulf. Tell me of his people.'

'The Gewisse? Well, they are a strong frontier people. They recently rose to dominate the tribes who were the West Saxons and incorporate them into a strong single territory. For most of the last century or so, they have driven the Britons westward. For a while the Britons held a strong kingdom that they called Dumnonia. As I told you, it is now almost vanished under Gewisse rule.'

'You are describing the very people we should be wary of, friend Eadulf,' Enda remarked.

'Well, they are a proud people,' Eadulf conceded. 'They make much of the claim that they have a kingship lineage from Baldaeg, son of Woden. The story is that their first king was Cerdic, who came to our country with his son Cynric in five great warships and defeated the Britons in the eastern part of their kingdom of Dumnonia.'

'And so Aescwine is their prince?' asked Enda.

'Aescwine is one of many princes who will want to take advantage of the scramble for leadership when Cenwealh dies,' Eadulf replied.

'He would get great prestige and status if he returned with the wife of our High King as a hostage, or even wife, for it would show the High King as weak. That would make a people like the Gewisse turn thoughtful eyes on this land of ours,' Enda remarked.

'This is true,' Fidelma admitted. 'But I still can't see how it fits in the conspiracy to overthrow Cenn Fáelad and the story that my family are involved.'

Eadulf glanced up at the sky, catching a glimpse of the moon behind the low racing clouds.

'Well, tomorrow will be the full of the moon and time is pressing on. We must find Grella and return her to the High King.'

Fidelma rose, glanced at the small fire and shrugged. 'There is little more we can extract from the information we have. I think we should make ourselves as warm and as comfortable as we can and try to refresh ourselves with some sleep. Tomorrow, I see no alternative but to carry on eastward towards Eochaill and continue our search.'

Chapter Seventeen

Fidelma and her companions were relieved to break camp early the next morning and leave the pathetic remains of the dead warrior in the cave. There was no alternative, as with the body of Áed, for they had neither tools nor time to bury the bodies. Fidelma hoped that they would eventually encounter some isolated community with perhaps a local Brehon or religious to whom they could report the bodies. She tried not to think about the alternative: that even in the cold winter, or maybe especially in such conditions, the bodies might not last long, for there would be wolves or ravens or other scavengers who might discover the remains and take back into nature what had come forth from nature. She shivered at the thought and hoped the others had not observed this expression of her feelings.

Once more they rejoined the stream and pushed eastwards. The forests gave way to another valley with brown hills and patches of bare gaunt trees. There were no fresh tracks or signs that those who had left Cluain had left the stream at any point. But there were plenty of stony places along the way and several well-used tracks leading from the stream, and Enda examined them carefully. Finally, he turned with a bitter expression to Fidelma.

'As much as I am loath to admit it, lady,' he said, 'I think we have already lost the trail long since. And the stream is going to become impassable a little way ahead.'

Fidelma saw what he meant – the bed of the stream became a series of beaver dams which would be impossible for horses to cross.

They came to a halt. Enda and Eadulf were looking at her with expectation.

'There must be a route to follow,' she said defensively. 'The question is . . . do we go north or south now that the path east has vanished?'

'South would lead us towards the great sea,' pointed out Enda.

Fidelma pulled a face. 'And within reach of Aescwine.'

The tolling of a bell close by caused them all to start. It was so unexpected and it was very close. Their reactions caused their usually docile mounts to shy a little. The bell continued, a slow, monotonous bass sound. It was not musical at all but harsh and ominous – warning and challenging at the same time.

'There must be an abbey nearby.' Eadulf frowned.

'I have not heard of anything near here worthy of being called an abbey, other than Cluain,' muttered Fidelma, trying to work out where the sound was coming from.

'That is not to say one does not exist.'

The bell ceased suddenly. But Enda pointed. 'In that direction, lady. Let us see what lies there.'

The warrior did not wait for her agreement but set off, picking his way along the narrow path. Fidelma realised that the sound of the bell had certainly come at an opportune time. At least it had given them a decision when they were about to argue over which way to go.

They moved northwards from the stream into wooded hills, soft undulating hummocks with only a few exceeding ninety metres or so. Enda, pausing now and then with his head to one side, led them through narrow passes, not really valleys, more like dingles or vales. But there was no further sound.

'The source should not be far away,' he called.

Indeed, as they skirted the base of the next hill they came to a secluded area, apparently accessible only by the small pass through which they had come, that was surrounded on all sides not only by hills but by numerous broad pedunculated oaks. Their massive crooked branches were bare of growth now but Fidelma could imagine their verdant spreading crowns, replete with green leaves and an abundance of acorns from which, she knew, one could make good bread. It seemed these oaks had taken over most of this little valley.

However, there was a clearing along one side containing a group of wooden *bothán*, or cabins. They could see that it was the oaks that had provided the builders of the cabins with their materials. Instead of being surrounded by a wooden stockade, the cabins were surrounded by another wood, not an unusual practice in these woodland communities. Elders grew thick and firm and had been carefully husbanded, their branches bent to intertwine into more of a hedge than individual trees. The mildness of the midwinter temperatures was shown by the fact many of them were coming into leaf. A distant childhood memory caused Eadulf to shiver: elders were often built round buildings as a rampart against the evil things of the world. Provided one treated the elders well, you were protected, but if you offended the 'Elder Mother', she would appear and take vengeance.

Within this rampart of elders were more than four cabins and between them a stream came cascading down the hillside almost like a waterfall in parts to provide water to whatever community lived there. There was no sign of movement among the huts. But as they halted and stared at the place, a single male voice began to sing. It was a clear tenor and the words were not immediately recognisable – then Fidelma realised they were being sung in Byzantine form, the words in Greek.

'*christos Anesti* . . .
Christ is risen,
From death he has risen
Victorious over death.
By his own death,
He has given life
To those who are in the grave.'

She exchanged a glance of surprise with Eadulf and then she motioned that they should ride forward to the entrance to the group of cabins. The entrance was not gated but simply a large opening in the elder hedge. Well, this was clearly some sort of religious community. She glanced up at the pale sun, which hung weakly in the sky, now and then obscured by white fluffy clouds.

'A curious time to hold a service,' she muttered. 'I fear we must intrude on it.'

She looked at the now-silent hanging bell and pointed to it, glancing at Enda. The warrior took out his sword and smote the bronze object. It moved only slightly, so heavy was it, but the sound it gave was deep and resonant and it had the immediate effect of stopping the singer in mid-sentence. For a long while there was total silence. Then the door of one of the wooden cabins opened and the tall, thickset figure of a man stepped forward. He halted and regarded them quizzically.

He was a curious religious, if religious he was, for he wore the garb of a warrior, and one of some wealth and position. His leather accoutrements were tanned almost black and a polished silver cross hung on a silver chain around his neck. His hands were clasped together in front of him, one over the other. He was tall, but carried himself with a stoop, bending slightly forward from the left shoulder. He wore a large but well-trimmed black beard, which, with his bushy black eyebrows, obscured most of his facial features. His eyes were black and fathomless. He could have been scowling or smiling.

He stood silently examining Fidelma and her companions as they dismounted. Fidelma moved forward to approach him. The dark man raised a hand, palm outwards, in the sign of peace.

'Welcome in the name of the true God. Come in peace and go in peace and remain at peace while you rest here,' he intoned in a his tenor voice.

Enda took her horse as she went to the tall man, raising her hand, too, in the greeting.

'We thank you in the name of the peace, in which we come. I am Fidelma of Cashel. What place is this, for we are travellers in a strange territory and the way is unknown to us?'

The man examined her curiously.

'Then welcome, Fidelma of Cashel, to my little sanctuary of Doirín. I am Éladach.'

Fidelma stared hard at the man. 'You are the brother of Glaisne?'

The man's mouth twisted a little. 'Ah, so you have heard of my dear brother? But, first, who are your companions?'

Fidelma inclined her head slightly in acknowledgement and indicated her companions in turn. 'This is Brother Eadulf, who is my husband, and that is Enda, a champion of the Golden Collar.'

'You say, lady, that you travel in strange territory and yet you know my brother's name and my relationship to him. How is that? Why do you travel through the land of the grey people, the Uí Liatháin?' Suddenly his eyes narrowed. 'Tell your warrior to be careful, for his hand seems uncomfortably near his sword hilt,' the tall man advised without a change of expression, but he raised one hand slightly. As if in answer, the door behind him opened and two young men appeared holding crossbows, cocked and aimed. They were certainly not dressed in the robes of the religious but of fighting men. One was hardly more than a youth. He had little facial hair and his head was covered in lanky corn-coloured curly hair. He looked nervous, his pale blue eyes darting to each of the newcomers. The second man was older, with a shock of red hair and wispy

PETER TREMAYNE

facial hair of similar colour. He seemed more of a fighting man than his companion. His eyes seemed to glint as if with fire – there was no way to be sure about their colour.

'In case you are wondering, warrior of the Golden Collar, glance outside. There are other bowmen beyond – you would not reach the gates of this little sanctuary.' Éladach smiled and indicated his own two companions.

'These are my right-hand men – Petrán,' he pointed to the elder first, 'and Pilib.'

'Your men bear strange names,' Fidelma commented.

'I have long been in the lands of the east and so, when I returned to my own people, I named them from the lands I had lived in. Petrán is "little rock . . . little Petrus", while Pilib's name befits him as a lover of horses. So, with introductions over and your acceptance that it would be unwise to attempt anything foolish while you are my guests, let Pilib take care of your animals and your weapons. Then I shall invite you to accept my hospitality.' He stood aside and motioned to the interior of the hut.

'You are most kind, Éladach,' Fidelma replied with irony.

They followed him into a large room heated by a central fire. Just inside the door was a flat stone slab and Fidelma was taken aback as Éladach suddenly went down on his knees and took up a jug filled with water. He looked up at her expectantly, saying 'Εἰρήνη σε σένα' in Greek. When she looked bewildered, he repeated in Latin: '*Pax tecum.*' Her mind had been distracted by the events of recent times and it took a moment or two for her to recognise the ritual. As she answered, '*Et tibi pax in domum tuam*' – 'and to you and your house, peace' – she kicked off her riding boots and pushed them to one side, stepping barefoot onto the stone while Éladach poured cold water from the jug over her feet. Then she held out her hands and the water was splashed over them and she was handed a square of linen to dry them. The ritual was repeated for Eadulf and Enda.

Éladach indicated seats before the fire, wooden seats on which animal furs had been draped to provide comfort.

'I am afraid we have no strong drinks,' he explained. 'But we have cold goat's milk, cooled in the mountain stream that runs close by, or cold water itself. Here we live frugally and close to nature, which provides for all our wants.'

They were served cold goat's milk by the young man, Pilib, who had abandoned his crossbow and taken up the role of attendant.

'Pilib is my steward,' said Éladach by way of explanation. 'Petrán is in charge of my bodyguard.'

'I thought you were a prince of the Uí Liatháin,' said Fidelma. 'Yet you seem to be a member of the religious and of the Faith of the East, while at the same time you bear arms.'

Éladach chuckled. 'You are correct in all accounts. When I returned to my people, having been converted to the rituals of the Eastern Churches, we decided to maintain our own little hermitage.' He chuckled again. 'Now, with all due respect, we wish we had picked a quieter spot.'

Fidelma shook her head. 'This spot could hardly be more secluded,' she observed.

'I think you are well aware of the conflict here, Fidelma of Cashel. I came here to contemplate life in peace, to observe nature and sing of our faith.'

'I understood that was supposed to be the role of your cousin Antrí?'

'Antrí?' Éladach grimaced sourly. 'It was the work of God to strike him down, and those who followed him.'

'Were you responsible for the deaths at Cluain?' demanded Enda suddenly.

'I am afraid violence is disturbing the peace of my beautiful countryside,' he reflected. 'But you already knew that. You are the Eóganacht *dálaigh* sent to investigate rumours and stories of a plot to overthrow the High King.'

'You know a lot, Éladach,' Fidelma remarked.

The man smiled. 'Violence seems to be a part of the storm of nature itself,' he replied.

'A short distance from here, in a cave by the stream on the other side of that hill, lies the body of someone called Áed, a bow-maker, and downstream beyond is the body of another man named Loingsech. Are you responsible for their deaths?'

Éladach seemed astonished and saddened in quick succession.

'Did they kill each other?' he asked.

'From the circumstances, we think not,' Fidelma replied.

'Áed was one of my men, but who was Loingsech?'

'He was a member of the Fianna, guarding the lady Grella, who arrived to stay with her cousin Antrí, who called himself Abbot of Cluain.'

Éladach grimaced as if she had spoken a dirty word. 'So that is what happened to him. Antrí is dead?'

Fidelma's eyes narrowed. 'Did you kill him?'

Éladach grimaced again. 'He was my cousin and my shame. Anyway, it might be that his death could be ascribed to my brother. Glaisne was the spawn of the devil and Antrí was little better, perhaps worse. Antrí mocked God when he and some of his thugs claimed to be re-establishing a religious community at Cluain; their aim was to abduct Grella as part of a plot to overthrow the High King, Cenn Fáelad.'

'Are you responsible for the destruction at Cluain?' Fidelma was shocked.

'As I have said,' Éladach replied almost in an offhand manner, 'the world is a better place without cousin Antrí. However, I should think it would be my twin brother, Glaisne, who found our cousin had decided to play his own ambitious game. Indeed, my brother was ambitious and not overly fond of his cousins, rather a ruthless person. However, in getting rid of Antrí he did the work of God.'

'As a *dálaigh*, I would take a different view.'

'I am sure that you would. But I deal in realities, not in law texts, no matter how many years ago they were written. Sometimes justice must take precedence over the law.'

'I have observed that your men arm themselves with crossbows?' Enda interjected.

Éladach smiled. 'A good and efficient weapon. My brother, Glaisne, adopted it after acquiring a number from a seafaring acquaintance.'

'Was the seafarer named Aescwine?' Eadulf suddenly asked.

'How perceptive,' agreed Éladach. 'I presume you have had some contact with that Saxon raider? I had seen that deadly weapon in use. It is unusual in these parts, but when I travelled in the east, the warriors there used them much. Are you saying that Áed and the warrior were killed by crossbow bolts?'

Fidelma leant forward. 'Your tone tells me that you are neither surprised nor concerned. I think you should be. I was a prisoner on board Aescwine's ship.'

'You have escaped, so I am concerned about Áed.' Éladach's voice tightened for a moment. 'He was a good man. Tell me how you found him, somewhere near here? I presume he also escaped after being captured by the Saxon at Eochaill.'

'You say he was your man,' Eadulf replied. 'You must know, then, that we escaped together.'

'I didn't know. That is why I am asking you,' replied Éladach sharply, as he turned to examine Eadulf with a keen eye. 'You seem familiar with events in this small corner of the world, Saxon.' He hesitated before the word 'Saxon'.

Fidelma decided to intervene. 'It seems we are playing word games with one another, Éladach,' she said, with a curtness equivalent to his. 'I was captured by this Saxon raider, Aescwine. Eadulf and Enda rescued me from the ship and rescued Áed at the same time. We found shelter at Baile an Stratha, but Áed left us overnight on an ass and rode in this direction. We followed and found him dead, just as we found the warrior from Tara.'

She paused for a moment or two.

'Now I will take a chance and be honest with you. You know who I am. I was charged by Cenn Fáelad to go to the Abbey of Finnbarr as Abbot Nessán was supposed to have discovered a plot by members of my family, the Eóganacht, to assassinate him. Further, I was told that Grella, his wife, had been lured away from Tara by the same information, and told to stay with her relative, who was supposedly Abbot of Cluain, while her companion went to consult with Nessán, who had sent the message. One thing . . . Nessán managed to tell this companion, a girl called Cairenn, that he had sent no such message.'

Éladach was listening intently. Then he said: 'One thing puzzles me. Why would Cenn Fáelad ask you to undertake this matter when you are sister to Colgú of Cashel, and therefore an Eóganacht?'

'You said that you had heard of me, and of Eadulf here. Then you will know that we solved the mystery of the murder of Cenn Fáelad's brother, the High King Sechnussach. My reputation is founded on the law and truth – whatever that truth is.'

Éladach seemed amused. 'You must be aware of the saying *veritas odium parit* . . . truth breeds hatred.'

'As aware as I am of the saying *vincit omnia veritas* . . . truth conquers all things. Now, I know that Grella is a cousin to Antrí, and therefore a cousin to Glaisne, your brother, and yourself.'

'Is there anyone in the Five Kingdoms who does not know she was of the Uí Liatháin?' he asked.

'Do we presume, from what you say, that Antrí entered a plot to abduct his own cousin? That your brother, Glaisne, killed Antrí and his followers, took Grella and involved himself in the plot for his own benefit?'

Eadulf was animated as he followed her questions.

'Glaisne's fortress is at Eochaill,' he said excitedly. 'That's why she was seen by Áed escaping with Glaisne when Aescwine's ship arrived at Eochaill. Of course!'

There was a silence, and then Fidelma shook her head slowly.

'That doesn't make sense.' She gazed thoughtfully at Éladach. 'You have said that Glaisne was in contact with Aescwine and his Saxons before this event. He was the leader in this matter, for I have heard that Antrí was his man and there to carry out his orders.'

Éladach sat silently smiling at her, watching her trying to piece things together.

'So this is it – Antrí tried to deceive Glaisne, who took his revenge on him.'

'Even a worm such as Antrí can turn,' Éladach said softly. 'Unfortunately for him, he was not as skilled as my brother.'

'So Glaisne took Grella to his fortress in Eochaill, having arranged for Aescwine to come there. He would hand her over to him and the deal would be complete.'

'So why did he ride away with her when Asecwine arrived?' asked Eadulf. 'It just doesn't make sense. Don't forget, Áed saw Glaisne riding towards Cluain with Grella . . . Ah, so he saw Grella riding away with you?'

'Of course!' Fidelma exclaimed. 'I presume Grella is a prisoner here?' she asked.

Éladach heaved a sigh. 'You have followed the path, Fidelma of Cashel. But, sadly, it does not end here.'

Enda was totally bewildered and struggling to follow the logic of the exchange. Fidelma took pity on him and said: 'Áed made one mistake. He thought it was Glaisne taking Grella to safety. It was Éladach. Don't forget, Éladach is Glaisne's twin brother. What happened?'

'Simple enough,' Éladach assured her. 'As soon as the news reached me about what happened at Cluain, I realised that it would not be long before Aescwine would arrive to conclude his part of the deal. I took my little band here and we went to Eochaill, entered by subterfuge and took Grella into my protection.'

'You pretended to be your twin brother? Did he not raise the alarm?'

'Alas, Glaisne was left in no condition to raise any alarm.'

There was a silence as they realised what Éladach meant.

'So you brought Grella back here? May we see her? The sooner she can answer a few questions, the sooner this matter can be resolved and I can report to Cenn Fáelad.'

Éladach smiled and shook his head.

'She is gone already.'

'What?' exclaimed Fidelma in surprise.

'Cenn Fáelad sent a special courier to search for her and bring her back safely to Tara. He arrived here last evening, having followed her from Eochaill. He insisted on taking her to where they might get river transport for the return journey.'

'River transport?' queried Eadulf.

'Just east of here is the River of Noise. It flows eastward until it comes to the Great River, north of Eochaill, the Hill of the Yew Wood.'

Fidelma's jaw had tightened. 'How did you know this courier was from Cenn Fáelad?'

'He bore a royal seal and as soon as Grella saw him, she readily identified him and agreed to go with him.'

Fidelma closed her eyes for a moment. 'Grella saw the courier and was happy to go with him? The seal that he presented . . . was it like this?' She reached into her comb bag and took out one of the gold seals she had.

Éladach glanced at it with a frown. The metal figure was a tall woman with a crown, holding on her right shoulder a solar wheel. Eadulf shivered slightly: he associated such figures and symbols with the pagan faith.

'That's it. It's the northern sun goddess Étain, the symbol of the Síl nAedo Sláine . . .'

'But that's not the symbol of the Uí Néill but a branch of the family. Was the courier a tall man, dressed in black religious robes and wearing a cowl?'

Éladach looked intrigued. 'He was. But Grella knew him, and greeted him as a friend. He introduced himself as Fínsnechta, an Uí Néill prince.'

'Fínsnechta! I think I can now tell you why Áed was found slaughtered near here. He seized this seal from his killer. We found it clutched in his dead hand. This is not the seal of Cenn Fáelad but the seal of his cousin, the leader of the conspirators who intend to overthrow him.'

There was a silence, and then Éladach glanced at Petrán.

'Take your horse and ride for the jetty on the River of Noise. Enquire whether Grella and that tall religieux in black have gone there; ask whether they took a boat and, if it is known, in what direction they are heading. Take a couple of men with you and send them on to see if there is any sign of the Saxon ship waiting along the coast.'

'I shall, lord,' the man said at once.

'Come back as soon as you can with the news.'

Petrán hesitated and said: 'I was just going to attend to the girl, lord. She seems to be getting worse.'

Éladach hesitated and an expression of irritation crossed his face. Then he relaxed. 'You go,' he said. 'I will have her seen to by Pilib.'

Petrán raised a hand in salute and was gone.

Eadulf looked quickly at Éladach. 'Did he say that you have someone here who is ill?'

'Last night a young girl came to our gates in a state of collapse. She seems to have taken a fever. She arrived looking as if she had been ill used and soaked through.'

'Ill used?'

'She had rope burns on her wrists and she seemed to have been hit. We have given her a warm bed.'

'When did she arrive?' Eadulf asked.

'We found her at the gates not long after the tall religieux left with the lady Grella.'

Eadulf rose immediately. 'If you take me to her, I shall see how I can help.'

Éladach looked surprised. 'What could you do?' he asked doubtfully.

'Eadulf studied the healing arts at the great academy of Tuaim Brecain,' explained Fidelma.

The Uí Liatháin prince looked impressed, so impressed that Eadulf felt obliged to explain: 'I did not finish the full course, for I then decided to make the journey to Rome to hear at first hand what there was to be learnt there.'

'Little enough, I fear,' Éladach gave a twisted smile. 'Usually everything one needs to know can be found where you are without making an exhausting pilgrimage. I know, for I have journeyed to many far lands in the east. Lands beyond Rome to Byzantium and even across the Southern Sea to the great city of Alexandria, whose learning was so feared that the great library there was burnt.'

'Well, I have some knowledge,' Eadulf said. 'We have to wait for the return of your man, Petrán. So let us not neglect the girl any further. If I can help, I will willingly do so.'

'She has been put in a corner of what we call our guest house, which I am afraid you must all share tonight as we have no other accommodation,' Éladach explained.

'That depends on what news Petrán can bring us,' Fidelma said. 'Then help yourself to refreshment and I will take Eadulf to the girl.' Éladach motioned Eadulf to follow him. He led Eadulf out of the wooden building and turned towards a fair-sized log cabin. He went up a short flight of wooden steps, opened the door softly and called:

'It is Éladach with someone trained in the healing arts, young lady. Can we enter?'

At the term 'lady', Eadulf registered that meant Éladach had identified the girl as being of rank.

There was a murmur in reply and Éladach seemed to take this as an affirmative because he led the way further into the dark interior. A fire was glowing at one end of the cabin, its red glow sending dancing shadows through the room, which was large with several beds in it. Some religious icons were arranged as decorations. The occasional sparkle of the reflecting fire showed that they were of silver. Even in such subdued light, Eadulf could see a figure stretched on a wooden bed in the corner.

A girl's voice seemed to be mumbling incoherently as she twisted and turned with sweat on her face and saturating her clothes. Eadulf listened carefully and then realised it was just 'fever talk', the product of an almost unconscious mind.

'I will light a candle for you,' volunteered Éladach. The winter day had suddenly grown very dark, because of the increasing bunching of the clouds by the wind rather than the hastening of sundown. Eadulf saw Éladach take up something from a table and go to the fire and, a moment later, he came back with a lighted taper in his hand. He turned and took up a candle that was on the table and lit it. Then he turned for the bed and came to stand at Eadulf's shoulder, raising the candle so that they could see its occupant.

The girl was obviously in a fever, for her face was deathly pale and drenched in sweat. Her head turned this way and that, and she moaned slightly. It was clear that she was in no condition to articulate anything. Yet she continued muttering, almost sobbing.

Eadulf reached forward and stretched out a hand to her forehead. Whether she saw his hand or felt it, she seemed to shy away as he touched her.

Her forehead was burning and wet.

'It's all right,' he said softly to the girl. 'I am here to help you.' He glanced at Éladach. 'Bring the light a little closer so that I can see her properly. It casts too many shadows where you are holding it. I think she has a fever but I don't think . . .'

He halted abruptly as Éladach brought his candle close to the girl's face. Eadulf had recognised her immediately.

He uttered an exclamation of surprise and then turned and issued a peremptory order in a tone that Éladach found unexpected. 'You may leave me to minister to her. Would you ask Fidelma to come here?'

When Fidelma entered, Eadulf turned to her immediately.

'I think you had better look closely at this girl,' he said.

She moved forward, peered down at the pale face lying on the bed and caught her breath.

'It's Cairenn.'

chapter eighteen

'The girl must have escaped from her abductors,' confirmed Eadulf.

'What is wrong with her?' asked Fidelma, leaning over the shaking, fever-ridden form.

'A malaise brought on by exhaustion, a drenching in a river or some other water and who knows what else?' he replied grimly. 'She must have had a bad time with her captors and then probably escaped from them, or they left her to die.'

'Can you do anything for her?'

'I can do only my best. At least I still have my *les* and I believe I have enough herbs that will help. The main thing is for this fever to break. Fever is often nature's way of burning up impurities in the body. But sometimes it needs help to break.'

Fidelma was torn between concern for the girl's health and the need to access her knowledge. But she accepted Eadulf's priority.

'I'll leave you to do what you can. It will be best not to identify her to Éladach until we are certain of all our facts. I feel that she might give us the final link in this mystery.'

'Hopefully the fever should break tonight,' Eadulf said. 'Perhaps by tomorrow she will be able to tell us her story.'

Fidelma turned to the door as it opened and Pilib entered.

'Prince Éladach told me to come here to see if I can be of service to Brother Eadulf,' he announced. 'I am not skilled in the healing arts but, when our *catha* is on the march, I usually attend to wounds if they are not grievous.'

Eadulf accepted the young man's help and so Fidelma left them. Under Eadulf's instruction, the young man fetched fresh water and a vessel in which to heat it. He put the cauldron on the fire while Eadulf rummaged in his medical bag. He realised that he did not have the essential herb he wanted and was about to give way to annoyance when a thought struck him. He turned to the young man.

'Do you harvest the elderberries from the bushes which surround these buildings?'

'We do, but it is months since the ripening season.'

Eadulf was about to snap that he knew that but forced himself to smile. 'I presume you dry and store the berries, flowers and some bark for later use?' he asked patiently.

Pilib's eyes lit up and he nodded eagerly. 'We do.'

'Then fetch some here.' He had hardly given the order when the young man went scurrying away.

Eadulf took from his *les* a small bag of a white crystal-like substance, a bit like the salt extracted and dried from the sea. He had acquired it from a travelling physician from the Uí Fidgenti country. He emptied the contents into the remaining water, watching it dissolve in a moment. He also took from the *les* a bag of dried nettle roots and leaves and a bag of dried white willow leaves and buds with some pieces of its bark.

Pilib returned, carrying the dried elderberries in a large bag.

'We only need a handful,' Eadulf said as the bag was held out enthusiastically to him. He took the amount he required and put them in the now-bubbling cauldron, together with a handful of the nettle mixture.

'We must wait a while,' he told the curious young man. 'Unless we have another vessel to boil the willow in, we will have to leave that until we have finished with this mixture.'

Finally, Eadulf turned to the young girl in the bed. She was semi-conscious, twisting and turning in her fever. At times it seemed her eyes were open and observing them, at others it was clear she was deep in the fever, with sweat pouring from her brow.

Eadulf had started to bathe her face, neck and shoulders with the sodium water and a linen cloth. She twisted and moaned a little as the cold water touched her skin. Eadulf glanced back to the fire and saw the mixture was boiling, so he ordered the boy to remove it and pour it out to cool in a drinking vessel. The boy looked at him quizzically.

'By boiling the herbs in the water,' Eadulf explained, 'they become what is called macerated, softened, and that produces a liquid which can then be drunk. That is the healing liquid.'

Meanwhile he continued to bathe the girl with the sodium solution.

'When she relaxes a little we will give her a drink of the elder-berry mixture.'

He bent over the girl and checked her pulse.

'She is coming up to the point where the fever will break,' he observed, touching her forehead,

The girl's eyelids fluttered for a moment. Eadulf realised that she was beginning to whisper in her delirium. He bent closer.

'All wrong . . .' The words came distinctly. 'It was all wrong.'

Eadulf sat on the edge of the cot and waved to the boy to bring over the herbal infusion he had made. He helped the girl to take a small sip, holding her head.

She moved restlessly, still mouthing words almost un-consciously.

'Wrong . . . betray . . . betrayed . . .'

Eadulf dabbed at her forehead with the cold damp linen cloth. Then he helped her to another few sips of the infusion.

'You are safe now, Cairenn,' he said gently. 'You are among friends.'

'No, friends betrayed . . . Wrong . . . it wasn't them . . . Wrong . . .'

Eadulf frowned. He doubted the girl was even listening but something prompted him to try to communicate.

'Who was wrong, Cairenn?' he asked.

'Wasn't them . . .' muttered the girl. 'Betrayed.'

Eadulf sighed and allowed her more sips of the herbal tea. Then he laid her head back on the pillow. He glanced up at the curious Pilib.

'It's all right. I'll stay here a while and attend to her. You can leave us.'

The young man left, reluctantly, and Eadulf turned back to the girl.

'I wonder what you are trying to say,' he said softly. 'I wonder what was wrong and who betrayed whom?'

He stood up and went to check the infusion of the willow bark, roots and leaves, which had mulched nicely into a strong tea. He poured some into a receptacle and took it to the girl. Holding her head again, he made her swallow as much of it as was possible. Then he bathed her face and neck once more. Some time later, the girl seemed to drift off into a deep sleep. By then, Eadulf's eyelids were drooping and he was just about to give way to tiredness when Fidelma entered quietly.

'How is she?' she whispered.

Eadulf blinked and stirred himself. 'The fever has broken and I think she is sleeping naturally now. If she sleeps without interruption, she should be better in the morning.'

Fidelma regarded him with approval. 'You should get some rest now.'

Eadulf shook his head. 'I think I should remain here, just in case. I would have liked her to drink more of the willow infusion . . .' He paused. 'Is there any news from the messenger Éladach sent to . . . what was it called . . . the River of Noise?'

Fidelma shook her head. 'Darkness has already come down. It is so early this time of year. Anyway, a wind has risen and started to blow away the clouds, so it will be a fine night.'

'If you can stay here a while, I could do with some fresh air, even the air of a winter evening.'

'I'll look after her. Anyway, I understand that this is Éladach's guests' accommodation, so we'll all be staying here tonight. At least there is a good fire and several beds.'

Eadulf went out and stood on the wooden steps, breathing deeply of the chill evening air. It was true what Fidelma had said. The quickening breeze from the west had dispelled the clouds and the sky was a dark blue canopy speckled with bright silver dots. The moon hung large and low in the sky but it had a curious red glow to it. Eadulf had seen the phenomenon often in his life and it always made him uneasy. He knew that before the adoption of the New Faith, the ancients had always described it as a 'blood moon' and predicted some historic happening, while the New Faith had converted it into a terrible act by God against those who had offended Him. He shivered slightly.

A figure emerged from the darkness carrying some bags. It was Enda. He saw Eadulf gazing up at the night sky and sighed deeply.

'*Ésca cró-deirg,*' he remarked.

'What?' demanded Eadulf.

'The blood-red moon.' Enda nodded towards the orb. 'It is a symbol that something is about to happen, that something important is about to be resolved.'

'So long as it portends nothing terrible,' Eadulf replied worriedly.

'I think we have had our fair share of terrible happenings in the last few days. Things must only get better.' Eadulf could almost see Enda smiling in the darkness. 'Is this where we are to sleep?'

At Eadulf's confirmation, Enda began to mount the wooden steps to the cabin.

'Try not to disturb the girl,' cautioned Eadulf.

'I am told she is Cairenn. Is her condition bad?'

'Bad enough,' Eadulf answered. 'But she should be in a deep sleep now.' Then, realising what might concern a non-medical mind, he added, 'There is nothing to catch from her.'

However, when the young warrior entered, with Eadulf following him, he took the baggage to a bed on the far side of the guests' hostel.

'Do you want me to look after her for the first part of the night?' Fidelma asked as Eadulf came to look at the girl.

Eadulf shook his head. 'Best if you and Enda get some sleep. When I am sure she is resting comfortably, I will sleep as well.'

It was still dark when the girl stirred, opened her eyes and clearly uttered the word: 'Water.'

Eadulf, half dozing, jerked awake. It took a few seconds before he responded to the request. He allowed her to swallow a few mouthfuls and then she lay back, blinking a little.

'I feel weak,' she said.

'You had a little fever,' he responded.

She frowned at him in the flickering half-light of the nearly exhausted candle.

'I know you.'

Eadulf smiled. 'I am Eadulf of Seaxmund's Ham.'

The girl's eyes widened little. 'You are the husband to Fidelma of Cashel. Where is she?' The girl was agitated. 'Is she safe?'

'Safe and well,' he replied. 'She is sleeping in that bed over there.'

'So she escaped from Tialláin?'

'Tialláin is dead. He was killed by the Saxon, Aescwine. You escaped, remember? We came to the place where you said you would meet us. But you had gone with some warriors, unwillingly by all accounts.'

'Glaisne's men. They were to take me to him, but then they found he had been killed and their plot discovered . . . They took their

vengeance out on me and then abandoned me to death. They . . .
they . . .'

Eadulf held up a pacifying hand. 'You can tell us in the morning,
when you have rested more. Don't waste strength now. Suffice to
say, you are safe. There is nothing to fear now.'

'But I must tell you now. All is not as it seems. The High King
is about to be betrayed, about to be assassinated. We must warn
him . . . tell him to seek his enemy in the last place he was expecting
betrayal. I was the distraction, I was expendable.'

Eadulf patted her hand soothingly. 'Yes, yes. Try not to think
about it for the moment. You are safe now. Just rest and get well.
The High King will be warned.'

'But it is his cousin Fínsnechta who is behind the plot – not the
Eóganacht.'

'We know that much, for Fínsnechta was apparently on board
the Saxon ship. But we'll talk about it in the morning,' Eadulf
assured her. 'There is no need to stress yourself.'

'The Saxon ship?' The girl groaned. 'Is it here?'

Eventually Eadulf persuaded the girl to lie back and try to relax.
When he was sure that she was asleep, he rose and went back to
where he thought Fidelma was sleeping. She was not. She was wide
awake. He was about to say something but she placed a finger over
her lips and shook her head.

She said softly: 'Tomorrow. Everything is clear to me, but
tomorrow we will have the last piece of this puzzle.'

Eadulf was disappointed but there was nothing to be gained from
staying awake and trying to analyse what the girl had said.

It was well after dawn when the hollow sound of the bell woke
Eadulf. He sat up and glanced around the guests' hostel, the large
single room with its many beds in which they had spent the night.
Enda was already up and crouched before the fire, stacking some
logs on its smouldering base. Fidelma was stirring beside him,
yawning in protest. He looked across at the girl, Cairenn. She, too,

seemed to be reluctantly waking at the sounds of the bell and of movement outside. It seemed that Enda had already washed. It was the custom of the people to wash only the face and hands in the morning. Eadulf moved to perform his toilet and, having done so, went to the girl's bed. She was awake, blinking in the morning light.

'How do you feel?' he smiled.

'A dry mouth and a strangely light head,' she replied.

He placed a hand on her forehead and nodded with approval.

'The fever is gone,' he said with satisfaction. He was standing up when the door opened and the young man Pilib entered.

'You have missed morning prayers,' he announced but his tone did not sound censurious. Eadulf thought he was conveying the feelings of Éladach. 'My lord is strict about his Eastern Faith and likes people to join in morning prayers.'

'I think your lord will appreciate that more urgent matters required our attention,' Eadulf returned drily. 'Has the warrior, Petrán, returned from the river yet? From his mission to see whether Grella and Fínsnechta had found a boat on the river and left the territory?'

'Not yet.'

'Is there anything else you need?' Eadulf asked – the young man seemed reluctant to leave.

'Has the girl . . .?' He looked across at Cairenn. 'Has she recovered from her fever?'

'As you will observe.'

Pilib stood there awkwardly and said: 'It was I who found her outside our gates the other night.'

'I am sure she will be most grateful,' Enda said solemnly, from his position stretched out by the fire. 'I am sure you now need to tell your lord that she is well.'

As the young steward left, Fidelma returned from washing and went to the girl. Cairenn was easing herself up on the bed and smiled awkwardly.

'No ill-effects from the fever?' Fidelma asked. When the girl shook her head, Fidelma said, 'Perhaps it is a good time to speak about what happened? Firstly, how did you get here?'

Cairenn shrugged. 'There is little to say that you cannot guess, I suppose. After you urged me to flee, I met your companions. I agreed with them to take the horses to Baile an Stratha and wait there for three days.'

'I understand you know that area of the Uí Liatháin country well?' interposed Fidelma.

'Not well, but I was a friend and companion of Grella long before she left the Uí Liatháin to wed Cenn Fáelad of the Uí Néill. We journeyed here together several times.'

Fidelma nodded slowly. 'Continue.'

'I was there a short time and arranged things with Báine. I went walking on the beach, only to be surrounded by a band of men. They were Glaisne's men. The leader told me that my lady Grella was ill and needed me to go to her immediately. They told me to mount behind one of them and, of course, I went. It was not until we came to Cluain that they were stopped by a tall religieux in black. Their behaviour changed at what he told them.'

She paused and there was a catch in her throat. Fidelma prompted her to continue.

'They took me to a cabin somewhere in these woods. Some of them rode off with the religieux. A few remained at the hut.'

'How did you escape?' asked Fidelma quickly.

'I did not escape until after . . . after they ill used me.' The girl shuddered and an expression of pain crossed her features. 'They tied my wrists and then . . . then . . .'

Fidelma reached forward and took the girl's hands.

'You are safe now.' Fidelma persisted: 'You escaped. How?'

'I finally loosened my bonds and climbed out of a window. Outside, it was dark and the wind was whipping the trees, and at one point I was so blinded that I fell into a stream. I was wet, cold and soon the chill was like daggers into my body. That was when I began to feel an ague come upon me.'

'Was the place from which you escaped far from here?'

'Perhaps on the far side of some hills. I was wandering for a time. I think a young man found me and brought me into this place.'

'That seems so. A young steward, Pilib, found you outside this compound and brought you here . . . the sanctuary, as he calls it, of Éladach, Prince of the Uí Liathán. He is the brother of Glaisne but, be assured, certainly no friend of his,' Eadulf smiled.

'I did not know where I went for it was dark, cold and windy. I was wandering without purpose other than to find shelter and warmth. My mind seemed to leave me, until I woke with Brother Eadulf giving me a warm drink.'

Fidelma paused thoughtfully.

'You said your abductors were stopped by a tall religieux in black robes and after he spoke to them their conduct towards you changed. Did you recognise that man?'

The girl's eyes immediately widened. 'How could I forget? He was at Finnbarr's Abbey. Oh, it comes back to me now. I saw him watching me closely at the abbey. The strange thing was that I was sure that I knew him, from before I was at the abbey.'

Fidelma's mouth tightened. 'From where do you think you knew him?'

'I can't be sure. But there was something very familiar about him.'

'Did Abbot Nessán or anyone else at the abbey know him?'

'I don't think so. I thought he was just a passing pilgrim who came there the evening after I arrived and claimed hospitality.'

Fidelma paused. 'Did you know that he left the abbey on the morning of the abbot's murder?'

The girl stared thoughtfully at Fidelma. 'Do you mean that he might have been the one who killed Abbot Nessán?'

Fidelma shrugged. 'It is not without logic. I was told that he left the abbey in the direction of Eochaill.' She paused. 'When he stopped Glaisne's men, after they abducted you from Baile an Stratha, did you hear anything of what he told them?'

'I could tell by their reaction that Glaisne was dead. He said that they should scatter and await further word. One asked what they should do with me.' She caught her breath. 'He said, "Whatever you want, but don't let her leave here alive." Then he rode off.'

Fidelma reached forward and patted the girl's arm. 'Let me take you back to what Grella told you in Tara. She said she had received a message from Abbot Nessán. Did that surprise you?'

The girl frowned for a moment and then shrugged. 'Abbot Nessán was an influential man in these parts. He was in regular communication with the High King.'

'But not necessarily with Grella. Did you not question that?'

'No reason why I should.'

'She told you that Nessán had warned her of an attempted assassination of her husband?'

'She did, and that he felt the Eóganacht were behind it. He gave instructions that she was to take me and a personal guard and seek sanctuary at Cluain with her cousin, Abbot Antrí. While there, she was to send me to Abbot Nessán to get details of the conspiracy.'

'Did she tell you that she had been specifically told to send you?'

'She did.'

'And you did not find that strange?'

'No reason why I should. She knew Abbot Nessán would trust me. I was a close relative.'

'But you said that when you arrived he claimed he had not sent the message?'

'That is true. By that time he had received a message from Cenn Fáelad, saying Grella had left him a note telling him she was sending me to hear the abbot's evidence and trusted me, even though I am an Eóganacht. At the same time Nessán received a message from you, Fidelma, saying you were on the way to see him. That was when he decided to say nothing until you arrived.'

'But Nessán said he had definitely not been in touch with Grella about this?'

Cairenn shook her head.

'Tell me . . .' Fidelma sat back. 'You spent time with Grella at Tara and you must have seen a lot of happenings at the court in recent months.'

The girl frowned at the abrupt change of subject.

'I was Grella's companion, as I have said. But I was not privy to the politics of the court.'

'But what about the social life?'

The girl nodded. 'There were a lot of foreigners coming to see the High King: Gauls, Britons, even Saxons, and so there was much feasting and celebration. Grella really enjoyed such occasions, and Cenn Fáelad was often absent on matters of the kingdom.'

'Were you ever aware of a Saxon prince who might have been an envoy to Tara,' queried Fidelma, 'a man called Aescwine?'

The girl's features tightened in recognition of the name. 'There were many envoys to the High King's court. I think he was one of them.'

'You know, of course,' Fidelma went on, 'that there were sections of Cenn Fáelad's family who were rivals to his claim to the High Kingship – that his own brother was assassinated?'

'And that is why Grella feared for his life,' Cairenn replied hurriedly.

'Did members of Cenn Fáelad's family ever mix with the foreigners . . . foreign envoys like Aescwine?'

'I suppose so. It would be natural.'

'Did you know a relative of Cenn Fáelad called Fínsnechta?'

'I was only Grella's companion and so did not mix with the Uí Néill princes but . . .'

'He was a tall man, I believe. Did you ever see such a man mixing with the Saxons at Tara?'

The girl's eyes suddenly grew wide. 'I don't know what you are saying . . .'

'No matter. I begin to see a picture now. All Abbot Nessán knew was that he did not send the warning to Grella, that she had misinformed you and that there was no Eóganacht plot to assassinate her husband. He was murdered and you were going to be blamed for it, but you thwarted the conspirators by managing to escape from the abbey. Thankfully, you left me a clue as to where you were going.

'You were an Eóganacht and trusted by Nessán. There is some betrayal here, but I do not know what it is.'

Fidelma was thoughtful for a moment. Then she relaxed and smiled at the girl.

'We will leave you to recover, Cairenn. We must join Éladach and you must now regain your strength. I will explain everything in due course.'

At once Eadulf intervened: 'I shall ask that some broth be prepared to restore you.'

The girl grimaced. 'I care little what it is for I am exhausted.'

They left her lying back on her bed with her eyes closed.

Outside the guest house, Eadulf glanced at Fidelma curiously.

'I suspect you have something on your mind,' he said pointedly.

Fidelma did not respond for a moment. 'I have to admit that I am beginning to see a pattern emerging.'

'We were worried about you,' Éladach greeted them as they entered his feasting hall. He was alone before a blazing fire. Cold meats, cheeses and freshly baked barley bread were on the table, with a jug of goat's milk. He waved them to be seated. Enda was already impatiently viewing the table.

'Has the girl recovered?' Éladach asked.

'She will be well soon,' Eadulf confirmed.

'What was she doing here?' queried the Éladach.

'Well, to be honest, she had escaped from some of your brother's men who had been holding her. She was Grella's companion.'

Éladach looked shocked. 'But if she was Grella's companion . . .?'

'She was not party to any conspiracy but was to be sacrificed by the conspirators. But it did not work out as they had hoped.'

A sound abruptly broke the silence. It was not the tolling of the bell at the gate of the community. It was the call of a military *stoc*, a trumpet. And it was close at hand.

ChAPTER NINETEEN

As Éladach and his companions rose anxiously to their feet, the young steward, Pilib, burst into the hall.

'It is Petrán returning, lord,' he announced breathlessly. 'He has a prisoner with him. My lord, the prisoner is your cousin Antrí.'

Éladach sat back in his seat with a grim smile of satisfaction.

'I had wondered where that vermin was hiding. I thought perhaps Glaisne had killed him but there is no such luck in the world. Vermin always seem to survive no matter their evil.' He paused. 'Pilib, tell Petrán to have him put under guard until we are ready for him . . .'

'Lord, Petrán is accompanied by another person. This one is not a prisoner,' Pilib added.

'Who is he?'

'Petrán says he is a lawyer.'

Éladach glanced at Fidelma in amusement. 'Another lawyer? Well, one is enough for the moment. Let Petrán come here first and make his report to us. This other lawyer can wait. I want to hear what has happened to the lady Grella.'

The young man left to fetch Petrán and Éladach suggested they all resume their seats. They did not have to wait long for the warrior to join them.

'Well?' Éladach demanded after Petrán had saluted him.

'The bad news is that Fínsnechta has escaped and taken the lady

Grella with him,' Petrán announced. 'Witnesses saw the man we know as Fínsnechta accompany the lady Grella onto a small river craft. They sailed downriver. It seemed they had been met on the jetty by Saxon warriors, who then accompanied them. But another man had appeared at the same time and an argument followed. This other man was knocked down by one of the Saxons and left behind when they boarded their boat.'

'I hope we will hear who this man was,' Fidelma said.

'We searched and found the man hiding after we arrived. My lord, the man was your cousin Antrí. We promptly made him our prisoner but he offered to make a bargain with us.'

'He would,' Éladach commented. 'What sort of bargain?'

'If we would give him his freedom, he would show us the place where Fínsnechta and the lady Grella were going.'

'Did you make such a bargain?' Fidelma asked sharply. 'Were binding promises made to the man for his freedom?'

Petrán shook his head with a smile. 'Thankfully, we had the advice of a young Brehon who pointed out that we would have been legally obliged to fulfil such a bargain if it were made. Anyway, I thought it was obvious where they would be going. So I insisted that he show us where first and said we would consider the matter afterwards.'

'You used the word "consider"? He agreed to that?' Éladach asked in surprise.

Petrán grinned crookedly. 'He had no option, lord.'

'Where did you find this astute Brehon?' Fidelma asked, frowning.

'He had recently arrived at the river on his way to Eochaill. He told us that he, too, was in pursuit of Fínsnechta, for the crime of murder.'

'For murder? Whose murder?' demanded Éladach.

'The murder of Abbot Nessán, lord.'

A look of satisfaction crossed Fidelma's face and she asked quietly: 'This lawyer . . . is his name Oengarb?'

Eadulf let out a gasp, and Éladach glanced questioningly in his direction. 'You know such a Brehon named Oengarb?' Then he raised his hand as if to silence a reply. 'First things first. Petrán, did you set out for the place you thought Fínsnechta was making for?'

'We did. Fínsnechta had had a good start ahead of us on the river. However, we had horses and rode across country. We arrived on a headland above Eochaill. Alas, we were just in time to see the Saxon ship hoisting sail and we could see Fínsnechta and Grella clambering aboard.'

Éladach smacked his right fist into the palm of his left hand and uttered a curse.

'So they managed to get aboard the ship. Has it sailed? There were no Uí Liatháin warships around to impede their sailing?'

'None, lord. But surely, even if the lady is taken as hostage, the High King will immediately negotiate a ransom to restore her to Tara?'

'The wife of the High King has been abducted and I am responsible for allowing this man, Fínsnechta, to take her out of my protection. It will mean war. Grella is now helpless in Saxon hands.'

'Not so helpless.' It was Fidelma who spoke quietly, with a thoughtful smile. They all swung round to face her.

'I don't understand.' Éladach gazed curiously at her.

'I think, apart from a few small points, I can resolve this mystery. Let's clear those small matters up first. Bring in Oengarb.'

Fidelma recalled that the young man was only a *dálaigh* and not a Brehon, and further was not as qualified as she was. The young man entered and halted, staring in surprise at Fidelma.

'Greetings, Oengarb of Locha Léin. I did not think your law circuit would bring you here.'

She referred to the fact that Oengarb had initially told her he was on a *cúartaigid,* a legal circuit of the territory so that litigants could bring their cases to him without the necessity of travelling great distances.

'No, lady. I was merely doing what you asked me to.'

'Which was?' Her expression showed that she already knew the answer.

'I was investigating the murder of Abbot Nessán, as you instructed,' the young man explained. 'I thought the girl, Cairenn, had killed him and then escaped from the abbey. You left the matter in my hands.'

'I did,' Fidelma acknowledged solemnly.

'Well, the girl was totally innocent.'

Fidelma allowed a pause rather than say that she had thought as much from the beginning. Instead she said: 'I understand that you were looking for the tall religieux who was at the abbey? How did you work out that this man killed the abbot?'

The young man shrugged. 'With no great thought on my part, I am afraid. I eventually learnt that the man who had come to the abbey disguised as a religieux and left just after the murder was, in reality, Fínsnechta mac Dúchado of the Síl nÁedo Sláine and first cousin to the High King. I did not know this until I had followed the girl all the way to Ard Nemed. Having found out who he was, I set off to track him and followed him to this territory. I had just missed him at the River of Noise. That warrior,' he nodded at Petrán, 'met me there while I was in pursuit of him.'

'So how did you know Fínsnechta was really the guilty one and Cairenn was innocent?' Eadulf rephrased Fidelma's question.

'It was part of a conspiracy. Cairenn was to be blamed for the murder to ensure she did not leave the abbey. Some of Fínsnechta's hirelings were left to guard the likely roads she would take from the abbey if she did escape and to make sure she did not complete her journey. They thought she would take the main road east to meet up with Grella.'

'How are you so sure of this?' Fidelma demanded. 'When it was thought she was guilty, you supposed she would head west to seek sanctuary with her family.'

'After you had left the abbey, the trackers that we hired reported that Cairenn had gone east. I set out to follow and came to the Great Island. Prince Artgal told me Cairenn had been there but insisted on her innocence. He also said that you had stayed with him and were in pursuit of her, too. The important matter for me was that he had some Uí Liatháin prisoners, one of which was a northern mercenary whom he had been questioning. The man admitted that he had been hired by the northern prince Fínsnechta.'

'I remember Artgal saying one of his prisoners was from the north,' Fidelma recalled with a frown.

'Artgal allowed me to interrogate him. The prisoner was talkative, hoping to negotiate a better future than that he was facing. He said he was hired by Fínsnechta to waylay Cairenn if she came into his hands. Fínsnechta wanted the girl to be eliminated. The prisoner said he was given a seal to identify himself among Fínsnechta's band.'

'And the seal was a female figure with a solar wheel on her right shoulder?' pressed Fidelma.

Oengarb allowed a momentary look of surprise to cross his face before he acknowledged she was correct.

Eadulf breathed out deeply. 'So the solution was there all the time . . . had we stayed and questioned those prisoners at Artgal's fortress we might have known it earlier!'

Fidelma shook her head ruefully. 'It never occurred to me to question Artgal's prisoners. Anyway, we would have had only an isolated part of the story.'

'An important part,' Eadulf observed quietly.

Éladach was examining Fidelma keenly. 'And you now have the entire story, Fidelma?'

'I will put it together for you,' she said, drawing an irritable look from Eadulf. 'It is a very complex and sad story. Let us first remember that Cenn Fáelad is in an unenviable position. He became High King after the murder of his brother Sechnussach. There are factions in his family that wanted the High Kingship for themselves – and none more so than his first cousin, Fínsnechta. He coveted Cenn Fáelad's power and status.' She paused. 'We must also remember that Grella was of the Uí Liatháin and knew this territory, being a cousin to you, Éladach, as well as to Glaisne and Antri.'

Éladach impatiently waved for her to continue.

'The idea of how to overthrow his cousin came to Fínsnechta while observing the behaviour of Grella at Tara. The fact was that Grella enjoyed the social life there whereas Cenn Fáelad did not. She enjoyed the feasting, the songs and dances, and especially the company of the foreigners . . . and she found one Saxon prince particularly attractive: Aescwine of the Gewisse.

'Had we but known it, Fínsnechta was probably involved in the conspiracy to murder Cenn Fáelad's brother Sechnussach – you'll remember that Eadulf and I were instrumental in solving that mystery. Fínsnechta now came up with a more subtle plot to overthrow the High King. He knew that Grella was having an affair with Aescwine – I concede it was probably more intense than just an affair. Fínsnechta put a proposition to her. We cannot know how willing she was to be involved in the overthrow of her husband. Perhaps Fínsnechta threatened to reveal her affair. Anyway, she made accusations to her husband about an Eóganacht plot, using Abbot Nessán as a source of authority. Fínsnechta's idea was to have Nessán killed to authenticate this. But who could get close enough to the old abbot to do it . . .'

'Cairenn?' finished Eadulf.

'Cairenn was an Eóganacht Raithlind. She was a useful person to take the blame on that account. She realised she was being used as a cat's paw and was clever enough to escape after Fínsnechta had killed the abbot. She had been meant to be identified as an agent of her people, which would have caused dissent between the Uí Néill and Eóganacht . . . even warfare.

'Grella told her husband she had gone to get the proof of the conspiracy and that she would stay with her family.'

Éladach was following Fidelma's exposition thoughtfully. 'I am not sure why Antrí went through this charade of being an abbot?'

'Grella had made the excuse to her husband that she was going to stay with Antrí, whom she pretended was abbot of a newly revitalised community at Cluain. I suspect Antrí's services were bought rather than having a political motive. That seems to fit his character. She was to hide there while she was supposedly, with Cairenn's help, gathering details of the plot against her husband. She was actually expecting to hear that Nessán was dead and Cairenn killed or a prisoner. The reality was she was awaiting the arrival of Aescwine's ship and was ready to be taken on board. She and Aescwine were to sail to his country, the land of the Gewisse, while the Five Kingdoms erupted in a war caused by the accusations and counter-accusations created by Fínsnechta with Grella's help. Fínsnechta and his followers – that gold seal was the symbol of the conspirators, as Oengarb identified – would have remained behind to continue to foment the idea that the Eóganacht, perhaps led by my brother, were involved in a plot to assassinate the High King and claim the throne, and they would be blamed for Grella's so-called abduction. That was why the Saxon ship took Grella on board here in my brother's kingdom rather than off the coast nearer Tara. A war between the Eóganacht and Uí Néill was essential – whether he won or lost, the High King would be denounced as a weak ruler to have allowed it to happen and be deposed by his nearest rival: Fínsnechta.'

She paused for a moment while they digested this, then added: 'But once we knew of Fínsnechta's involvement, he had no alternative than to join Grella and Aescwine and flee with them.'

Éladach sighed. 'I can follow it all, Fidelma, except how did my brother, Glaisne, become involved?'

'*Cinniud*,' she said simply.

Eadulf was puzzled, not sure of the meaning of the word.

'Destiny, fate,' Fidelma explained. 'Fínsnechta's cleverness backfired. Not really trusting Antrí, he thought to involve Glaisne in case things went wrong. Glaisne, equally corrupt, saw his chance to benefit either way – whether the conspiracy failed or succeeded. So he killed Antrí's men and took charge of Grella. If the plot did not work, then he could claim to have saved Grella from abduction. If it did work, then he would achieve wealth and position as a friend of the new High King. And again, destiny lent a hand because Antrí managed to escape Glaisne's massacre.'

'It's complicated,' admitted Éladach.

'And, I'm afraid, you made it more so,' Fidelma told him solemnly. 'You obviously heard what had happened to Antrí at Cluain but thought your brother, Glaisne, had abducted Grella and that she was entirely innocent. You are loyal to the High King, so you went to Eochaill to rescue her. During your rescue mission, your brother was killed. You then brought Grella here, thinking that it was to protect her. In fact, Aescwine arrived at Eochaill to pick her up as arranged, Fínsnechta arrived here, and tricked you into releasing Grella to his care. The rest Petrán has told you.'

Éladach sat shaking his head as he tried to come to terms with the conspiracy.

'And you are saying that the purpose of it all was for Cenn Fáelad to believe that his wife had been abducted? The High King would have been fed with the story it was an Eóganacht conspiracy and would therefore march on Cashel to seek retribution from Colgú. And even if Cenn Fáelad was victorious, he would still be seen as a weak ruler?'

'Defeat of my brother would not have been a foregone conclusion,' Fidelma pointed out with some asperity. 'You might remember that when the High King Cormac mac Art invaded the Eóganacht kingdom some centuries ago, the King, Fiachra Muillethain, and his army faced Cormac at Cnoc Luinge – the Hill of Ships – and drove them back to Tara, causing the High King to submit, apologise and offer compensation. That could happen again. But either way,

Cenn Fáelad would be made to seem a weak and unworthy king. Fínsnechta would find more enthusiastic allies among the Uí Néill. Complicated . . . but thankfully we have a good witness in Antrí – he is no fanatic and will quickly reveal his part to avoid the High King's wrath.'

Oengarb cleared his throat to attract attention. 'There is the warrior that Prince Artgal took as a prisoner on the Great Island and whom I questioned. He is also a witness.'

Fidelma smiled. 'That is true. We have his witness of Fínsnechta's involvement in trying to blame or eliminate Cairenn as well as her own testimony.'

There was a silence and then Eadulf sighed.

'The Uí Néill,' he said with a shake of his head. 'With a family like that, who needs to find enemies?'

Éladach was quiet, considering the case that Fidelma had put forward.

'Are you saying there is nothing else to do now? Fínsnechta and Grella have sailed safely off to the land of the Saxons with this Prince Aescwine?'

'There is nothing else we can do,' Fidelma agreed. 'All I can do is send my report to the High King and the Chief Brehon of the Five Kingdoms.'

'Then it means that we have lost,' pointed out Oengarb dolefully. 'The law has lost to this conspiracy.'

Fidelma smiled thinly. 'Not exactly. Truth has won by being revealed. It seems, for the time being, the perpetrators have escaped punishment, that is all.'

A week later, Eadulf entered their chamber in Cashel and saw Fidelma sitting before the crackling log fire, sipping a glass of mulled wine. She glanced up with a smile as he entered.

'I hear that there was a messenger arrived from Tara to see your brother today,' he announced, throwing off his riding cloak and moving to the fire, rubbing his hands before the flames. 'Has Cenn Fáelad made a decision on the matter?'

'The matter of Grella?' she asked. 'He has. I have just been discussing it with Colgú. The details of the matter are, of course, to be kept secret.'

Eadulf abandoned the fire and sank into a chair opposite her. 'Don't tell me that everyone has been placed under a sacred oath . . . what was it, a *geis*? I thought we had had enough of such things?'

Fidelma actually laughed. 'You need not worry about any sacred oath. It is just that we should be frugal with the facts of the case.'

'I presume that Cenn Fáelad will divorce Grella?'

Fidelma made an affirmative gesture. 'He has and that is the minimum that he could do in the circumstances. Grella, under law, is now regarded as one who has fled from her marriage contract without cause and thus has no protection under the law. She loses her honour price, her property and her standing in our society.'

'So that is an end to it? She has now fled this island and gone with her lover to the land of the Gewisse. No one will follow her, nor will they demand compensation.'

'No one will bother to exact justice. Compensation will be paid from her confiscated property and if that is not enough, from her relatives. Éladach is absolved from any part he played in the death of his brother. He is obviously considered the senior prince of the southern Uí Liatháin. However, he has already refused the title, preferring to consecrate the abbey at Cluain, establishing it to follow his concept of the rites of the Eastern Church. He cites the authority of the Bishop of Constantinople, claiming the Church there is of purer lineage than Rome.'

Eadulf sniffed disapprovingly. He hesitated for a few moments before saying: 'Grella would have been executed among the Angles and the Saxons. She would have been executed in the most extreme manner, as an example that fidelity in marriage is sacrosanct.'

'Not that conspiracy to assassinate a king is a crime unless it fails?' Fidelma observed cynically. 'Well, our law, as you know, is always concerned to protect women, and their children. There is no framework for physically punishing women even if they do wrong. We have seven legal concepts for divorce and seven more for separation.'

'It is hard to understand these from my culture,' Eadulf admitted.

'It is just as hard for a woman to become *deorad*, an outcast deprived of the protection of the law and her kin,' observed Fidelma. 'Apart from her plotting against her husband, Grella is guilty under two of the seven adultery laws and so she is deprived of such protection. Both those laws relate to her abusing her husband by sexually violating his trust. She loses her rights of protection and so her *coibche*, her dowry, is forfeit and she is made outcast. The confiscation of what property she has follows.'

Eadulf had long since had to come to terms with the fact that women in Fidelma's society could inherit and hold property on their own account as *banchomarbae* – female inheritors.

'What will happen to Fínsnechta?' Eadulf asked. 'After all, you made it clear that he was the real power behind the conspiracy. He was first cousin to Cenn Fáelad and could have easily stepped into the shoes of the High King he had deposed.'

At this question, Fidelma looked troubled and her mouth drooped in disapproval. 'I do not agree with Cenn Fáelad's decision. He and the Chief Brehon decided that nothing should be done. At the moment it is theoretical, because Fínsnechta has not returned to the Five Kingdoms, so far as is known. He remains in exile in the land of the Gewisse.'

'But what if he does return?' Eadulf demanded.

'He would be rebuked for helping Grella join her lover but no other charge would be made. It is considered better to ameliorate the tensions within the Uí Néill rather than exacerbate them – there are enough rivals for the High Kingship. So while he would not be welcomed in Tara, or anywhere in the High King's presence or personal territory, Fínsnechta would be allowed to return to his own fortress and estate without penalty.'

'That is not wise. That is merely storing trouble for the future.'

'I fear so,' Fidelma agreed. 'But the law is the law. At least he will be closely watched if he does return to the Five Kingdoms.'

'Better to eliminate the cause than wait for the effects,' Eadulf pointed out. 'Anyway, what news of Aescwine? What punishment was decreed for him?'

'Cenn Fáelad does not wish to provoke a war with the Saxons. Aescwine will be safe if he remains in the land of the Gewisse. I would be surprised if he came to our shores again with his ship and his crew.'

Eadulf lips formed a soundless whistle. 'I suppose that is good politics,' he said approvingly. 'But it is politics rather than law.'

'I am afraid sometimes politics becomes the law. That is why the law and justice are entirely different concepts.'

'What irritates me,' sighed Eadulf, 'is that this is the first case that you have been involved in where you have solved the mystery but the guilty seem to have gone free.'

'I am not sure what freedom they have,' Fidelma replied drily. 'Grella is now without the protection of the law here and, from what you say, her position in the land of the Gewisse will be far from a favourable one.'

Eadulf made a cynical grimace. 'Indeed, let us hope that she does not attempt any conspiracies against her lover,' he agreed. 'She will find the Gewisse are not as forgiving as your people, Fidelma.'

Fidelma regarded him with a slight frown. 'I trust, Eadulf, that you are now able to consider my people as your people?' she said quietly, but whether it was a comment or a question Eadulf was none too sure.

hISTORICAL AFTERWORD

A few years after these events, Cenn Fáelad mac Blathmaic, High King of Ireland, was killed by his first cousin, Fínsnechta mac Dúnchad. He died at a place named as Móin Aircheltair, near Loch Dearg (Donegal). Fínsnechta managed to secure the support of powerful nobles and churchmen and thus assumed the High Kingship in AD 674. He ruled as High King until AD 695 and even secured the epithet 'Fleded', meaning 'the bountiful'.

As for Aescwine, in the very same year that Cenn Fáelad died he claimed Cenwealh's throne and ruled the West Saxons for two years. His only achievement, noted by the Anglo-Saxon chroniclers, was that he defeated Wulfhere, the powerful King of Mercia, in AD 675. A year later, Aescwine himself was also dead but the historical records are silent as to the cause.

No attempt to attack or conquer the peaceful Five Kingdoms of Éireann was made by any of the Anglo-Saxon kingdoms for a further ten years. It was Ecgfrith, son of Oswiu, who had become ruler of Northumbria in AD 670, who led the invasion. He had risen to power as Bretwalda, or Overlord, after years of violent and bloody campaigns against his fellow Anglo-Saxons and the Britons, Rheged, the Picts and Dál Riada. In AD 684, his invasion brought forth protests from Bishop Ecgberht, who had decided to live in Ireland after the Synod of Whitby.

Ecgfrith's attempt to invade Ireland was made by landing on the coastal territory of Magh Breagh (Brega, south of Tara), part of the High King's southern Uí Néill lands. The Irish annals recorded: 'The devastation of Magh Breagh, both churches and territories, by the Saxons, in the month of June precisely; and they carried off with them many hostages from every place which they left, throughout Magh Breagh, together with many other spoils, and afterwards went to their ships.'

The monk and historian the Venerable Bede (d. AD 735) was among the Anglo-Saxons outraged by Ecgfrith's attempted invasion against 'a harmless race that had always been most friendly to the English'.

NIGHT OF THE LIGHTBRINGER

IRELAND, AD 671.

A man is discovered, murdered, in an unlit pyre in the heart of Cashel. He has been dressed in the robes of a religieux and killed by the ritualistic 'three deaths'.

When a strange woman named Brancheó appears in a raven-feather cloak foretelling of ancient gods returning to exact revenge, she is quickly branded a suspect.

In their search for the killer, Sister Fidelma and her companion Eadulf soon discover a darker shadow looming over the fortress. For their investigation is linked to a powerful text stolen from the Papal Secret Archives, and Fidelma herself will come up against mortal danger before the mystery is unravelled.

For more information visit
www.sisterfidelma.com

HEADLINE

PENANCE OF THE DAMNED

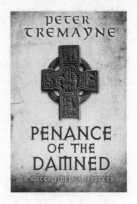

IRELAND, AD 671.

King Colgú of Cashel is shocked when his loyal Chief Bishop and advisor is murdered in the old enemy fortress of the Uí Fidgente. But as word reaches Cashel that the culprit will be executed under new law, a larger conflict threatens.

Dispatched to investigate, Sister Fidelma and her companion Eadulf discover that the man facing punishment is Gormán, commander of the King's bodyguard. Fidelma cannot believe he could carry out such an act – and yet the evidence is stacked against him.

To save Gormán and keep the peace, Fidelma and Eadulf must find the true culprit. As the threat of war looms, the date of execution draws ever closer . . .

For more information visit
www.sisterfidelma.com

HEADLINE

the second death

IRELAND, AD 671.

The Great Fair of Bealtain is almost upon the fortress of Cashel, and a line of painted wagons carries entertainers to the occasion. But preparations take a deathly turn when one of the carriages is set alight, and two corpses are found poisoned within.

As Sister Fidelma and her companion, Eadulf, investigate, they are plunged into the menacing marshlands of Osraige – where the bloody origin of the Abbey of Cainnech wreaks revenge.

What is the symbolism of the Golden Stone, and who are the members of the Fellowship of the Raven? Fidelma and Eadulf must face untold danger before they can untangle the evil that strikes at the very heart of the kingdom.

For more information visit
www.sisterfidelma.com

HEADLINE

DISCOVER MORE IN
THE SISTER FIDELMA SERIES

For more information visit www.headline.co.uk
Or www.sisterfidelma.com

HEADLINE